Other Stories

Table of Contents

Prologue Flight

"Good afternoon, I am Tom Smith with World News Today. I am here to interview a remarkable individual and his companions. While you might not know of him personally I can guarantee everyone watching or listening to this broadcast has in some way been positively affected by him."

"He and his family have been lauded as the founders of peace and prosperity in our world through their technological contributions. Tristali has pioneered development in iridium technology, synthesis, science, mathematics, physics and humanitarianism."

"So please let me introduce Tristali Verndactilia the 6th who has so kindly agreed to provide us with his story."

From the corner of the set the crowd can see four individual approach the stage. There are many gasps and intakes of breath. The young adults don't seem to have been old enough to have accomplished the enormous list of accolades just given.

The four walking toward stage consist of two males and two females.

The gentleman leading appears to be in his early twenties and close to two meters tall with a neat but slightly wavy steel blue hair, he has a lean muscular build and walks with dignity as he approaches the interviewer. As he turns toward the crowd you can notice his eyes are a vivid green and his smile and facial expression appears to call out to you as he waves.

The female directly behind him is close to the same height with dark auburn hair reaching her waist, she has a sleek stride. You would call her proportions perfect if she were a model. As she turns following the calls of the crowd you notice her smooth complexion and eyes that rival the color of the first gentleman. Even as she walks you can see a grace only granted those familiar with extreme athletic ability. While she walks you can see her show a slight hint of affection as she looks into the fist gentleman's face as she moves to stand next to him.

The third on stage is also a female, she is slightly shorter than the first, but her beauty would only be rivaled by her companion before her. She has straight waist length light brown hair, and you can see her kind smile without her even turning. She moves with almost feline grace and continues to glance at her surroundings. As she turns toward the crowd you can see her eyes are as blue as a pure deep pool of water.

The final guest approaching the stage is a male who is probably the tallest of the four. He looks much more imposing physically than the first gentleman. His hair is shoulder length curly brown and he seems to stride with purpose as he follows the group. When he turns slightly you can glimpse his steel blue eyes and a stern expression that seems to transform into a dazzling smile as the group shares a look before seating themselves.

Before the four sit Tom Smith extends his hand in greeting to each in turn. The smiles granted by the first and fourth would set even the hardest soul at ease, while the women appear to reserve their smiles for Tristali alone.

"Please be seated Tristali. I would like to thank you for appearing on our broadcast today." As Tom pauses for the crowd and to glance at the notes before him. "I wanted to thank you today for taking time from your busy schedule to give us a short history of your deeds."

"Thank you, Tom." Tristali says kindly.

"Would you like to introduce your companions?"

"I would." Tristali rises as he turns to the three sitting near him. As he slightly extends his hand toward the first female he begins.

"This lovely lady is Anistria Lastrande."

The girl blushes slightly as she peers up at Tristali's face with longing apparent in her eyes.

"She is one of those I consider to be closest to my heart."

At this comment you can see Anistria purse her lips and slightly look away.

"This second young lady would also share that spot."

The brunette next to Anistria visibly blushes as well.

"Her name is Tialinde Brocke."

Tialinde slightly nods to Tristali's introduction.

As Tristali approaches the final young man you can see a smirk on his face as they both share glances before Tristali turns to the crowd.

"This final gentleman is my closest friend Levan Lastrande. Yes, he and Anistria are brother and sister. Though sometimes you wouldn't be able to tell."

Levan smiles at Tristali as he slightly chuckles.

Tristali turns to again find his chair as he sits and looks toward Tom.

"Please, Tom to make our time together more personal call me Trist."

The other three announce in sequence.

"Ani, please."

"Tia, if you don't mind."

"Lev."

Trist glances back to Tom after the introductions.

"So, let me get this out of the way now. Trist, you look so young. Most of us remember the iridium technologies being introduced when we were children. You hardly look old enough to have pioneered that development." Tom asks with a curious expression.

Trist is smiling as he nods to Tom's question.

"Tom it's simple I just don't age the same as everyone else."

There are murmurs in the crowd.

"You see we aren't what you would classify as human."

The crowd is extremely excited, as the noise rises.

"Okay, I've heard stories already, but can you explain that comment to our audience?"

Trist nods, "I can. My friends and family originated from a planet called Paltius near the Velisus Nebula. Unfortunately, it is much farther than our astronomical observations can detect at this point."

Trist pauses as he considers a moment, "But thanks to our origins and our slow cellular growth I was able to work with our medical researchers to develop a vaccine capable of eradicating cancer cells."

"Oh, I was not aware of that!" Tom says surprised.

"I assure you that it was discovered by accident but once we found out we poured our own research into developing a cure. After we saw the suffering inflicted I couldn't turn my back to the people's needs."

The three companions watch the crowds exuberant cheering. Before turning back to Trist and Tom.

"Well tell me a little bit about what led you here today."

"Well, I am actually forty-three by your calendar…"

The crowd echoes voices expressing disbelief and low whistles.

Trist pauses while the crowd settles down.

"But as I mentioned we age much slower and due to that I am not surprised you saw the early benefits of our expansion into the different fields you mentioned earlier."

"How about to Earth? You said you aren't human, tell us a little about your origins?"

Trist contemplates his response, "Well functionally we are very similar. We are capable of intermarrying and even having children between our races. The one piece that separates us is the genetic attuning our race underwent long ago."

"What is this genetic attuning? Tell us a about that. Are you currently working toward that as well?"

Trist nods, "I think we always will be. If I can help the people of this planet I will, just as I have done the last thirty years. You see my ancestors were also stranded on Paltius over a millennium ago. They were pioneers and explorers looking for habitable worlds to develop or tera-form."

Trist pauses, "They were unable to return to their world so instead they began a new life on Paltius, sadly I have no information regarding their origin. But that led to the development of the Empire and the Tri-Moon Alliance with over a thousand-year peace."

Trist looks a little conflicted, "I am also the only known remaining prince of that empire."

The crowd is silent as Tom looks wide eyed himself.

"You mean you are royalty from where you came from, this Paltius?" Tom asks incredulously.

Trist nods, "That is correct. The early pioneers of my planet had their deoxyribonucleic acid (DNA) genetically attuned to enhance critical skills allowing each member of the original crew to excel at their jobs."

Trist shifts slightly in his seat. "Their genetic attunement also caused the cellular lifecycle to slow and extend our natural lives. This allowed the early deep space explorers more time to explore and develop worlds they encountered."

"My great-great-grandfather (GGF) was the commander of the exploration vessel that was stranded on Paltius. He was responsible for holding the crew together and led them to a prosperous alliance and a strong defense force." Trist's eyes grow somewhat dark. "Sadly, it also led to the collapse of a thousand-year peace and my ultimate arrival on Earth."

"Can you tell us a little more about your grandfather?" Tom asks inquisitively.

Trist looks to be fondly reminiscing, "I can, he was loved by the people and his successors were also. He led them in turbulent times and helped develop a city into an Empire where not one soul suffered. His reforms as their society grew led to their advancement and ultimate colonization of the two moons orbiting Titar, the gas giant in our binary system."

"He ultimately established the empire and though he initially refused was placed as Emperor by popular demand. He lived to be 335 years of age. To put that in Earths perspective it would be close to 800 years.

"During his prime he was known to say, as long as the people had a purpose and were happy then the empire was doing the right thing."

Tom considers Trist's words, "Well what led you to leave?"

"My grandfather's wish was to allow the people their freedom and that gradually led to the development of merchant and self-defense hierarchies. He supported their development but only made two requests. That was to ensure the safety of the people and not invite unwanted conflict from outside our system. You see he understood that eventually they might encounter explorers from their original world and didn't want strife or conflict to be brought to either side."

"It sounds like a utopia, what happened?"

Trist continued, "Well after several successive generations and the establishment of the Allied Alliance Military (AAM) their desire to expand the empires sphere of influence strengthened. Like all in my family line we desired peace most of all so this was never allowed. Unfortunately, this generated discontent in the upper cadre and ultimately led to a coup."

Tom nods slowly having seen historical accounts on Earth very similar in past societies.

"What I wasn't aware of at the time since I was, but a child was the intrigue being carried out between the merchant classes and the military. They both saw benefit in expansion but the true winners in any scenario would be the merchant class. That has led me to try to proactively limit similar circumstances on what I have done so far on Earth."

Tom looks interested, "What do you mean?"

"Well, if I make technology available to all and assist in the development equally there will be no opportunity for others to take advantage of less developed countries. That has been my primary goal, as well as to reduce the elements that I saw no reason for such as hunger, war, and intolerance. If everyone is fed and there is peace, society can truly develop. If we all have the same resources, there is no need to steal from others. I am not looking to create a global socialist society since micro economies will still exist. What I wanted to drastically reduce is the desire for nations to seeks resources through force."

"How do you plan on accomplishing this. It sounds wonderful…but human nature, even in your world will lead to corruption." Tom says passionately.

"I know, and I might never see it achieved. But that doesn't mean we can't dream about it as we work toward a communal goal." Trist pauses as he considers his next response, "Think about society in your lifetime Tom. What have you seen? Gone are the pointless deaths from cancer thought once as uncurable. What about starvation? War? Energy? Satisfying these needs has led us to a more peaceful existence."

Tom leans back in his chair, "I can't deny that fact. There have been fewer conflicts caused by energy needs and death rates from starvation have dropped drastically, you have even developed alternative materials that replaced once finite resources."

Trist is nods, "We will continue with your help. What I want to see is an Earth capable of standing with me. One Iridium Reactor alone is capable of powering an entire town."

The crowd has been eerily silent listening to the two speakers.

As Trist leans forward and places his elbows on the armrests as he interlinks his fingers resting across his knees. "I need Earths help."

Tom exhales as the crowd begins to murmur, Trist's companions are glancing around the crowd as well.

"I need help protecting my sister and defending Earth."

Tom leans forward in his chair as he glances out toward the audience. "Wait, why would you need our help when you have given so much already?"

Trist sits back in his chair as the girl next to him places her hand gently on his. "I am a threat to the AAM, they know that if I returned to Paltius the people would demand me as emperor. Because they see me as a threat they may choose to attempt to eliminate me and the only option I have is to defend, I have no desire to see harm come to my new home or to inflict harm on my previous world."

"Trist what you're asking is beyond our ability." Tom says with a worried expression.

"Not anymore." Trist smiles as he looks back as twenty-nine additional people walk out onto the stage.

"These are my classmates who shared my time when I first arrived. We studied together and cried together. They are pioneers in their own right and have developed the technology capable of creating a fortifying force enabling Earth's defenses."

"But what you're asking requires technology we can only dream about, the farthest we have sent a man to is Mars and that had varied success rates." Tom explained emphatically.

Trist nods, "But you forget, I came and now that Earth is ready I can help you achieve the next step in that development."

Tom calmed down a little with the audience, "How do you plan on achieving that next step and why spend so much time for a world that is alien to you?"

"I should first explain why I now hold Earth so dear, do you mind us telling a story?" Trist asked as he leaned toward Tom.

"Please by all means." Tom extended his hand.

Escape from Paltius

It was a day not unlike others that I had known, I studied, trained and practiced with my mentor before being allowed time to meditate and reflect on what I had learned. Today I decided to reflect in the palatial gardens, primarily to avoid listening to my sister's etiquette lessons.

That was one lesson I wished I could forget, they were so repetitive that I thought I would never stop dreaming about protocol and how to act in my grandfather's presence.

I mean really, why do I need to memorize which utensil to use while eating or how long to bow my head.

It was the raised voices that brought me back to reality coming from the hall connecting the gardens to the central reception foyer.

As I pondered why it felt like everyone in the palace was much more apprehensive over the last several weeks, even father had returned extremely late with a very distressed look. Mother told Emeri he was just busy when she asked if father was okay, however I've seen that look enough times to tell it was more than his normal being busy look.

As I attempted to focus on my meditation, I suddenly heard my teacher Shivan Lastrande call out to me from the entry way, "Tristali, where are you?"

I guess I should answer him, so I'm not subjected to another lecture, "I'm in here Shivan." I responded in a slightly elevated tone.

I saw Shivan briskly walk into the garden, and as I was about to ask what I could help with he suddenly grabbed me around my waist and tossed me over his shoulder.

This was a little startling since we never trained in the gardens but when I asked him to please put me down he ignored my plea.

"Tristali, I have orders from your father, we are taking a little trip." Shivan responded.

As he walked down the hall toward the transport hanger I heard him asking a guard if the Velisus was prepared.

With all the bouncing it was difficult to hear much more than that, "Where's my father Shivan?"

Shivan was quiet for a moment then told me he would meet us on the Regulous.

I felt it necessary to tell Shivan, "I can walk you know." Given this very undignified position.

I felt every stride as it gradually began to knock the air out of my lungs, "Will I be able to gather any belongings first?"

Gah, no response as he bounced me into the air to better position me on his shoulder. I can feel the tension in his very being echoed by the guards I see moving in around us. The more I glanced around as we passed the numerous halls leading off the main corridor and leading to the hanger I noticed the palace was abnormally active. The closer we drew to the hanger the more guards I noticed standing near the doorways.

Shivan paused before leaving the foyer to cross the path toward the hanger. I kicked my feet a bit and asked, "What's going on?"

Shivan's tone was unlike his normal playful banter when we trained, "Quiet! We are waiting for a messenger."

I heard footsteps on the polished floor, and someone briefly talked to Shivan in a hushed tones. I could only make out bits of the conversation, "The Emperor wishes you Godspeed, the other team will transport Emeri."

I could feel Shivan nod, "Understood, may Verndactilia watch over us all."

I was starting to panic a little with that phrase, great grandfathers name was seldom used lightly in that context.

"Shivan what did he mean Emeri is with another team, we are all going together right?"

What Shivan said next took my breath away, "My prince we must hasten, please understand and be patient. All will be made clear shortly."

With the words my prince, I immediately knew grandfather had passed. Being unable to grasp the entire situation I choose to trust Shivan, he had never lied to me and was trusted by my father and grandfather.

As Shivan entered the covered pathway leading toward the hanger I heard what sounded like shouts back through the corridor we traveled, followed by intermittent flashes of light and screaming. I had never heard screams like that, even during large gatherings and celebrations, it was as if people were dying.

I could see guards falling in behind us as we passed each branch leading off the pathway. As we entered the hanger door we immediately took the relay to the transport dock.

As Shivan engaged the relay the platform quickly faded away and I could see the light from the open-door blink out as the security door sealed. We shot into the afternoon sky and I could barely make out what looked like smoke hanging over the city.

We currently had three imperial guards with us, and they all looked incredibly tense as they kept glancing around and occasionally at me.

I must look an absolute sight in this undignified position, I thought, so of course they would glance at me.

When the lift finally began to slow Shivan hoisted me off his shoulder and set me in front of him, "My prince, we will soon be boarding the Velisus bound for the Regulous, there you and your sister will meet." Shivan calmly informed me.

"What about father and mother?"

Shivan briefly closed his eyes, "They will soon follow, once you are all together we will head for Sebanti for a diplomatic mission."

That was the first time Shivan ever lied to me. However, I wouldn't realize it until much later.

"Shivan, did the messenger you met with earlier say my grandfather had passed?"

He only nodded and gave me a quick glance as we walked toward the gangway of the Velisus.

"We will discuss much once we are on our way, but for now we must hasten our departure."

As we approached the entry I could see the Velisus through the viewing panes it was one of the newer ships christened in commemoration of the Nebula closest to our system. What I remember about battle identification was that ships of this class were used throughout the alliance and could fly virtually forever at light speed, given the conversion ratio once you achieved a factor of light.

The Velisus itself was capable of moving people or freight depending on the modifications. This ship had most recently been used as an entourage transport between the flagship and Paltius many times over the last couple of years. In its current configuration it was capable of housing close to five thousand passengers and dignitaries and could prepare enough synthesized meals to support all passengers in a matter of hours.

While capable of conducting deep space exploration, this class of ship seldom saw service outside of our immediate system. It also provided the necessary facilities for training, exercise, meditation, health, dining, sleeping and cryogenic support, it was extremely versatile.

I always found its shape a little peculiar, but I understood that had to do with the way it docked with the Regulous, and how its gravitational repulsion shields functioned preventing small debris from penetrating its hull at light speed.

Once the pressure regulated in the Velisus airlock the door quickly slid open allowing Shivan and I to enter. We quickly crossed the threshold and Shivan spun around and saluted the three guards who had accompanied us.

They quickly returned the salute and offered a bow, ...to me!? I quickly bowed back as I waved and thanked them.

The door quickly closed and Shivan beckoned me to follow. When we entered a large room with a glass table and numerous filament monitors hanging from the overhead framework Shivan asked me to wait for the others while he prepared for departure.

It wasn't long before Valdria, Shivans wife and his two children Anistria and Levan came from where Shivan had just disappeared.

Unlike Shivan's stern face, tall build and shining silver hair, Valdria was slender, with modest proportions and flowing brown hair with a slight hint of auburn highlights, both her and Shivan had steel grey eyes like my mothers. Anistria was about my height and very tomboyish, she had a childish expression that was beginning to mature, while her hair was a deep auburn and rested on her shoulders, her vivid green eyes could pierce your soul.

Levan was my closest friend, he and I competed in height and build, while my hair was steel grey his was a curly light brown and he shared the same eye color as his parents. It was nice to see Lev since he and I were the same age and often took the same training lessons, however Anistria was a little older and was always trying to pick on us, for some reason she always chose me as her target of abuse.

Once Valdria settled down in a large travel chair she told us all to do the same.

I asked, Valdria, "Do you know why we have to attend this diplomatic gathering? Does it have something to do with grandfather's death?"

She silently looked my way for a second with what seemed like deep sorrow in her eyes as she said, "Tristali I am truly sorry for your loss, I only wish I could tell you what is happening right now. Unfortunately, even I don't know the depth of damage done by the death of your grandfather or if this meeting is a result."

As Lev and I sat silently talking about the upcoming physical trial I noticed the filament monitors began to glow, indicating a change in status.

"I looks like we are off, I hope my sister isn't causing father or mother too much worry, she really hates these transport ships." I said quietly to Lev.

I noticed Ani looking in my direction with an unusual look of concern upon her face. That was when Ani moved over to the chair next to mine, when I looked at her as she sat down she avoided my glance with a somewhat unhappy expression. When she sat she did so with her back to me and I thought I heard her sniffle, but I wasn't sure.

I leaned over toward Lev and asked, "What's wrong with Ani?" Lev just shrugged.

"She is always strange around you." Lev replied.

As we were preparing to make the factor jump I heard brief announcements, status checks and updates over the internal communication network, just as the order was given to jump the Velisus shuddered very uncharacteristically.

This set off the blue strobe lights along the wall and I felt my ears pop and ache like when we were at high altitudes in the mountains on Paltius, but it quickly dissipated. We all continued to stay in our chairs until Shivan announced the all clear, confirming that our course was stable and clear. The time it normally took to reach the Regulous is no more than a few minutes, so this should be a quick trip.

However, when Shivan announced the all clear he requested we remain secured. He then dropped off the communication line.

I turned to Lev, "Isn't this taking longer than normal?"

He only responded with a "Humm..." almost as if he was thinking it was odd himself.

We had frequently taken a transport shuttle to the Regulous during the last couple years when father would visit the other worlds for trade and defense negotiations. Since Shivan and his family were known as close confidants and advisors of the Emperor it was common for us to travel together.

After several hours had passed it was apparent even to me that we were not going to the Regulous. I wasn't really able to demand answers and I knew Shivan was trustworthy and would never do anything to hurt the Empire so when we didn't meet with the Regulous I knew there was something dreadfully wrong.

Eventually Valdria removed her seat restraint and after she stood up she looked at us all and asked if we would like anything to eat, Ani glanced at me after I said please, and she responded with the same, while Lev's hand instantly shot up and he said, "Yes!"

After about thirty minutes Shivan and Valdria both re-entered the room, Shivan released a chair from the rails and slid it to be closer to us.

After a few moments of him looking at the filament monitors he turned to the four of us with a stern look on his face, "So, the situation is this. My prince ..."

I quickly interrupted, "Please Shivan call me Trist like always, there is no point in reminding me of my responsibilities since I know you would never let me forget."

With a slight nod, "Very well. Trist, I cannot express my heartfelt condolences regarding this situation, including the lie I told you while we were departing the palace."

I frowned, "The lie?"

Shivan silently bowed his head, as he looked back up into my eyes, he said the following, "The empire has suffered a traitorous rebellion." When Shivan noticed me about to break in he brought up his hand to motion me to silence, "Yes, I know this is very disturbing. However, it is the truth. Right now, another transport ship is taking your sister Emerila to a different destination."

"It is imperative that one of you survive so we couldn't risk transporting you together where the AAM could dispose of you both in one blow. This at least splits their forces and improves the chances of each of your survival. I do not know which direction they fled as it was your father's orders. What I do know is you must survive."

I could feel my heart pounding in my chest as my skin crawled up my neck in anger and fear before I asked the one question I was afraid of hearing an answer to, "What about father and mother?"

Shivan slowly shook his head as he glanced between the three of us, "All I know for sure is that your grandfather was poisoned sparking the coup, while everyone was attending to him the AAM made their move. It was neatly planned and something we never could have imagined. At this time, I fear your father and mother have likely been taken prisoner or even killed."

I wasn't capable of processing all that was being thrown at me, "Our planets alliance wanted for nothing, the people were fed, our technology allowed plenty of opportunities to enjoy life, then why!?"

I could feel my eyes start to burn as tears began to gloss over them, before I broke down further I unbuckled from the restraining harness and fled to the room adjacent to the tactical planning room.

I was taught that it was a prince's responsibility to be the strength of the empire and we should only openly show compassion never weakness. As I began to cry I heard the door open and close behind me, but I didn't turn to look. I expected it to be Shivan there to tell me to show strength, but it wasn't.

As I heard the soft footsteps on the carpeted floor a small pair of arms embraced me from behind.

It was Ani, she gently hugged me and rested her head on my back as she said, "I will be your strength when you must show weakness."

At that I began to sob until I was no longer able to remain awake.

When I finally awoke I heard a deep grumble, "Isn't it time for you to get up?"

As I looked up into her face she was extremely flushed, I giggled as she began beating me lightly with her fists.

I looked into her eyes and said, "I'm sorry Ani that you had to see me like that."

Ani just made a HMPHH sound as she turned her head away from me as she responded, "I meant what I said so don't forget."

As Ani and I re-entered the planning room, I noticed Shivan had gone as I approached my chair once again Lev quietly asked if I was okay.

I nodded then Lev broke into a grin and asked, "Did Ani give you a beating to bring you back to your senses?"

"Huh…! Like she could beat me." I casually said.

But when I glanced back Ani's way she offered a small smile before finishing her protein pack.

The Velisus, while capable of carrying many passengers and crew now only carried eight people. The current passengers consisted of Shivan, his family and one of the Empires best engineers, Talinde Brocke his son Jesende and daughter Tialinde.

Talinde looked well-built even though he appeared older, his dark brown hair had begun to grey at the temples, but his most distinguishing feature was his kind face and light blue eyes.

Jesende was twice our age so we hadn't met many times, he was somewhat solitary and very inquisitive regarding his father's work. He was close to two meters in height with the same curly dark brown hair as his father, thought he had his mother brown eyes, so I was told.

Tialinde was a sweet little girl who often joined my sister and Ani during lessons, she was a little shorter than me, with straight light brown hair and an innocent face, her eyes were a deeper blue than her fathers. Talinde had lost his wife shortly after the birth of Tia in an accident on the Sheila an AAM cruiser, while improving the surge capacity of the main reactor and weapon systems.

Unlike Shivan's descendants Talinde's blood lines were mixed, decreasing his genetic attunement and reducing his life cycle, while he was similar in age to Shivan he appeared to be several years older.

Talinde's features were somewhat strained when we all met in the planning room to discuss the current situation. Shivan asked about the status with the surge reactor.

Talinde replied, "Well the reactor is fine, but we lost the two crew who were in the reactor bay manning the perpetual drive mechanism when we were struck. I have the breach under control, but honestly, we don't have the manpower necessary or the time to drop out of factor to fix things. We are currently at factor three, but we would need to drop out entirely to even utilize the repair equipment."

Shivan looked like he was considering things, "What if we continue at our current rate, do you see any issues?"

Talinde readily responded, "Not immediately but since we don't know if the AAM is pursuing we can't take the chance. We are still within easy range of their scanners if we drop out, so I think we should continue."

Shivan slowly sat down, "Well, we are not on a known course so the odds of them hypothesizing where we will end up is slim. I am going to make a slow course correction once we verify the path, but our atmospheric scanners haven't sensed any habitable planets in the last week. I have a feeling this will be a long flight."

"Heh, well I'll keep us going for as long as you see necessary and if we survive a month I think we will be in the clear, at least for the time being." Talinde confidently declared.

Once the first month passed things began to relax a little, being settled into our cabins life seemed to begin to move forward more naturally. Due to the complex navigational logic routines it wasn't necessary to monitor the Velisus trajectory every moment, so to keep us occupied Shivan decided to renew our lessons. Valdria took the role of instructor in sociology, history and etiquette instruction, while Shivan taught the physics, chemistry, mathematical theory and physical training.

When he was able, Talinde also offered his services in basic mechanical theory, engineering and the importance of maintenance, what we didn't know at the time was he just needed a little help keeping things in order.

During one of the training sessions with Shivan, while covering quantum theory he paused during his instruction and told us not all actions could be explained.

I raised my hand, "But didn't you previously tell us that math and physics is nothing more than a puzzle we manipulate with knowledge? Does this mean if we can't explain something that the knowledge doesn't currently exist to solve it?"

Shivan smiled, since this saying was one he was fond of, "Not entirely, I literally mean sometimes our actions cannot be explained. For instance, you have all studied the impact of the genetic attuning conducted by our forefathers, yes? We can explain it, but we don't know how it works or why it passes on the way it does and we cannot replicate it, why?" Shivan glanced at each of us.

"Additionally, the tuning has evolved, some in the gentry in our society have found specializations that they are peerless in. So, each one of you will likely find your selves awakening to an ability that cannot be explained by physics natural laws."

Ani was the first to speak up, "Like being able to know where everyone on ship is without looking at a filament terminal?"

Shivan looked at his daughter, "Yes, that is likely a result of mutated genetics. Some don't recognize it right away but if you find yourself knowing or doing something unusual make a note of it, so we can tailor your education to strengthen and utilize these abilities to the fullest."

As the passengers of the Velisus settled into a routine, Shivan and Valdria began the groups formal preparation for the unknown. I buried myself in training and education wholeheartedly, each morning found me practicing in the cargo bay of the Velisus.

While I studied the rest of my companions focused on their physical activities which included endurance, agility, strength and balance training.

Currently, Lev and I focused on endurance and strength training with a traditional match of latch, the goal being to pin your opponent with one arm below and one arm behind preventing escape from the captor.

Lev and I were circling each other on the padded floor looking for a gap in the others defense. While we continued to circle one another, Lev noticed my eyes flicker toward the girls to my right and quickly closed the space between the two of us and was able to catch me when my guard was down.

Shivan shouted, "You can't let little things distract you in a real situation you could be captured or dead."

Ani quietly clapped as she and Tia walked by on their way to the balance course causing Lev to grin and me to wince.

The cargo bay had numerous areas allocated for various training regimes, the room itself was large enough for several structures to fit in and commonly would carry the land-based vehicles used by the Emperor when conducting diplomatic outings.

The Velisus was constructed in such a way that when it docked with the Regulous it appeared to be no more than a smooth extension of the surface. Design and functional aesthetics were extremely important in our society, even up to the city designs, each building complimented the one next to it, allowing for an open feel even though Paltius had a relatively high population density.

It also allowed for more even distribution of oxygen from the fields and fruit trees planted throughout the empire creating an effective logistics network capable of delivering goods the day they were prepared.

That night I had a horrible headache, and when I mentioned it to Valdria she took me to the infirmary for a brief medical scan.

As I sat in the examination cube Valdria said as she was looking at my scan, "Well I don't see anything wrong, but you have unusual activity throughout your frontal cortex, the scan doesn't detect any danger, so it could be the increase in activity due to the extensive learning curriculum so you're mentally exhausting yourself." As she lightly finger flicked my forehead, "I know you don't have as much time to relax and since you have begun to grow maybe you just need to try meditating after your lessons in the observatory. That might give you some time to process and rest, plus it's quiet."

I was a little unsure, "Anything to keep my head from this aching." The next day I noticed my headache had subsided a bit, so I felt it would be fine to continue my training after lectures.

Today it wasn't just Lev and I but also Jes who had been shooed out of his father's work area to exercise with the other boys. Jes was already at an age where he could become an engineering apprentice, so he spent most of his studies helping his father and occasionally sat in with the rest of us. But usually it was only when his father was doing something that had a component of danger associated with it.

Today's sport was catch dodge, the ball was oval and had an internal gyroscopic regulator which would cause it to make random direction changes midflight which worked off the momentum gained when it was thrown. Lev couldn't get near it but for some reason Jes was able to guess where it was going to land every time.

Noticing this, Shivan decided to change the velocity of the ball by just a few centimeters per second, this was just enough and Jes was flabbergasted when the ball took a turn he didn't expect. Shivan grinned to himself as he watched Jes make the very next catch. Shivan called us over, "So do you boys know why Jes is able to catch it every time?"

Lev and I shook our heads as we looked at Shivan then Jes and responded in unison, "No sir."

Shivan looked at Jes, and said, "Your pretty good with mathematics aren't you, how about physics and theory?"

Jes contemplated a bit, "I wasn't really good with math in school and I only took what was necessary in physics and theory."

Shivan responded, "Very well, you will be sitting through a few more lessons now. You might not have even realized it, but you were using math to determine the algorithm directing the balls flight." Shivan offered a rare grin, "Your father has been teaching you whether you knew it or not."

Jes nodded his understanding. Lev and I shared glances for a second and slyly grinned at each other. The next ball flew slightly toward the right of the field then shifted left as we all ran toward the center trying to predict where it would land.

This time however, we knew Jes was already watching for its landing zone, that was when Lev quickly cut in front of Jes and slowed causing Jes to veer off to the right to avoid a collision. As he did this I took the opportunity to catch the ball while it was in a stable spiral, so I jumped.

I didn't take much of an effort, but I was able to catch the ball and softly landed back on the field. Shivan noticed my movements and the height I jumped, and he quietly pondered this as he overheard Jes and Lev arguing.

"Hey that was unfair, you purposefully tried to cut me off." Jes decries.

Lev just grinned, "If you were faster I wouldn't have been able to do it."

As I walked back to the two I smiled at Lev and Jes, "Good game but you're too good at this, so let's try something else next time."

That evening after we headed to our cabins Shivan, Valdria and Talinde met to discuss the current situation.

* * *

Shivan was the first to speak, "After observing each of the children I can see a positive sign that they are all developing their own personal aspects. I think we need to continue to help foster their talents as we prepare for a destination that might be extremely hostile toward our kind."

Talinde asked, "Do we have any idea where we are going?"

Shivan silently shook his head pausing a moment, "We will have to eventually make a decision, while this craft can support us for many years do we want to do nothing but run? I say not, so then we must find those who would be sympathetic with our plight."

As if an afterthought Valdria asked, "What about the long-range scanners, can those help us find a habitable planet?"

Both Shivan and Talinde quietly sighed before Shivan responded, "No, that would nullify all the effort we placed into hiding our direction. While we can still use our passive receivers, it would be a giveaway if we used our scanners or communicator at this point."

"Yea, even if the long-range scanners only extend a light year the residual waves could be detected many times farther out." Shivan said.

"I see…" Valdria said.

Shivan sighed, "All we can do is prepare the children and ensure our prince remains protected. I fear we may never see Paltius again, but I must keep my word to my closest friend."

* * *

Time continued to flow as the Velisus hurtled through space toward an unknown destination. While I was focused on mental endurance training my companions were coached on self-defense using military confrontational and defensive training programs.

This was quietly conducted away from me.

My four companions stood before Shivan one day after training, "You four will ultimately be the princes armor soon enough, as I became his father's many years ago. Always remember though, there will be times when it will be more prudent to retreat. However, knowing the prince it may be difficult and you four will have to determine when it's wiser to disobey his orders and forcibly remove him from harm's way."

Shivan looked at the four gathered before him, as he thought about how they had grown so much, "You may all be young, and I know I am asking a lot of you but…"

Both Lev and Ani, were shocked when their father knelt before them.

"I humbly beg that you keep the prince safe so that we can someday return to Paltius and right the grievous wrongs perpetrated by the AAM."

All four nodded at Shivan's solemn words.

As the months slipped away and we grew accustomed to our regime of training and education, Shivan and Valdria began to turn toward secondary development. Having covered the entirety of the routine educational progression the only remaining options available were to focus on advanced literary works, history, sociology, psychology and tactics.

These fields would normally only be pursued if the individual was identified as a future emperor or candidate to become a high advisor. What I found disturbing was my ability to recall studies, though I never considered it a gift and assumed my teacher's ability was the result.

After working several weeks as a group the members of the Velisus soon became a force to be reckoned with in the virtual training simulators, not just Lev's, Ani's and Tia's martial prowess but also my ability to lead and command through each algorithmic derived situation.

On occasions when Jes was able to accompany the group he was always able to tune our gear in such a way that made us question our own strength and abilities.

Tia always seemed to be the skittish one when doing exercises, while she couldn't match the martial prowess of either Lev or Ani she was an incredible asset and had the ability to identify inconsistencies or traps incorporated into the training program.

Even when Shivan praised her for her foresight in keeping the group out of trouble she always looked like she wasn't satisfied since she constantly compared herself to Ani.

One training session when the group was put up against an especially difficult scenario, Tia found herself separated from the group when a cell of virtual elements flanked our perimeter. As she was pressed into a situation that would trigger a mission failure, Tia decided to try to lead the pursuers from her remaining team mates.

While knowing this was only a virtual simulation, the sights, sounds and tactile elements of the virtual program made it feel extremely realistic and generated heightened stress levels in each participant. These programs were designed to introduce explorers to extreme hypothetical survival situations while researching new territories or worlds.

When Tia had finally reached her breaking point she suddenly felt a presence immediately behind her. However, it was not projecting animosity toward her. As she slowly turned she suddenly felt someone grab her around her waist and then there was a feeling of being jerked up through the air only to land outside the range of the hostile virtual pursuers.

As she was gently placed on ground she realized the one who had rescued her from her situation was me.

"How did you find me?" Tia asked with a hint of moisture in her eyes.

I looked away as I slightly blushed, "You wanted me to help right?"

Tia looked almost ready to cry, "But I was leading them away on purpose, I couldn't let them near the rest of the group. Why did you come here? It was my choice!"

I placed my hand on her shoulder and looked into her tear-filled eyes, "Having even one of us hurt means we failed, I will not let harm come to anyone as long as I can prevent it so please rely on me a bit more when you need help, okay Tia?"

Tia silently nodded.

As the two were ready to head back toward the rest of the group we heard unnatural crashing noises and realized others were heading our direction.

As I prepared to defend myself Tia slightly giggled as she said, "It's about time you guys got here."

I looked to Tia then noticed the crashing noise was Lev, Ani and Jes coming through the simulated landscape.

As the three entered the clearing they all breathed a sigh of relief, then suddenly Ani stepped forward and slapped me.

"DON'T EVER DO THAT AGAIN!" She shouted.

I was totally unprepared for that and slowly brought my hand to my cheek as I looked at Ani who was in tears, "I'm sorry, but I knew you would all be okay without me and I heard Tia call for help, so I just…"

Tia looked a little perplexed after my comments as she glanced to Ani as she had her hands balled into fists.

"That's not the point, how do we know you're going to be okay when you run off like that?"

I quietly bowed and apologized to the group, "I will be clearer with my intentions next time, I am sorry."

As the other three quickly neutralized the remaining virtual foes and the simulation concluded, our surroundings immediately faded to the familiar sights of the cargo bay.

"Well, what do you think?" Shivan asked the other two overseeing the simulation.

Both Valdria and Talinde contemplated the outcome.

"They work well together, and I think they all understand the need to maintain a close eye on the prince, however I don't think he is being forthcoming in his aspect development. I have seen two aspects today that he has failed to mention, whether he understands them himself is unclear." Valdria quietly said as she pondered the outcome.

"Well regardless, they are very effective, so after getting to know them over the last several cycles I can say they are about as ready as we can get them." Talinde boasts beaming at his son and daughters performance, "Though I think Tia has a soft spot for the prince, she is a self-sacrificing type, so it worries me she may put herself in undue danger if it meant keeping harm from him." Talinde shook his head as he finished his verbal assessment.

Valdria smiled knowingly, "I know, I think Trist will have his hands full soon enough. He doesn't know it, but Anistria was being considered by Emperor Sendali as Trist's future match. So, I am proud but also conflicted in his ability to so easily sway the hearts of his companions."

* * *

When Shivan checked the Velisus's course and the passive sensors he noticed the system had detected several low frequency analog transmissions.

He immediately called Talinde to the command center, "Talinde what do you make of these frequencies and messages?"

"Well they are very low power and seem to come from a very early stage technologically developed society. The compression rate of these messages is horrible, there is so much distortion it is difficult to decipher the content and direction it originated." Talinde shook his head as he muttered, "How long ago did we start picking these up?"

"I have no idea, the system just recognized them as intelligent patterns. Well, we better spend a little more time monitoring the scanners, I will check every few hours from here on out." Talinde promised.

"Do we risk using the active sensors?" Valdria asked.

"I can detune the sensor array, that will reduce the active scanning range, but it will also reduce the residual wave. I still can't promise it wouldn't be picked up by any pursuing ships if they are within several factors." Talinde pondered as he scratched his chin.

"How about transmitting behind a planetary body, will that help disperse the waves residual distance traveled?" Valdria asked.

"That's easier said than done at our rate of speed, it's not like we can slide in behind a celestial body on a whim. Unless you want to drop out of factor speed for a bit. I could also repair the damage done when we departed Paltius. Since we never know what will happen in these unchartered systems I really would like to have the Velisus in top condition."

"Okay, let's do it. Once you're ready let me know. We can find a large celestial body and sit in its gravitational shadow while we repair and listen for other transmissions." Shivan said as he intently watched the monitors that automatically mapped, calculated location and direction of travel, "It will give the system time to process the frequency and decipher the messages as well."

Once Talinde reached the reactor bay he ensured the shields were solid before checking statuses for the reactor and perpetual drive mechanism. Using the direct communication link to the command center Talinde gave the ready confirmation as he slipped out of the room in case of the fields shoring up the prior breach failed.

Shivan slowly began the power reduction to the perpetual drive mechanism and gave status updates to Talinde, "Current factor three, factor two, factor one, main directional engines coming online, directional engines green, dropping out now."

As Shivan eased the Velisus into solar navigational normal he watched as the light flashing past the viewing monitors began to slow in intensity, "Talinde we're in solar navigational normal now, how does it look on your end?" Shivan asked over the communication link.

As Shivan waited for a response the doors to the command center slid open and Valdria entered glancing at the monitors, "I noticed a fluctuation in our drives, is there a problem?"

Shivan glanced at Valdria, "No, we are picking up unknown low frequency transmissions, so we wanted a chance to listen and at the same time repair the damage done during our flight. Keep this to yourself for the moment. I will talk to Trist tomorrow since we can't hide the fact we stopped but the transmissions could be anything so let's not get them excited just yet."

*   *   *

Once Talinde entered the planning room of the Velisus, Shivan began to speak. "As you all may have noticed we have dropped out of factor and are now preparing to conduct repair operations." He glanced around those sitting around the clear filament table and smiled slightly, "So today Talinde will begin your engineering training in earnest."

Shivan motioned for Talinde to begin.

Talinde looked toward his son, "Jes, I am going to have you work in conjunction with me. Tia and Ani will monitor the reactor room pressure. Trist and Lev will help loosen the support beams and replace the internal panels as we secure the repair panels on the exterior. The fun part is you will have to wear zero gravity enhanced suits as a precautionary measure. Shivan, can I have you keep an eye on the shield and hull monitors in the command center?"

"I would be happy to." Shivan responded.

Talinde nodded, "Okay let's get ready, Tia, Ani come with me and I will show you how to read the room sensors. Trist, Jes and Lev I will meet you in the decompression room for fitting."

As everyone prepared there was a heightened sense of excitement since all were included in the repair operation.

Once everyone was suited and organized in their positions Talinde and Jes slowly stabilized the pressure in the entry corridor while Trist and Lev waited inside the reactor room with the door sealed.

When Talinde approached the aft damage, he gave a status update, "It looks like we were grazed, there is less residual damage from the impact and more from the decompression. Trist are the internal shields still showing active?"

I glanced at the power module, "All green in here."

Talinde and Jes moved into position near the closest panel joints, "We are releasing the first panel now, Shivan can you keep an eye on the Velisus internal pressure. Let me know if you see any fluctuations."

Shivan responded quickly, "Understood, currently monitoring."

As Talinde went through the same process for each panel they slowly completed the exterior repair. Each ship is equipped with replacement interior and exterior panels in case of damage during inter planetary travel, even small debris can be extremely damaging if it made it past the repulsion shield. Though Talinde never thought he would have to repair damage due to an attack from an AAM ship.

Once the last panel was in place Talinde and Jes moved down the port side of the ship well out of range of any potential danger, "Trist, Lev are you two ready for us to decompress the reactor room?"

A quick yes followed, "Okay then, Tia, Ani slowly decompress the room like I showed you, so Trist and Lev can remove the barrier."

Tia squeaky voice quickly came over the communicator, "Decompressing now father."

After a few moments Shivan added, "All clear so far."

"Looks good out here too, okay Trist, Lev go ahead and remove the barrier and remove the three interior panels like I showed you and replace with the new ones."

As Talinde continued to direct the interior replacement he tracked the progress through his visor monitor, "Yup, just like that. Now make sure all the damaged panels are secured to the floor and stand back by the door. Now, Tia, Ani can you slowly pressurize the reactor room, go in increments of quarter atmospheres at a time. Wait for the okay for the next pressurization command."

Tia responded, "Okay."

"It looks good on our side." Shivan said.

The pressure is gradually increased to a full atmosphere slowly to ensure there will not be a catastrophic failure of the repaired sections, that ensured there was minimal risk to Lev and I who would risk being violently ejected from the ship.

With the repairs completed and the ship holding pressure we were now safe to continue. Shivan let out a quiet sigh once the process was completed. He turned to Valdria, "Well now that the ship is repaired I feel much better. You never know what type of atmospheric environment we will find ourselves landing in."

Valdria smiled and asked, "What about the low frequency transmissions, any new signals?"

"Nothing for the time being, but all the lower frequencies are static, normally there would be nothing, but waves generated by electromagnetic radiation and the system filters those out." Shivan responded.

"For the time being let's sit tight and see what we detect. Let's use this chance to teach the kids how to decipher radio waves, we can use their help in analyzing without coming straight out with our discovery."

* * *

Over the next several days the crew found themselves taking classes on wave theory and how to identify patterns outside normal electromagnetic interference.

This line of study had numerous benefits for the group, first it helped identify incoming transmissions that might indicate intelligible life, second it could assist in ascertaining the origin of a signal, and lastly it would allow them to differentiate between beam and wave transmissions, beam being the type used by the Empire.

Shivan would intermittently add random segments of different types of communication to the pattern being analyzed by the group.

Typically, Tia was the first to pick up pattern changes the quickest, then as Shivan was about to introduce a merchant wave to the sound bit Trist suddenly stood up, "Did you hear that!" He quickly said looking excitedly around the room.

Shivans hand hovered over the transmit button as he looked at me. The rest of my companions seemed to be listening even more intently now.

"What was it you heard Trist?" Shivan asked as he stood and approached me.

"I thought I heard a short binary code, but just for a second. It definitely wasn't static or from the Empire." I stated.

Shivan stood behind me and slowly replayed the last minute of recorded sound, "It definitely isn't random."

"Okay now try to determine which astronomical direction it derived from. Can you do that Trist?"

"I can try but I'm not…"

Jes suddenly interrupted my response, "It came from these coordinates." Jes simply stated as he pointed to an astronomical map.

"Very well then, Valdria can you continue to watch over things here?"

"Of course."

As Shivan made his way toward the command center he called Talinde on the personal communication link, "Talinde are we okay to head out?"

Talinde's response was brief, "Let me verify statuses." After a brief pause, "All good in here. Are we moving out already?"

Shivan terminated the link and entered the command center. Shivan shook his head to himself as he pondered how talented each of the kids had become. He began to enter the desired course into the navigational logic terminal and began to process our next destination.

Shivan mumbled to himself, "That code was deteriorated, I'm amazed he even picked up the pattern. From the sound of it we still have a ways to travel, I wonder how the transmitting worlds technology has grown since it was initially sent. Let's hope they are still there and sympathetic."

As the Velisus began to come about toward the preprogramed course the surge reactor began their pulse sequence that would thrust us to factor one. Once the Velisus reached factor two and the perpetual drive took over Shivan confirmed with Talinde on the all clear.

Shivan then set the scanners to active notification, so we wouldn't miss any change in frequency or duration from the course we were traveling.

As Shivan left the command center he said, "For now I guess we are back to training." Since he knew the time was quickly approaching for us to make an assessment if this led us to a world capable of supporting our needs.

* * *

Several days after changing course it became apparent that this was indeed the right trajectory. The number of transmission waves grew much more consistent and with a clarity not previously apparent. Some of the weaker transmissions even contained what sounded like verbal communication though it clearly differed from Paltian. As the waves frequency increased Shivan decided after discussing with Valdria and Talinde to reduce speed to factor one.

This allowed more time to decipher and strategize before we approached an unknown transmission source. While the transmissions were still very low power that did not dissuade the crew from becoming excited whenever a new transmission was received.

One afternoon as we recovered from our most recent training program Tia voiced what had not previously been said out loud, "What will we actually do when we arrive? Will we have to fight like the simulations when we set foot on the surface?"

Shivan had just walked into the dining hall from the main corridor leading to the dignitary quarters on the Velisus, "Let me answer that Tia." Shivan said as he walked up to the group glancing at each member present before he asked for a moment of time as he called Valdria and Talinde to join him on the communication link.

As we waited Shivan remained silent as we all continued consuming our individual meals.

Valdria entered the room right after Talinde who pulled up a chair and sat adjacent to Jes and Tia while Valdria sat next to Shivan.

Shivan sat with his hands clasped in front of him resting on the table, as he slowly straightened from his contemplative posture, he looked out among us as we sat before him.

"The education, training and physical activities you have been performing over the last two solar cycles have held several purposes. The primary purpose was to give you the education and development you would have normally received on Paltius which also helped take your minds off our current situation. The secondary reason was to build camaraderie between each one of you, so that regardless of where we ended up you would be able to work together and survive."

"Since we still have no clue as to the nature of the inhabitants who transmitted the waves we have been monitoring, you may truly be forced to defend yourselves when we land. If that is the case I wanted to prepare you for a worst-case scenario. Regardless, you will all find what you have learned since our departure from Paltius as an incredible resource. Regarding the nature of the inhabitants, we might have obvious differences in physical traits, so we don't even know if this world will accept us, let alone support our atmospheric needs."

Shivan continued, "So, once we determine if the populace of this new world is sociable we will take every opportunity available to prepare for a smooth integration into their societal structure. However, if the risk is too great then we will be forced to continue on our search."

Talinde spoke up next, "We have the ability to maintain our voyage for a long time if necessary, so we are in no rush to land and place you all at greater risk. Shivan and I have been putting together fragments of language we have received and have classified at least twenty dialects on this world."

Valdria spoke up next, "I am sure you all know the repercussions of this information correct? With so many apparent languages there are bound to be multiple societal structures in place. Our challenge is to find the one which will provide the least resistance to our integration."

Shivan sat quietly nodding as Valdria finished, "Also we will make our integration as peaceful and anonymous as possible. This will give us a chance to gauge their capabilities for growth and understanding more clearly than what we can gleam through wave transmissions."

"I am certain they are technologically inferior to our current level, so it should be easy to remain hidden from their detection while we study the necessary languages and cultural idiosyncrasies before we land. However, we still have no idea what the planet surface is like, so this is all under the assumption that it is at least a similar atmosphere to Paltius."

Shivan paused a moment as he clasped his hands together, "Okay, let's not get distracted and remember there is a purpose for your training and study."

The others in group except for me began to excitedly chat amongst themselves, while I sat quietly contemplating what Shivan just said. Based on Shivan's discussion there are several disqualifying factors for us settling on this upcoming planet. But what he said about gauging their capabilities for growth, I wonder…

* * *

I stood before Shivan and Valdria's quarters later that evening as I depressed the call button.

Shivan appeared in the doorway within a few moments and smiled at me, "What can I help you with my prince?"

I sighed quietly, "Please just Trist, that could be dangerous on a different world if you let that slip you know."

Shivan smiled with a chuckle, "So you are thinking about our conversation earlier aren't you? Well that's good, we need to seriously be prepared."

"Can we chat?"

"Sure, come in, what would you like to discuss? Quantum theory maybe?" Shivan offered a mischievous smile.

"Ugh, please no. I still see the equations floating in my head from our first lesson. What I wanted to talk about is gauging capabilities. If this is a low technology world do you really plan on assisting in their technological development?"

Shivan sat among the cushions of the sweeping semicircular ottoman as he motioned me to have a seat. Valdria came into the room from the sleeping chamber and silently seated herself across from me as she offered a smile and nod.

Shivan continued to explain, "I have one goal and several secondary priorities, the first and foremost is keeping you safe. The others range in importance, but many support my primary goal. Keeping you safe is going to require allies so we will need to determine who can be trusted and how we will release technology without it causing strife in this multicultural world."

Shivan paused, "Next, what technology do we share, we don't want to release something so advanced that it disrupts their existing social and technological development too much. So ultimately if we determine this world is adequate to support our physiological needs we then need to catch them up."

Shivan continued, "We are at a disadvantage as well, we will need to find a way to obscure our ship from their world since the technology we have is vital to our survival. If you or one of the others were injured, without our ability to repair our cellular structure our bodies would take cycles to fully heal."

Shivan then looked at me with a slight smile as he continued, "Plus, you may not know this, but my great aunt's daughter is your mother Gialena, so we are blood related after all, so I look at you as being my very own son."

I blushed after hearing what Shivan said, "I knew that but didn't want to mention the genealogical link to others since if you didn't make it openly known it could cause undue resentment from other families."

Shivan nodded and said, "I figured as much. But Trist, I want you to enjoy what remains of your youth among others outside of this stuffy transport. I want to take pride in your growth in your father's stead. So, when he and I meet again I can tell him all the milestones I was able to observe while you matured. And Trist, you will become a great uncle here in the next solar cycle."

Both Shivan and Valdria began to smile as I sat there with a blank look on my face trying to discern his meaning…

"WHAT!?"

Shivan openly laughed at my reaction as Valdria covered her smile with her hand.

"Con... Congratulations!" I stammered.

"So, Trist, I too have a selfish reason why I would like to find a world we can grow with." Shivan said more seriously.

I nodded quietly as I thought about family.

*   *   *

As the signals-maintained consistency it became more apparent that we were within a few lunar cycles of our destination. With the entire crew gathered Shivan announced we would be dropping out of factor and approaching the upcoming system at solar navigation full, so we could more easily maneuver the Velisus into a distant orbit of the proposed world.

"Once we maneuvered into the solar system containing a small white star we quickly identified the third orbital planet as being the origin of all the wave transmissions received over the last few lunar cycles. While continuing to use passive scanners we identified a planetary body circling this new world in a relatively stable orbit."

Shivan paused as he looked at each of us, "I propose using this moon to mask our presence while still utilizing active scan dampeners to avoid electromagnetic detection. This world is relatively small, but not much smaller than Paltius itself. Unlike Paltius this world was not tidally locked and has a slight wobble to its axis creating variants in seasonal change." Shivan stroked his chin as he glanced at the filament monitors.

"The most surprising discovery we made was that the solar cycle for this planet is approximately 365 days. External short-range scans reported numerous contaminates and degradation of the atmospheric sheath protecting the planet from electromagnetic radiation." Shivan considered his next words.

"The planet is a blue world with 70% of its surface in water. Population densities vary; however, we have identified the language origins from the first several transmissions we received. The planet itself is awash in low frequency radio waves which we identified by observing the electromagnetic spectrum. We will be attempting to capture and analyze these waves soon to assist us in understanding the cultural diversities as well as their languages."

As Shivan concluded, he turned the filament monitor to low power mode, "Any questions?"

Talinde was up first, "The atmospheric contaminates, are they toxic? How about the remaining atmosphere is it a nitrogen oxygen mix like ours?"

Shivan looked to have expected this question, "Well good news for both of those questions, the contaminates are toxic but the quantities are minute enough that our purifiers could easily eliminate them. As far as being out in the open, even in these quantities at ground level you wouldn't be affected, in fact due to the increase in oxygen levels on this planet you might even feel better than when you lived on Paltius."

Valdria spoke after Shivan finished, "The communication wave network was extremely simple to infiltrate, we are currently analyzing what appears to be a simple digital knowledge network, as well as two-way communications so this will allow us to begin compiling instructional material for all of us on the primary languages of this world."

Shivan thanked Valdria and continued, "Finally once we decipher their language and have a deeper understanding of their cultures we will make an assessment based on strategic value, which land mass would be most appropriate to ensure survivability, and the local ability to institute technological advancements. That way it will be easier for us to initiate gradual improvements to bring the technological median up across all cultures."

* * *

It was early morning as the entire group focused on learning the primary languages of this new world when I suddenly asked, "So, if this world defines a year by revolutions around their star how old does that make us and what do we tell others about our age if we eventually live on the surface? I mean according to our solar calendar I am about to turn eight, but I don't look like any of the pictures of eight-year old's we have seen from this world, nor do I look nineteen if we go by a 365-day solar calendar."

The others looked up as I voiced my concerns and began discussing the potential problems if they were placed in classes with those who looked visibly older than them.

Tia sheepishly raised her hand as she said, "I don't want to be separated from everyone if we go to a school on this world."

Jes was about to say something but I stood up causing him to pause, as I walked over to Tia and placed my hand on her head, "Tia we are close enough in visible age to probably be in the same institution. Plus, do you think we would leave you separated from us?"

Tia quietly shook her head as she lowered it to her chest with visible signs she was fighting back tears of relief.

I then turned to Shivan, "What do you say Shivan, it's apparent our appearance won't be an issue, other than that how difficult will it be to infiltrate their society, and what types of documentation do they use?"

Shivan responded to my inquiry, "It will be simple to create documentation, the only problem is it won't stand up to critical review. We can generate registries in any system for each person and even adjust age to alleviate Tia's earlier concern; however, if they keep physical copies of this documentation then at some point we might be discovered."

Jes finally spoke up, "I understand Tia's fears but what about those of us who look visibly older than the school age of those on this world?"

Talinde responded, "I was actually thinking of that as well, since we will have to have some sort of income to subsist on based on what I have understood of their culture. This will be a new concept to at least everyone on this transport since none of us ever worked outside the royal palace. But I was thinking while we are still unsure of our final settlement I think that once decided we can immediately investigate small level technological introductions. This will not only create a source of income it will help open doors to more resources, so we don't exhaust our synthesizer."

As the group continued to discuss the languages and debated the merit to each culture, the decision on where to settle was finally made. Over the next several lunar cycles the adults worked on researching objects of value on this planet which we have discovered the inhabitants called Earth.

During our research we realized that the inhabitants of Earth only had identified 115 elements, most being simple and easily replicatable given the right circumstances. Among the known 115 elements Earth contained many currently unidentified elements including artificially created compounded elements.

These elements lose all their characteristics when combined, melding into a completely irreversible mixture. Of these new elements many would gradually need to be discovered and introduced so we could develop and introduce certain technologies.

Once we determined the best material to initially fund our integration we decided to look to the moon currently concealing our presence. Using a short-range personal skip, typically used for shuttling small groups between space bound craft to avoid the lengthy docking process, the group took to the moon's surface with tools used to identify mineral resources.

After setting up the equipment and activating it, the team returned to the transport allowing the ore collection unit to collect and prepare selected materials in an auto sequence. Of the minerals being mined titanium was the primary ore with the collector set to gather rarer metals as it sifted through regolith in the process.

By the time the Velisus received the short-range transmission signaling gathering completion we had a good amount of material to fund our settlement on Earth.

Once the material was transported back to the Velisus the group took stock of what had been collected. Looking at the contents of the collection vessel Shivan and Talinde weren't very impressed.

"We expected to gather more of the rarer materials unknown to Earth, unfortunately we only have a few metric tonne of gold, rhodium, silver, platinum and several metric tonne's of titanium. Well it's a start, do you think this will be enough?"

Shivan looked over the gathered materials, "Well based on what we have seen of Earth's monetary system I think this will be enough to last us at least a little while."

"So where do we go from here?"

"We need to make sure we are all fluent in the local languages. We have quite a few to learn and considering the population distribution and our observations there are at least ten languages we have been focusing on. This should allow us a fair amount of flexibility when dealing with this worlds governments."

*   *   *

As time approached for our initial contact, Valdria was busy replicating documentation in the style of the designated country, "They really should consider bio-registration, it is much more difficult to forge." Valdria said as she prepared documents.

"Have we identified a way to mask the signature of the ship as it enters the atmosphere? It's much denser than Paltius isn't it?" Valdria asked Shivan.

Shivan nodded as he added, "While it is denser I think the Velisus has plenty of gravitational thrust to evenly maneuver in atmosphere with no issues."

Talinde laughed when he overheard Shivans comment, "That might be the case, but I still think we need to break atmosphere well over a large body of water. This monster makes a horrendous racket when it enters atmosphere, and the thrusters kick in."

Upon hearing Talinde's recommendation Shivan paused a moment, "Talinde, what about in the water? Could it function under the surface?"

Talinde totally stopped what he was doing and glanced at Shivan like he was crazy, "Are you serious?"

Shivan gave an uncharacteristic shrug of his shoulders, "Why not. I mean if we can. This whole time I was wondering how we were going to get the ship to land without everyone seeing us. I mean we can avoid scans, but it would still be optically visible. Not to mention the space it will take to land."

Talinde quickly turned and headed out toward the engineering station mumbling to himself the whole way.

Jes walked into the planning room just as his father was mumbling and walking out, "What's fathers problem he looked like he was in a hurry?"

Shivan smiled, "I just gave him a challenge he couldn't turn down."

Jes eyes opened a little bigger as he smiled and turned to ran after his father.

Shivan smiled and thought to himself, "Like father, passed to the son."

* * *

When Talinde finally poked his head out of his station he looked haggard.

Shivan looked at the exhausted Talinde, "Hey there old man, don't overdo it."

Talinde just slumped into a chair and slapped a portable filament monitor down on the planning table, "I think I may have made a mess of our landing circuitry, but all the simulations give a green. Considering this planet's gravitational forces, the atmospheric pressure, the density and dynamics of the water I have reprogramed the drives to work using your scenario."

While Shivan thought it was impossible this old man, known as one of the empires best engineers had done it, "Seriously?"

"Well, these drives were designed to work in heavy mist, so the moisture isn't an issue, what I was concerned with was maneuvering in water and being able to escape the atmosphere once we actually landed. Since we will have no issue reaching water. Gravity will do most of the work in that situation." Talinde paused as he thought.

"But how do we maneuver without damaging the Velisus, or ensure she remains submerged since she will maintain a fair amount of buoyancy in the water. So I converted the engines fore and aft to be able to turn more than normal, this will give us the right/left/up/down thrust under water. After that keeping her down is easy to remedy, we can always flood the cargo bay to reduce buoyancy until we achieve depth. Once there we have the grapples that can secure our position. Then we simply pump out the water."

Shivan just shook his head, this crazy old man did it, "How about re-entering orbit, wouldn't the water act like a vacuum when we tried to lift off?"

Talinde shook his head, "At first I struggled with trying to modify our shields to project the surroundings over the ship like holographic communicators used on ship to ship transmissions. But I gave up, honestly there's an easier solution, we just re-flood the cargo bay and use thrusters to take us far enough out to sea then pump the water out. Once we are on the surface we just use full navigational thrusters. Once we're clear we can use navigational thrusters like we would entering atmosphere. If we get to a point where we have to depart it won't really matter if we're seen after all."

Shivan must agree, "That's true at that point either they know, and we do it with the planets full knowledge or we are fleeing. Well, I am still impressed you came up with the idea regardless. What additional help do you need?"

Talinde looked at Shivan with heavy eyelids, "No need I put Jes to work. He passed out as I was heading up to the main deck."

As Talinde began to softly snore Shivan pulled a blanket from the side storage closet and covered him, "Good job old man."

As the time approached to enter Earth's atmosphere, the entire crew was busy manning each sensor. Navigating through the debris in low orbit was quite troublesome however the shields easily deflected stray particles.

There was no way to do this to keep attentive eyes from seeing the re-entry however, the Velisus could mask its presence from any electronic detection but it would be a visible spectacle.

Shivan's voice sounded throughout each communication link, "Each department status check."

Talinde was the first to respond, "All green, but take us down slow otherwise it will be a scorcher."

Next was Valdria, "Medical ready."

My voice sounded out clearly, "Shields full, focusing power on lower shields."

Jes came next, "Electromagnetic shields full."

There was a long pause before Shivan asked, "Lev, Ani, Tia status?"

Lev's voice sounded out, "Sorry father, passengers secured and pressure green."

With the final check complete Shivan eased the Velisus toward an entry orbit and slowly headed through the outer troposphere. As the craft passed through the stratospheric layer it began to hasten its descent being dragged by Earth's gravity. As the Velisus passed through the heavier air the exterior began to heat.

I quickly announced, "Exterior temperature approaching one thousand degrees."

Shivan came across the communication link, "Everyone prepare for retro propulsion bursts."

As the Velisus passed the thermosphere the craft temperature began to stabilize due to the propulsion burst slowing the descent. As the turbulence began to pick up Shivan noticed the Velisus suddenly began to feel heavier.

Jes voice rang out, "We are seeing numerous pings against our electromagnetic shields."

Shivan hurried the descent as the enormous freighter was buffeted by high altitude winds, "Bringing us down faster."

Suddenly the entire crew can feel the full weight of gravity ease up signaling a rapid descent. The girls reached out to hold hands with each other as they felt themselves easing away from the chair and the restraint applying increasing pressure.

"Hold on, slowing descent."

Suddenly the gravitational force seemed to intensify as it began to slowly force each passenger deeper into their seat.

Then with a sudden jerk we all felt and heard a loud noise like dropping a large rock in a shallow pool. Suddenly the feeling eased as the ship violently bobbed on the sea surface.

*　　*　　*

From a great distance a unique astrological sight was observed. Numerous craft and radar installations made reports of a hole in space according to readings from their monitors. Observatories throughout the Pacific region reported a strange shooting star that seemed to bounce and descend slowly toward the earths South Pacific Ocean.

The strange shooting star could be seen from New Zealand, Hawaii and all along the West Coast of South America. This strange phenomenon was enough to cause the United States to deploy components of their Third Fleet to investigate the peculiar phenomenon.

*　　*　　*

As the waves around the Velisus begin to calm Talinde made his way to the command center.

Once Talinde walked into the command center the literal brain of the ship Shivan was adjusting the Velisus's navigational coordinates.

Talinde expressed his urgency to relocate, "So, I think we should move from this location quickly. We received numerous detection probes on entry, it is likely they will send whatever they have available to investigate."

Shivan almost clicked his tongue, "Yea, that was not as smooth as I had hoped, are we good back in the engineering rooms?"

"We're fine back there, but we need to move, and I would recommend submerged so we are out of sight."

Shivan reached for the communicator, "Trist, Lev, and Jes make sure all the lower doors are sealed."

The three responded in near unison, "Will do!"

Talinde finally asked, "Do we have oceanographic layouts for this sea?"

"No, we were too busy elsewhere and honestly I didn't think about it since we initially didn't really plan on navigating submerged."

"Well, I don't think it will hurt to use our scanners, I will reduce power on the scan anyway just to be sure. For now, I will look for an isolated location where we can plan our next move."

Talinde turned and headed toward the planning room. Shivan continued to run through checks waiting for the all clear on the cargo bay and lower levels.

The communication link lit green as Sivan received my report, all green.

"Well here we go."

Shivan slowly opened the cargo bay outer door as he watched the cargo filament monitor. The Velisus began to list to the stern and slowly rocked forward as the cargo bay began to fill with water.

As the ships buoyancy dropped Shivan attempted to balance the intake of water to create a neutral buoyancy which would allow the Velisus to submerge and easily maneuver.

"For the time being let's wait for the dust to settle." Shivan quietly said to himself.

The Velisus slowly settled into the South Pacific Basin as Shivan maneuvered it toward its destination.

With a safe retreat from the South Pacific Ocean, the Velisus slowly approached the east side of a small island and settled into the depths. As the passengers of the Velisus gathered in the planning room it was finally time to discuss first contact.

*   *   *

Shivan started the meeting, "We are 75 kilometers from the coast of a country named Japan, currently sitting in an area known for geologic activity. The known activity in this area will aid in masking our presence temporarily. However, we cannot remain here for too long. Later this cycle we will venture into the town of Kamogawa and attempt to find a broker for the material we prepared. That will give us some local currency."

Valdria looked at all the faces watching Shivan intently and finally asked, "How will we approach the city?"

Talinde answered, "The suits we use for zero gravity activities will work but they could be a little heavy, especially if you want to deliver the ores we gathered."

The trepidation of the group was apparent, since the first contact could very well define their relationship with Earth.

Tia and Ani whispered to each other as Lev and I shared questioning glances, "…if they attack us what would happen…" I could barely overhear.

Shivan began to lay out a plan, "While I agree with Talinde the suits will be extremely cumbersome we have little choice for now. We first must determine where we can exchange the ore before we even consider hauling it to the surface. So, in addition to myself, I would like to take two others who feel they have a firm grasp of the local language."

Valdria said, "It would be best if at least one person who knew how to pilot remained to offset a worst-case situation. I think that rules out Talinde, so I will volunteer it will also look more natural for a man and a woman to be together."

As the other members glanced around at one another uncertain of their ability, I raised my hand, "I think I will be able to help, not only have I memorized the characters I can easily read and pronounce them."

Shivan looked at me as he pinched the sides of his chin, "Very well, while I don't particularly like placing you in an unknown situation we need to be fully prepared to negotiate."

As the group began preparation Lev and Ani met up with me in my quarters.

The typical quarters on the Velisus were not much more than ninety square meter rooms. However, since the crew of the Velisus is so small we all have taken up residence in the larger dignitary quarters.

My cabin was even more lavish than theirs. Being closer to five-hundred square meters and including finely spun rugs, furniture and artwork depicting Paltius cityscapes and landscapes throughout.

As Lev and Ani entered my cabin they noticed me sitting at my desk immersed in studies and looking through what appeared to be maps on the filament monitors.

Lev spoke up first, "Isn't it a little late to cram? You guys are leaving in less than a cycle."

I straightened as I turned toward the two. Then sighed as I saw the faces of my friends, "You guys. It's not like we are walking out to face the AAM, everything we have studied shows this society to be relatively peaceable. So, could you refrain from the distressed look Ani."

Ani frowned slightly, "What, I can't worry about father or mother. I'm not worried about you in the least."

Lev let out a sigh as he looked at Ani while she responded, "Anyway, I think father is ready and he is checking over the suits with Talinde, something about differences in pressure. Are you ready?"

I shrugged slightly, "About as ready as I was to board the Velisus."

Both Lev and I grinned at each other, while Ani just looked at me worriedly.

As we met up in the same airlock we previously used to initially enter the Velisus, Talinde was going over the final adjustments on the suits. The three of us began slipping on the suits over our clothing which was chosen to be closest to what those on Earth normally wore. Grey jump suits with patches of yellow along the sides and shoulders.

Once fully equipped Talinde went over the final control changes, "The communication system was the same, what I did adjust was the pressurization and thrust of the suits since you will be working in much heavier and a thicker atmosphere than in orbit."

Shivan quickly latched his helmet in place and ran through a quick suit check and announced over the internal link, "Looks good, okay finish suiting up and evacuate the air lock Tal."

As Talinde exited the room and walked toward the panel controlling the dual wall airlock my companions looked on as the doors slowly slid closed and sealed.

Shivan looked at the monitor panel and once it read green he then slowly depressed the linked control on his suit that would begin the decompression and flooding of the room.

I began to feel the water as it rushed against my legs making me feel a little unsteady. The feeling while not as cold as space made me think of a cold hand grasping my leg as it moved up my body. As the room finished filling there was an earie noise as the super structure groaned with the change in pressure against its inner walls.

With the dark water before us, we exited the ship and immediately engaged the thrusters which worked as water jets propelling us in the direction of land. The journey took several cycles.

Shivan's voice suddenly came over the link an hour into our journey, "Let's begin a slow ascent, we have about two hours to shore, so set your rate of ascent at two meters per ten traveled. That should put us near the surface close to shore."

Both Valdria and I respond accordingly. As we noticed an increase in illumination we realize we were nearing the surface and slowed our ascent to maintain depth until the rocky outcroppings began to force us up.

The feeling of traveling through the water was extremely unique. I had never been in a body of water as large or deep. What was peculiar were the variety of sea life we saw along the way, all of which scattered as we grew close.

Once we determined we had reached the coast we stopped and scanned for movement above the surface, "Looks clear now let's break surface." Shivan announced.

As all three of us gradually broke the surface, water drained down from the viewing visor and we could see rocky outcroppings that appeared to be manmade.

As we fully exited the water we noticed a steep hill covered in lush foliage. We moved toward the base of the hill to assess our location, which was no more than three kilometers from the densest part of the city. No one appeared to be within visual range of our emersion either.

As we quickly began to remove our suits we neatly concealed them within the tree like foliage growing at the base of the hill.

As we slowly scaled the hill we suddenly came to a short wall flanked by a smooth black surface which appeared to be a road. Glancing in both directions Shivan motioned us forward.

The light seeping over the horizon told us it was early morning, there were very few inhabitants out this time of morning, so we made good time as we rounded a curve in the road and approached the most populated part of town. As we started to see increased activity I notice an excessive number of looks passing our direction.

As I looked up at Shivan and Valdria I could tell they had noticed them as well. I spoke in a low voice, "Did we do something to draw excess attention?"

Shivan frowned and said, "I don't think so, but the looks are beginning to make me warry."

As we continued walking I noticed a decline in the number of people along the pathway. Even the vehicles no longer traversed the road to our right. Shivan suddenly said, "I think we may be in trouble."

As he stopped walking he placed his hand on my shoulder to pull me toward a building entry.

Valdria moved to my right as there were now several people flooding out of a vehicle in front of us. The man directly in front of Shivan had his hands out in a peaceable fashion although he was flanked on both sides by what could only be described as nothing less than military personnel.

All three were wearing blue jump suits and black body armor, the two on the right and left of the man directly in front of us had what must be some sort of weapon. The man closest to us who initially motioned us to halt looked to be a little under two meters tall with a solid build, muscular arms were exposed past his body armor and he showed us an unreadable expression.

As he silently appraised all three of us he suddenly asked if we spoke Japanese.

Ahh, I understood that I thought to myself, "Yes, we do, how can we help you?" Shivan responded.

The man then nodded to himself as he began to talk, "I would like you to come with me. We would like to ask you a few questions away from prying eyes."

"We are just looking for a chance to visit your town, we have done nothing wrong." Shivan responded.

As he finished his sentence I noticed the two men behind the man who first approached us slowly begin to move their weapons closer to firing position.

"This isn't really open for debate, would you please get in the vehicle."

Shivan looked back at me then at Valdria and up again, "Do I have your word we will be unharmed?"

The man nodded with a short, "Yes, you have my word."

The two flanking the speaker moved to either side of the vehicle side door.

As we loaded into the vehicle I quickly noticed that it appeared to be well armored and the seats seemed to be arranged in line with a monitoring screen located against the front of the vehicle separating the rear from the operator.

As the three of us climbed in the man who first approached us followed while the two soldiers slid the door closed and returned to a different vehicle.

It wasn't long before we began moving and as I looked at the interior of the vehicle apprehensively Shivan began to speak, "I seem to have failed to catch your name earlier, if we are to be detained I would like to know the name of our captor."

The man leaned forward a bit as he detached the side restrains on his armor and pulled it over his head and quietly placed it to the side of the vehicle wall, "I can't tell you much, but I don't suppose knowing my name would cause any harm, I'm Hidekazu. I am sure we will be able to answer your questions soon enough. I hope you will be able to answer ours."

As the vehicle progressed I noticed Valdria sharing a concerned look with Shivan, but he remained silent with a very serious look on his face.

When the vehicle began to slow in speed it was obvious we were going through some type of checkpoint from the voices that could be overheard outside.

As the vehicle came to a full stop and the vibrations ceased I heard the door open in the front and quietly looked to Hidekazu and my two companions.

When the side door to the vehicle suddenly slid opened Hidekazu motioned us to stay seated as he exited the vehicle and closed the door about halfway.

I looked to Shivan and quietly asked, "What do you think is going to happen?"

Shivan just nodded, "I am unsure, but if we wanted to make contact this might be the opportunity we were looking for, I only hope..."

As Shivan was about to finish he quickly cuts short his response as the door slid open again. Hidekazu stood in the doorway and asked us to exit and to follow him. As we exited the vehicle I looked from right to left and realized we were in a large hangar, about the size of the cargo bay of the Velisus.

The walls were grey and appeared to be insulated and the floor was painted grey with lines leading in different directions. The perimeter of the building is surrounded by guards with similar weapons to those we first met, but these guards don't appear to have the same color uniforms.

As we fall in behind Hidekazu we began to walk toward a separate doorway not marked by lines on the floor. As we approached the door I noticed Hidekazu punch in a code next to the doorway. This must have a similar function to our doors I thought, then to my surprise Hidekazu pulled the door open.

Once we passed into the room I noticed several individuals standing behind a semi-circular table. Hidekazu motioned us to take the three seats at the head of the room.

As the door was closed and I looked back, two soldiers had entered and were standing in front of each exit. I looked at Shivan as he looked at each person deliberately as if he was making an assessment.

He then turned to Valdria and I and said in Paltian, "It's okay let's hear what they have to say." This caused a few in the room to nervously glance at each other.

As we seated ourselves in the chairs provided, Hidekazu walked around the table and stood in front of a chair to the far right.

Once Hidekazu found his position, the older gentlemen at the apex of the table cleared his throat and said, "First off, let me welcome you to the Japanese Aerospace Exploration Organization (JAXO). I hope you weren't too inconvenienced in your trip to our facility. Now I believe introductions are in order."

The Deal

"I am Tomomi Hitoshi, I have been delegated as the representative of Japan and as the president of JAXO, I would like to formally welcome you to Japan." The elderly gentleman said.

As each in turn introduced themselves I began to feel overwhelmed with so many names and the different positions they held.

Final as it came to Hidekazu he looked in our direction and said, "I am Tenshin Hidekazu, I am the representative of the Japanese Maritime Defense Force."

As the final introduction was completed and following protocol I began to stand but as I leaned forward I glanced toward Shivan, he was already standing and looked back at me as if mentally telling me not to give myself away.

Shivan gave a formal bow and as he straightened up he slowly passed his eyes across each individual before him as if memorizing their faces, "It is my pleasure to meet you all, I am Shivan Lastrande."

As he motioned to Valdria, "This is my wife Valdria and…" Shivan paused a moment, "And my son Tristali." Once he completed the introductions he turned to the others in the room and said, "I would like to formally request asylum in your country for my family and crew."

Those in the room stirred briefly, Hitoshi was the first to speak, "And exactly what are you seeking asylum from?"

Shivan silently contemplated his question, "We have lost our home and have been searching for a place we can quietly settle and begin to build a new future. Of the locations we researched, Japan seemed to be the best suited to our propensity for peace."

The room remained quiet for a few moments before Hitoshi sighed and asked his next question, "Can you tell me if these are yours?" Hitoshi motioned for the guard to open the door as a new face pushed a hand cart with what appeared to be our suits.

Shivan's face looked somewhat strained, "It appears you watched us for a while. Yes, those are our suits."

Hidekazu is the next to speak, "Well it is not often we see a ship the size of yours enter our atmosphere." He said with somewhat of a smile on his face, "While it seems, you were able to mask your entry by blocking radar waves you couldn't mask your visual. Did you really think you could land a ship that large without being noticed?"

Shivan was also wearing a slight smile, "It is exactly as you say, we knew the chances of being detected visually were high, so we choose to land as far from land as possible. We did not detect any craft in the area, might I ask how?"

Hidekazu just pointed a finger toward the ceiling, "You choose to land in an area that is known as the spacecraft cemetery. Plus, we began detecting what appeared to be an abnormality in our scans. Since you seemed to be attempting to be stealthy about your entry we merely watched, your ship had a large infrared signature, so it was still easy to follow once you submerged."

Valdria sighed and quietly said, "I thought we accounted for all possibilities, I didn't even think about satellites, I guess we underestimated their abilities."

Hitoshi glanced around the room then spoke, "It appears my colleagues have many questions that they are unwilling to ask. So, let me be blunt, what are your intentions if we refuse asylum?"

The room was silent for several moments as people awkwardly shifted in their seats as they waited for Shivans response, "Given Earths unwillingness to grant us respite we would be forced to depart your system."

Hitoshi looked toward Hidekazu then toward each representative sitting at the table, "It appears we will have no choice…"

I made my decision, "Excuse me!" I said as I stood.

As I looked to Shivan who was casting a stern glance my way, "Trist don't get involved." Shivan hastily said.

I look at Shivan and continued, "Shivan we have no choice, you know fairly well that we are likely not to find another world capable of supporting us as readily as this one. I have made my decision for the betterment of us all."

I suddenly stood a little straighter and performed the official diplomatic introduction used by the empires royal family, "I am Tristali Verndactilia, the first prince of the Tri-Moon Alliance and descendant of Remali Verndactilia the 1st. I hereby formally request asylum as a representative of Paltius. We will not let your generosity go unrewarded."

The representatives at the table seemed to be whispering amongst themselves as Hitoshi leaned over to listen to his advisors then straightened and leaned back a little in his chair, "Well, let it not be said that JAXO turned away the Prince of Paltius. Tristali, if I might call you that."

I responded as I remained standing, "Trist is fine."

"Well then Trist, we already recognized the benefit in granting you asylum could bring our country. While I appreciate you being forthright with us, you have much to learn in holding your cards." Hitoshi slightly smiled.

As I noticed his smile I quickly glanced toward Shivan who was leaning over. As Shivan straightened up he glanced my way with a sad but proud expression on his face.

Over the next several hours we were asked numerous questions regarding the location of Paltius and capabilities of the Velisus and finally the number of crew. Shivan deftly responded to each in turn but I noticed he didn't provide any more information than what was asked.

As the questioning appeared to come to an end Hitoshi finally asked if we would be willing to take a physical examination, his reasoning was to ensure there was no fear of us introducing unknown illnesses.

Shivan looked to Valdria before she responded, "I can provide you a detailed list of each passenger and a summary of their most recent examination. This will be the first cooperative information exchange in our new partnership with Japan."

Several of the members of the meeting began to excitedly chat amongst themselves.

As Hitoshi stood so did the other members of the session, he suddenly bowed prompting other members to follow suit, "We look forward to a prosperous partnership then."

As he raised his head Hidekazu stepped away from the table and approached us, "Please follow me."

As the three of us glanced at the departing members then at Hidekazu, Shivan asked, "What would you have us do now?"

"Well, since we don't know much about you we might as well start from square one. It is sort of an assessment of your immune system, since we have no idea if you could be harboring bacteria that would be harmful to us, just like you don't know if you are fully immune to bacteria on Earth."

We began following Hidekazu as he walked through the doorway used earlier to bring in our suits.

"What about our belongings?"

"Ahh those, well they are remarkable pieces of technology, but they are biometrically encoded, aren't they?"

Valdria smiled, "So you checked them already."

"We would be poor scientists if we didn't, right?" Hidekazu glanced back with a slight smile.

We traveled down a long corridor painted grey with high ceilings, and as we approach a set of doors on opposite sides of the hallway Hidekazu stopped and opened the right door, "Please come this way."

As we passed through the doorway the room looked to be what would resemble a basic medical examination room. There were three small tables and two chairs at each station. Next to them stood a physician waiting to take vital signs and from the instruments on each table, blood samples, "I do apologize for the request to draw blood, but you see everyone you have encountered will have to be quarantined for thirty days minimum. Having your blood samples will allow us to run tests to shorten that time."

Hidekazu grunted a short laugh, "Actually, everyone you have met knowingly agreed since it's not every day we have visitors like you." As we found chairs as directed by the physicians they began to take heart rate, pulse, respiration and temperature and finally blood samples.

The physicians looked perplexed as they each found oddities deviating from what they expected. The physician attending to Valdria nonchalantly asked, "So I understand you are the one who offered examination details on each passenger."

Valdria looked at the physician, "That is correct. I am the Emperors royal medical consul. I now attend to Trist and the others on the Velisus."

"Velisus, is that your ships name?" Hidekazu asked from the corner of the room, "I apologize, I didn't mean to eavesdrop."

Valdria shook her head slightly, "Yes, it is, but if you wish to know more you should speak to Shivan or Talinde."

"Hidekazu, when can we expect to be able to contact the Velisus?"

"Please, call me Kazu, we will probably be working together for the duration of your stay in Japan. Once the examination is competed we will arrange an opportunity to contact your vessel."

As Kazu finished Valdria again faced the physician attending her, "I am sorry, I can provide you all the most recent examination results for each passenger. I can also provide information that will allow you to conduct these archaic tests noninvasively." Valdria finally said.

The physician was preparing the draw site on her arm as he began to explain what he would be doing.

I looked over at Shivan and Valdria as I winced and yelped a bit not expecting the pinching and burning sensation I felt, as he stuck a needle in my arm. As I looked down I saw him slowly back out the needle that had a clear tube attached to it until there was a squirt of blood.

When the tube was nearly filled he pulled the tube from the needle and placed another vial in its place. Both vials filled quickly with light red blood.

Once the physician was done, he placed a gauze over the draw site and slowly slid the needle from my arm.

"Trist keep pressure on that, it will take several cycles to close." Valdria told me.

The physicians looked at Valdria then at me. The one physician attending Shivan asked, "Do you have problems with wounds closing?"

"Once you analyze our blood you may find many things that differentiate us from humans."

As the three physicians finished up and picked up their samples they bowed and quickly retreated.

Kazu laughed once as the doctors exited the room, "They are probably tripping over each other trying to get to the laboratory right now."

Each of us continued to keep slight pressure on the draw site as we all intently focused on Kazu.

Once he noticed our looks he stood up and carried his chair to sit in front of us, "Now, that the unpleasantness is over where should I begin, and what are we going to do with you?"

"Luckily for you, we have received no requests from the United States (U.S.) regarding your arrival, it could have been blind luck that they weren't watching your landing sight. They tend to have bad taste when it comes to flaunting their technological ability to see everything. They were probably focusing on North Korea for all I know. Which is good for you."

"How is that good for us? You still saw us, should we be afraid if the U.S. saw us as well?"

Kazu shook his head, "No, they would probably still work with you, we are allies after all. How should I say this tactfully? Their idea of cooperation might deviate from what we offer. While we would prefer a long-term outflow of new ideas, they would prefer to take a lump sum cash out."

Kazu looked as though he was searching for an example, "That really isn't fair either I guess, let's just say we have different views on our expectations regarding visitors."

Shivan looked like he was perplexed.

As Kazu was explaining the differences in Japans treatment of what he referred to as visitors, there was a knock on the door. Kazu paused and looked back, as he slowly rose and walked to the door.

The door opened partially but not enough for us to see who was there. Occasionally we could see Kazu nod as he silently listened to the unknown speaker.

Kazu suddenly bowed and said, "Please leave it to me." The door silently closed as Kazu returned to the seat before us, "So, shall we discuss information sharing?"

Shivan looked to Valdria and I then he turned to Kazu and said, "Yes, that would be acceptable."

"I have just been granted the authority to negotiate and provide you residency and help you settle into society. This transition would be supported by the government of Japan with the understanding it will equally benefit due to its support."

"Will we be able to bring the rest of our companions as well?" I asked.

Kazu glanced at me as he nodded, "That is my understanding, I would ask that we have a chance to visit your crew to make our expectations known."

Shivan narrowed his eyes as he said, "What expectations might those be?"

"Well, I don't think you will find them unjust. You are to remain silent regarding your origins and if it becomes known you are from a different world we will deny knowing of your presence, and you will be treated as invaders. If you do anything to jeopardize the citizenry of this country, you will be dealt with severely." Kazu paused a moment.

"Any technology shared must be vetted through myself and approved by the Head of Technology before released, and the form of release must adhere to the prior restrictions. I will be honest, we will place higher value on productive technologies to include what we deem as defensive capabilities. We are very interested in your shielding abilities."

Valdria asked, "What about knowledge, we of course can replicate technology but if we shared knowledge and left the development to others would that be acceptable?"

"As long as it isn't detrimental to the Japanese government or places us at a disadvantage that would be acceptable." Kazu said, "Now, if I could trouble you for a list of passengers and your lodging requirements I will forward that to the team currently tasked with locating a suitable location."

"Can you locate something near the coast? Since you didn't demand the surrender of the Velisus I assume we can still utilize its facilities, right?" Shivan asked.

"Yes, that is correct. While we would love to investigate it thoroughly we will still leave it in your care. Perhaps a time will come when we can discuss your interstellar technologies but for now let's work on building trust." Kazu smiled earnestly.

Valdria looked to me as she handed me the tablet Kazu provided, "Trist, while I have been able to master the spoken language you have proven much more adept at the written. Could you please note the number and names of each member?"

I quickly wrote the names of each member in the Velisus for Kazu, noting name, gender, family structure and age. As I hand the tablet back to Kazu he glanced at it.

He appeared to really be focusing on its contents before he let out a deep breath and looked up to each of us, "Is this correct?"

I offered a quizzical look, "Did I make a mistake in the characters?"

"No, that's not it, but…are you really 89 years old Shivan, and Valdria, you're 64?"

Shivan and Valdria nodded, "That is correct, however by your solar calendar we would be 2.4 times that old. Our world orbited a binary star system, so our year was 876 days."

Kazu, coughed to clear his throat a bit, "Okay… I will relay that information. Maybe we could use more information on the history of your world, so we don't have any more surprises."

Shivan began to layout our requests, "If possible, we would like lodgings near the coast, so we can easily access the Velisus, off deep water would be best. We would like to keep the crew together, seeing how there is only eight of us the dwelling shouldn't need to be too big. And, we have three other passengers who are near Trist's age. Also, we would like to offer them the chance to interact with children near their age and physical development. Lastly, unlike our world, we understand you still work on a currency-based system."

Kazu nodded as Shivan continued, "We have a stock of supplies we mined prior to arriving on Earth. We had intended to search for a way to sell them. Is there any way to broker a sale? It would provide us the necessary currency to help establish our household necessities."

Kazu's eyebrows raised, "Oh… I think we can do that."

As Shivan finished discussing our requirements Kazu continued to note each request. When we finished he asked, "Well, let me pass this on so they can begin working on some of it, and I know it must be getting late for you. We have provided a place for you to rest, it's not much but it should suit your needs until we take you back to your ship tomorrow."

Shivan offered a slight bow in thanks, "For now, please follow me." Kazu stood and paused until we all did the same, we followed him out the door opposite from our initial entry and into a corridor flanked by large windows.

This was the first glimpse we had of the exterior of the building we were brought to. It appeared to be surrounded by lush grasses with gardens circling the perimeter. I noticed a unique cylindrical object laying sideways off in the distance next to a building with the abbreviation JAXO on the sign.

We were led to another room with what appeared to be reclining couches, the blinds to the room were drawn and as Kazu explained where the facilities were he paused, "Have you eaten recently? I am terribly sorry for not thinking of it sooner."

Shivan responded, "We ate prior to departing the Velisus, we have not eaten since."

"Well, let me take care of that. Do you have any dietary requirements? Will a few sandwiches be okay? Our cafeteria is likely closed so while we have the staff bringing your suits to the room through that door I will have something prepared." Kazu had pointed to the door adjacent to the personal facilities.

Since I had a chance to finally relieve myself I noticed extreme differences in designs for the same purpose, at least the cleansing function was similar. As I ran my hands under the dispenser water rushed out to cover my hands, so much so that I thought it was broken.

I quickly pulled my hands back then slowly looked for a drying mechanism. Unlike the Velisus or home, we used a system that dried and sanitized your hands without moisture since water was a precious commodity.

As I re-entered the resting room I noticed Valdria had already returned and Shivan was now sitting on the edge of a couch.

When Shivan saw me he quietly said, "I wish you had not voiced your heritage earlier. We must remain diligent from here on that it remains a secret even in the direst of circumstances."

I quietly accepted his chastising advice given out of his true concern for my wellbeing as I nodded in understanding.

After about one hour there was a knock on the door, Shivan was the one to answer, "Enter."

The visitor was Kazu with what appeared to be a bag. He carried it over to the table at the head of the room and began to sort many different objects wrapped in paper.

Once he finished he beckoned us to the table as he began to explain what he had brought, "Since I wasn't sure what you would like I brought an assortment. This is yakisoba, this one here is steak, and this is egg and this one is a katsu sandwich. I assure you they are all delicious."

As I began to think about food my stomach made a grumbling noise and I immediately blushed as Valdria and Shivan snickered. As I reached for the egg sandwich I noticed Shivan pondering his choice when suddenly I heard another muted grumble.

Shivan quickly decided on the katsu sandwich as he turned away in embarrassment. Both Valdria and I began laughing.

As I unwrapped the sandwich I looked at it curiously, we didn't have anything like this in the palace. The soft white exterior and golden interior seemed to beckon as I took my first bite.

I have never enjoyed a sensation as pleasing as this, as I took another bite I swore I would never eat another synthesized meal again.

As I looked over at Valdria she was slowly chewing what appeared to be the yakisoba sandwich while Shivan chose the katsu.

They both appeared to be thinking the same thing I was. I suddenly asked Kazu, "Can we take some of these when we head back tomorrow?"

Kazu offered a wide smile you could even see in his eyes as he said, "I think we better."

As we finished eating I finally started to calm down. This had been a hectic ordeal, but it looked like we would finally be able to settle in. As I sat on the edge of the couch I pulled the cover Kazu provided up to my chest and slowly laid back, I didn't even realize how tired I was and soon fell asleep.

As I dreamt I thought I heard the voices of our remaining companions, specifically Ani and Tia crying for us.

Once we awoke and began taking care of our personal hygiene chores we heard a knock on the door. Kazu announced, "It looks like you guys are good, in fact you have fewer bacteria on you than a clean room."

As another face appeared from around the corner. Kazu introduced the person with him as Warrant Officer Toshi. He explained he would be the person in charge of taking us to our destination.

Kazu showed us to our suits and asked if we would like them transported or if we would like to carry them.

Shivan responded, "We can carry them, they aren't too heavy."

Kazu raised his eyebrows, "Very well, then let's depart."

As we traversed some of the same corridors we had yesterday I overheard Shivan ask Kazu, "How do you plan on getting us to our ship?"

"We have a vessel located near your position to keep other ships from the area conducting what would appear to the casual observer as military drills."

As we exited the building the same vehicle was already prepared with a door open to accept us. As all five of us entered and the door closed we began the first part of our journey back. It was a much quicker trip this time, no more than fifteen minutes before the vehicle came to a halt.

As we waited the door soon slid open and two men clad in green jumpsuits and helmets and visors directed us toward another strange vehicle.

This one appeared to be white with a gold stripe on the tail and had a rotating blade attached to the top and rear of the vehicle. As the operators guided us into the passenger compartment they slid the exterior door closed.

They handed us protective headwear to mute the noise of the vehicle. It was very peculiar, we didn't have anything like this on Paltius. When I tried to ask what this vehicle was I realized I couldn't hear my own voice.

As we all settled into seats the vehicle began to whine louder and it suddenly began to list forward and gradually picked up momentum. This was a spectacular feeling, being able to fly in something that didn't use thrusters but used a totally different power source than what I had learned about.

The flight took over an hour, I didn't realize we had traveled that far when we first had left the Velisus. As I noticed a change in the momentum I looked out the window to see several vessels scattered about around a ship with a flat surface.

Toshi's voice came through the headwear, "That's the carrier we are going to." As he pointed in the direction of the largest ship.

I tried watching out the window, but we had changed angles, so I could only see the open water.

We began our descent and I could feel a slight jerky motion as we contacted a firm surface and bounced a bit. It wasn't long until the whining of the engine began to subside to a dull whirring noise.

Once the rotation of the blades stopped a group of men dressed in what appeared to be uniforms opened the door and assisted us in removing the headgear and escorted us to a small ready room in the ship where we were asked to wait.

As we found ourselves separated from Kazu and Toshi we looked around and took seats among the numerous chairs lining the room.

As Shivan and Valdria talked I found myself taking in all the maps lining the wall, there appeared to be a banner near the front of the room with the name Ryuuga spelled out.

After about forty minutes Toshi returned, "Please follow me, I will take you to an area where you can suit up, and we will meet with Kazu who is preparing now."

We followed Toshi deeper into the storage bay for the vehicles, I learned were called helicopters, to an area that opened above the water line of the ship. Here Toshi asked us to prepare.

As we all began to slide the suits over our clothing Shivan adjusted my suit and checked Valdria's before he finished pulling his on. Once we were adjusted all that remained were our visors and to do a final pressure check.

We waited a few more minutes before a small vehicle arrived carrying Kazu, who appeared to be in a very cumbersome suit that looked like an exoskeleton surrounding a hard-lined pressure suit.

"Sorry that took so long. They had to adjust the suit and give me instruction on how to use the propulsion system. These are definitely heavier than yours, will this size be an issue entering your vessel?"

Shivan glanced over the suit Kazu wore and said, "It should be fine, the decompression chamber is fairly large."

Once Kazu was ready we all put our visors on and sealed the seam. Shivans voice came over the communication link, "Okay do a pressure and link check and give me a status."

Valdria and I responded with, "All green." As he motioned we were ready to Kazu, the two men who accompanied him helped attached a winch line to a hook on his back, and they slowly lifted him up and moved the boom out over the water. We could see him give a thumb up sign as he started to enter the water.

Shivan said, "Let's go." And we all jumped into the sea. Shivans calm voice again prompted for a propulsion check and we waited floating below the surface for Kazu to be released.

Once they released Kazu he began to descend rapidly until he was able to adjust to the use of his thrusters. Once he began to control his descent Shivan motioned us to follow and he began to lead the way.

It took several minutes before we could make out the dull outline of the Velisus in the dark waters. As we approached the flooded decompression chamber Shivan motioned Kazu inside.

When the doorway was cleared he began to initiate the pressurization sequence from the control panel inside the room.

As the water level began to decline I was about to take off my visor but Shivan quickly stopped me, "Wait until it is clear, what would you do if the chamber started flooding again?"

As the remaining water sloshed around our ankles I could hear a slight creak from the super structure of the Velisus. Once the panel turned green, Shivan engaged the seals along the wall so we could remove the suits. As Shivan finished he motioned for Kazu to turn around as he assisted in removing his helmet, "So how do we get you out?"

As the helmet cleared Kazu's head all I heard him say is, "My GOD!! This is the Velisus? It is much larger than the infrared signature we detected."

Shivan chuckled as he continued unfastening the joints holding Kazu's suit together, "Most of the ship has extensive shielding since it was often used as a transport vessel for the Emperor, you probably were seeing the heat signature from the thrusters."

As the last retaining seal was removed Kazu was finally able to step out of the suit. Shivan faced Kazu, "Please let me do all the talking." Shivan locked his stare with Kazu's.

"While we have an agreement, our companions will most likely be concerned and possibly hostile since we failed to return in the time frame we initially discussed. They do not know about your offer yet so please allow me time to explain the situation. When I ask you may answer my questions but don't interrupt. Don't be alarmed if you don't understand what they say either. They have all been studying your language but may not immediately speak it."

Kazu nodded solemnly.

As Shivan moved to the panel that would sync pressure in the room with the rest of the ship he noticed Talinde and Jes to the side of the door. Once the pressure equalized the door quickly slid open.

Shivan responded in Paltian, "Tal, Jes it's okay I brought someone who is going to help us with a new start on Earth in a country called Japan."

Talinde stepped back away from the side of the door until he could catch Shivans eyes, "Shivan look at me and say that again."

Shivan inwardly smiled at his old friend's caution, "The human with us is named Hidekazu, he was instrumental in helping us broker an agreement with the Japanese government for asylum." Talinde stared in Shivans eyes a moment but saw no coercion present.

As Shivan walked through the doorway Talinde quickly grasped arms with him, "We were so worried! While you were away several vessels began to converge above us, then when you failed to return we feared the worse."

Valdria and I walked into the hall and Talinde gave Val and I a huge hug, "I am glad to have you all back."

I saw Jes in the corner holding back on his welcome out of respect for his father. Talinde must have been incredibly worried.

I hoped Lev, Ani and Tia were okay, I thought to myself.

As Talinde and Jes finished expressing their concern and introductions, the group slowly made their way to the command center. I smiled as I watched Kazu wearing an expression of utter awe as he took in his surroundings. As the door to the command center slid open I saw Lev, Ani and Tia sitting around the table.

As soon as their eyes meet mine Ani and Tia began to run toward us and they both… tackled me!?

"Hey what was that for!" I suddenly asked only to realize they both were openly sobbing while squeezing me like a drowning man would squeeze a buoy.

As I looked toward Lev, I noticed he was also is crying, "Come on guys it was only a couple days."

Shivan, Valdria and Talinde watched quietly. I could tell Talinde was close to showing his emotions as well, now that his daughter had finally been able to release the tension and worry built up over the last two days.

As I slowly sat up assisted by Ani and Tia moving with me I quietly put my arms around them both and quietly said in their ears, "I'm home. I missed you guys too."

As I tried to stand it was like they were permanently attached, as they stood with me, "Umm, Ani, Tia this is a little embarrassing. Could you stop squeezing me so tight?"

They finally stopped squeezing but continued to cling to me as Lev finally walked over and joined them, "We were so worried about you guys, and suddenly there were those vessels and we had no contact. I'm just glad you made it back safe."

As Lev, Ani, and Tia continued to cling to me I overheard Shivan talking with Talinde along with Valdria, "I think this is our best opportunity, they only expect us to adhere to their principals and to maintain silence about our origins…"

As they continued to talk I looked toward Kazu who was still trying to take in his surroundings as a tactician would memorize a battlefield.

* * *

As I encouraged and guided my friends toward my cabin we all quietly entered. So, I could be somewhere comfortable I sat on the ottoman, Ani and Tia plopped beside me as I sighed quietly.

Lev found a seat in a single chair located across from us, "Are you going to be silent this whole time?" I asked Ani and Tia. Both looked like they were nearly asleep once we sat down so I gently stroked their heads one at a time.

Lev quietly cleared his throat, "They haven't slept much since you left so they are probably tired. They were both a handful yesterday."

Lev said as he glanced in turn at the two girls, "When you were gone they couldn't sleep even though Talinde tried to convince them to, and at one point I guess they both had a similar dream and woke up crying for you."

Lev finally couldn't hold back his curiosity, "So, how was it. What does the surface really look like? Are there a lot of people, how about some of the pictures we saw? Did you see…"

As it looked like Lev would continue with his questioning I laughed and held up my hands in defense.

"Let's do this slower. Anyway, I need to change my clothes." I looked down at Ani and Tia and could clearly tell they were asleep by listening to the sound of their breathing and how their grasp on my suit had lessened. As I leaned into each in turn and position them against the ottoman pillows, I then slowly sat up and quietly moved toward my changing compartment.

When I returned I was wearing a lose fitting shirt and comfortable pants, I softly sat on the far edge of the ottoman so not to disturb the girls and pulled on my comfortable indoor shoes.

As Lev watched me sit back with a big sigh he asked, "Well, how was it?"

I leaned forward slightly as I contemplated his previous barrage of questions, "It wasn't as busy as the photos we found, but the people we interacted with were polite enough. Though I didn't see anyone our age. We were detained shortly after we arrived in town."

I thought about when we first stepped foot on land and when we saw the gardens outside JAXO, "I think their foliage is much different than ours, I noticed a deeper green than anything on Paltius."

I slowly shrugged as Lev and I talked, "Once we got into town and were detained I didn't see much until we arrived at a facility called JAXO." Lev and I continued to talk about the experience as the two girls rested, but at some point, I must have nodded off myself.

*　　*　　*

As Shivan and Talinde finished their conversation Valdria exited the command center for the infirmary. Shivan turned toward Kazu, "I apologize, it is much easier to communicate in our native tongue."

Kazu looked startled as Shivan began speaking in an understandable language, "No, that is quite alright. To be honest I wasn't really expecting so much, I'm a little intimidated."

"Kazu, this is one of the brightest engineers of Paltius, and my old friend Talinde."

Talinde gave a brief bow and spoke in an awkward fashion, "I am pleased to meet a representative of your country."

"Now that you have at least met each member of our crew how about a tour?" Shivan casually asked.

Kazu's eyes widened, "You would be willing to show me around." Being used to a little more secrecy in the technology field, Kazu was a little shocked.

Shivan looked at Talinde and back to Kazu as Talinde smiled slightly, "Well it's not like we have many places to go and since we agreed to work with you it makes sense." Shivan paused, "What would you like to see first?"

Kazu, continued to glance around before he spoke, "If it's not too much to ask, I am very interested in your source of power."

Talinde smiled, as he glanced at Shivan, "I told you he would want to see the engines, maybe he is an engineer at heart."

Introductions

As the three men made their way to the rear of the ship Shivan offered a brief explanation for each area they passed, "Unfortunately this ship is very undermanned. Normally it would carry a crew of close to a thousand. During special events or large-scale diplomatic conferences the Velisus can carry as many as five thousand passengers and crew."

Kazu continued to follow as he silently contemplated a vessel capable of transporting so many people.

As they approached the mechanical sections of the Velisus, Talinde took over the explanations, "The areas to our left, house the storage for synthesizing capabilities, while the right here..."

Talinde stopped and faced a door with a strange script that Kazu could not decipher. Talinde described this as the vaporization processing facility.

"This equipment is responsible to processing moisture exchange within the ship. The ventilation caries all air through the exchange before it is treated and recirculated. This allows us to replenish oxygen and purify our environment."

Talinde motions to a gauge, "This gauge indicates a change in filtration particulates, it looks like you might have brought some friends from the surface."

Kazu offered a puzzled look, "From the surface you say?"

Talinde nodded, "This system is so efficient it even analyzes particles and neutralizes foreign substances. The air is recycled and purified at a microscopic level."

"This also processes and provides all of our moisture recovery. As it is separated it is recirculated into our water stores." Talinde paused, "But you were more interested in the power source, so let's head back out."

As Shivan exited the room he began to walk back down the corridor toward the stern of the Velisus with Talinde and Kazu in tow. They continued to talk about different functions as they proceeded until they finally reached what appeared to be the final door at the end of a long corridor.

The door opened when Talinde approached before he suddenly paused as if he just remembered an important point, he turned to Kazu as he reached into his side pocket and removed what appeared to be a coiled metallic bracelet, "Put this on if you don't mind."

Kazu curiously looked at the object he received, "What is it, a radiation monitor?"

Talinde cocked his head to the side, "Radiation? Of course not." He snorted, "There is no worry aboard the Velisus. This is a temporary biometric access band. It could be bad if you ended up locked in a room or got lost on the ship. This will allow you through most every door except assigned personal cabins. We will also be able to locate you in case we are separated."

Once Kazu placed the band on his wrist it emitted a slight blue glow and quickly faded, "Okay, it is now registered to your biometric pattern. It has a limited duration but should be good for our purposes."

The three then walked into the main engineering portion of the Velisus. Talinde approached a table with filament monitors spread out before it. As he touched the counter the monitors came to life.

Talinde explained to Kazu the purpose for each monitor and the functions they tracked, "The Velisus has four propulsion functions, the primary is the surge reactor which is responsible for achieving factor, the perpetual drive maintains this process which uses less power than the initial jump. The other two functions provide interstellar propulsion and our thrusters which are only used when landing or breaking atmospheric orbit." Talinde continued to explain excitedly as if he had found a new student.

Shivan finally spoke up interrupting Talinde, "I think you are losing your student." Shivan said with a smile.

"Ahh, I am sorry. I didn't mean to explain so enthusiastically."

Kazu who is still trying to comprehend the conversation finally asked, "When you say factor, what do you mean?"

"I'm sorry, I wasn't thinking of your unfamiliarity with our technology. Factor is just that a factor of light speed. The initial surge provided by the surge reactor provides the necessary thrust to move us to light speed. Breaking that barrier is the most difficult. However, using the burst reactor at light speed allows us to increase the speed at half the energy consumption. It also becomes easier to maintain a higher factor level, unfortunately the factor a vessel can travel is limited to the computational ability of the navigational processor. It must be able to process and interpret forward calculations to ensure that a collision with a foreign object doesn't occur. Fortunately, we can shield against most minor objects we might encounter that are too miniscule for the navigational system to detect. The Velisus is capable of factor four but that pushes her limits."

As Talinde finished up Kazu just shook his head, "Amazing…"

Once the trio departed the monitoring station they approached the starboard bulkhead and traversed the corridor leading to one of the two primary reactor bays. As they approach the door leading to the reactor bay it quietly slid open and the group entered. Talinde motioned toward the wall containing several monitoring screens and announced, "This is the reactor bay and perpetual drive link."

Kazu looked at each monitor, unable to make out the displays and asked, "Is this the control panel?"

Talinde shook his head as he walked up to primary panel and decreased the power draw on the starboard reactor. Then he made a few deft adjustments on the panel to the right and a section of the lower wall slid away, "This is one of numerous reactors that power functions on the Velisus."

Kazu noticed a change on the hairs on the back of his neck as the panel slid open and Talinde made his announcement, "Is this safe?" Kazu asked quietly.

Talinde smiled, "It is probably safer than being on the surface of your planet."

As the group made their way back toward the command center Kazu continued to listen to both Shivan and Talinde as they went over individual functions and purposes of the mechanical portions of the Velisus.

As they entered a larger corridor signaling the start of the passenger quarters Shivan asked, "While we are close I would like you to get an idea of the ores we previously mentioned if that is okay?"

Kazu raised his eyebrows, "That's fine with me, then I know roughly what we will need to transport them."

As Shivan verified the cargo had not shifted on the monitor outside the small storage bay he then opened the door. As Kazu turned the corner of the storage area he realized that Shivans idea of a little was extremely skewed, "What do you guys consider a lot?"

He found himself verbalizing before he realized, "I'm sorry, I didn't mean to sound rude. It's just everything we have seen is on a much grander scale than I had expected, or you led us to believe. I think we might have to wait until you find a more permanent docking location before we can move this."

The mountain of stored ores was immense, considering the quantity there must have been several metric tonne's.

"Well, shall we head to the command center?" Shivan asked next.

"Please I would enjoy that, but before that do you have a bathroom?" Kazu asked pleadingly.

Both Shivan and Talinde asked, "Bathroom?"

Then Shivan had an, ahh moment, "You mean the personal facilities. Yes, let me show you the way. I will provide a quick explanation since I noticed yesterday ours differ slightly from yours."

"I would really appreciate that. To be honest I have been so busy since we met that I haven't had many chances to relieve myself. But after talking with you and Talinde it appears our concerns were unfounded. You have been extremely open." Kazu bowed in thanks.

Once Kazu finished the three headed back toward the planning room on the way toward the command center, "Would you like something to eat before we head forward?"

"Well I am a little thirsty, your ventilation system is extremely effective." Kazu said.

Talinde departed momentarily while Shivan and Kazu discussed the purpose of the planning room and the numerous monitors functions.

When Talinde returned he handed Kazu and Shivan a small foil looking pouch that had a straw like protrusion.

As Shivan looked toward Kazu he grinned and said, "Don't expect much."

After tasting the food Kazu provided yesterday he knew this would be somewhat of a disappointment for him, "You bite down on the center of the protrusion and can squeeze the pack. It provides a meals worth of nutrients and liquid."

Kazu looked at the packet and slowly brought it to his mouth. As he bit down on the straw he noticed moisture fill the straw as he squeezed. The taste and sensation was like drinking blended konnyaku.

As they finished the meal they disposed of the packaging in the processing disposal receptacle and began walking toward the command center. The tour continued but now focused more on security and crew quarters in this portion of the ship. Kazu inquisitively asked, "How many floors does the Velisus have?"

Talinde glanced his way as they continued walking, "There are twelve levels below us and four above not counting the cargo bay. Those are primarily crew and passenger cabins, however, there are activity chambers close to the cargo bay which the crew who is assigned or the passengers could use."

Kazu let out a slow whistle.

When they reached the command center Shivan continued walking knowing the door would open. As it slid open and the interior came into view Kazu's eyes widened.

The room was literally a wall of monitors with chairs surrounding a large arching semi-circular console, "How did you pilot this monster with so few crew?" Kazu asked as he looked at the numerous monitors and guidance panels.

Shivan laughed rather amused at Kazu's expression and remark, "The Velisus is designed to be maneuvered with very little guidance. Since we were not navigating a busy space port it required fewer eyes watching special location and individual maneuvering thrusters. When this ship would dock with the Regulous it is nearly automatic and uses location sensors to align with the docking clamps."

Kazu heard a name he hadn't heard previously, "The Regulous, is that a ship like the Velisus?"

Shivan's eyes widen, "By no means, the Regulous is the empires flag ship. The emperor would normally use that ship when traveling between worlds, the Velisus is only a transport freighter. Next to the Regulous the Velisus would look like the helicopter we used next to the Ryuuga."

"What about other functions of the Velisus like, scanning, shields, and navigation calculations?"

"Those are all handled in this room. Each console can adjust accordingly so all command adjustments and can be handled by one person given the appropriate circumstances."

"What about weapons?" Kazu asked as he leveled his gaze at Shivan.

"Sorry, there are none." Talinde responded, "At least not lethal ones."

Kazu glanced over as Talinde who is wearing an awkward smile, "This is a transport freighter; do we have craft capable of engaging in battle? The answer to that is yes. However, you will only find personal weapons on the Velisus. And those are only to handle matters that occur on board, so they are intended to incapacitate rather than kill."

"I hope that isn't the type of technology you are looking to receive from us." Shivan flatly stated.

Kazu felt somewhat relieved, then a thought occurred to him, "Do you have communication capabilities strong enough to reach the surface?"

Shivan laughed out loud for the first time, "In what galaxy would you like to transmit too?"

Shivan wore a smile as he apologized to Kazu for his disrespect, "I say that but none of your receivers would be able to pick up a transmission directed that far away. We can transmit on some of your lower range frequencies…"

As Shivan turned to the panel to his left he quickly keyed in the communication frequency range, "Well? What frequency would you like?"

Shivan looked at Kazu before he pulled out a tablet he carried on the interior pocket of his jump suit and quickly thumbed through as he slowly paused on a specific page. Shivan entered the frequency as Kazu relayed it, "This is an encrypted frequency, so they won't respond right away."

"No worries, the Velisus can decode the encryption and even adjust the intensity so it is only a close-range transmission."

"This is a modulating encryption code, are you sure?"

Shivan nodded, "The Velisus can compute and plot a course at factor four, decrypting a simple code is nothing."

Kazu sighed, "Okay I guess that was silly question."

Shivan moved to the side to allow Kazu to sit in front of the communication panel, "When you want to transmit place your finger here, it will detect the signal from your biometric bracelet and allow the panel to operate, and release while you wait for a response."

Kazu nodded, as he placed his finger on the firm panel though he felt no movement. The filament monitor signaled outgoing transmission in progress, "This is Commander Tenshin Hidekazu aboard the Velisus, Ryuuga do you read?"

The signal went silent once Kazu moved his finger.

A moment of static came through, "This is the Ryuuga, code phrase?"

Kazu spoke an odd phrase, "A skilled hawk hides its talons, I repeat, a skilled hawk hides its talons, over."

There is another pause, "Thank you, commander."

A few moments pass and then a new voice sounds over the communication line.

"Commander Tenshin, this is Vice Admiral Otonari Naoya, good to hear your voice. I take it things are going well."

"Yes Sir, my hosts have been most generous. I think we will have a prosperous relationship. How are things progressing on your side?"

Shivan and Talinde remained silent as they listened to Kazu's conversation, "The sight is almost prepared; can you make a determination on the depth and size necessary to maintain full submersion?"

Kazu glanced back at Shivan with a slight smile before he responded, "Well Sir, you probably won't believe this but the Velisus will need to have about 150 meters worth of vertical and horizontal clearance to maintain an appropriate buffer from sea floor to surface."

The communication line went silent a moment.

The line came back to life, "I can't wait to see this monstrosity."

Shivan suddenly spoke before Kazu continued, "The ship can be farther out to sea if necessary, we can build a shuttle system to shore if it becomes too difficult to find a coastal location."

Kazu nodded and looked back to the panel as he contemplated Shivans suggestion, "Sir, how about the canyons off Furigawa? It is close, and we can easily patrol the area, it would be easier to camouflage their ship as well."

The line went quiet, "Let us look into it Commander. Give us a couple days."

Kazu finally broke the silence, "Sir, permission to remain onboard until you can identify a location."

The line remained with intermittent static for a few moments before there was a response, "Granted, keep the line open if possible and we will contact you once we have coordinates for your next move. Out."

Once the conversation was over Shivan almost felt like he wanted to sigh, "Hopefully you don't mind me staying a few days with you." Kazu said as he looked up from the console chair.

Before Shivan could answer Valdria's voice came over the communication link, "Shivan, Trist can you come to the infirmary please." Her voice faded into silence.

"So Kazu, care to visit the infirmary before we find you a temporary cabin?"

Kazu sheepishly smiled, "Well I guess I did infringe on your hospitality, so I guess I don't mind keeping you company."

They all departed the command center and as they approached the planning room Talinde said, "I am going to look into the docking mechanism on the top levels, if we find ourselves having to frequently come and go that may be easier." Talinde turned and departed for the main lift.

* * *

For some reason I found myself on Paltius, near the gardens where I usually meditated on lessons. As I was walking through the Palace back to my room I had a strange feeling. I felt as though I was being followed. But as I glanced over my shoulder there was no one there. In fact, there is no one anywhere. I suddenly began to panic and ran from my parent's room to my sisters shouting their names.

This can't be happening, I shouted for my father and mother, and I immediately sensed something nearby, the bloodlust it projected my way was oppressive. I began to flee to the only place I felt safe, but the more I ran the hotter my surroundings became. I stopped to see if it was me or if the air itself had increased in temperature.

Then suddenly something jumped toward me from the corner of my vision. As I tried to dodge I felt as if my legs weighed a hundred kilograms. Suddenly I was pressed to the ground as if I was being smothered. It felt hopeless, just as the air left my lungs for a final scream… I awoke.

My eyes weighed heavily as I looked around me I realized it had been a dream. But it was hot, too hot for the Velisus. As I attempted to lean forward to stand I suddenly realized why I was so hot.

Both Ani and Tia had moved next to me again and were leaning against me sleeping awkwardly. Even Lev was asleep across from me curled up in the chair, some help he was.

I silently told the two, "What am I going to do with both of you." As I looked at their sleeping forms with deep feelings.

I stroked their heads and tickled their ears with my finger hoping they would awake. No luck, I finally resolved myself to waking them, so I began to stand as they slipped from my side and slumped onto the ottoman against a pillow. The way they were sleeping now looked incredibly uncomfortable, so I did the only thing I could think of.

I pulled the covers back from both sides of my bed and while telling myself they were light, I was easily able to lift them up as I carried them to the bed and gently pulled the covers over each in turn.

As I was about to head out for something to eat I remembered the wonderful sandwiches we had the night before and wasn't really looking forward to a nutrition pack. When my door slid open and I entered the hallway I had the strange sensation that I heard Ani and Tia's voices in my head.

I made my way toward the planning room the most obvious place to find Shivan and our guest, when I thought I heard Valdria call.

It sounded distant, so I figured she was calling from one of the planning ante rooms. I hastened toward the sound of her voice and as I was about to approach the infirmary I hear Valdria over the communication link, "Shivan, Trist can you come to the infirmary please."

That was odd, if she was going to call why not just use the link first.

As the infirmary door opened I saw Valdria sitting at a small white desk. She looked like she had the portable molecular stabilizer on the table next to her. As I approached her she turned to see who entered.

"Oh, Trist, that was quick."

"I was already on my way after you called me the first time."

"The first time? I only called once." Valdria said with a puzzled expression.

"I was pretty sure I heard you call but not on the communication link."

Valdria looked contemplative, "I did think I needed to call you however…Trist, have you had anymore headaches recently?"

I thought a second, "No not since the one day, though sometimes…It sounds odd, but my brain feels like it itches. That's the only way I can explain it."

Valdria had a serious look on her face, "Trist first have a seat and remove the wrap from yesterday."

I obediently complied, Valdria was in full medical consul mode. As I exposed the puncture wound and slowly pull the cotton away it apparently had continued to seep blood.

Valdria wiped the puncture sight clean as a bubble of fresh blood broke the surface. She then held the molecular stabilizer over the wound as she activated it. My arm had a peculiar sensation not entirely uncomfortable.

As she lifted the instrument from my wound a small stain remained from the drop of blood, but the puncture was sealed, "Thank you."

Valdria grabbed my hand as I tried to stand, "Not so fast." She pulled me over to the examination cube and had me enter and sit. She then walked to the panel located on the side of the machine as she began to run a scan.

Just as the lights dimmed on the machine I heard the outer door open followed by Shivans voice. Valdria opened the door and said I could go.

I stood up and stepped out, Shivan was getting the same treatment as I had just received.

Kazu looked my way and smiled so I returned his smile and left the room. I had a sleeping target waiting for me.

* * *

Once Valdria finished with Shivan, Kazu said, "That is amazing. Would that technology work on humans as well?"

"Would you like to find out?" Valdria asked as she twirled what looked like a pointed object.

"Umm, not right this moment, no!" Shivan laughed at Kazu's response.

Shivan chided Kazu, "You should be careful Kazu, she wasn't too happy about the blood drawing."

Valdria smiled brightly at Kazu.

"I will pass that information on, heh, heh." Kazu laughed weakly.

"Anyway, I am glad you're here." Valdria motioned Shivan to follow her. She had two medical scans open side by side on the display screen. As she touched the stylus she had in her hand it expanded an area of the scan, she repeated the process on the second.

Shivan frowned, "Is this Trist?"

"Yes…I thought he had abnormal activity when I took this initial scan. I wouldn't even have seen this if he hadn't complained about a headache." She paused, "You can see the density increased in these areas of his brain."

She expanded sections showing significant development, "I'm a little concerned, earlier when Trist first arrived he said I had called him twice. Do you remember when we had the kids working on the survival exercises?"

"You mean when Tia got separated from the group?"

"Yes, I didn't think anything of it at the time, but he might be developing a telepathic link." Valdria said as she looked at the scans intently.

Shivan let out a slow breath, "When did we last have an Emperor with telepathic abilities?"

"It's not known by many since he used it to strengthen alliances but Lestanali Verndactilia 2nd was the only one in our recorded history." Valdria said as she stood staring at the scans.

"Do you think he will have similar aspects?"

"Until Trist recognizes them himself we can't do anything for him. If we try to interfere in his development, it could stunt his potential."

As Shivan and Valdria discussed the scan Kazu felt totally lost, "Is the young man okay?"

Valdria glanced back at Kazu and nodded, "Oh, he is more than fine. In fact, I wish there was a problem, so I could at least help with it. But this…he must work this out on his own. I will do some research and investigate it some more, I am sure there are records in the Emperor's private medical file. That aside for now, why don't you have a seat Kazu."

"Huh?" Kazu questioningly asked.

Valdria opened the examination cube door and motioned Kazu to take a seat.

Shivan just grinned, "Quite fair don't you think?"

Kazu's shoulders slumped a moment, then he straightened, "Well you were more than cooperative with us, so why not." He tentatively stepped into the cube then asked, "Now what?"

"Just have a seat, it will only take a moment."

"Do I need to take off my shirt or shoes or anything? Oh, I have a bullet…" Kazu began to explain.

"Yes, I see in your right buttock."

"Huh? You are already scanning?"

"Why yes, unlike your barbaric methods we prefer to know what's going on inside our bodies before we poke or prod into them. That was the one aspect of studying your medical development I really cringed through."

The light went dim as Shivan opened the door, "Care to hear how long you'll live?" Shivan asked solemnly.

"You can tell that?!" Kazu asked somewhat excitedly.

Valdria shot Shivan a quick look, then glanced at Kazu, "No, we can't, but we can do many things to assist in the healthy development and aging of the body."

Kazu glanced at the scan Valdria placed on the primary filament monitor, "It looks like you have been operated on before. You really should have that removed you know."

"Wow!" Kazu said as he looked at a scan that took a matter of moments, "The clarity is incredible, kind of embarrassing and a little earie looking at my body like this."

Valdria sat back and turned her chair to face Kazu, "Your current methods are the main reason I so readily offered to share medical knowledge. I can provide instruction and engineering diagrams that explain the circuitry and assembly process for every piece of equipment in this room. That alone would be worth the lives of hundreds of thousands a year."

Shivan spoke next, "And I have access through the Velisus data base on technologies necessary to create the circuitry for those instruments and many more. Our food synthesizers, while not as delicious as the food you might be used to, provide all the nutrients a person needs to survive."

"Now that you have seen the crew and what we have to offer, we will all be in your care." Shivan and Valdria both bowed.

It was late when the three left the infirmary. They guided Kazu to one of the guest rooms and showed him how to link the room to his biometric bracelet and voice commands. As they explained each amenity his eyes widened more, "This is a guest room? It's bigger than my apartment back in Tokyo."

Shivan was unsure what to say, "These are accommodations for a mid-level dignitary. We have larger rooms if you like."

"No, no, this is fine. Smaller perhaps?" Kazu looked at Shivan and realized he was joking.

Shivan and Valdria began to walk toward the door, they turned and wished him a good night before they exited. As Kazu changed into the night clothes Shivan provided he wondered just what the next year would bring.

* * *

After I left the infirmary I made my way back to my bedroom, I felt it would be best to let Shivan entertain Kazu since there were so many things that needed to be discussed. As I turned the corner and my door opened the lights dimmed to simulate the transition from day to night.

I was beat, while I had a short nap, the dream I had earlier erased all the relaxation it provided. As I slowly undressed and prepared for bed I gave the command to extinguish the lights and walked to my bed in the darkness, having done so every night for the last two years.

The room immediately began to cool when the lights went out as I slowly slid between the sheets.

The bed in the emperors room was ridiculously large, I never seemed to use much more than one side. As I lay thinking of the hectic last few days sleep finally claimed me. I slept with the sensation of being cradled by my mother when I was younger as I rested the remaining evening.

The faint light now present in my room was the sign that morning had come, as I laid on my back and gave a sigh, the rest I had gotten last night was probably the best I had in months.

At least since we stopped training every day. While lying there on my back I decided I should go ahead and get up.

As I attempted to pull my arms from under my pillows I realized it was pinned, then I suddenly noticed something. I was surrounded!! As I glanced to my left I saw Ani facing toward me as she breathed softly.

Her head was on the pillow my arm was under. No problem I thought I can pull it straight out. Nope! As I looked to my right I noticed Lev was in the bed too. Okay, this is awkward. Okay, I had enough. I pulled my right and left arms under the back side of each pillow and turned toward Lev and pushed.

As he surreptitiously landed on the floor with a thump he immediately sat up as I slid to the side of the bed and hung my legs over the side.

The look on his face was amusing, eyes at half-mast still mostly asleep as he slowly surveyed the room. He was like a scanner panning from right to left, once, twice…oh he stopped.

"Where am I?!"

"Wake up you sleepy head! Why were you in my bed?"

Lev turned toward me as if asking what I was doing there. Then his eyes darted around some more, "This isn't my room!"

"I know, that's why I asked, why were you in my bed!?"

"Ahh, I woke up while it was dark and just though I fell asleep in my room." Lev started to grin, "Sorry ha-ha."

I smacked him with a pillow.

"Hey, that wasn't fair." Lev grabbed the pillow from my hand as he began to take wild swings at me, so naturally I reached back and grabbed the other pillow not thinking about Ani and Tia still sleeping.

Ani's head plopped onto the bed as I pulled the pillow out from under her. As Lev and I continue to take wild swings at each other Ani and Tia slowly sat up.

I noticed Lev stopped swinging as his eyes focused behind me, "Wide open!" I said, as I smacked him along the side of his head.

When I realized he hadn't even noticed I looked behind me and saw both Ani and Tia looking at me wide eyed.

It was quiet for a few moments then Lev said with a funny expression on his face, "I slept with my sister…" He suddenly stood up and bolted out of the room in pure embarrassment.

He was always sensitive about things like that since he hated stories of how Ani would hold him when he fell asleep when he was a baby.

I laughed inwardly at Lev, then turned to Ani and Tia, "Good morning, do you both feel better?" I guess they hadn't slept at all since Shivan, Valdria and I left so I wasn't too surprised they slept as much as they did.

The two girls were just staring at me for several minutes, without saying anything. Finally, I decided to get up and get dressed.

I went into my wardrobe and choose a set of comfortable clothes, pants and a pull over shirt. When I came back into the room I noticed Ani and Tia had left. As I tossed the pillows back on the bed I engaged the automatic function to make the bed. I then headed toward the planning room to see if everyone else was up.

As I entered the planning room Jes was the only one sitting at the table, "Morning Jes."

Jes looked my direction and grunted, "Morning."

"Anyone else up yet?"

"Father was up late last night going over schematics for lift technology. Not sure what he has planned but I'm sure he will let us know soon enough."

I nodded as I walked over into the side room for a nutritional pack. I walked back out and keyed in to the terminal on the table top as I slowly consumed my breakfast, "I don't see anything on our training schedule. I sort of expected it to continue."

"Well the cargo bay is still flooded to provide ballast, so we don't have many places to train." Jes said as he continued to read the text he had displayed on his monitor. I begin to read over Japanese and Earth history as I sat down and finished my breakfast.

Not long after my arrival Kazu poked his head into the planning room, "Good morning." I said as I looked up, "Hopefully you slept well."

"Like the dead, this place is much quieter than any ship I have ever been on." Kazu said as he yawned and stretched.

I got up and walked to the synthesizer and grabbed a nutrition pack. As I reentered the room, Kazu glanced my way as he stood waiting. I tossed a nutrition pack his way and he barely caught it as he fumbled a bit before he had a firm grasp.

"Thanks."

I nodded as I resumed my reading, "You can use any of the monitors just key in your desired search. We are on the local information network now."

Kazu walked over to the table still holding his pack and placed it next to the monitor.

He glanced down at the table then over at my monitor, "How do I start it?" Kazu asked after a moment.

I stood up and walked over next to him, I showed him the initiate button and the monitor flickered on as he touched it.

Once Kazu felt comfortable he began to really focus on what he was doing. He had a curious look on his face as he looked up and asked, "How are you accessing the network?"

I looked his way as I recalled what Valdria said about the local network virtually crisscrossing the globe, "This planet is being bombarded by signals, once you can identify the one with the best flow you can attune our receiver with it to actively monitor virtually any network. At least that's what Valdria said."

As Kazu, began to type in keywords he crashed his forehead into the table. Jes and I both jumped, we didn't expect that, "What was the purpose in that?"

"Oh, it seems I can even access my email and secured networks from here." Kazu sounded defeated.

"Oh, is that bad?"

Kazu looked at me with a puzzled look, "Well, it's supposed to be hosted on our most secure network." Kazu sighed, "I guess I should have known this was possible after touring your ship yesterday."

When Jes finished he stood, "I'm going to see if father is up." Then he departed for his family's cabin.

As Kazu and I remained seated I continued my studies.

I heard Kazu clear his throat after a while, as I looked up he appeared to want to say something, "Bathroom?"

"No!" He just shook his head with a defeated look on his face, "I guess this is normal for you."

"Not really, we have really relaxed training and lectures since we arrived in your solar system. Normally by now we would be working in the physical endurance course or practicing survival training."

"What type of survival training? Like camping in the mountains and fighting wild animals?"

I thought for a moment to place an image to the words he just used, "Ah, no, more like hand to hand survival. We were unsure what type of habitable planet we would ultimately be on, so we had to be prepared for any situation. Do you fight wild animals in Japan?"

Kazu laughed, "No, just was curious what your idea of survival training was. I'd love to watch you guys next time."

As I was about to respond Shivan walked in from the main corridor, "I think we can arrange that."

I sat fully upright as Shivan walked over and asked me to fetch my training partners. As I stood I discard my empty nutrition pack and headed off toward Lev's cabin.

* * *

"I am sorry I was out late, Valdria wasn't feeling well."

Kazu perked up, "She's not suffering from something from Earth, is she?"

Shivan shook his head, "No, she is dealing with her pregnancy, nothing can really be done."

Kazu's eyes widened, "Congratulations!"

Shivan offered his thanks, "Not the best of timing but once we were traveling there was no way of knowing when we would find a home. Plus, child birth is an auspicious event in our culture. I only regret we are unable to celebrate as we would have on Paltius."

"When is she due?" Kazu asked.

"Due? You mean when the child will be born?".

"Yea."

"Due to our longer than normal lifespans fetal development can take close to a full solar cycle."

"You mean a year?" Kazu's eyebrows raised.

"That is correct, but on Earth that is approximately two and a half years."

Kazu mouthed an "O" and remained silent a moment.

"When is she expecting based on our calendar?"

"Based on my understanding of your calendar she still has close to fourteen months."

"Well, we will have to celebrate with you since this will indeed be auspicious having your child born on Earth." Kazu made a mental note.

"Shivan, I have another request for you pertaining to your asylum." Kazu said with a solemn face.

Shivan can sense the change in the atmosphere, "And what would that be?"

Kazu turned to the monitor in front of him and keyed a search, "If this got out you would be hunted by every country on Earth."

Kazu motions to the monitor that has a window to every top-secret network in the world.

Shivan glanced down at it, "They have nothing we need anyway. We only used it to understand the different cultures on Earth, and that is why we ultimately approached Japan as a possible home."

Kazu nodded, "As long as you understand and please let the others know."

*   *   *

As I approached Shivans cabin I depressed the call button, and the door immediately slid open.

Valdria was still in her sleeping attire, and Lev was sitting on the ottoman teasing Ani who turned my way as soon as she noticed and retreated to the changing room.

Lev began to laugh louder.

"Please come in Trist." Valdria offered.

"That's okay, Shivan just asked me to notify Lev and Ani that we were doing physical training today. I need to get Jes and Tia next." I waved as I stepped back into the corridor, "Meet you in the planning room Lev."

"Got it!" Lev responded.

I then began heading toward Talinde's cabin located in the larger rooms closer to the engineering section. I gradually broke into a run to cut down on travel time.

I could never get away with this in the palace, not only were there too many people, but Shivan and my father would chastise me for acting in an undignified fashion. I finally arrived at Talinde's cabin and depressed the call button.

A few minutes later the door slid open and Tia stood before me. As she saw me her face immediately blushed, "Is Jes available?" I asked her.

"No, he left when father woke. They are working on identifying the materials for a relay platform." Tia quietly said.

"Ok, well are you ready?"

Tia looked perplexed for a second, "For what."

"Shivan is going to start up physical training again and wanted us all to come." Since she looked ready, I grabbed Tia by the hand and started to lead her into the corridor.

At first, Tia struggled against my grasp then finally began to walk with me. As I went to release her hand, once we were on our way I noticed she slightly tightened her grasp.

Tia remained silent as we walked to the planning room, as we entered she reluctantly released my hand. We both walked up to the planning table and found a seat.

"Is Jes occupied?" Shivan asked.

"Yes, he is helping Talinde with a relay materials list."

Shivan nodded upon hearing my response, "Good, he's thinking ahead."

Shivan glanced around those seated, "I would like to provide Kazu a view of your normal physical training. We will be using the lower deck training simulator since the cargo hanger is currently occupied."

"We will make it a simple scenario this time, but I want you to take it as serious as if the difficulty was increased."

We all seemed to nod at the same time.

"So, grab year gear and meet at the fifth-floor training simulator."

Kazu followed Shivan as the rest of us headed toward the lowest level to don our protective gear. Once everyone was suited up we all met by the lift, "Make sure we stick together, and this should be quick." I told everyone.

Ani rolled her eyes, "Yea make sure you stay together Trist." Ani seemed a little more herself, in fact she almost seemed upset. I will probably never understand her, I silently thought to myself.

Once we exited the lift it was a short walk to the simulation room, which was roughly fifty meters squared. This simulation room was typically reserved for the crew to enjoy on longer missions away from Paltius.

Over the last two solar cycles it had been primarily used by the girls when Valdria worked with them.

As the four of us entered the simulation room we saw Shivan and Kazu near the scenario terminal. As we gathered close Shivan began to give us the normal situation we would be up against.

"Don't forget your team work and give it your all." Shivan began the program and the simulation room appeared to be a city scape like what we saw when we first walked into Japan.

Shivan must have added this last night knowing Kazu might want to see our training.

As the virtual elements coalesced at the far side of the street they immediately scattered. Whoa, this isn't like our normal engagements. I noticed most of the buildings were single story, but to our left was a multi-story building with roof access.

"Lev, Ani, Tia watch our flanks, we need to move to an area less open, follow me." We quickly advanced to the closest multi story building.

As we entered we did so in groups of two, Ani, Lev then Tia and I. Ani moved to the interior doorway and looked for access points. As we made a quick assessment of the ground floor as I passed out directions.

Tia and I moved to the second story, while Lev and Ani remained concealed in the closet opposite the stairwell. I quietly whispered as we prepared to head up the stairs, "Let the first two enemy by."

Lev and Ani nodded.

Knowing the response patterns, Tia and I quietly observe the city from the upper windows. Within a matter of minutes, we began to observe the virtual aggressors who appeared to be nothing more than shadows in human form darting to and from buildings making their way toward our position.

I counted, one, two, three, four, Five, SIX…why are there so many? I thought to myself. I tapped six times on the floor knowing Ani and Lev would understand. As the first opponents neared the doorway I purposefully knocked a small pebble to the ground from the window.

As Tia took position along the wall next to the doorway I remained near the window slightly visible from the stairwell. As the first two made their way toward the stairs I took position in the corner opposite Tia.

The aggressors flooded into the room as they noticed me, however the second one noticed Tia first, but it was too late. She engaged at the same time as me. Our opponents dropped almost immediately.

I could hear combat below and I pulled Tia with me out the window, as we landed we immediately entered the room Lev and Ani were defending. We quickly flanked our opponents and left then dissipating on the floor.

Shivan and Kazu watched the progression, "Have they only been trained in hand to hand?" Kazu asked Shivan as he nodded.

"The weapons we have on board are limited, plus I never planned on putting any of them in harm's way on a hostile world. Even the most peaceful world can require you to defend yourself."

"I'd like to try going up against them in a hand to hand match." Kazu said.

"That can be arranged I'm sure. Lev is excellent in offensive combat, Ani excels in defensive combat, Tia is decent at both, Trist however is probably the weakest of the three."

"Humm, interesting."

As the city scape faded once the final foe was eliminated we walked toward Shivan, "Shivan, that wasn't fair. They had half again as many as we did."

"No one ever said fighting was fair." Shivan grinned, "What are you worried about you did fine. So…" Shivan programed a new scenario which produced a mat on the middle of the floor closest to the group.

"Trist how about a hand to hand match with Kazu?"

"Huh, why?"

"It will just be a simple match, I would like to test your ability to see if it differs from our hand to hand training." Kazu announced.

I thought for a minute, "Well, I don't really mind but isn't this a little unfair?"

"I'll go easy on you." Kazu smiled as Trist frowned.

Kazu used the changing cabin attached to the simulation room. As he appeared he looked much more fit in the training gear than the clothes he was previously wearing.

While Kazu's initial appearance was a male in his early forties, once in training gear his physique looked much more imposing.

Kazu and I walked out onto the mat and faced each other. As we found our positions Kazu turned and bowed to me before Shivan announced the start of the match.

I think I will just test his strength with a grapple Kazu thought.

"Begin." Shivan announced.

Kazu cautiously approached, as I waited for his first move.

I kept my defensive stance as I looked at Kazu slowly circling me as he closed the distance between us, when he was within a long stride he lunged.

He was much broader than the virtual foes I had fought in the past. As he tried to encircle me with his wider reach I ducked and spun to my left sweeping my leg around which placed me to the right of his lunge as he jumped slightly. I tried to think of myself as being lighter, so I could reach the necessary height.

I jumped with my elbow aimed toward the back of his neck and shoulders. As I reached the apex of my jump I tried to make the force of my elbow as heavy as I could. As my elbow collided with his upper back, combined with his forward leaning posture he dropped almost immediately.

Kazu silently laid on the mat as I took up another defensive stance a few meters away. When he reached out and slapped the mat I could tell the match was over.

I leaned over and asked Kazu if he is alright.

He just grunted, "What did you hit me with?"

"I only used my elbow, but you were already off balance."

He groaned, as he began to push himself off the mat.

Shivan reached out to offer Kazu a hand, "Well, what do you think?"

"I don't think we will need to worry about a guard detail, that's for sure."

Shivan laughed quietly.

Kazu stood and looked at the four, assessing each in turn. Then turned to Shivan, "Okay, I'm satisfied."

Once Kazu returned from changing, Shivan sent the four of us off.

As Shivan accompanied Kazu back to the planning room they made a quick stop by the infirmary.

When Shivan entered Valdria was sitting at the table translating medical documents. She turned toward Shivan and Kazu as they entered.

She could tell Kazu was in pain just from the look on his face, "Now what did you do?"

"He wanted to check Trist's skills, and it nearly killed him." Shivan explained with a slight smile.

"It looks like you really want to experience our technology first hand. Okay have a seat." Valdria opened the examination cube for Kazu. As Valdria conducted the assessment scan, "Well, his shoulder blade is fractured, it is probably due to Trist's height difference, so he didn't land a solid blow."

Shivan nodded at Valdria's assessment.

Valdria opened the door and asked Kazu to seat himself near her table.

As Kazu sat Valdria asked him to relax as she used the molecular stabilizer over the fracture and bruised muscle. To Valdria's surprise the process completed much quicker than normal, "Try sitting up straight Kazu."

As he did the pained look on his face dissipated as if he was expecting pain that didn't come, "Oh, the pain is gone." Kazu suddenly said as he rolled his shoulders, "Not that I wanted to find out first hand but I'm glad that works on humans as well."

"Well our structures are fundamentally similar after all."

Once Shivan and Kazu left the infirmary there was an alarm announcing an incoming transmission, "What's that?"

"It appears you have a communication incoming."

Shivan and Kazu hurried to the command center. As they entered the room, the panel they used previously indicated it had picked up a transmission on the programmed frequency.

Shivan motioned for Kazu to sit.

Kazu slipped into the chair and gently placed his finger on the transmit button, "Ryuuga, do you copy?"

There is a long pause, "Ryuuga, this is Commander Tenshin do you copy?"

The static broke for a moment as they heard a response, "Commander Tenshin this is Vice Admiral Otonari."

"Sir, this is commander Tenshin."

"How are things going Commander?"

"Very well Sir, I have had additional opportunities to observe their technology and have verified the children's capability to defend themselves."

"Very good Commander, we have finalized the location details for all requests and look forward to your confirmation."

"If we transmit details via coded frequency, do they have the capabilities to receive?"

"Yes, Sir I don't think it will be a problem."

Shivan moved to the adjacent panel and prepared to input the frequency.

Once the Ryuuga began transmitting, the encrypted message was immediately translated and appeared on the filament monitor.

"Your ability to treat encryption like that scares me." Kazu said as he watched the message appear on the screen.

"Commander, I will leave the remaining negotiations in your hands. Let us know when you plan to depart."

"Will do Sir. Give me some time to go over the message with the crew. Out." Kazu closed the transmission.

As Shivan, Valdria and Kazu went over confirmation they also addressed items needed by the government of Japan to generate the appropriate documentation.

"Regarding their ages, we can't really just convert to Earth years. But their knowledge levels will probably surpass children of their same physical stature." Valdria said as she looked at the requested information.

"I was thinking about that. While I agree they are either too small or too smart for high school or middle school respectively, what do you think of a compromise."

Kazu paused, "I propose starting them in middle school. This might not be very challenging intellectually, but it will allow then to establish societal bonds easier. Since other students will be in a new environment as well, it will level the playing field from a social standpoint."

Kazu looked to Shivan and Valdria for their thoughts, "While they might be less physically developed their intellect and mannerisms should be adequate from what I have observed."

Shivan is quiet a moment before voicing his thoughts, "I think Trist would already excel in an advanced educational institution, but I agree this will allow then to develop bonds."

Valdria nodded as Shivan spoke, "I agree, it will give them opportunities to make mistakes before they are considered adults as well."

"Well that's settled, now we have secured and are preparing an older ryokan which should provide a decent amount of space, unfortunately it is not on the coast. However, it places us within distance in the event of an emergency and there are several industrial capabilities in that region."

Shivan is nodding while Kazu goes over each detail, "The difficulty is the Velisus, it's a big vessel and there is an active fishing community in that area. So, concealing it is the challenge." Shivan looked a little unsure where Kazu was going with this.

"We are in the process of reclaiming an area off the coast of Furigawa. It is being labeled as a foundation for Tsunami relief measures. At least that is the public view."

Shivan is silent a moment then asked, "Are you making a docking foundation?"

Kazu smiled, "Exactly, but these things don't happen overnight, and the people have to be carefully chosen since we don't want word to leak out about the unique nature of this sight."

Kazu continued, "Once complete we should be able to tug the Velisus into position, we will have to construct some sort of fabricated exterior, but it can be done. Pre-fabricated structures are not uncommon on Earth. The prefabricated unit will be built where we plan on having the Velisus surface, so it will be invisible from prying eyes."

Kazu sighed, "And lastly, this will likely take a few years to complete."

Valdria was the first to voice her concerns, "How about removing the necessities from the Velisus, or the ores we planned to sell?"

Shivan glanced back at Kazu, "In order to fulfill our part of the bargain we will need access to the Velisus, I hope Japan doesn't expect unlimited access."

"Of course not, we are already aware of your biometric measures and the technology would be meaningless if we didn't understand how it inter-related to each function."

"We have personal belongings and I would like to take a monitoring trans-link, so we can still utilize the Velisus's functions for surveillance as well as some of the medical technology. Earths medical capabilities are still lacking and as you saw we heal slower so even minor injuries take an abnormal amount of time to heal naturally."

Kazu agreed with Shivans request, "We will construct a secure portion within the Ryokan to be utilized as your external command center. We just expect your technology to remain behind those walls."

Shivan asked, "Back to the Velisus, would you like the external specification to simplify the planning for the exterior structure facade?"

"That would help greatly, just be sure to only include the dimensions nothing else. They will need to know the above and below water measurements."

"We already have those with and without ballast, but preferable I would like to utilize the cargo bay, so we will calculate without ballast."

As they continued discussing logistics the problem of getting personal belongings from the Velisus still remained.

Just as they were approaching an impasse Talinde entered the planning room, "I might have a temporary option for that."

As he walked up to the table he pulled up his plans for a temporary relay link, "If we modify the existing equipment we use for ship to ship docking we might be able to make it work. It will be a slight stress on the ships ventilation system, but it should do okay."

The three listened intently as Talinde explained the process, "We can use the same docking enclosure we use in ship to ship transfers, we have enough material to easily reach the surface. We will have to create an air lock at the surface to maintain pressure in the relay link. Then we pump in air, and it will extend until it reaches the surface. We just need to keep a positive pressure, so it doesn't collapse due to the forces at greater depths. We can even repeat the process in reverse when we are done offloading."

"How long would it take to get this going?"

"I could probably start attaching it tomorrow."

"How about it Kazu, do we have a way to mask our surface activities in the next day or so?"

"Well the Ryuuga is still there and considering we announced we were conducting rescue exercises and anti-submarine drills there won't be any other boats nearby. We could probably drape a tarp over the side near the entry we exited the ship last time. If we requested permission to conduct emergency repair drills with headquarters, we could easily conceal recovery operations."

Kazu contemplated the entire discussion and scanned the information on each member necessary to create registration documents, "I think we have what we need, if I can get Shivans help sending this to the surface we can request approval for Talinde's suggestion."

Shivan and Kazu headed to the command center and contacted the Ryuuga. Within a matter of minutes, the information was relayed, and they only waited for an approval on Talinde's proposal.

Awakening

The response from the Ryuuga was received within an hour, they were prepared and standing by waiting our proposal implementation. As the crew readied for relocation each member went about their personal organization, being directed to bring only items that would not link them to Paltius. In addition to securing our necessities, Shivan also was responsible for bringing the necessary items to link them to the Velisus.

Valdria packed the medical technology in their transport containers and linked her medical data base with the portable filament scanitor capable of relaying data to the Velisus medical bay and providing a diagnosis.

The difficult job was left for Talinde and Jes. They were left with assembling the necessary components to extend the relay shaft and prepare it for connection to the exterior of the Velisus.

The crew brought their necessities and packed them in a single container used for long term storage. These containers were usually stored in a vacuum environment in large trailing ships frequently used by merchants to transport delicate materials, so they were very stable.

The last crew members to pack their belongings was Talinde and Jes. As Kazu documented each box by member he noticed the one Talinde loaded was a little larger than the others.

Talinde noticed Kazu's glance so he smiled, "Tools of the trade."

Kazu nodded and said, "As long as it won't give you away, you know the restrictions."

Once the storage container was sealed Shivan left Lev and I in charge of moving the ores into position outside the interior air lock.

As Lev and I headed toward the storage where we secured the ore Lev asked, "What do you think? Are you nervous at all?"

I consider his question as I thought about my first trip to Japan, "Well, not really. I'm looking forward to the learning institution since I was always privately instructed so it will be a change. Though we won't be starting until spring, in April if I remember their calendar correctly."

"Humm, well I'm kind of scared, I only ever knew the kids in the palace."

"What's to be nervous about? We will still be together, that was one of the conditions remember?"

Lev nodded a few times, "I guess you're right." As he put his arm on my shoulder we continued walking.

Once we arrived at the storage room we removed all but one center cargo restraint and engaged the electrostatic lift stabilizer. The cargo shifted slightly, and I ensured its stability before disengaging the final restraint.

The lifts allowed cargo to be easily maneuvered so it was a simple task for us to relocate the six containers to the corridor outside the air lock. Once we moved the last two containers in place we deactivated the electrostatic lifts and went to inform Shivan.

When Lev and I entered the planning room I noticed everyone was sitting at the table watching an external feed. It was our external docking monitor, they nervously watched Talinde and Jes as they finished the final connections for the relay link. It was a somewhat slow process since neither was used to working in an environment other than space.

As Talinde's voice came over the link, "Looks clear down here, heading back."

There was a noticeable ease in the tension in the room. After Talinde and Jes cleared the airlock and returned to the planning room, we had one final meeting before the day closed. The plan was to begin transfer operations once it grew dark on the surface, so we were forced to use this time to rest prior to the events ahead.

Shivan took a moment with Talinde and Kazu to inspect each suit as well as the loaner suit for Kazu who had initially used a very cumbersome diving device.

Kazu was looking at the suit he would be wearing tomorrow and shook his head, "I am amazed that this is all you need, our deep-sea exploration technologists would turn green with envy if they saw these."

Shivan inspected the remaining suits, "They were initially designed for toxic atmospheres, but they are very versatile. Well, try to get some rest Kazu, I will meet you in eight hours in the planning room."

As we made our way to our individual quarters I found myself feeling anxious. My room lacked my normal personal belongings, so I couldn't really study or sleep. I knew sleep would be the right choice but for some reason I just couldn't settle down.

I thought about the time when everyone fell asleep in my bed and how I slept so well. I almost wished Lev, Ani and Tia were here to at least provide companionship even if we just sat enjoying each other's company.

It wasn't long before I decided to get up and just read from my primary filament monitor near my desk. There were so many topics and languages not to mention a whole new world waiting for us. As I began reading a compilation of old poetry I heard someone at the door. As I turned around to face the door I said, "Enter." As the door slid open.

"Yoh!" Lev stood there with his hand in the air with Ani standing next to him.

"I though you guys were told to get some rest. I'm not complaining though, come in." As they both entered and headed toward the ottoman I inwardly felt relieved.

As the door silently closed there was another chime. I thought it was odd, but I still said, "Enter."

Ahh, Tia was here too, and she looked like she was a bit out of breath, "Tia, what are you doing, are you okay?" I asked as I stood up to approach her.

She looked up at everyone, "I tried to get here before Ani and Lev entered but I was too slow." I laughed to myself, how do they know when I need them?

When we all settled down the two girls sat on the side of the ottoman facing me holding pillows in their laps. Lev was sitting in his normal chair across from the ottoman, "It's funny you all showed up, I had just been thinking it would be nice if you were all here." I said more to myself than anyone else.

Tia looked at Lev and Ani then back to me, "I felt like there was something wrong, it was like you were calling me. So, I just had to come check."

Ani's face looked contemplative as she was thinking of what Tia just said then quietly asked, "Did it feel like he was calling, or he was lonely?"

"I guess like he was lonely, I don't know why but I just had a strong feeling he wanted to see us and then when I came I saw you and Lev at the door."

Lev glanced between each girl as they talked, "What are you guys, Trist psychics? Just admit it, Ani you just wanted to see him."

Ani swung the pillow in her lap toward Lev and let it fly.

Lev was expecting it, so he quickly caught her pillow, "Thanks, I was hoping you'd do that." As he stuffed the pillow behind his neck.

Ani shot him a frustrated glare then looked at me, "That's not true, I was just worried. Like Tia, I had a feeling you were lonely. Not that I really care but it would be a hassle if something was wrong."

I personally thought it strange, Lev didn't seem to have the same feeling, or he just wasn't being honest.

Just then Lev stood up and walked around to Tia, "Let's try something out." He grabbed Tia by the wrist and pulled her up.

"Hey, wait, what are you doing!" Tia said as she tried to pull away.

Lev continued to pull her toward the changing room, "Just come on, let's try something."

She looked back to Ani and me with a pleading expression.

I frowned as Lev continued to pull Tia, "What are you doing?"

"I want to show her it's her imagination, so she won't worry." Tia finally stopped as Lev paused to explain, "Let's see if it really was a coincidence. Tia will go in a different room and come back in when she thinks Trist is calling."

This would also put me at ease as well, since I thought it was strange they always arrived shortly after I'd thought of them, "Sure, I don't mind. It's better than just staring at each other."

Lev pulled Tia into the next room once she stopped resisting and slowly closed the door once he exited, "Now Trist, wait a bit then try calling her into the room or think you want to see her or something."

I think this is sort of amusing, but I will play along, "Okay, so how long should I wait?"

Though, as I asked I started thinking of Tia and mentally called her to the room.

"Just wait a bit then…" Tia emerged from the room before Lev finished.

"I felt like he called." Tia shyly said with an embarrassed look on her face.

I was a little shocked, but I didn't say anything.

"Did you call her Trist?" Lev asked after glancing between Tia and me.

I nodded with an uncertain frown, "Why don't we put Ani and Tia in there and I will think about one, that would be easier wouldn't it?"

Lev thought a moment, "Yea probably."

"Okay Ani, off to your closet!" Lev said with a grin.

Ani quietly stood and headed to the side room. As she passed Lev with his amused smile pointing toward the changing room she unexpectedly punched him in the stomach.

"Ugh…!" As he doubled over and slipped to the floor, "I am so telling now Ani." Lev said in a gasping voice.

Ani looked down at Lev as her expression turned threatening, "Don't you dare."

Ani then turned toward Tia who was standing near the changing room entrance and they both entered and closed the door behind them, "Come on Tia."

Lev slowly got up and sat on the ottoman, "You know Trist you are in trouble."

"Huh, what did I do?"

Lev just shook his head, "I can't say."

After a minute or two I cleared my mind and thought about all the fun we have had even though the situation was due to tragic circumstances.

As Lev looked in my direction he sat up again as I made hands signs like we would in training indicating Tia. I then called out to her in my mind. Tia again opened the door.

"Okay, that was just a coincidence!" Lev said in an elevated voice, "Try it again!"

Tia looked at both of us as I smiled, and she smiled back and stepped back into the closet.

This time, I will try expressing it through desire I thought. I looked at Lev and give the signal for Ani. I then held my hand out and counted down from five, four, three, two, as I reached one I thought how I would like to see Ani's face again like the morning we both woke sleeping next to one another.

Ani walked out of the room with a completely blushed face. Lev's mouth dropped open, "You are a Trist psychic!"

I mentally called Tia, and she suddenly poked her head around Ani. Okay this could be a problem, I thought to myself.

Lev sat with his arms crossed but didn't say anything else for a while after Ani and Tia came back in and sat down.

Ani sat with her arms crossed and a faint blush still on her face as she looked at me and suddenly said embarrassedly, "Not happening!"

"What do you mean?"

She just looked away toward Tia and Lev.

"What did you hear when you thought I called?" I asked both girls.

They both remained quiet a few moments then Tia responded, "Both times it was like you just called me to the room."

Ani was looking at Tia as she explained, "It wasn't the same for me. It was more like a feeling. Like you were telling me you wanted something."

I thought back on the times I heard people in my sleep or dreams, there was also that once during training I thought I heard Tia calling me asking for help.

I sat with a contemplative look until Ani broke the silence, "Have you ever thought we called?" She asked tentatively.

I see no reason to be embarrassed, "Yes, a few times."

I looked at Ani and Tia, "Want to try it again? I will go in the changing room?"

Tia immediately said, "Yes."

While Ani just nervously nodded.

So, I stood and walk toward the closet when I paused to look at Ani, "Do you want me to try or not?"

"What do you mean?"

"I just felt like you were asking me not to go."

The blood drained from Ani's face.

I held her gaze a moment then turned and entered the room when she didn't respond. Once I entered the room after a few moments I felt like I heard all three voices call me at the same time, so I opened the door, "That was fast, even Lev called me."

All three were silent like they didn't really believe what was happening. Well, at least a few things made more sense now. I will need to be a little more cautious in my desire to see then so I don't worry them when we are apart.

I guess the girls talked Lev into trying at the same time. He just didn't think it would work.

"This could be fun." I said out loud to no one specifically, "Let's try something. I will think of a number and name. If you think you know it raise your hand." I had all their attention now. So, as I looked at each of their faces I began to think of the number 42 without assigning a face to it.

No one responded, how about this. I began to think of the same number and mentally told Tia.

Tia timidly raises her hand, "Forty-Two I think."

"Wow, okay, yea that was it."

Tia beamed a smile for a moment as she looked a little excited. Lev is still sitting like he doesn't totally believe what's going on.

"Let's try something else." I began to think of a direction, more than that but directions on how to get to the planning room. I did the same thing I previously had and thought about it without seeing a face or name. No one responded.

This time I repeated the directions in my mind and told them to Lev.

"Okay if you just told me how to get to the planning room I am a little disturbed."

Ani looked at Lev then me, "So do you mean you can talk without saying anything?"

I frowned a bit, "I have no idea, I have heard you guys when I was far away but thought I was imagining things. This might be worth looking into, I thought to myself. "How about you guys? Just think of a number, name, or object and assign a face to it, but don't all think of me. Let's see if it goes between you guys too"

As the three of them began to think I focused on what each person before me was thinking. As I closed my eyes and focused on emptying my mind and extending my senses I tried to reach out for my friends thoughts in front of me. My head suddenly began to ache, then I was bombarded with three different voices as if they were shouting directions, numbers and names, I wasn't familiar with.

My head started pounding and I subconsciously placed my hand against my forehead. Before I knew it, my head was spinning then Lev, Ani and Tia were shouting in my mind asking me what was wrong, I sensed overwhelming worry, fear and dread before I collapsed.

When I woke up Valdria was sitting next to my bed. She noticed me open my eyes then sat the scanner on the bed, "How do you feel?"

I looked around the room a bit, then back to Valdria, "I feel fine now, just sleepy."

"Can you tell me what happened?" Valdria quietly asked.

"Umm, yea. We were trying to determine the extent of our ability to communicate telepathically. I asked Lev, Ani and Tia to pick something and try to send it to each other instead of just me. When I tried to clear my mind and extend my senses, my head began to ache then suddenly it was like their thoughts began flowing into me with great force."

I leaned forward a bit and Valdria moved to the side a little, so I could swing my legs over the beds edge.

As I glanced around the room I noticed the three were sitting against the ottoman on the floor sound asleep, "When did they fall asleep?"

"It was only a bit ago, I sedated them."

I looked confused, "Why?"

Valdria placed her hand on my knee as she began, "Trist, what you did was very dangerous. Before I explain more promise, me you won't try this again until you are older."

I am not sure why this is dangerous, but I prefer not passing out, "I promise."

"Your great, great, grandfather Verndactilia 2nd had the same problem you're having right now. He was blessed with the aspect to communicate subconsciously with his close family and friends." Valdria watched me contemplatively.

"However, as he grew older and his brain continued to develop, through his ability he found he could not just hear friends but was also subject to the thoughts of all those around him."

Valdria paused, "So, I say it is dangerous because you are unable to filter what bombards your subconscious. When you purposefully tried to listen to the others you inadvertently broke a barrier allowing you to freely hear their thoughts."

Valdria sat back a bit, "Their thoughts overwhelmed your senses and caused you to pass out. I had to sedate them since they continued to worry about you even after you collapsed. But your brain didn't stop receiving their signals. Until they calmed down you would remain open to their outflowing thoughts. And as I suspected you awoke a few moments after they fell asleep."

Valdria looked at me intently, "Is there anything else you have noticed regarding aspects of your own?"

I don't recall anything that really stands out, "Not that I am conscious of."

"Listen Trist, from now on you need to start working on mental discipline. Having this happen so early is unexpected, so if you don't begin now this will have long term negative impacts and possibly incapacitate you at a very inopportune time."

I slowly nodded, "I understand."

When Valdria was sure I was going to be okay she left, leaving the three asleep on my floor. I really worried them I guess, I know Valdria said to restrain myself, but I couldn't help it. I mentally told each Lev, Ani and Tia I was fine and wished them a good night's rest.

I awoke a few hours after Valdria had left, and I noticed the three were still sleeping though they were now laying on the floor against each other instead of the ottoman.

As I pulled myself out of bed I began the automatic bed making process and walked over to the three. I really had some great friends in these three.

Ani was closest to me while the other two were leaning on the person next to them. Since Ani was always hassling Lev and I, it wouldn't hurt to earn her good graces. Since she looked the most uncomfortable the way her body was twisted resting on the floor with Tia resting against Ani's hip and Lev leaning against Tia's side.

I picked up my portable filament monitor and sat on the floor next to her as I gently lifted Ani's head up to rest it on my leg. After a few moments she nestled against me a little more putting her hand slightly under my knee. I smiled, she must think she had a pillow. I continued to read.

After about an hour I heard Shivans voice over the internal communication link, "Talinde is preparing to deploy the relay, there may be some fluctuations in ventilation. The rest of you should meet in the planning room in three hours." Shivan's voice faded out.

From where I sat I could reach Ani and Tia's heads. I slowly rubbed their heads in turn and said, "Hey Ani, Tia wake up." Ani moved her other hand to the top of my knee after a moment. I tried again, and gently rubbed their heads again.

As I rubbed Tia's she began to stir. I suddenly noticed Ani go stiff and her breathing changed as Tia attempted to sit back up.

Then suddenly Lev slid off Tia and plopped to the floor behind her. Lev rolled to his back and began to stretch. While Tia sat up and looked around.

As soon as she looked at me and then down to Ani resting her head on my leg I could see a frustrated look cross her face for a moment. Out of nowhere Ani pinched the back of my knee.

As I yelped and jerk my knee up it forced her to face me, "What was that for?!"

"I was just checking to see if I was asleep."

"Then pinch yourself."

As Lev was glancing back at me with a slightly worried look, I smiled, "I'm fine but thank you for worrying."

Lev just nodded, and I could see relief in his facial expression.

When I looked at Tia and Ani I smiled as I thought about last night.

I pointed to Tia, "7."

I then pointed to Lev, "The personal facilities are that way." As I pointed to the door.

I finally pointed to Ani, "Sebanti." I finished with a triumphant smile on my face.

"Wait, I wasn't directing that toward you last night." Lev suddenly shouted.

"And I was trying to tell Ani my age." Tia said.

"I know, Ani was the only one trying to tell me something. Sorry that turned out the way it did."

"So, what did mother say once we fell asleep?"

"Just that it is better that I don't try doing that again for the time being."

"We were all really scared." Ani said as she looked up at me.

"Are you going to get up?"

Then she suddenly sat up and elbowed me in the shoulder. I will never understand her I thought as I rubbed my left arm.

Once we all had fully woken we arranged the cushions and took a last look around before we headed down to the planning room.

We all arrived at the same time, just as they were observing the final deployment of the relay shaft as it slowly expanded toward the surface.

I looked around and saw Valdria, Talinde, Jes, but Shivan and Kazu were nowhere to be seen, "Where's Shivan?" I asked Valdria.

Valdria looked my way and smiled, "He and Kazu are in the command center talking to the Ryuuga. The relay shaft should reach the surface soon. After that they will begin draining and pressurizing."

I looked over at Talinde who is intently watching the deployment. When I glanced over at the monitor it looked almost completely extended.

A few minutes later Talinde let out a big sigh, "That's it, Jes can you check with Shivan if we can begin pressurizing?"

Jes started running toward the command center as he said, "Yup."

Jes returned after about 15 minutes, "They say it is secured to the Ryuuga now and we can begin the pressurization process."

Talinde nodded as he watched Jes deliver his message then glanced back down and began to pressurize and drain the water from the relay shaft.

I felt my ears begin to have an unusual pressure as they popped.

I walk into the synthesizer room and grabbed four nutrition packs and handed the others one, "Does anyone else need one?" No one seemed to be in the mood to eat at the time.

Besides a few odd sensations I couldn't really sense a big difference in the ships internal pressure. After about two hours there was only a small amount of water visible near the external docking door.

When Talinde finally took his eyes off the monitor he again called Jes over, "Can you tell Shivan it's complete. We just need to test it."

Jes nodded again and quickly headed back to the command center. A short time later Shivan, Kazu and Jes returned. Shivan glanced around the room before he began his final speech.

Shivan's eyes rested on me a moment, "How do you feel?"

"I'm fine now."

He nodded and sighed, "Okay, in this is next phase, we have seven loads to get to the surface. There will only be one person per lift in case there is an issue. Kazu agreed to take the first lift with our belongings, after that it will be…" Shivan continued to detail the order we would ascend. He planned it so that if there was a catastrophic failure only one person would risk injury. "…once the external hatch opens and the relay is in place we will roll the cargo into place and reseal the exterior door before the relay heads up. The last relay will be Valdria and I. I will set and secure the door, so the functions will be externally accessible. I plan on turning the atmosphere to minimum to reduce the heat signature if anyone happens to pass over." As Shivan finished his instructions he asked, "Any questions?"

Shivan looked to Kazu, as he stepped forward to address the group, "First, let me welcome you officially to Earth, and Japan. I know I have only been with you a few days now, but my government plans on treating this ship as the diplomatic property of Paltius and therefore an entity outside our laws."

Kazu looked around at each of us, "However, that doesn't mean you won't be held accountable for actions that deviate from our national laws. As long as you adhere to the agreement I want you to consider Japan your second home."

Shivan looked anew to the group, "Kazu has arranged for a suitable structure to meet our everyday needs as well as necessary furnishings. They will work to broker the ores, so we will have a short-term supply of their currency until we can find ways to replicate and market our technologies through the government. I also understand our documents will be provided when they transfer us to our residence, as well as the schools you four will be attending in April."

Shivan directed his gaze toward Lev, Ani, Tia and me, "For now, I want you all to suit up and prepare to depart. Any questions?" Shivan paused a moment as he assessed the expression of each crew member, "Then let's get ready."

When Shivan concluded his directions we all began suiting up. Having worn this suit previously there were very little changes I needed to make. As I stood with my suit fully adjusted I just waited for Shivan to give the final okay.

I noticed Lev floundering with his, "You've worn that once already, what's wrong?"

Lev crawled back out of his suit as he turned it upside down and shook it. As he did several nutritional packs came tumbling out and scattered across the floor. I looked up at Lev then at the drinks and began to laugh.

Lev's faces went red, "What? I thought it would be nice in case I got hungry."

As I was still laughing I asked, "How were you going to consume them in your suit?"

He looked at me a second then picked them up and set them on the shelf where he stored his suit. I slowly wiped a tear from my eye as I finally calmed down. Lev then began to climb back into his suit.

I looked around the room and saw Talinde helping Tia while Valdria was verifying Shivans, so he could in turn verify the rest of ours. I looked toward Tia, now that Talinde had moved to getting his suit on I walk toward her.

She seemed occupied with adjusting the fit, "You ready Tia?"

She jumped a bit and smiled, "Yes but I'm nervous going by myself."

I ruffled her hair, "It will be fine, the food there is really tasty."

She giggled at my mention of food.

Once Tia had settled in I looked at Kazu who appeared to be able to don his suit without much assistance. As my eyes scanned the others I noticed Ani off near the cargo containers trying to balance herself as she tried to don her suit. I walk over to her and as I got close she looked like she began to lose her balance but couldn't pull her leg out, so I quickly grabbed her arm, "You okay? Need some help?"

"Please." Ani quietly said.

She held onto my arm as she slipped her last leg into the suit and began pulling it up and adjusting the clips as necessary. Once Ani had her suit on I helped with minor adjustments before Shivan verified.

As the others milled around the airlock I moved a few items from my suit locker, so I could sit on the small seat attached to the wall. I noticed Shivan helping Kazu and explaining suit functions before he slipped on his visor. As Shivan and Kazu walked toward the airlock I got up to follow.

Shivan glanced at me, "Can you turn on the electrostatic lift?" I nodded and moved into position to power the lift on.

When Shivan nodded I engage the lift and it began to easily move under our guidance. We moved the lift into position in front of the exterior lock. As I waited for Shivan to give the next command I showed Kazu how to power on and off the lift. He nodded in thanks. I could see him say something but didn't hear without my visor on.

Shivan turned to me, "Let's make sure you're good."

I slipped my visor over my head and adjusted the locking mechanism. I then turned around to allow Shivan to verify all the fittings and I then I pressurized my suit.

As Shivan closed the forward airlock bulkhead I heard his voice over the internal link, "Kazu, are you ready?"

I see Kazu turn toward us and mouth a response but there was no sound. I heard Shivan again giving directions on suit communications.

Kazu looked down to his wrist terminal as he fumbled with the settings, "Can you hear me now?"

Shivan gave a nod, "All clear."

A moment later, "I thought you said these suits were light." Kazu complained as he raised and lowered his shoulders.

"Normally they would be but since we are using the lift we needed to take precautions so please bear the burden." Shivan said apologetically.

Shivan motioned me to wait next to the remaining crates as he engaged the aft airlock. Once the seal was completed I saw him giving directions to Kazu as they engaged the remaining external lock.

As the door slowly opened I could see the lift waiting. Once the door fully open Shivan assisted Kazu in moving the first crate in place and disengaged the electrostatic lift. As Kazu moved into position the door slowly began to close. With the door fully closed we could do nothing but wait for the lift to make its way to the surface and back.

On the third load it was Tia's turn to ride the lift with the crate. I could tell she was worried by the look on her face. As Shivan helped her with the visor he explained the internal link to Tia as she listened intently. Once the aft lock began to close again I heard her voice echoing in my head. I smiled through the window and tried telling her she would be fine.

Let me know when your safe I added. I had an overflowing sensation of thanks coming from her, I thought to myself, "I could get used to this."

Next up was Jes, then Lev, Ani and finally me. As Shivan helped maneuver the final crate in place I powered off the electrostatic lift and stepped onto the platform.

Shivan gave a single wave as the external lock closed. Once fully closed the lift began its upward ascent.

As I traveled up with the last crate I thought about Lev and Ani's worried voices until they were at the surface. They are probably in for some surprises, I thought. I smiled to myself as the lift continued to move me in the direction of our new home.

As I approach the surface the lift slowed, until it inched its way to the point just beyond the last seal. As the seal behind me slowly began to close I looked down into a translucent tunnel with moon light rippling off the sides into deeper shades of bluish green.

The moon reflected into the enclosed area shining somewhat translucently as the tiny waves rippled and occasionally crested.

The crew of the Ryuuga approached the transport container as I helped unsecure and engage the electrostatic lift. We slowly eased the container onto a platform that gently rolled with the sea. Once I fully exited the lock, it began to close, and I could see the interior partition re-open and the lift hurtled back into the dark waters where Shivan and Valdria waited.

The crew deftly attached lines to the crate and they gently hoisted the cargo up as they swung it into the waiting ship. As the boom came back around it was now holding what looked like a cage with a door.

A sailor guided me to the entry point, and they began hoisting me up. Once they had the lift secured they unlatch the door and I let out a sigh of relief as I stepped onto the dimly lit lower deck of the Ryuuga.

When I turned I could see the men peering over the edge waiting for the final passengers of the Velisus to emerge. I slowly began to unfasten the restraining latch on my visor as I pulled it over my head. I noticed a slightly pungent scent as I look around I realize it must be coming from the Ryuuga's workshop.

I glanced around and noticed a group of sailors securing our belongings and wrapping tarps over the surface. As I looked around for my companions I realized I didn't even see Kazu. One of the sailors noticed me searching and told me my escort would return shortly and to please wait, that I would be taken to the ready room shortly.

While waiting, I attempted to take in as many of the sights as I could. I moved closer to the hoist, so I would have a better view of the crew waiting for the final lift. As the exterior tarp fluttered gently in the cool breeze I heard someone say it's coming. I stepped a little closer but was motioned back by the sailor operating the hoist. After several minutes the hoist swung the basket over the side. I could see the cable wobble indicating it had found a temporary cargo. Once the hoist began reeling its line in I saw Shivan and Valdria standing in the cage. I could hear what sounded like a whooshing noise and looked into the water as the airlock slowly began to bleed off its pressure and slowly filled back up with sea water.

As Shivan and Valdria stepped from the cage for the first time I noticed they looked extremely tired. Finding a nation as understanding and willing to cooperate must have lifted a huge burden from his shoulders. For two years nonstop he taught, trained and prepared us for the unknown, but now he will have an opportunity to take some time for himself and Valdria.

As Shivan and Valdria removed their visors Shivan sighed, "Well the easy part is over, now for the challenging part."

I frowned inwardly, "I thought we just finished the hard part."

Valdria smiled and Shivan looked to me with one of his kinder expressions, "No, I think you will find that is incorrect. The challenges we now face will be akin to our ancestors having to build and develop a society with their knowledge but not the tools."

I contemplated his response as I remembered our early history of the time when my great grandfather first landed on Paltius, "I think I understand."

As Shivan and I were talking I noticed a sailor walking toward us in formal looking attire. Once he got closer I suddenly realized it was Kazu. I motioned toward Kazu and Shivan turned.

With Shivan, Valdria and I standing Kazu bowed, "Welcome aboard the Ryuuga, everyone else is waiting in the ready room. The smell was giving the girls a headache, so I took them in ahead of you."

Shivan glanced around like he was unable to identify the source before Kazu said, "What you smell is probably the fuel used in the helicopters, I understand it is fairly potent if you're not used to it."

Shivan nodded, "It does seem strange, I don't really know what to compare it too."

Kazu nodded his understanding, "Well, shall we meet with the others?"

He turned without waiting and began to walk toward the doorway he initially emerged from.

While we were walking I glanced around noticing the muted colors of grey, the occasional helicopter glinted in the faint light and I could barely make out the gold stripe on the tail, but many more were a similar shade to the Ryuuga.

When we approached the door, I thought it looked different. The door itself was very heavy with a bar attached to the exterior that appeared to open several internal latches at the same time.

Once we passed through we traveled down several narrow hallways and up multiple levels of narrow stairs until we came to a more spacious area with a door that led to the same room we previously encountered.

As we entered the room I saw all our companions, Kazu stepped aside and motioned us to enter as he followed us in and closed the door behind him.

"We will be departing our current position soon. Once we head out we should be back by mid-afternoon. It will be an unannounced port call, so we will have to move swiftly. The cargo will be inconspicuous enough, but you eight won't be."

Kazu looked down at a schedule he pulled from his pocket, "At dawn, we plan on flying you inland close to a facility they have ready to host you for a couple of days until your belongings are shipped and repacked in normal moving boxes." Kazu paused as he glanced back at his notepad from his inner coat pocket, "When you arrive we will take measurements, photographs and have the younger members take an assessment test designed to understand where your educational gaps lay."

Kazu cleared his throat, "Once that is done we have a few people who would like to meet you."

Shivan interrupted, "Who will we be meeting with?" Shivan seemed to narrow his eyes as he watched Kazu.

"They are heads of their respective fields of study, anatomy and physiology, physics, medicine, engineering, and electronics." Kazu smiled, "The normal people you would expect to meet when someone comes along and negates many of your known principles."

Shivan looked at Kazu questioningly.

"They are all trusted with many of the nation's most vital secrets so please don't worry about them leaking your information." Kazu paused, "If that happened you would not be held responsible."

Shivan nodded as the rest of us glanced at each other wearing concerned looks.

As I considered the implications of increasing the number of people knowledgeable of us, "What would Japan do if our identity was unintentionally leaked by one of these representatives? Didn't you previously say that you would deny our existence and treat us as invaders if our presence became known? This seems like an unnecessary risk."

After I spoke Shivan also voiced his concerns, "How will you ensure there will be no leaks?"

"If that did happen they would of course never be privy to information you provide, plus they would cease receiving funding. The government would of course deny your existence and if necessary we would relocate you, but we wouldn't show any hostility toward you. You will likely become the foundation of our…"

Kazu paused in thought, "No that's wrong, how about the foundation of the worlds technological revolution."

Shivan relaxed visibly, "That is our goal. We would have all benefit from our knowledge. The happier the people are the less chance for violence."

Kazu nodded his understanding, "I wish for that as well." Kazu noticed the vacant looks from the others before he sighed, "For now, let me bring some blankets so you can rest until we are ready to depart."

Valdria looked at Ani and Tia as they breathed quietly out of sync from one another, "I think that would be best, they look very tired."

Kazu departed and returned a few moments later with another sailor carrying eight blankets.

As we all took a blanket Valdria began to cover Ani and then turned to Tia as she draped her with the second blanket. Lev stood after Kazu departed and walked over and sat next to me with a look that clearly said, "Now what?"

I return his look and offered a slight shrug.

I leaned back in the chair clearly not intended for sleeping and found myself slowly blinking as my eyes failed to open a little less each time until I finally fell asleep.

After what seemed like a matter of moments I heard the door latch and gradually opened my eyes. The room was dimly lit by the light coming through the open door as Kazu peered inside.

As I leaned my head forward I glanced around the room. Shivan also sat against a wall with his arms crossed, Valdria seemed to be leaning against his shoulder. I looked next to me and Lev's head was tilted back with his mouth wide open.

I suddenly wished I had something to drop in his mouth.

I scooted up since I seemed to be sitting on the edge of my seat as I slept, this alerted Kazu someone was awake.

As he looked my way he reached in and turned the lights on, "We will need to depart in the next hour. Do you think you will be ready?"

As I was about to respond I heard Shivan say, "I will see to it." As he gently rubbed Valdria's head as if to wake her, "Trist can you rouse the others."

"Sure." I told him.

I pulled the blanket from around me and smiled as I draped it over Lev's head.

I slowly woke each in turn starting with Talinde and moving to each member of our group until I reached the girls who I gently patted on the head instead of shaking, "Hey, wake up Ani, hey Tia wake up."

They slowly opened their eyes then Ani sat straight up. They both were looking around probably trying to get their bearings, I walked back over to Lev who was still sleeping.

I felt bad, but I had to do it, I gently nudged Lev's feet and as he began to slip from the chair he immediately began to flail around not knowing what had happened and having a blanket over his head. Finally, he was able to scoot back into his seat and pulled the blanket from his head. I only grinned but I was laughing inside as he glanced around.

About the time the last blanket was folded Kazu returned, "Are you guys okay? Do you need something to eat or can you wait an hour or two?"

As Lev was about to say he was hungry, Shivan cut him off, "We will be okay a little while longer."

Lev looked dejected as his stomach complained.

"Very well, if you would follow me we will head to the craft transporting you to the next location."

As we all filed out I glanced back at the room and thought so much had happened since I was first on the Ryuuga.

As we approached the flight deck we were stopped just inside the hatchway, "They are moving your craft now."

We continued to watch the crew prepare the helicopter, as they conducted their checks and removed the little red flags.

A few moments after the crew finished their inspection a sailor approached us with protective headwear. I was familiar with them from last time, so I slipped mine on. Jes after looking my way followed suit. I showed Lev, Ani and Tia how to strap them on. Shortly after we had donned our headwear the helicopter began to whine, and I could smell the same pungent scent as when I boarded the Ryuuga yesterday.

Once they motioned us out we quickly filed toward the door of the craft and they helped us each in. It was much more crowded this time, you could tell these weren't made for many passengers.

After we were all fastened in the turbines began to whine louder as the blades began to rotate at an increased speed. When I felt the helicopter begin to roll forward it slowly pulled from the deck and began speeding toward our next destination. We all sat without speaking since it was difficult to even hear yourself. However, everyone began showing excitement once we approached the coast.

It was no more than an hour when we began to feel the change in altitude and momentum as the craft took a descending path toward an open green field next to what looked like a three-story building shaped like a simple rectangle.

The building looked like it was made from red rocks or bricks stacked on top of one another in an overlapping fashion with windows appearing at regular intervals. The main entry was in the center of the structure facing our landing sight. As we landed I noticed several individuals waiting outside the building for our arrival.

Once the craft landed it was several minutes before the turbines began to wind down and the blades slowly came to a halt. As the crew opened the door from the exterior Kazu jumped out and began giving directions to those waiting. When we all were unloaded, we walked toward the building entry. Upon entering I noticed it was a large entry with staircases on the right and left leading to the upper floors. The floors looked old but still shone with a high gloss.

When we were all inside we were instructed to remove our headwear. As I unbuckled mine I slipped it off and sat it on the table they had placed for them. Tia looked to be struggling with her buckle, so I helped her quickly and slipped it off her head and placed it next to the one I wore.

Lev had his unbuckled and was helping Ani with hers when she pulled her headwear off I though her hair looked a bit more vibrant auburn, almost glowing. I figured it was due to the helmet so didn't think much of it. As Kazu stood talking to the person wearing a white coat I glanced around and saw the others who met us were waiting outside the door.

When Kazu finished talking he turned to us, "I would like to introduce Dr. Moriyama, he will help assess the children's learning needs and will direct discussions the day after tomorrow with our panel of experts."

Dr. Moriyama stepped forward a bit, "I am Moriyama Kenchi, please call me Kenchi. I will help determine what educational levels each of you are at, and direct preparations for your move this week. Last I heard your new home was nearly complete, they were preparing a secure room within the house for more sensitive belongings. For now, please follow me, we would like to fit you with some more appropriate seasonal attire."

I looked at each of us as he finished and though we were all wearing simple clothing for Paltius. Now that I thought about it the weather had been cooler since we arrived.

As he took us to a room a short way down the hall he opened a door and allowed each of us to enter. As we walked in I noticed the windows were darkened to prevent outsiders from seeing in. Inside was a man and woman waiting to take our measurements.

When we stepped in they began calling us individually over, they asked our names and began writing numerous measurements on sheets of paper, they went from neck, chest, underarm, waist, leg, and finally inseam. The process was much more efficient than when I saw them once measure my mother for clothing on Paltius.

As the two finished up Kenchi asked us to follow him, the next room had several beds and assorted personal belongings in some type of wrapping on a long table near a door marked restroom. As we entered Kenchi paused, "Please take some time to refresh yourselves as you can, dinner should be here soon."

As we all looked around I noticed this room also had blackened windows.

I hadn't previously noticed but when I entered the restroom I realized I really shouldn't wait so long. There were several rooms with green tile located to the side as I walked in, each enclosure had a cloth like covering. As I peaked in I could see a knob and a faucet like protrusion from the wall about two meters high, there was also a metal grate in the floor. I would have to ask about the purpose when Kenchi returned. The other fixtures appeared to have a similar function to the personal facilities we encountered in the JAXO building.

As I relieved myself I found the faucet was manual after I initially tried placing my hands under it and water failed to run, then as I adjusted the valves on the side I figured out one side was cool and the other warm. Not having a function that dispensed water at body temperature was a little inconvenient since it wasted water till you found the ideal mix. When I exited,

Kenchi was waiting near the door for the remaining members of our group to finish preparing.

When we all had relieved ourselves and straightened our clothing we followed Kenchi to a room at the far end of the building. The room was about as large as the room we would be using for the next few days, but instead of beds, it had tables lined in four rows the length of the room with a raised platform to the right wall and the left had a door leading to what looked like a smaller room with people occasionally coming in and out to set objects on a table.

As we all entered the room Kenchi motioned to the closest table, "Please have a seat and they will bring out your meals shortly."

I began to smell something unique but strangely tantalizing. I closed my eyes and tried to imagine what it was and suddenly I heard Lev's stomach growl. I looked at him and smiled knowing he must be hungry, "The sandwiches they served when we first arrived were tasty, but they didn't smell like this."

Lev grinned as he stretched, "As long as it has more flavor than a nutrition pack."

When they started bringing food to our tables it was apparent it was much different from my first meal. I suddenly thought I heard Lev's stomach again, but when I looked his way he was just watching the servers bringing in our meals. I glanced further down the table and could see Ani's face, it was bright red, as she was looking down in embarrassment. When she looked up and noticed me smiling at her she quickly turned the other way.

What they sat in front of us was a tray with five different dishes. There was a slightly scorched object with an inner white meat on the larger plate while the bowl next to it looked to be a steamed grain. The smallest bowl had green vegetable like contents and the largest bowl had a mix of orange, tan, green and translucent strips mixed with finely sliced meat. The last bowl contained a soup like liquid with small white square contents and a green leafy substance.

Once the last tray was placed, Kenchi glanced at the servers who then brought pitchers with condensation forming on the exterior and a clear glass for each member. When the serving was completed Kenchi continued, "While Japan is very proud of their culinary diversity the meal before you best represent a traditional Japanese meal. The utensils are unique to Japan and neighboring Asian countries." Kenchi then gave an example of how to use what he called chopsticks. When he finished we began trying to use them ourselves.

Surprisingly they were somewhat difficult to master. Unlike the utensils we used on Paltius these served a variety of functions.

While we tried to familiarize ourselves with the new utensils there were various levels of success. Valdria seemed to master then the quickest as she began to taste the different culinary dishes before her. Shivan looked to be faring better than the rest but I noticed he occasionally had his chopsticks pop out of his hand.

Talinde had given up on mastering them and was using them to stab the softer foods. The rest of us were finally able to eat as we became more comfortable with the positioning of our hands. As Kenchi observed us for a few minutes I could detect a slightly amused look on his face until he exited the room and returned with a tray for himself.

The scorched meat or mackerel was extremely delicious, the interior was flaky and melted in your mouth while the crust had a pleasantly crispy taste. This was the first time I had ever eaten fish before. The grain was a staple food source called rice and was grown in Japan.

The greens were slightly sweet and sour with a crisp texture and was called sunomono, the largest bowl contained cooked carrots, onions, potatoes and grilled meat, that I heard was called beef. The potatoes and carrots seemed to melt as you bit into them and carried a slightly sweet taste. The soup Kenji explained was miso shiro and was slightly salty with small white chunks of tofu that absorbed the flavor of the cleansing broth. It was by far the best meal we had enjoyed these last two years. I occasionally glanced around the table between bites and noticed a variety of expressions from my companions, ranging from puzzlement to bliss.

When most us had completed our meal the group began to chatter amongst ourselves regarding taste and the desire to try different aspects of the meal again.

Kenchi stood, "Now that we have had the opportunity to eat I would like to discuss our schedule for the next couple days."

Kenchi paused in case there were questions, "We will not burden you further today since I understand you have not had much rest since yesterday morning. Tomorrow however we will begin at 07:00 with breakfast, it will be much simpler fare than today's meal."

"At 09:00 we will split up into groups for different activities." Kenchi began to explain the individual activities, it appeared Shivan, Valdria and Talinde would be meeting with experts from multiple fields to determine what areas we could provide immediate influence.

The rest of us would be tested on our general educational understanding. This would assist them in determining if additional instruction would be necessary prior to enrollment in a learning center or school.

Most of us would end up in middle school due to the similarities in our physical development to those in the seventh year of instruction, or so we were told. I didn't really mind but worried that Lev, Ani and Tia wouldn't score adequately on general studies pertaining to Earths cultural and societal history and more specifically Japan related topics.

Jes however was going to be assessed for higher education given his age and physical build. He didn't seem to be too concerned since he was more interested in engineering than playing or training with the rest of us anyway.

"At 12:00 we will break for a lunch and will return to testing the children afterwards. Testing should be complete by 15:00 unless we identify discrepancies."

Kenchi paused a moment as Kazu quietly entered the room and pulled up a chair near Shivan, "The following day will be used to conduct any remaining evaluations and a final question and answer period for our panel of experts."

Kenchi looked in Shivan and Valdria's direction, "If you have any questions regarding the current state of our technologies this will be the time. After that you will be able to assess how best to initiate knowledge and technology sharing."

It sounded like the experts weren't so much coming to ask Shivan, Valdria and Talinde questions as they were for us to assess their understanding of anatomy and physiology, physics, medicine, engineering, electronics and mathematics.

This way we could target the translation of written knowledge, so we could gradually improve their understanding of concepts we would ultimately introduce.

"With that I would like to have Kazu explain the transition process to your new home." Kenchi motioned to Kazu.

"Thank you, Dr. Moriyama. The Ryuuga should be in port this evening, once they off load your cargo we will pack your belonging in a vehicle that will accompany you to your new dwelling. We will do it this way, so it presents a more natural appearance to those residents who might observe your arrival."

Kazu paused a moment as he glanced at his note pad, "You will have enough clothing to accommodate your initial transition, however you will be responsible for purchasing additional items once you settle in. I have some reference guides outside that cover basic principles such as years, seasons, a history summary and Japanese geography. This will assist you tomorrow, so I suggest you at least browse through them."

Kazu pulled out several small objects and thin red books, "We took the liberty of opening an account for each of you so that we can deposit funds as necessary, here are the books and stamps." Kazu slid them toward Shivan who nodded but did not reach for them yet.

"I should have your registration paperwork tomorrow, including identification documents and the necessary paperwork for enrollment in school once your assessments are complete. After the assessments are reviewed and an institution is chosen we will provide the necessary supplies and uniforms if applicable." Kazu paused as if considering any items missed.

"Oh yes, there is also a transportation schedule for the local area near your home, try to familiarize yourself with it. We will also provide you with passes necessary for utilizing the bus, and train network. There are other transportation modes but those will be left up to you to fund."

Kazu looked to Shivan, "Once you feel more comfortable we have a boat registered in your name capable of reaching the Velisus in case of an emergency. I will give you the details later." As Kazu finished he lightly slapped his hands on the table and stood, "Any questions?"

He glanced at each member of the group. As no one seemed to have anything Kazu cleared his throat, "I will be your liaison between the Japanese government so if you ever have questions or an emergency please call. You will have phones provided so you can easily communicate with each other. Think of these as our communication link, you will also be able to access the internet or local network." Kazu smiled, "Though it won't be quite as efficient as the Velisus." Kazu paused, "I know you must be exhausted after the last several days, but the hardest part is almost over. The next challenge will be determined by your individual abilities to assimilate into society."

* * *

While Shivan, Valdria and Talinde discussed the upcoming meeting with the representatives of Japan's academic and technological community with Kenchi and Kazu I took this opportunity to retreat to our temporary room.

As I exited the dining hall I noticed a small table on rollers near the entrance and silently thumbed through the reference guide and pamphlet containing timetables. I picked up one of each and made my way to our temporary room. As I walked down the hall I contemplated the method of testing they would employ to determine educational development.

I knew that Lev, Ani and Tia conducted lessons with Shivan and Valdria, but very seldom did we study jointly. I was worried about their understanding of Earth's history not to mention Japan. I wonder if there was a way I could help so we could stay in the same class.

I slowly thumbed through the book as I thought on my options. The book while it was only a summary and not too heavy gave me a strange sensation since having a physical object was in itself unique. I had always used a filament monitor or a personal network terminal to study with, so a book made of paper was a new concept.

The reference guide included days of the week, a calendar of months, and a listing of years, both in standard and Japanese. It detailed holidays which were celebrated and gave a brief description of the origin. Other topics included lunar cycles and seasons associated with the months of the year.

Unlike Paltius, Earth only had twelve months numbering from 28-31 days, equaling 365 days per year. The other guide also contained a brief history section dating from what was called the Jomon period through Japans current history, it noted significant events and names associated with different points of historical interest.

It was a very simple document, one which should be easy for Lev to understand. As I sat the book on the table next to my temporary bed I laid back and could feel a sinking sensation as the bed accepted the additional weight of my body. While different than our sleeping accommodations on the Velisus I didn't find it uncomfortable even though it was somewhat soft.

As I blankly stared at the off-white ceiling I thought about the inherent differences in our solar cycle. Having a binary solar system, we experienced seasons much more differently than Japan.

Earth broke down their months based on lunar cycles but Paltius and the other two moons didn't orbit quite the same as the Earth and its moon. While they were satellites of Titar they were tidally locked and didn't experience any rotation.

Though when Titar progressed in orbit it slowly rotated giving a variation to seasonal periods. Based on Earths seasonal calendar with four seasons Paltius would have what would have been eight seasons.

While we didn't call them specific names instead we identified them as phases. Paltius and the other two moons in our alliance shared similar seasonal periods though they were somewhat accentuated by the distance and synchronous orbit they held with Titar.

When I began to contemplate the differences, I wondered what I would encounter on Earth which maintained a stable orbital rotation. During my contemplation I noticed the door open and Ani and Tia returned to the room. As I turned toward their direction I asked, "Are they still talking?"

Ani nodded as she walked over to her bed and Tia came to sit next to mine facing me.

She looked to have the small reference book in her hands. As I glanced down at it I noticed her clenching and unclenching her hands on it. She had a strained look and was avoiding my gaze somewhat.

Knowing Tia, she had something to ask she was either embarrassed about it or she needed help with something, "Tia, what's wrong?" I quietly asked.

Her lower lip seemed to be quivering a bit as she glanced from Ani to me, "Trist!" Tia said in an elevated voice.

That was a little unexpected I thought.

My eyes opened a little more as I twisted to my side propping up my head on my knuckles looking her direction, "Yes?" I calmly answered looking more interested now.

"Can you help us study?"

I looked over toward Ani and she was staring into a corner of the room but didn't say anything.

As I glanced back at Tia I smiled kindly, "I would like that."

When the words left my mouth, I saw Tia significantly relax and I heard a soft sigh from Ani. I pushed myself up and slid to the edge of the bed as I reached for the reference book I had gone through previously, "What do you want to study first?"

Ani jumped off her bed and walked over and sat next to Tia, "I don't know any of their history and there are too many names." Ani said as Tia silently nodded.

Next Tia asked, "I don't understand some of the words or the reasons behind some of the holidays. Even before that what will they be asking about in the examination? What if they put me in a different class than everyone else?"

Tia's eyes were beginning to moisten as Ani spoke up, "I have a hard time studying anyway, and now I have to translate the words and it is hard to memorize then and retranslate them into the proper symbols." Ani also looked near tears, "Will they let us still go to school if we don't know everything?"

I can feel the desperation in their thoughts, so I try to focus on them and block my desire to mentally reassure them while they sat right in front of me. I know a better way.

I stood up and stepped closer and slowly embraced them both and quietly said, "I will make sure we stay together, I won't let us be separated. I promise." As I pulled away with my hands still on each of their shoulders I can see tears streak down Tia's cheek, and I looked to Ani who seemed to be trying not to show her moist eyes as she turned away and quickly rubbed her eyes with the back of her hand before looking at me again. Ani nodded as Tia smiled. I slowly stood and caressed each of their cheeks as I came fully upright and stepped back to the edge of my bed, "Now let's get started."

As we began going through the brief historical account I heard the door open again.

Lev entered the room and glanced at us sitting near my bed, "What are you guys doing?"

I look up, "Just going through some of the history."

Lev had a hurt expression on his face, "Why didn't you tell me?"

"I just did, how were seconds?" I asked with a smile on my face.

"Oh, they were good, why didn't you tell us about the food?"

I just smiled with a mischievous grin, "I figured you would find out soon enough."

"Oh, that's right the book. Be right back." Lev quickly ran out the door leaving the room.

Ani was slightly shaking her head. Lev returned shortly and was thumbing through the pages as he walked over to where we sat and plopped down on my bed next to me. I glanced at him and told him where we were.

When I looked back toward Ani and Tia they were both staring at Lev with intent looks as he thumbed to the same page.

"Okay, so…" As we progressed through the different historical periods I helped them use associations with the names of significant figures from each era. While it only seemed to be a short time I noticed even the faint light that shone through the darkened windows earlier had faded signifying the coming of night.

When the three seemed like they had a decent grasp and could identify the different names with the date and events we decided to call it a night.

Shivan, Valdria and Talinde were still occupied when I finally decided to head to bed. As I prepared and slipped into the simple night clothes provided I returned to my bed and enjoyed the sensation of the cool sheets though somewhat rough with a slight floral fragrance.

"Are you nervous Trist?" Lev quietly asked as I was about to drift to sleep.

"I'm only nervous for you. I'm sure Ani and Tia will be fine."

"Ha-ha, well Ani is only good for her brute strength, I think her head is even full of muscles."

I heard an, "UFFFF!!" noise coming from Lev's direction. As I looked over my shoulder at his direction I saw him balled up and Ani slipping back into her bed. As I contemplated the assessment I unknowingly fell asleep.

The next morning arrived quite quickly, I awoke to the sounds of Shivan talking to Valdria regarding the meetings today. As they continued their discussion I slowly rolled to the right side of my bed and sat up. I sat up on the edge of my bed a few moments with my elbows resting on my knees as I tried to force the rest of my body to wake. When I finally stood up I slipped on the shoes they had provided and made my way to the restroom to prepare for the day ahead.

After I washed my face I decided to try using the shower I had investigated yesterday. Kenchi had the staff provide towels and gave us a brief explanation and purpose for these rooms. As I removed my clothing and wrapped a towel around my waist I walked to the shower room. When I slid the curtain open I twisted the valves and cold water came gushing out in a dispersed stream.

It seemed very cold, but when I twisted the other valve the water gradually began to warm to a comfortable temperature. I hung the towel next to the door, so I could easily reach it once I was done and slowly began to moisten myself under the streaming water. I used the soap provided and quickly began cleansing myself. So not to waste much water I completed the process quickly and rinsed the residue left from the soap. Unlike on Paltius, where bathing required minimal water usage this was almost luxurious. When I turned the valves off my skin felt slightly tight and a little squeaky.

After drying with the towel, I wrapped it around my waist and slipped my shoes on as I walked back toward my bed to grab my clothing. As I gathered my things from the shelf next to my bed I looked back toward the restroom. Ani and Tia exited the women's restroom talking quietly about what sounded like todays assessment. As they looked up they both immediately noticed me and stopped, with odd looks and blushed faces reminding me of the time when they found themselves in the same bed as Lev and me. As I passed and smiled, I walked toward the privacy of the restroom to don my clothing for the day's activities. Ani and Tia can sure act odd for us knowing each other for so long.

When everyone had dressed and returned from breakfast we had about an hour before we would break into different groups. I looked at this as much the same as attending a normal lesson, so I wasn't too worried regarding the testing. It was a different story for Jes and the others. While I was relaxed, Jes was going through the reference guide trying to commit the dates and names to memory. The other three seemed to be doing the same with different levels of success.

Lev would sigh from time to time as he flipped through each page. Ani had a look of utter concentration and Tia was silently saying the names and dates as she read through the guide.

When there was a knock on the door Shivan glanced around the room before responding, "Enter."

As the door opened Kenchi stepped into the room with Kazu, "Are you ready?"

I sat up and headed toward the door with the others. When we stepped outside Kenji asked Shivan, Valdria and Talinde to follow him, while Kazu motioned to the rest of us.

As we headed toward a different section of the building I looked back and saw Shivan and the others turn the corner heading toward the entry.

The room Kazu brought us too was a similar size to the dining area though it was the opposite side of the building. It had three rows of tables lined from front to back, they looked wide enough to fit two people though each only had one chair. As we entered another gentleman in a dark blue set of slacks and a white button up shirt with pale stripes wearing a blue tie directed us to find a seat.

Kazu watched as we all found a chair then he turned to the gentleman at the head of the room and motioned toward Jes, "He will be taking the advanced assessment, the others start with the entry level and increase in difficulty if they do well."

Kazu turned back toward us, "Remember this is only so we can assess what areas your strengths lie so we can assist in preparing you for your upcoming institutions."

Kazu turned toward the proctor, "I leave them in your care."

The man nodded, "Leave it to me."

As Kazu stepped out of the room the gentleman began writing on the green board behind him. It appeared to be a name, as I watched him write I put the characters together…Murakami Shotaro is what I thought it read.

"Good morning, I am Murakami Shotaro. As Commander Tenshin said I will be conducting your assessments. You will have one hour for each test and I will check them as you finish." He paused a moment and turned toward the chalkboard. As he detailed the timeline and topics on the board he continued to speak, "Not only will this determine your knowledge gaps it will also allow us to more appropriately place you in an institution geared toward your abilities."

As we listened he outlined the content for each session. When he finished I wasn't too nervous since I had previously read over many of the topics while we were preparing to land on Earth. He walked to each of us and provided a couple sheets of white paper and a yellow cylindrical writing utensil I found out was a pencil, shaped similarly to a stylus. Once we all had a writing instrument he placed our assessments face down on the table and asked us not to turn them over until instructed. When he completed and returned to the head of the room he glanced at his watch, "You may begin."

It wasn't too difficult. The history questions revolved around major events and noteworthy individuals associated with them. When I began the mathematics portion I didn't even really need to think of an answer, so simple was the math. There was a section on English, while we didn't practice much we had prepared for this language since many of the documents we reviewed were written in it. The only topic I hadn't delved as deeply into was on social studies but after looking into the different cultures the information what was asked was basic. The science was simple and covered basic principles.

It wasn't more than twenty minutes before I sat my pencil down. As Murakami noticed my pencil down he stood and began walking my way. He quietly asked if I was done and then took the papers when I nodded. I heard Ani sigh.

As he looked at my paper as he walked to the front he paused before he turned then sat my sheets down and immediately returned with three more fresh sheets. "Try this level next. Complete what you can in the remaining time."

I took the sheets and placed them on my desk and quickly browsed through them. It was pretty much the same set of questions, though the depth range increased.

It covered more on history and looked to specific individuals and contributions, the math was still overly simplistic, the language covered many more characters called Kanji, but I was familiar with most already, though I sometimes noticed my pronunciation was off. The science was a little more complex but still lacked any reference to complex elements and focused more on natural science. The English again was complex but still at a lower level of difficulty. This time there were also components of government structure and history and geography with more of an emphasis on Japan. As I finished answering the final question I sat the assessment down. I glanced around and Jes looked to have just finished. The others were either on the last page or thumbing through pages checking their responses.

As I looked around Murakami announced the end of time, "Please put your pencils down. Pass your papers up and please take a short break."

As I stretched I turned my chair toward Jes, "How was it?"

Jes shrugged, "There are areas I could only answer based on my current understanding. Their science is easy since they only work on a 115-element periodic table. The physics and mathematics were simple compared to Shivan's lessons."

I nodded as Jes finished explaining. I then glanced at Lev, "Well?"

"How did you finish that so fast?"

"Most of the problems were very basic, what did you have a hard time with?"

"The translation from Japanese to English, the history, however the math and science were pretty easy."

Tia quietly affirmed her own opinion, "I thought the same. I just wish I had listened more when Valdria taught us science and English. I have a hard-enough time sorting out Japanese let alone translating it to something else."

Ani just gave a glazed look and rested her head on the table. She looked like she was close to crying.

It was about an hour of discussing the assessment test when Murakami cleared his throat. After Murakami completed his review he quietly exited the room while we continued to chat. When he returned he had a new set of papers ready to hand out, "Are you ready for the next session?"

We all responded, "Yes."

He then began passing out the next set of assessments. When he finished handing the others their papers he placed a stack that looked to be a considerable number of sheets on my desk.

As he returned to the front he glanced at his watch, "You will have two hours for this portion of the exam. Begin."

I flipped the pages over and immediately noticed the questions had changed significantly. No longer were they simple responses or multiple choice, now they required a significant amount of thought. This must be the advanced middle school questions; the others were too simple. I grinned to myself and began writing.

The format was organized much differently as well. It immediately started with math and progressed into physics. As I finished up the physics it began to transition into a much more complex science and chemistry. While I noted the compounds that would finish the formula in one question I also wrote a simpler combination to the side including compounded formulas with a brief explanation.

As I progressed, the test covered world and Japanese history, geography, world and local politics, economics, though the portion that took me the longest was translating into the different languages. There were several language questions and I was truly thankful for our previous preparations. This time I was only done a few moments before Murakami announced the end of time.

I wish I had been better prepared, I would have liked to review more.

"Please put your pencils down and pass your papers forward."

As he collected the different piles he began to shuffle them and looked out over each of us, "I apologize I ran that into your lunch break, but I did ask the staff to wait for you to complete this current set. Take the next two hours to eat and relax, feel free to review as necessary." Murakami took the assessments and departed the room.

As we all stood and began to walk toward the dining area, Tia and Ani discussed the most recent assessment I could tell Ani felt better on the last round. I laughed to myself, or it could be lunch.

Lev, ran up behind me and jumped up by pushing off my shoulders, "Well how did it go? You didn't finish as quickly that time." He had an earnest smile on his face as he rested his elbow on my shoulder as we walked side by side.

"I know, that last test was a little more intense. The content wasn't too bad, but the time limit was tight."

Tia glanced back as we talked, "I think I did okay with the Kanji, I was worried, but it was pretty easy."

Ani bumped into Tia's shoulder purposefully, "No it wasn't."

As we entered the dining hall the servers had placed several trays with sandwiches on the table. There was water and pitchers arranged next to them. I walked over and picked a half egg sandwich but this time I also wanted to try the katsu sandwich I saw Shivan try the last time.

The others watched me and finally asked, "What are they?"

I realized they hadn't tried these yet, "Oh, right. We were given sandwiches when we were at JAXO last time." I pointed to each as I called them by name, "The egg sandwich was very good but Shivan and Valdria both seemed to like the katsu and yakisoba sandwiches."

Ani glanced at the selection of sandwiches, "Which one is the yakisoba sandwich?"

"I don't see it this time."

As the others made their decision I walked over to a table with my plate and glass of water. When I sat I tried the katsu sandwich first. It had a wonderful tangy taste and crisp crunch that made my mouth water as I chewed. I really could get used to these, I thought. As we ate Lev plopped his plate down across from me.

When I looked up he was glancing to my right and left, and when I turned I saw Ani and Tia standing at my sides, "Are you going to sit?"

They both smiled brightly, "Yes." They said in near unison.

As I continued to eat Lev looked at me and shook his head.

When our break ended Murakami entered the dining hall and looked around, "Tristali, could you come with me a moment?"

I responded with a brief, "Yes."

I stood and took my plate and glass to the table set aside for used dishes. The others were still eating but seemed to continue to watch me as I walked over to Murakami and exited the room. We walked down the hall until we came to a door just past our sleeping quarters. Murakami opened the door and asked me to enter. As I did I saw Kazu and Shivan sitting in the room already while Kenchi was behind a desk. I thought it odd that there were so many present. Murakami motioned to a chair next to Shivan for me to sit, as I did he sat in a chair behind us.

At first, I felt a little apprehensive, Shivan wore a solemn face, usually the look he showed before he discussed an unpleasant activity.

"Thank you for coming Tristali, let me get down to the issue at hand." Kenchi slid a few sheets and a pencil in my direction, "Could you answer these for us really quick?"

I looked down and glanced at Shivan. These were fairly simple calculations. I took up the pencil and jotted down the answer and silently slid the paper over to Kenchi who watched intently.

As he took the sheets and glanced down at my answer he silently shook his head, "Can you explain how you came to these answers?"

I didn't really understand why he was asking such a simple question, "Well, the problem leads to this result."

Kenchi then began hand writing an equation, "How about this one?" It was more complex than the last but also had a relatively simple solution. I began writing the answer as Kenchi seemed to be leaning over his desk watching me.

As I finished I slid the paper over to him as he just stared at the answer. Several minutes seemed to pass before Kazu cleared his throat.

This startled Kenchi who seemed to be deep in thought. He suddenly looked up to me as if my head had spun around, "Umm, well I knew from talking to Shivan about Physics and mathematics that you were advanced, however…"

He paused as if in thought a moment. "…I will need to have this verified."

Kenchi placed the paper on his desk as he seemed to let out a long exhale, "Tristali, this is the situation. Based on the last assessment you would be a suitable candidate for our national university. The expenses of doing so would be covered by the government, we would even include a stipend for housing and a food allowance. There are many benefits to studying at the University of Tokyo. With a little instruction you could easily pass the entrance exam. I would like you to strongly consider our recommendation."

I glanced at Shivan who turned his head to me, "It is your life, I am only here to guide and protect you."

"What about the others?"

"Based on their scores so far, they have shown they will have few difficulties in high school let alone middle school. At this point it will primarily be to assist in the socialization aspect."

I knew my answer, but I wanted to explore other possibilities, "What will happen if I choose to stay with my friends?"

Kenchi leaned back and clasped his hands in front of him while he looked at me quietly contemplating, "It would be a disappointment I am sure for our instructors. And to have a prodigy of your age would undoubtedly create a stir in the mathematical community. So, having the additional notoriety would probably be a disadvantage of taking our offer. If you choose to stay with your friends, there will be no negative consequences."

Kenchi showed a slightly disappointed look, "Honestly, I see more disadvantages to our offer when I think of your situation than I see benefits. However, I would like you to at least consider it. Even if it doesn't happen right away."

Kenchi looked me in the eyes and then slowly picked up the problem he just had me solve as he mumbled. "…I'm not even sure we can verify this yet."

As Kenchi continued to look at the answer Kazu slowly pushed his chair back as he stood, "Well, shall we head back Shivan?"

As I turned and looked toward Shivan I saw him looking at me, "Trist, you will have to walk your own path at some point, and there will be those that follow without reason who you can consider friends, those that follow because of your words who will be looking for inspiration, while there will be some who follow you because of your deeds, those will be the ones to be cautious of." As Shivan finished he silently stood and followed Kazu out of the room.

I slowly pushed my chair back.

As I stood I looked toward Kenchi, "I must politely decline your offer at this time. Though I will keep it in mind and if later date there is a need I will let Kazu know."

Kenchi glanced up at me as he silently nodded, "It's a shame but I understand."

When I turned toward Murakami he stood and followed me out of the room and back toward the assessment class. As we walked Murakami sighed, "You can sit out the remaining assessment if you like. Your success will be secure in any school we place you in."

I offered a short nod, "I will ensure my friends succeed as well."

"Well, then shall we?" Murakami said as he opened the door and invited me to enter.

Moving In

The next day found us meeting after breakfast to receive our registration documents. As Kazu provided our papers he also handed us a small card with our individual photos and other information pertaining to physical characteristics.

"These are your registration documents, please keep them safe. The residence card will be your primary form of identification. It should be with you at all times. In the event your identification cards are processed it will flag my office as your guarantor, but I would hope you avoid situations that would require my intervention." Murakami finished passing a set of identification cards to each of us.

Murakami also passed an envelope to Lev, Ani, Tia and me, "These documents contain your school registration information. You will all be attending Furigawa Middle School. Classes don't start until 9 April, so you have a month to settle into your new home."

Murakami handed Jes a similar set of documents, though they looked heavier, "Jesende, you will be studying at the University of Tokyo, in the engineering Department. You will probably have to work at some of the prerequisite classes, but I have faith you will do wonderfully."

Jes glanced down at the envelope and I could see his brow slightly furrow.

Kazu explained, "You will be able to commute, or we can secure lodgings closer if you prefer."

Jes looked up at Murakami then to Kazu, "I prefer to commute for the time being."

Kazu continued, "I was informed late last night that your dwelling was completed, and we will take a van to your new home tomorrow morning. Your personal belonging will arrive after we do. The movers are part of my staff, so they will assist in placing your belongings to ensure confidentiality and sight security."

Kazu paused as he considered his next words, "It has been a pleasure to spend time with you over the last week. I hope we can continue working together." Kazu bowed deeply.

Shivan responded in kind, "You have been a tremendous help and I hope our partnership is fruitful." Shivan offered a bow in return.

As we each said our thanks Kazu added as an afterthought, "Oh, your clothing will also be delivered tomorrow, as well as your school uniforms. I had them set aside some clothing for you to wear during your move tomorrow. It should be more comfortable than wearing what you arrived in, plus it is more to what you might consider normal attire."

Once we finished it was about time for the evening meal. After I had eaten I retreated to our room. I would be exaggerating if I wasn't apprehensive regarding the upcoming changes.

While having finally secured a place to live should be a relief, there were so many unknowns in our future it was more than I could really handle. I felt like I needed time to think. We have been moving toward this for so long that now that it is upon us I almost fell like running away. What would school be like I thought.

The fear of being in close proximity of so many students my age was nothing I had ever had to contemplate previously. Will my friends be accepted? There were just too many uncertainties to process at once, so I decided to lay down for a while and sort through the complex emotions surging through my mind.

Shortly after I began doubting my ability to comprehend our transition I heard the door open. As I lifted the arm I had resting across my forehead I glanced toward the door.

As Lev, Ani and Tia slowly poked their heads into the room they looked my way then proceeded into the room when they saw my glance.

"Are you okay?" Lev was the first to ask.

Ani and Tia both showed deep concern.

I glanced back to Lev, "I'm fine why do you ask?"

"Well you know, I got one of those feelings, like you were…I don't know how to say it. It felt like I was sharing your anxiety."

I looked over to Ani and Tia who were holding hands, they both looked close to tears.

I tried to give them a reassuring smile, "Really, I'm just thinking about the challenges we will face. So maybe I let my subconscious slip a bit, I'm sorry if it worried you."

Ani offered her encouragement, "Well, I am really happy we all will be in the same school. I was worried when I took the first test, but the others weren't so bad."

Tia let Ani's hand go as she walked over to my bed and sat on the edge.

She looked conflicted then suddenly she laid down next to me on my pillow and put her arm over me in a half hug, "Thank you for keeping your promise." She quietly said then quickly sat back up.

Ani seemed to be looking toward the wall deep in thought.

That night I slept fitfully and woke several times as if I was being called. Each time I thought I heard Ani and Tia talking in their sleep. However, I would quickly slip back into a fitful slumber.

When morning came I felt somewhat exhausted. I figured I should prepare to start the day off right since this was going to be the first day in our new home.

Once I had showered and brushed my teeth I looked at myself in the mirror. To me it looked like I was a little thin, as I thought back I did remember eating less since the first trip to Japan, before we were captured.

There had been so much happening the last few weeks that I hadn't even noticed. My hair was getting slightly wavy, I probably should ask Valdria to help me trim it, but as I looked closer my eyes also seemed to be a deeper green. I didn't think much of it of course, as I wiped the sink out and headed back to the bedroom.

As I returned to our room it looked like Jes was the only one still sitting on his bed. I could tell he was tired and probably a bit worried about his upcoming entrance to college. When I finished placing my few personal belongings, including the reference guide and the clothes I had worn until last night away in the boxes Kazu provided I heard Valdria and the girls exit the restroom.

I offered them all a smile and a good morning. Once my bed was straightened I collected my belongings and carried them to the entryway until we left for our new home.

I took this chance to grab something to eat since I wasn't quite sure if we would have an opportunity later.

When I walked into the dining hall I noticed Shivan, Talinde and Lev were already eating. Once I chose a few items from the serving platters I walked over and sat with the three.

Talinde was discussing the moving process and how they would go about determining which information would be foundational for Earths technological improvement.

They continued talking as I noticed Lev sitting casually with an empty plate. When I began eating, Lev slightly kicked me in the shin, "Hey, will we have a food synthesizer when we get to our new place?"

I laughed as I continued chewing as I thought, "I doubt it, they don't seem to have those. Do you remember when Kazu first was on the ship? He was really interested in it and said he hadn't seen anything like it before."

Lev frowned, "Doesn't that worry you a bit?"

Kind of caught off guard I asked, "Why?"

"Do any of us know how to cook?" Lev asked with a questioning expression.

I thought on all the meals I had in the Palace, but never once had they been prepared by Valdria or by the other adults.

"Maybe we need a guide on how to prepare Earths dishes." I responded since I had never even thought about it before.

When I stood to leave Lev followed. As we walked out the doorway we collided with Ani and Tia who were quietly chatting as they headed to the dining hall. I stopped hoping they would notice, but they were so absorbed in their conversation that Ani ran right into me.

As we collided she almost fell backwards but I was quick enough to catch her by the wrist, "Careful." I said as she quickly regained her balance.

She looked about to say something then quickly walked past Lev and me. As Tia passed she offered a quick smile and followed Ani.

I looked at Lev and he shrugged, "I guess you surprised her."

I smiled at Lev, "She did seem excited about whatever they were talking about. I hope she doesn't act like that when we start going to school." As we walked toward the entry I noticed there were several more boxes near the entry.

Since we had some time, we walked out and enjoyed the cool morning, spring was slowly causing the trees to bloom with colorful flowers. I noticed several on the perimeter of the grassy field that looked covered in a muted fluffy pink cloud like surrounding the individual trees. There were occasional lighter and darker pink blossoms interspersed among then.

As we sat enjoying the scenery a grey car pulled up along the driveway and parked slightly past the steps. When the driver door opened I noticed it was Kazu who stepped out. As he noticed me sitting on the stairs, with Lev leaning on the handrail.

Kazu looked toward us and held his hand up in greeting, as he approached, "Are you ready?" He asked with a smile on his face.

"I think we're all ready, it will be nice to finally be able to establish ourselves."

"Well, the van should be here within the next few minutes. Are the others preparing?"

I looked back, "I think everyone is packed but not sure if they are done eating."

Kazu nodded as he continued up the stairs and into the building. I leaned forward and stood up, "Want to go inside?" I asked Lev.

"I think I'm going to stay out here and wait."

I nodded and opened the door and walked to the dining hall to see if anyone was left. As I glanced in I only saw the servers cleaning the remaining food from the serving table. I left and headed toward the room we had been using as the door opened and Kazu exited followed by Shivan and our remaining companions. Valdria was smoothing the top of Ani's head as Tia talked to her father. I stopped and waited for them near the entry.

As I waited I heard Lev come through the door, "It looks like the van is here."

Everyone collected their belongings from the entry hall and moved outside to a small van. The driver wearing a dark short brimmed hat and blue suit looked almost bored as he stood near the back of the van and took our personal belongings and stowed them away.

The side doors were already open, so the girls were the first to move toward the vehicle. As they tried to climb in the driver closed the back doors and walked around to the passenger side and showed us how to move the seats allowing better access to the back of the vehicle.

Once all but Shivan were in the van the driver looked back toward Kazu and asked, "Anyone else?"

Kazu held up his hand out toward Shivan, "One more."

I could slightly overhear Kazu telling the driver he would meet us at the address. When Shivan finally climbed into the passenger seat the driver closed the door and we were off.

As we left I noticed we passed through a gated area with a small building next to the road, it appeared to be a secured access point for the property we had been staying on. We traveled through several narrow roads with the occasional small house scattered about the landscape. It looked to be a secluded area with several green fields and some smaller orchards. It was difficult to tell what they were growing but I noticed several different varieties of crops.

When we finally merged onto a wider road I started seeing an increased number of vehicles and even larger trucks and buses, if I remember their vehicle types correctly.

The number of people gradually increased to more than what I had previously seen. They were heading both directions along the walkways adjacent to the road. The buildings began changing from small narrow shops to a more robust business district. There were signs indicating a number of different functions along the road.

There were restaurants, shopping malls, grocery stores and a brightly lit sign indicating an arcade. As we traveled through we occasionally had to stop for other vehicles, crossing traffic or for pedestrians crossing the road. We continued and started to see more dwellings and fewer shops. The taller multifamily dwellings were also scarcer.

After we had driven for an hour or, so we entered a slightly less populated area nestled into a wide valley that slightly overlooked the town. The houses in this area looked older with somewhat faded exteriors. The roofs were made with a faded blue-grey tile that seemed to slope up slightly at the eaves. Most had some type of fencing and large gardens in various states of activity.

When I saw the driver look at Shivan and point I glanced in the direction he was indicating. What I saw was an older home that was much larger than the houses we had passed. It was a two-level dwelling and was surrounded by the same pink trees I saw earlier in the day. The driveway was a circular design allowing you to pull in and circle around.

The property looked to be surrounded by shrubbery and well-maintained miniature trees. The entry to the house was a wide slate path set in gravel. There were two steps up to the platform before the sliding double doors.

Once the driver brought the vehicle to a stop the doors on the passenger side opened and he exited the vehicle and walked to the back.

As we all filed out of the van I heard a quick beep sound and noticed the car Kazu was driving earlier turning into the driveway for our new home.

As he pulled in and parked he got out of the vehicle retrieved an object from his trunk. It was a large box with a colorful exterior. He carried it over to the porch and set it on the top deck, "I thought you guys could use a celebratory gift for finally moving in. It isn't much, but you should find the contents useful."

He looked back toward the road and then toward us gathered before him, "It appears the moving van is running a little late. Why don't we explore the property before it arrives?"

Shivan spoke first, "That would be appreciated."

I was also looking forward to looking around the house.

The driver of our vehicle finished setting the last of our belongings on the porch of the house and bowed as he departed.

The exterior of the house looked to be made of wood and a white plaster. There were areas that looked recently patched as the wood had a brighter more vibrant red hue than the darker weather worn exterior.

The porch also had areas with new planking that seemed to extend around the perimeter of the house. As we walked around the exterior I noticed there were several well-groomed miniature trees and shrubs.

The garden steps we passed over seemed to meander around, so you could enjoy the beauty of the lush greenery. While it was still early spring many of the shrubs were already budding with bright green shoots.

The property looked to extend several meters into the thicker untrimmed bushes, I also noticed a large amount of bamboo growing around the perimeter creating an artificial enclosure.

The back of the house had a wider open area that was closely cut deep green grass surrounding a small fountain and pond.

The flat gravel area behind the rear of the building had a small area that looked like it could accommodate several tables and chairs. This would be enjoyable in warmer weather. It reminded me of the area where I would sit and mediate in the palatial gardens.

When we came around the right side of the dwelling I noticed a larger number of door panels capable of exposing the interior of the house. As Kazu explained the surroundings I could occasionally hear voices off in the distance, as well as the occasional car passing down the road. When we made a full circle, I realized this house was much larger than I initially expected.

As I looked down the driveway I could see an occasional pink blossom flutter to the ground. I was admiring the greenery while I thought the trees and bushes would probably provide protection from the heat of summer.

When Kazu stopped in front of the house he motioned us to follow him in. As the double doors slid open the entry was made of a similar slate to the walkway in the driveway, though it seemed to be a much smoother surface.

The slate entry extended about three meters into the house and was close to three meters wide. There was a well-worn dark wood case sitting along the wall in the entry. As Kazu stepped in he removed his shoes and placed a set of soft looking slippers on.

He explained that it was a cultural expectation in personal dwellings. It was also intended to help in keeping the finely woven tatami mats clean by not traipsing in dirt to spaces where you would be residing.

The entry led into the center of the house but hid the exterior rooms. As we walked up onto the wood floor we came to an open area with a decent expanse to the right and left. To the right I saw what might have once been a lobby but had been remodeled somewhere in time. There was enough room for several chairs and tables.

When we went back toward the left it led into an open area that looked like a kitchen. The equipment was obviously new and there were new fixtures and the walls were a smooth white tile. The kitchen had a wide walk in pantry capable of holding a large amount of supplies.

Kazu motioned us closer, "In order to keep a secured area we built in a false wall to the right of the panty entry." He flipped the two switches in opposite directions and the door slid open revealing a large square room.

The room was probably six meters square and had a table built along the wall with a monitor that showed different views of the property. As Kazu took us to the monitor he provided a brief explanation, "In order to maximize your security and keep the chance of outsiders from discovering your identities or technology we provided security cameras built into the exterior of the property so not to be readily visible."

When we were exiting Kazu paused and rapped on the wall, "The walls have been replaced with reinforced concrete, the door we passed through is also extremely sturdy so there should be no fear of intruders reaching this room. You can also lock it. I will show you how when we move your belongings in."

I took a last look around the room and noticed a fair number of outlets along the wall, I wondered if our equipment could be integrated to use or if we could even use their power system.

As we left the kitchen we moved toward the wing of rooms extending toward the left side of the house, the larger room on the left appeared to be a bathing facility, it was a wide-open area and had a room dedicated to changing and wood racking capable of holding several baskets. On the other side of the doors was the bathing room. The floors in this room were also slate as well and extended a meter up the wall.

The floor had a few drains along it and several faucets protruding from the wall about a meter high on both sides. Attached to each faucet was a shower head similar to the building we left earlier today.

At the end of the room was a large area that was about a meter deep with a small ridge extending above the floor. It looked big enough for several people to use at once.

Kazu explained the bath and briefly told us how to fill and drain it, he made a point to explain how it was traditional to wash prior to bathing.

The exterior wall of the bathing room was white plaster above the slate and extended to about chest height, after that there were panels you could open to allow air to freely move through the room.

As we exited the bathing chamber Kazu opened a door across the hall, as we entered this room I noticed a long cabinet containing several sinks and a mirror attached to the wall.

Near the door to the left was an area with a machine used to wash clothing and a small area for sorting and placing laundry. Across from the sinks was a set of double panel doors that hid a closet for linen.

The next room Kazu showed us was the toilet, it was in a small enclosed area with an opaque glass panel in the upper corner. It included what looked like a new toilet that contained a number of controls along the side.

Kazu explained, "We had to remodel the restrooms to accommodate you since the original building only contained a communal area with several partitioned toilets. We enclosed and sealed that area for the linen closet and reinstalled two toilets off each hall." Kazu pointed to the glass, "You can tell if it's occupied by this panel."

As we walked down the end of the wing there were two rooms on opposite sides. Each of these were bedrooms that were close to eight meters squared. The first thing I noticed was the flooring, it was made from tatami mats, which had a slight give to them as you walked on them.

They were softer than the wooden floor and covered much of the room, with the exception of a small nook and the exterior side that looked like it could be enclosed with the panels. As we walked in and slid the panels open you could see the meandering path and lush surrounding foliage.

There was an air conditioner in the upper corner of each room, it appeared each room was equipped with these since the house was older and didn't have much insulation. The opposite room was much the same.

As we made our way back to the central lobby as we explored the right wing. It was similar but instead of a bathing chamber there was an additional bedroom looking out the right-side exterior garden. It also included two-toilets. There were three more bedrooms at the end of the hall for a total of four in the right wing.

Kazu slid the final door closed since each was almost identical to the others, "Would you like to see upstairs?" He asked next.

As we returned to the main lobby there was a hallway with stairs leading up located next to the entry by the first hall we explored.

As we ascended the stairs they looked to be a dark polished wood with slight indentations in the center probably from years of wear. When we entered the second floor it was much more open than I expected. There was an area capable of holding a few chairs or tables with a window allowing a decent amount of lighting in.

The halls on this floor also extended to the right and left. As we started down the right wing we glanced in each room, they appeared to be much smaller, these were most likely used for single guests when this was an active ryokan. The other wing led to a single room roughly the same size as the lower level rooms. The second floor also contained a single toilet making it more convenient for residents on the upper floor.

As we started back down I heard a larger vehicle outside. When we approached the ground floor Kazu announced, "Well it sounds like they're here."

As we all finished descended the stairs I looked around the corner as someone approached the doorway.

"Good afternoon the man said, we are here to deliver your belongings." The mover announced.

Kazu approached the man, "Can you bring in the marked boxes to the one room." The driver nodded understanding the request.

As Kazu turned back toward us, "So now that you have had a chance to tour your home, do you have any ideas where each of you would like to settle?"

I looked toward Shivan, "Wouldn't it be better if you took the bigger room considering?" As I glanced at Valdria with a smile.

Shivan smiled as well, "That would be adequate."

"I wouldn't mind the left-wing rear." Talinde said.

"Can I have the one opposite father? That way if I return late once school starts I will disturb fewer people."

Shivan nodded, "I have no objections. How about you Trist?"

"I wouldn't mind having an upstairs room, the view looks very calming from that side of the house."

It ended up being only me on the second floor, Lev, Ani and Tia were on the right wing. They initially wanted upstairs but since the remaining four rooms were quite small they decided on the larger downstairs rooms.

When the movers began carrying in the boxes labeled fragile they slowly worked their way toward the secure room Kazu first showed us. Kazu excused himself and exited the house. We made sure to stay clear as the movers did their job and waited for them to carry in our new belongings.

After several minutes Kazu returned and handed each of us a small package, "These are your phones, they will appear to the casual observer as a normal smartphone, however they have additional functions."

Kazu pulled a similar phone from his pocket, "These have all the normal capabilities you would expect, but they are also equipped with an emergency function and a direct line to me." Kazu explained the phone operation and told us there were detailed directions in the package he provided.

Once the movers started bringing in furniture we all gathered our personal belongings and placed them in our rooms. After several hours the movers completed their job and began wrapping up the equipment and packing materials remaining.

As I went upstairs I wondered where to begin, I took a few moments to enjoy the view. As I watched out the window I saw Kazu talking with the movers and then the movers saluted Kazu and he quickly returned it before they departed.

While I was going through boxes I noticed how each had a label indicating contents, this made it easier to determine which order would be the most efficient. After the third box I heard Kazu's vehicle leave the property. I slowly stood up and glanced out the window and saw Kazu driving down the road. I noticed for the first time that my room had a view overlooking town.

While we were outside of town, I still could hear the occasionally bus pass by the front of our house. At least there was a regular transportation network near us, I thought.

The closet in my room had several deep shelves, along with the dresser, desk, chair, bookshelf and single bed. Even with the furniture arranged in my new room there was still an adequate amount of space.

While it was much simpler and smaller than my room on the Velisus this had a more comfortable feel to it.

The desk was large enough to hold the small portable computer that was provided and allowed for room to place a large book or filament tablet on its surface, additionally it contained several drawers along the side which I slipped my personal filament monitor into.

Next to the closet there was a nook with a hard wood elevated platform where I placed the viewing monitor they called a television. I was unsure how to connect the equipment, so I probably should read the directions provided first. But first I had to finish going through the last few boxes.

After a while I started to notice the shadows growing longer and it was getting close to sunset. I had gone through all the boxes and sorted out the clothing they had provided.

While the clothing served the same purpose there were subtle differences, the pants contained spaces to store small objects in the front and back, the material seemed durable and made from natural fibers but not quite like our clothing which used synthetics and was capable of resisting wear and acted as a natural armor.

The clothes identified as school uniforms were the most elaborate, there were two sets, one intended for warm and the other for colder weather.

The uniform consisted of a button up long sleeve white shirt, a pair of grey pants and a grey blazer with a black tie. The summer uniform differed slightly, and it included a white button up short sleeve shirt and pants that felt like a lighter material more suited to warmer weather.

On the pocket of the blazer and the summer shirt was an embroidered patch which must be a school design and moto stitched below the emblem. As I smoothed out the uniform I hung them in the closet, I still needed to read through the acceptance paperwork to determine the expectations for our new school.

As I finished laying out the bedding and sorting my personal space I broke down the boxes and sorted the trash to carry down stairs. Once that was done it was dark enough that I needed a light, so I could read through all the different directions for the different devices provided today.

As I was ready to pull out the chair my stomach decided to object to my chosen activity. I guess I should see what we plan on doing for dinner. I laughed to myself, maybe I should have brought some nutrition packets like Lev tried to do. As I smiled to myself I turned the light off and walked downstairs.

Acclimation

When I entered the kitchen, I noticed a number of boxes still needing to be unpacked, it looked like they provided all the possible necessities to equip our kitchen. Since I wasn't sure how we wanted to organize our cooking space I decided to check on Lev instead.

I headed toward Lev's room I saw a box fly out of his doorway and land in the hall. I poked my head around the corner and peered into his room.

"GAHH!" I couldn't help but muttering. His room was in all sorts of disarray, "What happened in here?"

Lev turned toward my voice, "Oh, hey Trist." He then continued dumping the next box out on the floor before him.

"You know if you read the labels you would know what each box was right?" I stated as I looked at the furniture shoved to one side and his pile of clothing, and boxes scattered about haphazardly.

As he was about to toss the next box through the doorway as he paused, "Oh yea, your right." He said as he glanced at the label on the top.

I shook my head and smiled as he was looking out over the floor. He noticed my smile and broke into a mischievous grin himself as he tossed the box at my head.

I pulled my head back just in time for the box to pass harmlessly by to thump the opposing wall.

I heard Ani shout something then could hear her opening the door. As she said, "Would you stop throwing…" When she left her room, she noticed me and went bright red.

I noticed she was wearing clothes I hadn't seen her in before. Her shirt had a very feminine cut and she was wearing a shorter skirt. As she noticed me looking at her she quickly turned around and retreated into her room.

When she left I looked back into Lev's room and he was laughing out loud, "This is going to be interesting."

I had a puzzled look, "What is?"

He just shook his head, "Nothing really. I can't wait to see her in front of you with her uniform on."

"Are they that unusual?" He just shook his head as I entered his room, "Want help?"

"Sure." Lev said.

I went ahead and picked up the box that included the bedding and sat it on top of the bed as I slowly unpacked the remaining boxes.

As I finished laying out his bedding I slid the bed toward the wall away from Lev's pile of chaos. Once that was completed I moved the other items to locations I found convenient for myself.

When the last box was opened I left Lev sorting clothes and went to the hall and began flattening all the boxes, so they wouldn't be in the way. Once I placed the boxes in a stack with mine I returned to Lev's room. Lev still sat slowly sorting the different clothing, so I figured I would see if anyone else needed help.

I walked toward Shivan and Valdria's room and lightly knocked. I heard a rustling noise as the door quietly slid open, "Evening Trist, please come in."

As I stepped in, "Can I help with anything?"

Shivan was sitting in a two-seat sofa and reading the manuals for the electronics as he looked up, "I think we are almost done."

Valdria smiled as she stood, "We just put the final items away. What do you think of the clothing?"

"They seemed pretty light, but there are also heavier pieces if the weather gets cooler. Want help with the boxes?"

Valdria nodded, "No we can take care of those."

"I stacked Lev's and my boxes near the entry, I'm not sure where to place them though."

Shivan looked up, "I will have to ask Kazu when he returns."

"Is he coming back tonight?"

"Yes, he was going to purchase some groceries for tomorrows meal as well as dinner this evening." I let out a thankful sigh, at least my stomach will have something to do.

I exited their room and slowly slid the door closed. I wonder if Tia needed help, since Ani looked to be opposed to me seeing her right now.

As I passed Ani and Lev's room I paused in front of Tia's. I knocked gently and heard Tia, "Yes?"

I slowly slid the door open and saw her sitting on the edge of her bed. She was sorting through her new underclothes, "Do you need any help with boxes or anything?"

Tia looked around her room, "I think I am almost done." When she realized she was holding her underclothes she suddenly hid them behind her back as she looked down blushing slightly.

I was getting ready to slide the door closed I noticed her glance up at me with a bashful smile, "Thanks Trist."

When I closed Tia's door I decided to unpack and arrange some of the furniture located in the entry. We now had several chairs and a three-seat couch.

The television was still in a box, so I unpacked it and placed it on the table. This would probably be a nice area to entertain guests given the opportunity. I need to remember to ask Kazu about the internet connection.

As I was walking down toward the left wing I heard a car door close outside. I stopped and back tracked. I headed toward the door and slid it open just as Kazu was about to press the chime, "Oh, perfect timing. Evening Trist, would you mind helping?"

"Sure, let me grab my shoes."

He handed me few plastic bags containing several different items in each bag. As I slipped my shoes back off I carried the bags to the kitchen. I guess Kazu's idea of help was me being the relay to the kitchen. After several trips Kazu finally slid the door closed behind him as he carried a single book and an overstuffed plastic bag in the other hand, "Are you hungry?"

I was a little embarrassed since my stomach had growled after he walked in, "A little. I wasn't sure if we had plans tonight."

Kazu smiled, "Could you let everyone know?"

I turned around and headed toward Shivan and Valdria's room first thing.

As we all entered the dining room we noticed Kazu had already set out several black rectangular containers with clear lids. These were different than the meals we had tried previously, Kazu called then bentou boxes.

Each one contained a different combination of food. The one I chose had cold rice, steamed vegetables and small round pieces of breaded protein, what Kazu called chicken. They were simple but tasted good, even more so since we hadn't eaten since early morning.

As we were eating Kazu was sitting with us enjoying the different looks each of us made as we ate, "You can get these at most convenience stores, there is a Family Cart down the street near the next bus transfer station. You will probably pass by it every day on your way to school."

This was the first time I had heard of a convenience store, the more I heard the more interested I was in exploring town.

Kazu stayed for a couple hours, he helped organize the small kitchen appliances and assisted me in connecting to the internet the government of Japan was kind enough to provide. He also showed us where and told us when the different refuse pick-up days were. I guess they attempt to recycle what they could to reduce waste here as well. There were so many things we still had to learn about Earth and Japan.

Before Kazu left he promised to show us the different markets closest to us, so we could purchase our own groceries.

His final parting gift that night was a book with different recipes called a cook book.

Once Ani and Tia finished looking through it I glanced through a few recipes myself, Lev wasn't the least bit interested in learning how to cook. To me they didn't look too difficult, I would like to learn how to cook at some point, I thought.

As the others left for their respective rooms I figured it would be a good time to read up on some of the items I received today. When I entered my room, I noticed it had cooled significantly so I closed the inner doors to limit the amount of cool air coming into my room.

It took only a few minutes to attach the television and connect it to the house network, this allowed me to access several different programs but nothing that I saw was really interesting. I turned the television off and began reading about the functions of my new phone, then the laptop I was to use for school. I attempted to connect to the network using my portable filament monitor but being outside of the Velisus range it only had a blank screen.

Sometime after midnight I crawled into bed. The comforter that was provided was very thick and warmed up shortly after I pulled it up to my neck. I thought about everything that had happened today and remembered how nervous I had been the night before. It's funny how we can see so much fear in the unknown.

Over the next few days Kazu proved to be extremely helpful. He would check-in on us daily and even helped cook one meal, this was one of the few nights he ate with us.

The girls seemed interested in helping Valdria when Kazu was showing her how to cook.

Shivan and I would occasionally sit and talk as he deftly prepared a meal. It was a very relaxed information exchange. We talked primarily about food and recipes from Paltius while he would describe different meals from his hometown in northern Japan. This gave him a better understanding of the types of foods we were used too.

Once everyone was settled in we slowly began to set up the monitoring equipment for the Velisus. When it came time to connect the equipment to a power source Talinde was at a loss, "The power source here is to erratic."

Apparently, the electrical current fluctuations varied to widely, the equipment we utilized worked on what would be considered low voltage continuous flow and didn't require a large amount of voltage.

This was similar to quantum field theory discovered by Earth during the early 1900's known as the Meissner effect. The flow is so smooth that the transmission source can be finer than a hair and still provide enough current to power the heaviest machinery on the Velisus. Due to the lack of electromagnetic fields a spool of filament fibers could contain millions of independent signals without any electrostatic interference.

Talinde continued to piece the equipment together when he finally let out a deep sigh, "I guess I have no choice." As he stood and turned to the one remaining box he had packed with our personal belongings.

When Talinde unpacked the reactor Shivan's eyes widened a little. An uncharacteristic display of surprise for my mentor. As he took the backup reactor from the packing material he carefully positioned it under the counter near the corner below the security monitor.

He then began unspooling the cabling used in emergency repairs to run a connection to the equipment that would power the link to the Velisus. Once it was connected he and Shivan verified the inputs to the transmission receiver then Talinde powered on the reactor. I noticed it began to emit a faint blue light. The panel indicated no flow even though the equipment quickly powered on.

Talinde stood with a look of triumph on his face. When he turned to Shivan he had a mischievous childlike grin on his face, "I'm glad we brought this. It is drawing so little power it would probably power this equipment indefinitely."

As the link powered up the filament monitor began running through a status sequence displaying environmental and external anomalies detected around the Velisus since our departure.

I was a little curious now, "Will our portable monitors be able to access the Velisus database now?"

Shivan nodded, while Talinde said, "Yea, this will allow us to link up as well as program translation data as we become more familiar with the different languages on Earth. Shivan can you power on the other terminals? I want to make sure we have these pulling from different links."

As Shivan connected the remaining monitors the table began to look like a smaller scale planning room. Shivan and Talinde continued to work on the setup while I exited the room and moved into the kitchen where Valdria was organizing the different utensils and planning the evening meal.

When I offered to help she shook her head, "I'm good for now, I just am trying to get used to all these new tools and functions." She said as she looked at a pamphlet she picked up from the counter. It didn't appear I could offer any help, so I decided to check with the others.

As I came around the corner of the dining area Jes was exiting the washroom and drying his hands on his pants as he walked my direction, "Morning Jes, are you settled in?"

Jes looked up and nodded, "Yea but I am wanting to look around town to get an idea what it's like. I want to try using the bus as well. I don't want to get lost the first time I go to college."

That made sense to me, then I had a great idea, "What about going to town now?" I asked somewhat excitedly.

Jes contemplated a moment, "Sure, it would give us both a chance to see things, plus we could go to the post office. I wanted to try withdrawing some money for lunches and incidentals during the next week."

"That sounds great, we could both do the same thing, mind if I ask Lev and the girls if they want to go?"

"That's fine, I will check with Father and Shivan while you grab them."

It was our first outing, I was excited but also a little trepidatious about being out in town. I headed toward the right wing and lightly knocked on Lev's door, "Hey Lev, want to head into town with Jes and I?"

I heard a muted crashing noise and heard Lev mumble something.

When he slid the door open he was rubbing the back of his head, "Yea! Let's go." He said excitedly.

I glanced in and his chair was on the ground. He got up so fast he fell backwards in his chair. He was such a klutz it's amazing how he's changed since we left Paltius.

While Lev was gathering his belongings, I knocked on Ani's door, "Yea, you can come in."

I slid the door open and looked in and saw her reading the cook book, "Hey, were heading into town, want to go?" Her eyes widened a little as she looked back toward her book with a serious face. It was like she was trying to get over her fear.

She nodded slightly and turned back toward me, "Sure, that would be exciting."

"Okay, Jes is checking with Shivan and Lev is getting ready, bring your bank book so we can stop by the post office." Ani nodded and opened her desk drawer and provided a small red book as she flashed a satisfied smile.

When I headed back toward Tia's door I was about to knock when her door slid open, she looked rushed as if she was late for an important event, "Can I go too!?" She said, with anxiety showing on her face. Like a small child being excluded from a game.

I gave her a bright smile, of course, I was just about to ask, we wouldn't leave you behind, "Bring your bank book, we intend on stopping by the post office."

She nodded and quickly retreated into her room. I took this chance to head upstairs to grab my bus pass, bank book and smartphone.

After I returned everyone was gathered at the entry, including Shivan. He looked over each of us, "Jes will be in charge." He said as he looked us over, "Understood?"

I nodded and glanced at Jes who looked somewhat nervous with this additional responsibility.

I'm not sure he expected this, I thought. When we had all slipped off our indoor slippers and donned our new outdoor shoes we headed off.

I pulled the map function up on my phone and set a home point in case I ever got disoriented, this would allow me to find my way back as we all began walking toward the street.

We made our way toward town at a leisurely pace. I had ample time to observe the nearby houses and people outside engaged in various activities.

When one of our neighbors noticed me glancing their way they stood and offered a wave that I returned, "Good morning." I offered in an elevated voice they could hear. We saw a number of other people along the way, but not many others our age.

As we came to a more populated cross road I noticed the convenience store Kazu had mentioned, Family Cart diagonally across the intersection. There were people near Jes's age exiting the convenience store and talking as they stood near a bus stop, "I think Kazu said the post office was a few blocks in this direction."

I glanced toward where Jes was indicating so we approached the intersection and paused for the vehicles to stop. Ani and Tia looked to be chatting and quietly pointing at different shops as we walked. When the lights changed color, the sign changed indicating it was safe to walk and told us the light had turned blue. I wasn't sure why it said blue, so I added it to my list of questions for Kazu.

When we crossed we continued down the street observing all the side shops, some seemed to be closed but most were open. As we passed several shops I noticed the exterior of each was decorated to the tastes of the shop owner. Some had signs painted on their windows others hanging over the sidewalk.

It was nearing mid-morning on a Tuesday if I recalled correctly, this was in the middle of the normal work week. Most of the people we saw walking in town were older, so we stood out a bit. The road next to us continued with a steady flow of vehicles, off in the distance I could hear what sounded like a train. About a block away I saw the red sign indicating a post office. Jes seemed to notice at the same time.

When we arrived, we all made our way inside, there were several machines in a side room used to automatically withdraw currency.

The post office interior had a wide front counter with areas for the staff to interact with customers. You could purchase items or have letters and packages delivered from here as well. I was the first of our group to find the line. As I waited for two customers before me another staff member motioned me over to their window.

I handed the cashier my bank book and asked if I could make a withdrawal.

She asked for my identification and verified it to my bank book as she punched in my information on her computer. I may have been mistaken but her eyes opened a little wider when she saw my account.

She asked what I would like, and I was at a loss, "We are doing some shopping I will take what you think would be best." I asked since I had minimal understanding of their monetary system.

"Are you clothes shopping?" The teller asked.

"No, we are trying to get used to town, we just moved a few days ago."

She nodded her understanding and quickly punched in numbers on the terminal, she then counted out twenty thousand yen, "This should be good for a while if you are just looking around."

She handed my bank book back and I noticed she had adjusted the amount to reflect a new balance. As I bowed and thanked her I stepped back and waited outside for the others.

I looked closer at the bank book Kazu had provided and noticed the amount was very large. Though I had no understanding of the current inflationary factors in Japan I couldn't tell if the amount was small or large in comparison.

I placed the money in the wallet provided by Kazu with our clothes and glanced back into the building. Jes and Tia were at the counter now. Ani was standing back with Lev.

As Tia finished she came out with her bank book, "I hope I got enough, I wasn't sure what to get." She said as she walked up to me with a smile.

When Lev finally finished it appeared we had all withdrawn different sums of money.

Ani and Lev both had ten thousand, Jes withdrew thirty thousand and Tia had a thousand.

We walked a few blocks toward the station before Jes paused, "I guess I will be coming through this way every day, I'm glad it's not hard to find."

There was a fairly large crowd exiting the train terminal, as we looked down the street we saw a number of new shops. This street looked busier than the one we had previously traveled down. We walked parallel to the station as it was approaching mid-afternoon.

We found a shop that looked to have a number of people entering and exiting. When I looked in I saw several independent shops, plus a bakery that was selling a variety of different breads and premade sandwiches.

"Hey, let's go in." As I pointed to the shop entrance. After I asked I saw Ani and Tia give excited looks and they agreed immediately.

Jes pointed up the street, "There is an electronics store up ahead, I'll meet you guys back here in an hour, will that work?"

We parted with Jes and planned to meet in front of the bakery in an hour.

That should provide a decent amount of time to look through the store. As we entered the shopping area we were overwhelmed with the aroma of freshly baked breads with a number of other scents mingled in.

Ahh, my stomach is making noises already as I placed a hand over it to calm the grumbling.

The first floor contained a number of shops selling tea, a local coffee shop, a Bunkin Donuts, a bakery with a fancy scrawled name I didn't recognize as being any of the languages I had studied.

We walked around the main floor as the area opened to a wider space containing several benches and an escalator leading up and down, "I'm going to start from downstairs."

Lev followed me, but Ani and Tia headed upstairs. When we arrived on the basement level it looked like there was a food court selling a variety of different style of foods, as we walked through I made a mental note to return when we had more time.

Lev was heading toward what looked like a grocery store based on the description Kazu had given us. We walked through a produce area and they had a wider variety of vegetables than I ever recall seeing. There were several isles with different types of packaged foods sorted by categories. I would have to tell Valdria the location of this store, it could meet all our needs. When we reached the far side of the store it had changed to a bakery and a place that made food and packaged it in take home containers like the bentou's Kazu brought previously.

As we left we headed back up the escalator to the main floor. Since the shops looked to be food and gift related we decided to go to the second level.

The second floor was entirely different, now the shops looked to be clothing and one side was small appliances and housewares.

As I looked around I tried to remember what the school entry notification had suggested bringing on the first day of class. We had been provided most of the necessities including a small satchel for our school supplies. So, until I discovered a need I would wait to purchase additional school related items.

Lev on the other hand was looking in the housewares section as he would pick items up and see how they worked.

I laughed inwardly at how easily he found things to amuse himself. Right now he seemed so distant from the reliable team mate when we practiced hand to hand training.

The third floor was pretty much the same type of things though it was a little sparser, while there were a number of people the goods were larger and looked like self-assembly furniture pieces.

After Lev and I saw our fill it was coming close to an hour so we both started back down stairs. We talked about some of the more unusual items and the electronics that were intended to simplify your daily existence.

When we reached the entrance closest to the bakery I noticed Tia standing out front looking frazzled, anxiously glancing from left to right.

As Lev and I exited I called out to her, "Tia, what's the matter?"

She turned suddenly hearing her name called. She looked like she was about to cry as she ran up to me and grabbed me by my arms, "I can't find Ani, she was going down stairs to look for you guys, but she hasn't come out yet!"

I pulled her toward me and gently embraced her as I rubbed my hand on her back, "Don't worry, she couldn't have gone far. Did you try using your phone to call her?"

Tia stepped out of my embrace and glanced up at me with moisture glistening at the corners of her eye as she cocked her head, "How do I do that?"

I inwardly sighed, I will have to show them how the phones work I guess to keep this from happening again.

I pulled my phone out and looked at the numbers programed in contacts, currently there were eight numbers, our immediate family and Kazu's.

I selected Ani's number and called. The phone began connecting and gave intermittent sounds as it rang. After a few moments there was a noise indicating a connection and I could hear Ani fumbling with the phone, "Trist is that you?" Was the first thing she said.

"Yea, where are you right now?"

"I'm looking for Tia, I think she got lost." Ani said somewhat anxiously.

I smiled as I noticed Tia and Lev give me curious glances since they only heard one side of the conversation, "Ani, Tia is with us, do you know how to get back to the entrance we first came through?"

"Umm, I'm already outside but I don't see the bakery near me."

"Okay, don't move we will walk around the side of the building we should see each other soon." I motioned the others to follow.

As we walked down the sidewalk to the next corner we saw Ani standing near another entrance. Tia immediately ran toward Ani and gave her a hug. Ani looked a little embarrassed but hugged Tia back.

When Lev and I reached her I said, "You guys need to remember the resources you have so you don't panic. I will show you how the phones work once we get back if you'd like."

In near unison all three raised their hands and said, "Please!"

I looked over to Lev who had a silly grin on his face as I just shook my head, "Let's head back to the other entrance so we don't miss Jes."

As we all walked back with Ani and Tia holding hands we saw Jes standing out front looking down at his phone and holding a small plastic bag in is other hand, "Jes! Sorry for keeping you waiting."

He looked our direction, "No trouble. I was just exploring some of the functions, we can actually track each other, so I knew you guys were heading this way."

I was a little surprised, I hadn't noticed that yet. I need to play with it a little more I guess.

On our way back, I asked Jes if he minded me going to the convenience store we saw earlier.

Jes looked at us and asked, "You okay getting back from here?"

"Yea, it is an easy route from this point." I was ready to part from the group, but Lev, Ani and Tia insisted on going with me. So, as we parted with Jes we crossed the street toward the

Family Cart. As we began to enter there were a few people exiting so we stepped aside as the door slid open.

When we entered we were immediately greeted by the clerk behind the counter, "Welcome to our store." I looked his direction and smiled as he watched us enter then continued his current task.

The store was much smaller than the one we previously explored but it had a large variety of goods. It looked like the main purpose was single use items or snack type foods. As I was looking at the different drinks I heard the clerk greet the next set of customers, as I looked back I saw two girls who looked about the same age as Jes, walk in happily chatting.

They came down the same isle I was on and both looked over at me and glanced at each other as one smiled. I smiled back and continued to make a choice of drinks. I choose an item called green tea in a small squarish bottle. As I looked though the store Tia and Ani were still browsing, so I approached the clerk and sat the drink on the counter.

When he noticed me, he gave me a short greeting and scanned my purchase and announced a price. I removed a thousand-yen bill from my wallet and handed it to the clerk. He announced the price again and what I had handed him then the amount of change owed. As I took my change I walked toward the entrance of the store.

As I walked out I saw Lev eating something on a wooden stick, he said it was a popsicle. It was a blue frozen snack from what I could tell. This is probably an item intended for warmer times of the year, but Lev never adhered to what was normal.

As we talked about some of the items in each of the stores we had seen, as well as, the different experiences I heard the door open next to us.

The girls who had smiled at me earlier departed but this time they both turned and smiled and said, "Good bye." They both coyishly smiled and waved.

I smiled and said, "Have a nice day." As they turned and continued walking I could hear them giggle as their voices faded away.

Lev looked at me, "Do you know those girls?"

"No, they just smiled earlier so I smiled back."

"Humm, people seem pretty nice so far."

When Ani and Tia finally came out they both had a small bag containing a few personal items they bought.

As we started off toward the intersection I noticed the position of Lev, Ani and Tia had changed. Ani was now on my left and Tia on my right. I didn't mind but I could tell Lev was a little annoyed.

While walking home Tia shyly asked, "Trist, did the girls in the store talk to you?"

I hesitated a moment since I thought it was an out of the blue question, "They said good-bye when they exited. Why do you ask?"

"Oh, it's nothing." Tia slightly blushed.

I turned toward Ani to ask but I noticed she turned her head away when I looked her direction. Humm, these two are difficult to grasp sometimes.

When we got home I finally opened the tea and took a drink. It had a slightly bitter taste and left a refreshing clean feeling in my mouth. I sat it on my desk as I started thumbing through the different applications on my phone. I found the locator application Jes mentioned earlier and set it up.

I could locate others in my address book if they had location sharing turned on according to the directions in the app. I pulled out the change from my purchase earlier and looked at what remained of the first thousand yen. I had a little over eight hundred yen left. This gave me a somewhat more realistic gauge of costs and value of the Japanese yen.

Once I considered it a bit more I thought we should at some point take the bus to the school grounds, so we had an idea of time, distance, location and what type of neighborhood surrounded our school.

That way we could familiarize ourselves with the route in case we ever became separated or took the wrong bus transfer.

As I sat my phone down I decided to test the connection to my portable filament monitor, it immediately connected and updated my normal searches and study material. I sat it on the table and attempted to access the network through the Velisus.

While I looked through different locations of the town we lived, I noticed it used satellite imagery to view Earth. I was able to zoom in and search by location. As I zoomed in I noticed the vehicles were moving in the scan. I must be seeing a live feed, I guess the Velisus is accessing the local networks. I closed the map and decided to review current events in Japan and related countries. As I picked up the monitor I carried it with me as I lay down on the bed and continued to read until I fell asleep.

Settling In

Over the next few weeks we gradually settled into a routine, Valdria and the girls became better at cooking, Lev and I helped maintain the property, Jes even challenged himself with a solo visit to the campus he would be attending.

Shivan continued to monitor the Velisus daily while he worked on translating different texts pertaining to well know principles among Paltians.

During her free time, Valdria converted medical documents into Japanese. Before these could be released however, the technology to recognize the symptoms needed to be identified. This placed more emphasis on developing technologies achievable with Earths current capabilities.

To hasten improvements Shivan released several hypotheses related to microprocessor and filament capabilities. These would lead to better transmission, processing and power savings.

Shivan told Kazu the only way Japan could improve was to develop their base knowledge by letting their scientific community slowly test and understand these theories.

Kazu solemnly nodded and relayed Shivans message. To Kazu's surprise after receiving Shivans first papers the government immediately agreed.

When the first of April arrived Lev, Ani, Tia and I convinced Valdria to let us try braving a trip to visit the school campus. It was a mild spring day and the cherry trees were in full bloom.

Little pools of blossoms would gather as the wind dislodged them from the trees leaving them drifting like a fine pink snow in places. Over the last couple weeks, the four of us had ventured into town and helped with shopping and errands. This helped us become somewhat familiar with the local community.

When school entered its recess term before the start of the new year we saw a larger number of students our age wandering around town. So, the morning we decided to make our way to Furigawa middle school, we encountered a number of students present for club activities.

The first time on the bus was challenging but the driver had patience with us. It was Lev who seemed to be the biggest challenge. He didn't understand why he had to tap the card to the reader when it was in his pocket. Ani gave him a firm scolding for embarrassing her since she had to show him as the driver explained.

The time necessary to travel by bus wasn't much more than thirty minutes so we wouldn't have to leave extremely early in the morning. As the driver announced the Furigawa middle school stop we all prepared and slowly walked toward the front of the bus. Today the bus wasn't too crowded, but I expected mornings on school days would be much worse.

When the bus came to a halt we filed off, each tapping our passes to the scanner to register our fare. As we walked toward the main gate we realized the school was a relatively large institution.

We noticed a number of students on campus running laps around the sports field. There were also people sprinting between orange cones and back.

When we passed through the main gate I noticed a polished brass plaque that included the name and founding date of the school. The main building was wider than it was deep with wings extending toward the north and south.

As we nervously walked onto the campus we circled the perimeter of the school. When we walked around the back we also noticed a wing extending toward what must be the gym.

On the north side of the gym there was a smaller two-story building that had several rooms with signs on each door. There were a large number of people wearing track suits around the building and in the sports fields.

The gym was closed but we could hear voices and shouts coming from inside. When we made our way around the south side of the building, there was a concrete area with several vending machines and benches surrounded by trees interspersed among the area.

The far end of the property included an older more traditional building, but we didn't see any signs on the exterior, so we had no idea what it was for.

When we finished circling the entire campus an older gentleman who was walking from the sports field noticed us and called out.

As I heard his voice I turned. I could tell he was beckoning us since we were obviously the only ones in the direction he was walking.

As I turned the others stopped with me, while we weren't in uniforms or track suits it was apparent we were potential students. As the gentleman approached, he appeared to have a jovial expression on his face.

"Good afternoon. Are you here to tour the campus?" The man asked.

I nodded, "Yes, we will be starting here next week so we wanted to get an idea where the campus was and how long the commute would be."

"Very good, I am Murakami Mitsukuni, I'm an instructor here but I also advise a couple clubs. So, you can call me Murakami-sensei."

I recognized his name and wondered if he was related to Murakami Shotaro the gentleman who proctored our exams, "It's a pleasure to meet you." I began to introduce my companions, "This is Levan and Anistria Lastrande." As I motioned to Lev and Ani, "This is Tialinde Brocke, and I am Tristali Verndactilia, but you can call me Trist if it's easier Murakami-sensei." As I completed the introductions we each bowed in turn.

"Your Japanese mastery is extremely good, have you been in Japan long?"

"No, we arrived a month ago, we are from overseas." This was a generalized response Shivan decided on after researching physical traits and one that would best fit our physical look since we knew several languages we could field general questions if they arose.

"That is wonderful, could I show you to the office? They could arrange for a student to show you around I am sure."

I looked back toward Lev, Ani and Tia and they both offered no objection. In fact, they looked interested, "That would be most kind."

"Then please follow me." Murakami turned and headed toward the main entrance. This instructor provided a good first impression for all of us, he had a kind face and appeared to be in his late thirties to early forties, he had black hair that had thinned slightly, and he looked to be about 172 centimeters tall.

Today he was wearing less formal clothing, he had dark blue slacks and a short sleeve button up shirt with no tie.

As we followed him in I heard Tia talking to Ani in the background while Lev took his normal place next to me. The main entrance was a wide space that had a number of lockers arranged in several rows, Murakami took us to a set of open lockers and loaned us each a pair of indoor shoes.

While we quickly swapped our shoes, he led us down the central hallway to a set of offices past the teachers' lounge signifying administration offices. As he entered the room he called out to another one of the teachers, "Is the student council president still here?"

The teacher who responded directed him toward the gym. As he beckoned us to follow we headed out the back-east entrance toward the gym we passed by earlier.

I noticed the few students milling about were paying close attention to us. I could imagine with hair as vibrant as Ani's and brown hair like Lev and Tia we must stand out quite a bit. The guys seemed to be watching me and the girls would stop and whisper between each other as we passed, I could tell our first day would likely be interesting. I hoped it didn't bother Ani and Tia too much.

As we exited the building and passed under the covered portico leading to the gym I noticed the activities were still going full bore. As Murakami opened the door I could see there were several students playing what I recall being called volleyball. As Murakami paused at the entrance I was able to get a decent look inside.

The interior looked like it had three volleyball courts lined up with a raised platform on the far east side. There were a number of backboards raised up out of the way. I couldn't see the north and south side but overall it appeared to be a decent size gym.

As Murakami recognized the person he was looking for he called out, "Haruka, come here a moment please." One of the female players stopped and turned to her team mates and another player came in to replace her.

As a girl near our age approached I noticed she was quite tall, she had short black hair that just covered her neck, dark brown eyes, and a petite figure. She was also wearing a grey track suit like the other students.

When she approached Murakami, she stopped before him, "Yes sensei, how can I help you?" I saw her glance back at us as she listened to him explain his request. For some reason her eye's lingered on me for several seconds.

"Haruka, I am sorry I disrupted your practice, but could you show these four around? They will be starting first years next week."

"Sure, thing sensei." She bowed briefly and walked around Murakami.

As Murakami turned, "You will be in good hands, I look forward to seeing you four next week." Murakami nodded and he walked back toward the main building.

We all bowed as he passed and thanked him.

Haruka stood before us as Murakami departed, "My name is Haruka, I'm a second year. It's a pleasure to meet you." She directed her introduction to all of us, but she seemed to be looking at me, since I was standing in front of the others.

I bowed briefly as I turned slightly toward my companions, "This is Levan, Anistria, Tialinde and I am Tristali but please call me Trist." Lev offered a wave while Ani and Tia a slight bowed and then they watched Haruka closely.

As I introduced my companions I noticed her eyes widen a bit, "Your Japanese is very good. Have you studied long?" She asked.

I was beginning to get self-conscious since that was the second time someone said that.

I shook my head, "No we recently moved her from overseas. We are living on the outskirts of town."

Haruka cocked her head slightly as she listened to me explain, "We would appreciate you showing us around."

She smiled shyly, "Please follow me." We started heading toward the smaller two-story building. As we walked she asks several questions about sports, hobbies, likes and favorite foods. I thought this was a little more than small talk, but I answered without much thought.

She turned to wave at other students as I noticed her hair had a slight blue hue to it as the sun shone on it. As we approach the club building she waved to a few girls standing outside near the water fountain.

"These are the club rooms, when you start you are expected to join a club after the third week of school. We have a lot of different sport clubs, do any of you play any sports?" Haruka finally glanced at the girls and Lev.

When I turned toward them no one was responding, "We are all fair at athletics but nothing you would recognize as a sport."

When I responded I noticed Ani had a sour expression and Tia looked somewhat tense. When I noticed their looks I decided to inquire about other activities, "Does the school have other activities available?"

Haruka smiled, "Of course, there are a number of them. There will be a recruiting day during the first week of school. Take your time to look at the options." As she finished talking with a couple of the girls that were watching us, Haruka turned and began to lead us to the main school building.

When we reached the main building Haruka showed us the first-year classes which took up the upper most second and third floor in the south wing, "We have close to seven hundred students so many of the classrooms are used. The empty classrooms are used for non-sport related clubs as well."

When she was done showing us the first-year classes she then moved to the second-year and third-year classrooms as well as the cantina where you could purchase lunch items during the day, though she said many students still brought their own lunch and ate in the courtyard during nice weather.

Once she finished showing us the courtyard we walked toward the older building on the south part of the campus, "This is the dojo, they conduct judo and kendo on alternating days. We are one of the few schools who have both." She paused as if to consider other areas she could show us, "That is pretty much it, did you have any questions?"

As we all nodded, "You have been extremely helpful." I bowed slightly.

Lev finally spoke up, "Thanks." He said with a bright smile.

Ani provided a brief bow and looked toward the sports fields while Tia shyly thanked Haruka, "I appreciate you showing us around."

"It was a pleasure, I look forward to seeing you next week Trist." Haruka smiled and turned toward the main building.

As Haruka departed I turned toward the three, "Well what do you think?"

"I don't like her." Ani immediately offered.

I was a little surprised.

"That's surprising, what about you Lev, Tia?"

"I think it's a pretty nice place, it's pretty big and seven hundred students doesn't seem like that many.

Tia is a little less critical, "I am interested in the clubs. I don't really like sports unless I can do it with everyone, so I hope we can do something together."

"Why don't you like Haruka, Ani?" I asked wanting to know if she sensed something I didn't.

"I just don't! Okay!" She said passionately.

I didn't really know what to say, Ani was usually easy going. I mean she used to pick on me and Lev but recently I thought we got along great, "Well, with so many students I hope we all have the same instructor." You'd think I had hit each of them in the stomach when the words left my mouth.

They all turned toward me with faces screaming, "WHAT DO YOU MEAN!!"

I couldn't help but be set back a second, "I mean they usually place students in their classes based on scores, so there is a chance we could be in different classes."

"Wait a second, that's not what I understood, didn't Kazu say we would stay together?" Lev was the first to ask.

I nodded, "That's true and we are staying together in the same school. Right?" It made sense to me since everything I investigated the last few weeks pointed to the fact classes were geared toward keeping students with higher aptitudes in a faster paced class environment.

Tia looked about ready to cry as she clasped her hands in front of her mouth, while Ani was standing with drooping shoulders staring off into space, "Can we ask Kazu to help?"

I shrugged, "I'm not sure, but we could try if you are really concerned." As I responded Ani turned and started walking with purpose toward the crosswalk, "Hey Ani, what's the rush?"

"We need to ask Kazu right now! I don't want to be in a different class."

I began to follow Ani toward the crosswalk. Hopefully Kazu could do something.

The bus trip back was tense, Ani stared out the window the entire time, and Tia looked deep in thought with a somewhat worried face. Lev on the other hand continued to chat with me until something caught his attention.

It seemed to take less time getting home than to school. The moment the bus stopped at the convenience store Ani was out the door. We all hurriedly exited to follow her.

When we reached home, Ani went straight to her room, while Lev and I walked into the kitchen with Tia.

Tia glanced around for Shivan and then her father. When she didn't see either, "Trist, I am going to change. Do you think Kazu might stop by today?"

"I'm not sure, he doesn't come by every day so there is no way to tell. You could probably call him."

Tia's eyes widened a bit and she had a smile on her face.

"Thank you for taking me with you today." Tia smiled brightly as she turned and headed toward her room.

As I watched Tia go Lev was eating a carrot stick. He always seemed to be nibbling on something when he wasn't in his room, "What do you think?"

"About what?" Lev asked.

"The school, it doesn't look like a bad location and the sensei was nice."

Lev contemplated a moment, "I thought it was nice, the people we met were friendly. I would prefer we were all in the same class but even on Paltius we trained apart numerous times, so I don't see much difference."

When Lev and I parted I headed back to my room. I figured I could do more reading on social expectations. I still had a little difficulty with the differences in polite form in the Japanese language. What I couldn't understand was when to use it. I knew I was older than the students we would be with but in order to maintain our cover I would have to identify and utilize polite form with teachers and second and third years, so I needed to understand when it was and wasn't appropriate.

As I was reading I heard the stairs creak slightly, so I knew someone was coming up, what I didn't expect was it to be Ani. Several minutes after I heard the creaking there was a light knock on my door, "Yes, you can come in."

Ani slowly slid the door open and stepped in while sliding the door closed. She seemed to be glancing around my room since this was her first time in here. I turned my chair to face her as I looked at her face I could see her eyes were a little red.

When her eyes stopped wandering over everything she clasped her hands behind her back and quietly began, "Kazu said there was a chance we could end up in different classes as well. When I asked if he could help he said influencing the school like that could cause undue speculation toward the governments intervention in our instruction."

I also thought it would be difficult for him to intervene. Since others knowing the government was helping us could lead to the discovery of our origins, "I think he made the right decision, but Ani we don't even know if we will be in different classes yet or not." When I mentioned different classes I could see Ani squinch her face a bit as if trying to keep from crying.

I stood up and pulled her toward the bed and had her sit. I sat next to her and put my arm awkwardly around her shoulder as she leaned into me. I could feel the occasional drip of a tear on my wrist as I held her left hand with my right, "Regardless, I will be with you as long as I can. You know how important all of you are to me. Even in another class we would see each other several times a day and think of the opportunities to meet new people."

"But I don't care about that." She hick-upped a little, "I want to be where I can keep you safe, I don't want people to get too close to you and take you away from me."

I frowned slightly, "No one will take me away."

"If others see how wonderful you are I'm afraid you will have so many people wanting to be with you that we won't be able to." She said as she twisted her face into my shoulder a bit.

I smiled now as Ani expressed her feelings, "Ani, we live together so we will always be with each other, even if school demands keep me occupied and unable to play or study with you guys I still come home with you. Right?"

She nodded quietly. I sighed a little as I hugged her a bit tighter with my right arm. As her hand seemed to relax I continued stroking the top of her wrist and hand trying to sooth her fears. When I began hearing her irregular breathing I could tell she had fallen asleep.

I gently rose and slowly let her lay back down, as I lifted her legs up, so she looked more comfortable I covered her with the blanked I used at the foot of my bed.

When she was settled in, I slowly sat back down to avoid making any noise.

After thirty minutes or so I could detect a change in Ani's breathing though I continued reading over the different sports played in different schools. As I heard the blanket rustle I turned and see Ani sitting up, "Feel a little better?" I asked in a compassionate voice.

Ani nodded slightly, "I'm going back to my room."

I smiled, "Okay see you down stairs shortly." I said as I looked back to my filament monitor. Out of the corner of my left eye I saw Ani's brilliant auburn hair and suddenly felt a soft sensation on my cheek. Then she quickly stood upright.

"Thank you, Trist, for always having so much patience." Ani quickly left the room.

I was a little bewildered, Ani always seemed to leave me somewhat at a loss for words with her erratic actions, but this was a first.

The next few days we spent enjoying our free time around the house or exploring the area up the hill behind us. When the four of us were in town Ani and Tia seemed to always position themselves next to me.

I felt a little awkward for Lev who just accepted it like his life was in danger if he opposed his sister.

The Saturday before school started we decided to visit a fast food restaurant that was a block away from our first bus stop heading to school. When we entered there were several students in the dining area, most looked older than us. We each ordered, I had a small hamburger and water. I couldn't handle the drinks with carbonation, for some reason the bubbles made my nose burn.

When I carried my tray to the dining area I found a seat between a group of students.

The table to our right had three girls and the table to our left had a mix of boys and girls. As I started to unwrap the burger I could hear the girls whispering after I sat down.

As I looked up I saw Tia with Ani following heading toward me. When they approached the boys to my left were talking about Ani and Tia. I could barely overhear some of their comments, "She's cute, look at the other girl's hair…"

I didn't really mind because I also thought they were cute from time to time, but I still felt a little nervous that they attracted so much attention. While they wanted to keep me safe, I felt there may be a need for me to protect them as well.

* * *

On the 9th of April school started. I heard Jes preparing late the evening prior and he was walking out the door before the sun rose. I slowly woke myself before six, then I gathered my personal items and made my way to the washroom to brush my teeth and straighten my hair.

We had taken turns using the bathing room the prior evening however we still had not filled the bathtub, it held so much water we were a little hesitant to be so wasteful, even though the water could be used multiple times.

When I entered the washroom I quickly brushed my teeth combed my hair and washed my face to help me wake up a bit. As I headed back toward the stairs I saw Tia and Ani making their way toward the bathroom in a disheveled state, "Good morning Ani, Tia." I said as I ascended the stairs.

"Mooorning." I heard Ani say as she yawned.

Tia was a little more with it, "Morning Trist." She said in her usual quiet tone.

When I got to my room I slipped into my clothing and checked to make sure I had all the items I was supposed to bring the first day of class. Today class didn't start until nine since it was the first day and entrance assembly, but I wanted to start things off right. When I verified all my belongings I headed back down stairs for something to eat.

Valdria was still not out yet so I took the liberty of trying what I had learned over the last few weeks while helping in the kitchen. The meal was simple, eggs, toast, sliced banana and bacon. I made enough for Lev, Ani and Tia since I was the first down stairs.

As I turned the burner off and set the pan aside I walked over to my companions rooms and knocked on each door. Ani and Tia responded quickly. I told them there was breakfast and they seemed a little disappointed but nodded and started heading to the kitchen. I knocked on Lev's door again and he didn't answer. I slowly slid his door open to check if he had gone to the washroom, but he was still asleep in bed. With a big sigh I walked over to his bed and grabbed his covers and pulled up sharply. As the covers under him acted as a lever he slowly rolled off the opposite side of his bed with a thump!

"Ugh, ouch."

He slowly sat up and looked over the bed at me dressed and ready for school, "Where are you going?"

I laughed a bit, "School, get up breakfast is ready."

"Oh right, that starts today. Okay give me a minute." He stood and started pulling his night clothes over his head as I stepped out and shut his door.

By the time I got back to the kitchen my breakfast was cold, but it still tasted good. I was pretty proud of myself actually.

Lev came into the kitchen about ten minutes later, he had wildly curly hair and sleep lines still showing on his face. I just smiled as I saw him and slightly shook my head.

Tomorrow I would need to wake earlier but for today we had plenty of time. When it hit eight o'clock I knocked on Lev, Ani, and Tia's door again, "Hey we should be leaving soon."

Shivan finally opened his door and asked as he exited his room, "Off for school?"

"Yes, it's a late start and we should be home early."

"You guys have fun, remember this is more for socialization than learning, don't try to stand out too much."

I nodded and let Shivan pass, "I will meet you guys at the entry."

I could hear rustling in their room, so I headed toward the entry. I slipped my shoes on and sat on the short bench we placed next to the shoe rack. Lev was the first so as he started putting his shoes on I began to walk outside. Lev quickly joined me as we began talking about the first day.

He was interested in if we would be in the same class but didn't seem to worry if that wasn't the case. The door suddenly burst open as Ani and Tia looked frantic.

"I thought you guys started walking!" She said in a desperate voice.

I just smiled, "Why would we do that on the first day?"

As Ani composed herself we all began walking to the bus stop, the morning was cool, and I glanced at Ani and Tia, "Are the skirts cold?"

Ani was self-conscious about it in front of me as she kept smoothing the front of it even though it came to her knees. I don't like these that much but it's not really uncomfortable."

Tia also nodded, "The socks are pretty thick, so they keep my legs warm."

As I looked their way I thought they looked very nice. The skirt was a grey plaid and matched their jackets, "I think they look great on both of you."

Ani began to blush, and Tia just quietly looked down as we continued to walk.

As we approached the bus stop there was a fair number of students wearing the same uniform. When we were walking up many of the students glanced our way, some were openly staring, and others just had curious looks on their faces.

When we neared the bus stop Ani and Tia stood to my right and left while Lev was behind me. I felt sort of surrounded but didn't really mind.

The bus ride to school, took a little longer than the first time we visited. Primarily due to the larger number of students. When we arrived, I saw several students approaching the front gate.

Once we exited the bus we made our way to the main entry and we noticed a poster board just inside to the right. There were several students standing around and I noticed this was the class assignment roster.

As the four of us approached I could feel tension emanating from Ani and Tia. I quickly scanned through the extensive list of first year names and spotted my name in class 1-A, "So now which class are the others in?"

A quick look showed Lev in class 1-B, how about Ani and Tia. They were both in 1-B as well. Humm, at least they were together even if it wasn't with me.

Lev sighed in disappointment, "Well it looks like I get the short stick again, I'm in the same class as Ani."

At least Lev is keeping the mood positive. I glanced over to Ani and Tia and they both look dejected, "It's not that bad." I encouraged them, "We can still see each other every break and will travel home together."

They both just nodded slightly.

Class Assignment

I had a plan to get me moved to the same class, if only I could sell my proposal.

I left my companions at the front, "Well I need to take care of some business in the office. I will meet you inside."

I hurriedly changed my shoes and made my way to the office.

When I opened the door, I noticed Murakami-sensei talking with another instructor. When Murakami noticed the door close he glanced back at the entrance and saw me, he offered a smile, "Good morning."

I bowed slightly and returned his greeting, "Murakami-sensei, I have a request, would it be possible to meet with the principal?"

Murakami's eyes widened at such a request on the first day of class, "Is it something I can help you with?"

"I am not sure, it's about class assignments."

"If I remember correctly you're in 1-A. I looked into the assignments after we met last week."

"Yes, that is correct. However, I feel the school could best benefit from moving me in with my friends."

Murakami had an interested look on his face, "How might that be?"

"I would be happy to share with you and the principal." I smiled.

Murakami laughed, and excused himself from his conversation, "Follow me then Trist." We made our way out of the office and toward the gym until we reached the last office door with a plaque stating, principal's office.

As Murakami knocked and paused he then opened the door. Inside there was an elderly gentleman sitting behind a plain wooden desk. As he looked up he offered a good morning to Murakami.

"How can I help you Mitsukuni?" As the principal noticed me, "Ho-ho, do we already have a troubled student?" He jokingly asked.

"Sir, this young man requested a moment of your time regarding class assignments."

The principals eyebrows rose, "I'm sorry son, but the assignments are set based on merit, I can't move you into a higher ranked class."

"Um, Sir, Tristali is already in class 1-A, I doubt that is his request."

"Sir, I would like to step down to class 1-B, I have several family members attending that class. I can guarantee having me do so will improve the class average above that of class 1-A."

The principal was taken aback and thought about my comments a few moments before he responded.

"How do you think you can do that?" The principal asked.

"If you doubt my word, you could evaluate my abilities. I would be willing to take the 3rd year final assessment."

Murakami's eyes were open wide as the principal just sat looking at me. He finally sighed, "Okay, now understand if you don't score 100% then you will remain where you are. Understood?"

I nodded my understanding.

"Murakami, could you prepare the end term 3rd year test for this young man."

Murakami was somewhat surprised, "I could, what about the assembly?"

The principal rubbed his chin, "Well if he passes you will be responsible for him. Have one of the new teachers guide your class to the assembly, better to get this out of the way while we can. Since this young man already came recommended by reputable sources."

Murakami looked at me as he turned, "Follow me Trist."

As we exited the principal's office we headed back to the administration offices. As we entered Murakami motioned me to take a chair as he disappeared into a side room. When Murakami returned he had several papers. "Let's find a quiet place."

We headed to the next room through the side door. It looked like a simple breakroom with several short tables and chairs. Murakami had me sit, "Listen Trist, you have nothing to gain by doing this, if you don't score 100% on each test you will remain in your class and those that recommended you will lose face in the principal's eyes considerably." Murakami paused as he looked directly into my eyes, "Well, what will it be?"

"Murakami-sensei, I promised my friends that when we moved I would keep us together, I have studied so I can make that happen. I have a responsibility to live up to my word and I refuse to disappoint my father any more than I already have." I said with resolution showing on my face.

Murakami posted signs on the two exits that simply said testing. When Murakami returned he explained the tests, "Trist, you will have several hours to complete these tests. However, if you finish early we will move to the next subject and restart your time. Is that acceptable?"

I nodded and said, "I am ready."

Murakami provided the first test, "You have an hour. Begin." He simply said as he glanced at his watch.

The test he handed me appeared to be a bit easier than what I initially took during our assessment period. It covered Japanese and world history. I was able to finish the test in about twenty minutes. As I sat my pencil down Murakami looked up from a magazine he had found on a chair, "Have a question?"

"No sir, I'm finished."

Murakami had a look of disbelief on his face, "Seriously?" He asked as I nodded. He stood up and walked over to the table and slid the papers into his hand. As he flipped through them his eyes continued to open wider as he progressed. He stepped back to his table with the remaining tests and handed me the next, "Okay, same time limit. Begin."

The next test was science and physics. This time I only provided what was asked even though many of the formulas had simpler equations. The test itself contained relatively easy problems but the answers were not multiple choice.

After about thirty-five minutes I completed the second test. When I sat my pencil down Murakami frowned. As he stood and walked over he picked up the completed pages. When he glanced over each problem he was shaking his head.

"Here are the next two sets, you have ninety minutes for these." Murakami glanced at his watch, "Begin."

This time Murakami watched me much closer, the tests he gave me were mathematics and economics.

I was able to answer the problems simply by looking at them. The economics problems were a little more in depth since they were situational word problems that needed to have information extracted before calculation.

While there were a large number of problems both sets only took thirty minutes, "Complete, how many more?"

Murakami almost snorted when I said I was done, "If I hadn't been watching I wouldn't believe it. You have language, geography and social studies next. Need a break?"

"No, I was just curious." I responded and glanced up at the clock.

He sat the remaining pages on my desk, "I would say you have ninety minutes, but you will probably be done sooner. Begin."

The final subjects were the easiest so far. I was able to finish within forty-five minutes. I glanced back over the English and was sure the geography questions were correct, the social studies questions were the most difficult so far, it covered principles that were known to me especially since my family played an integral part in Paltian government and politics. On Paltius we had a single ruling body for close to a millennium.

I quietly sat the papers down and looked up at Murakami, "Well Murakami-sensei, anything else I need to complete?"

As Murakami stood he sat down across from me, "Just why are you here?"

My eye's narrow a bit as I returned his glance, "To ensure my friends and I stay together. I will make sure you are pleased with the results after moving me to 1-B."

Murakami sighed, "Well let's get these checked. I would like to do it with the principal. The assembly should be almost complete."

As we exited the faculty lounge Murakami removed the signs and I followed him to the principal's office. When Murakami knocked I heard the principal reply.

Murakami opened the door and stepped in as he waited for me to follow before he shut it behind me, "Tristali, have a seat." Murakami motioned to a chair against the wall.

The principal was looking at Murakami with a questioning glare as he walked to his desk and placed the test papers for the principal to review. As the principal shifted his gaze from Murakami to the pages he slowly picked them up, "He finished them all?"

"Every single one of them." Murakami said.

"And you verified this yourself?"

"In this situation I paid closer attention than I normally would since he was finishing in half the allotted time on most tests."

"Have a seat Mitsukuni." Murakami pulled the chair out and seated himself. As the principal reviewed each page, he glanced my direction occasionally.

When he reached the math, he paused and looked my direction, "You didn't show any work. Why not?" The principal glanced to Murakami, "Did you provide him scratch paper?"

"Principal, he just wrote the answers down I was watching, I haven't seen anyone do that before."

"Is that true young man?"

"Yes, the problems were fairly simple." I said.

"Murakami, can you grab the mathematics textbook on that second shelf?" The principal pointed to a bookshelf along the wall.

Murakami stood as he walked to the shelf and gathered the requested book and handed it to the principal. The principal then began to thumb through it and paused on a page, "I am going to give you a few problems, is that okay?"

"As you wish, I will do my best."

The principal wrote a few problems on a notepad he had on his desk, when he looked satisfied he turned to me, "Give these a try." He asked as he slid the pad in my direction.

I stood and walked to his desk. The problems while complex have several answers depending on what you wish to solve for. "What would you like me to solve for?"

The principal smiled, "Solve for each value if you would."

As I begin writing the answer for time, distance, velocity I glance over the answers and set the pad down and slid it back.

The principal looked at the answers and compared them to his text book. After he reviewed them he set the book down and began to go through the remaining test pages.

After several minutes he sat the pages down and let out a deep sigh as he slowly leaned back in his chair and turned to look out the window.

I glanced over at Murakami who sat watching the principal. After a few minutes the principal cleared his throat while still glancing out the window, "Tristali, I accepted you and your friends based on the recommendation of a very close friend. He told me he couldn't say much but he said your knowledge was verified. I don't know where you came from, but I will probably never doubt Kenchi again."

After a long pause, "I approve of moving you to class 1-B. If you can improve the class average above that of 1-A, you will have impressed me again, and that doesn't happen much at my age." The principal turned to face us. As he looked at me and then to Murakami, "He's in your care from this point Mitsukuni, don't let me down." The principal again turned his chair toward the window.

At this point Murakami rose and motioned me toward the door. I stood and followed him out, "Well Trist, I hope you continue to show the same passion and drive in class as you did today."

"Murakami-sensei, you haven't seen anything yet."

"That's what I'm afraid of." He chuckled as we walked down the hall to the administration offices to pick up my satchel and bag.

Murakami left me in the hallway as he walked into one of the staff offices. As I glanced in I could see him motion toward me during his explanation. The lady nodded then Murakami returned, "Shall we?" He opened the door and I followed him to the second-floor classrooms.

When we approached the classroom marked 1-B he paused and quietly opened the door. He motioned me to follow him in and to wait by the door.

I heard a deep intake of breath as I noticed Tia sitting at the desk closest to the door. I looked over at her as she held her hands over her mouth and I offered her a sincere smile.

Oh no, Tia is going to start crying I thought. I looked up to the others in the class and all eyes seemed to be on me including Lev who had a huge grin on his face while Ani looked in the same state as Tia sitting right behind Lev.

Murakami finished talking with the instructor leading the class and once they finish talking in hushed tones the temporary instructor departed through the same door. Murakami turned to the chalk board and wrote his name down, "Sorry for my absence I was evaluating a last-minute addition to our class." Murakami motioned to me, "Please introduce yourself."

I stepped into the room a few paces and turned toward the class, "I am Tristali Verndactilia, please call me Trist. I will be in your care." I bowed once my introduction was completed.

"Tristali, for now please have a seat at the desk in the back, tomorrow we will move you in line with the other students."

I made my way down the first isle of desks and turned the single remaining desk to face the front. As I placed my satchel and bag next to the desk, I sat. When I looked up I still noticed several eyes looking my direction. While glancing around I could somewhat tell the seating was in alphabetical order, this would probably place me on the last row close to the front I thought.

Once Murakami finished writing the remaining schedule for day he turned toward the class, "We will be going to lunch break shortly, but afterwards we will be choosing class representatives. So, think about your nomination during lunch." As he said this the lunch bell chimed signifying the beginning of break. Murakami gathered his planner and exited the room.

Several students quickly departed the room while some continued to mill around. A few students tentatively approached me but were too intimidated by the presence of Lev, Ani and Tia, "How did you get them…"

I held a finger up to Ani's mouth before she could finish her question, "They made a mistake is all. No one else needs to know." I looked at Ani and Tia as I gave them a serious look. Both Ani and Tia nodded, "There will be consequences to me being in your class. I hope you're ready." I grinned as intimidatingly as I could.

"What does that mean Trist?" Tia asked with a questioning look.

"I promised to raise the class average above 1-A, so I expect you all to do your part."

Lev just sulked, "I thought this was going to be easy." Lev said as I grinned at him.

"So, what did I miss?" I asked the three.

"Not much, just a speech about our new school, making bonds and achieving the impossible. It sounded like something Shivan would say." Lev imitated in his best Shivan expression.

Ani elbowed Lev, "It was more than that."

As Tia was about to speak two girls approached from behind Tia, "Um, excuse us." They quietly asked.

I smiled at them as they stepped closer, "Hello, can we help you with something?"

They looked extremely timid, "My name is Edamitsu Aiko, you can call me Aiko."

The second girl also spoke up, "I'm Ikeda Anju but please call me Anju."

"It's a pleasure to meet you Aiko, Anju." I bowed slightly from my chair as I said each of their names.

Anju looked to her friend, "Since you weren't here for introductions we thought we would introduce ourselves."

Aiko looked toward Ani and Lev, "Did you by chance move into the old Furigawa Ryokan?"

My eyebrows must have raised a bit because Anju looked a little intimidated, "We did. How did you know?"

Aiko looked a little embarrassed as she responded, "Both of us live up the road from it. We saw it being renovated, and last week we saw you walking down the same street as ours while Anju and I were going to dinner with her parents."

"Oh, we're neighbors, that's nice."

They both looked a little more excited as I smiled at them.

Anju glanced sideways at Aiko as she said, "Maybe we can go to school together occasionally, not many students live that way."

Anju quickly looked toward Ani who seemed to have a somewhat disappointed look on her face then to Tia who looked a little anxious.

"That would be nice." I responded with a smile.

As I smiled again they returned a smile and turned to head back to their desks as they quietly chatted occasionally looking our direction.

Ani let out a deep sigh, "I can't take this much longer."

I furrowed my brow, "Take what?"

Lev began laughing, "Give it up Ani." Lev said as he slapped her on the back.

Lev is suddenly doubled over from Ani's backhand as it lands in his solar plexus.

Once the first lunch bell rang to signify the end of lunch students began filling back into class. The remaining class time Murakami went over expectations, class rotations and school rules.

When he completed going through the remaining rules he paused, "Okay now I hope you have thought about representatives. We will be choosing one male and female to represent the class for the semester. Do we have any nominations?"

A few hands were raised, and each student nominated their ideal candidate.

Once there were a few names on the board Murakami spoke again, "Anyone else?"

The girls who approached us earlier Aiko raised her hand finally, "I would like to nominate Tristali."

I suddenly felt intense looks being pointed in my direction. As I looked around class I saw Ani and Tia glancing back at me. What am I being nominated for, what is a class representative? I thought to myself.

Her friend then raised her hand as well, "I would like to nominate Aiko." Aiko reached over to smack Anju. As she just quietly giggled.

Murakami wrote the new names on the board, "Anyone else?"

After several moments with no responses Murakami passed out small square sheets of paper, "Please write your choice of male and female class representative on these sheets and pass them forward."

After a few minutes the papers began to move forward. I didn't really know many in class yet, so I chose the name of the only person I knew. I picked a random male name without knowing who the person was.

As the slips were collected by Murakami he began tallying the votes. At first, I looked to be in the clear since votes seemed to be going to the others on the board. Though as Murakami approached the halfway mark there were a few votes for me.

One, two three…five six, seven, I looked at the five other names with tally marks next to them, four, five, five, six, and three. This doesn't look too good I thought. The girls had four nominated, and their distribution was a much wider gap, three, four, five and nineteen. It looked like Aiko had the largest number of votes. I heard a thump on a desk and looked toward Lev and saw Ani's head resting on the desk.

* * *

As Lev watched the situation he was amused. When Murakami announced Trist and Aiko as class representatives I wanted to laugh. I thought to myself he was in for a rough time, if Ani was able to tell him how she felt Trist might look at her a little differently. But like always his kindness was just second nature.

Even his father had the love of the people without making an open effort. If Trist needed to raise the class average this was going to be a huge help. I glanced across the room at Tia, she was another issue, what were her feelings for Trist? Had Ani and Tia talked? I thought to myself. Well as Trist's best friend I will support him in every way I can, Lev promised himself.

* * *

Why!! Why did it have to be Trist? Ani thought. He already seemed to be attracting people left and right. Why does everyone watch him? He's ours, he said he would stay with us. We don't need more in our group. Will Trist have time to still head home with us? I worried nervously.

As I heard the announcement all those thoughts crashed through my head and I couldn't take it, so my head crashed to the desk. As I turned my head to the side facing Trist I saw him wide eyed looking at Aiko.

Please let him continue to be oblivious to her feelings. I can so easily tell when people approach him. Their eyes almost shine as they look up at him, mine do as well, so I do everything I can to hide it but sometimes it's just so hard.

His steel grey hair, his wonderful green eyes, the kind look he always shows, I can understand why people follow him but it's so frustrating. I reminisce on all the times his gentle touch has comforted me, even when we were on Paltius he was so gentle I couldn't help but target him.

I just had to have his attention. As I sighed to myself I turned my head toward the window. What will this bring now, Ani asked herself.

* * *

Tia glanced back at Trist. When I heard the girls behind me whispering I knew Trist was in trouble, but I didn't know what to do.

They planned to get Aiko elected as representative, so she would have more time with Trist. I was surprised when they walked up to us earlier. Most people had until now just watched him from a distance.

I felt so privileged when I found out we were on the Velisus together. I wanted to show him how much I cared but I know Ani liked Trist too. I felt guilty sometimes when I had opportunities to be next to him or when he held my hand, it's was like a dream.

I guess as his companions we needed to figure a way to keep Trist from falling into a situation where he is out of our range to keep him safe. Being a class representative with Aiko might be our first challenge, Tia thought.

* * *

Aiko smiled to herself, when my friend nominated me I was extremely embarrassed, I don't like to stand out. But for once I was super happy she did. I am so excited inside, this isn't the first time I've seen Trist.

Anju and I saw him when Haruka was showing him around school last week, but I don't think he remembered. The smile he showed Haruka was stunning, I want him to smile at me the same way. But I think his companions Ani and Tia are also vying for that smile.

He seemed like a kind and supportive individual, one that would do anything for his friends. I wanted him to support me as well, I am really looking forward to the next year, we will have plenty of chances to develop our friendship, and I live close as well.

Aiko wore a slight smile as she continued to fantasize about the future.

* * *

Murakami stood before the class, "Tristali, Aiko please step forward."

As I stepped forward not even realizing what I was stepping into I noticed all the student's eyes on me while I approached the head of the class. Aiko reached the front first so as Murakami directed I stood next to her.

"I would like to present your class representatives. Please give them a hand of applause." The students clapped briefly as we stood at the front.

Aiko looked up to me, "I'll be in your care." She said as she offered a broad smile.

I returned her smile, "I hope we can get along."

"You two may take your seats."

As we made our way to our seats Murakami detailed the non-school activities for the rest of the week, "Also, you will need to decide on a club over the next two weeks. The class representatives are of course excused from mandatory club activities, but you may join one if you wish."

Murakami looked at Aiko and me. As the bell rang he announced the end of the class, "Be safe going home. Tristali and Aiko could I have a few minutes with you to go over your responsibilities?"

"Of course, Murakami-sensei." I quickly offered.

Aiko also replied, "Sure."

As Lev, Ani and Tia walked over I gathered my belongings, "I will meet you downstairs unless you want to wait up here."

Murakami was waiting at the head of the class, Aiko was already there, "I need to go, I'll be right down." I said as I stood and started walking.

"Sorry for holding you up guys. From now on you will be responsible for the classroom journal and occasionally I will have you run errands and make printouts for class activities. The job shouldn't impact your daily activities too much, you can do the activities together or you can take turns, but I will leave that for you to decide." Murakami looked to both of us then rested his eyes on me, "I have a feeling this will be an interesting year."

"You can go for the day, I will take the journal down this time but starting tomorrow you can find it in the administration room in the class 1-B box. Any questions?"

"No sensei." Aiko replied as she glanced sideways at me.

"No questions, Murakami-sensei."

Murakami nodded and excused himself as we both bowed.

I looked at Aiko, "Well my friends are waiting for me. Were you going home now?"

Aiko shook her head reluctantly, "I am meeting Anju for track practice."

"Oh, you're on the track team?"

She quickly waved her hands in front of her, "No! I'm not fast enough to be on the track team. I have several friends from my last school who are though. I just like to watch."

"Well, I'm not sure if I'm the fastest runner but I know Lev, Ani and Tia have quite a bit of stamina, maybe I should have you introduce them sometime."

"That would be wonderful." She said as she clasped her hands excitedly in front of her, "Thank you, Trist, I look forward to working with you." Aiko said as she turned and departed.

I wondered why she was thanking me, but I didn't have much time to think about it before Ani burst back into the class and walked up to me, "Why didn't you refuse?"

I look at Ani then over to Lev and Tia waiting inside the room now, "Who did you vote for Ani?"

Her brow furrowed a bit as if she wasn't expecting the question, "Well, I voted for you of course."

I looked to Lev and Tia, "You guys?"

Lev looked at Tia as she returned his glance as they both said, "You."

I looked back to Ani, "Well why should I refuse when you voted for me?"

With a frustrated face Ani ran her hand through her auburn hair as she gritted her teeth, "Because I didn't know it was going to turn out this way."

I placed a hand on her shoulder, "Ani, first I could tell you were going to vote for me the moment my name was announced, and secondly this will help me keep my promise to improve the class average. I accepted not out of a desire to do so but out of necessity."

Ani seemed to reluctantly accept my reasoning and followed me downstairs, "Oh, by the way, what club do you guys think might be fun?" I asked as we descended the stairs.

"Hadn't thought about it." Lev said as he bounded down the last several steps.

Ani looked at Lev as he landed, "I don't really want to join a club honestly. If I have to I would prefer something challenging, little judo or maybe even running."

Tia glanced at Ani then turned to me, "I don't know what I want to try. I don't really want to be outside and I am not sure what all the indoor clubs do yet."

"Well, we can always check out the different clubs after class this week, it would be fun to join something we could all do."

"You're going to join a club too?" Lev asked a little surprised.

"Why not, Murakami said I could, and I promised we would stay together right?" I bowed teasingly, "I am a man of my word after all."

The four of us made our way to the judo clubhouse, but today it appeared to be set aside for kendo practice. While we sat a few moments watching, Lev looked interested but after a bit he said, "Lets head to the other clubhouses."

As we approached the rear clubhouses there were many more students than the first day we toured the school. It looked like club activities had been going continuously throughout the year.

As we watched one of the groups run sprints back and forth between several cones I heard a voice calling my name. When I looked toward the water fountain outside the clubhouse I saw Aiko waving. I quickly waved back and continued watching the runners, "It doesn't look really difficult to me."

When the coach blew a whistle and the teams finished their last lap, several students dropped to the ground to catch their breath. When the coach noticed us, she said something to the other students and some of them stood up and walked toward the fountain while others laid back on the grass, "Are you first years?" The coach asked as she walked our direction.

Ani was the first to respond, "Yes, we were looking at the different sports clubs."

The coach nodded, "Why don't you change into your track suits and you can practice with us a bit, to see if you like it."

Ani looked over at me as if to ask if it was okay, "I don't mind." I said responding to her unvoiced request, "Where can we change?"

The coach pointed to the club house, "The end two rooms are changing areas, the doors are marked girls and boys. The prospective members are taking a short break, so we have a few minutes. The regular members have today off."

I looked at Lev who shrugged and Tia who looked like a mouse caught in a trap as we all headed toward the changing rooms. When we separated Lev and I entered the boys changing area and found a spot to place our satchels and clothing.

Once we changed we headed back out toward the field. We arrived before the girls, so Lev and I began stretching like we would before one of Shivans physical exercises. I noticed the other students watching us until Ani and Tia joined.

As Ani was walking in our direction she had tied her hair up in a pony tail, it was a nice look on her since it made her hair appear to be an even deeper auburn. Tia had also tied her hair up, but instead of a pony tail hers was wrapped in a bun, so it didn't sway as she ran.

There was somewhat of a crowd moving closer to the area where we would be practicing. I didn't know it, yet but Lev, Ani and Tia had caught a lot of people's attention during the morning assembly.

While the four of us stretched the instructor returned and nodded her approval, "You seem to be used to physical activities."

"Not like this, only hand to hand training but the judo team didn't have practice today." I said as we finished stretching.

"Interesting, well. Let's see what you can do. The practice will be a shuttle run. You will run ten meters, then back. Once you reach the line you will run twenty meters. You will continue this until we reach thirty meters. We usually do several sets like this. It will be a test of your stamina and acceleration." The coach explained.

Sounded easy enough to me, as the instructor called the other students back she told them they would do two sets this time. Some of the students looked like they already wanted to quit.

I wondered how hard it could be, we often ran for hours on end when Shivan trained us. "Endurance will be the one attribute that can't be taught, it must be developed." He would say.

The four of us lined up at the end of the starting point. The cones were spaced out at the ten, twenty and thirty-meter intervals. The coach looked across all the students standing at the starting point. She suddenly blew the whistle and we started running, Ani and Lev pulled out ahead of me while Tia remained close to my speed.

As I hit the ten-meter mark and began to return Ani had just pulled away from Lev and was heading back while he was still turning.

When I reached the starting position and turned for the twenty-meter stretch I was about two meters ahead of Tia. I just couldn't keep up with Ani, she was a monster when it came to our usual physical training, it looked like this would be no different.

I was about to hit the thirty-meter mark on the second set as Ani reached the finish line, with Lev about ten meters behind. As I finally came to a stop I turned and yelled at Tia, "Come on Tia your almost there."

Tia finally crossed the finish and walked around a bit before she came back to stand with us, "I can tell we haven't exercised a bit, but I don't feel as out of breath as I normally would be."

We stood and waited for the others to reach the finish. I thought they were on the same set or were we supposed to do more than two?

The coach walked over to us, "Did you guys use to run a lot when you were training in hand to hand?" She glanced at each of us noticing we were not even panting like the students who just reached the finish line.

She turned and waited for the remaining students to finish. Once the last student crossed she asks us to move to the track located near the rugby field.

As we all walked from the grassy area to the packed earthen track I notice there were several lines in concentric circles surrounding the field, "Everyone take a moment to catch your breath. We are going to do one lap. I want you to run as fast as you can, this will give me an idea where your talents lay, in running long distance or for shorter sprints." The coach explained.

As she instructed us to line up she prepared the whistle. One of the other students was holding a stop watch this time next to the coach, "Get ready, Go!" She blew the whistle.

As we all began to run I saw Ani slowly pull away. I tried to keep up with her but fell behind when we reached the first turn. Lev had been keeping pace with me, but he too gradually passed. I kept pushing my body to move faster as my muscles protested, and I couldn't move past my current speed.

When we were reaching the final turn, I noticed Tia had caught up with me and was ever so slowly pulling ahead. When I crossed the finish, I slowed my pace and walked over toward Lev, Ani and Tia, "You all beat me that time."

Tia was smiling and seemed to be extremely happy she wasn't last, "I didn't think I would catch up, but I'm happy I wasn't the slowest this time."

I patted her on the head and smiled at her grin.

Ani looked a bit indignant, "I was first, doesn't that count for something?" She said somewhat offended.

I walked to Ani and patted her head too with a grin on my face, she just swatted at my hand though I could tell she was just embarrassed.

As we finished teasing each other over our performances the final students completed the run, "That's it for today guys, make sure you stretch to keep your muscles from tightening. You four, can I talk to you?" The coach asked.

We gathered near the coach, as she looked at the recorded time for Ani, Lev, Tia and me, "Why don't you guys join the track team. I can't guarantee you will run any events your first year, but you are already faster than most of the third years."

"I am not sure I want to do track, I still want to see the other clubs." Tia responded quietly.

"I wouldn't mind joining but let me look around first, we all sort of wanted to be in the same club anyway." Ani responded.

Lev just started stretching as the others talked to the coach, "By the way what are your names?" The coach asked.

"I'm Anistria, this is my brother Levan, that's Tris…Tristali and this is Tialinde." Ani said.

"Tristali?" The coach looked over at me, "Humm, so you are the missing student of 1-A. I'm sorry for not introducing myself earlier I am Miyoshi, I am the homeroom teacher for class 1-A." She appeared to be making a visual assessment, "Why did they move you to class 2-B?"

"I requested the move, so I could be with my friends."

"Huh! And they just moved you?" She looked a little incredulous. She was shaking her head now, "Well regardless, I want you to strongly consider joining the track team. We usually do well in regionals, and some have even progressed to national events. If you show positive results it will help you get into a better high school."

As Miyoshi started walking back toward the school we decided to change and make our way home. Lev and I finished first and were waiting outside for Ani and Tia. When they finished changing we all headed toward the bus stop.

While we waited with several students Ani asked, "Why did they suddenly move you to our class? I wanted to ask earlier but so much happened I didn't think about it."

"He promised we'd be together, isn't that enough Ani." Lev said as he just glanced down the road.

"That might be true, but how? I mean this morning you were in class 1-A and before we knew it you were being introduced to 1-B. It doesn't make sense they just moved you because you asked."

As I watched Ani, I tried to decide what to say, "Let's just say I had to prove my ability to convince the principal. I told him I could help boost 1-B's class average over 1-A. So, I will be counting on each of you to help fulfill that promise."

Ani sighed, "That still doesn't tell me how." I offered her a smile that told her I had no intention of saying.

"Regardless, I am very happy we can be in the same class, I hope we can find a club that we can all be a part of." Tia said with a grin.

As we continued to talk about the day I noticed students beginning to line up. As I glanced to the right I saw the bus with our stop on the signboard.

I shouldered my bag and moved into line followed by the others. When the bus departed I could hear students talking quietly to each other, occasionally there was a stray look in our direction.

When we finally reached our stop and crossed the street Lev asked, "Why does everyone look at us? I've been noticing it much more frequently since we visited the school the first time."

I didn't really have an answer that I could accept but I offered possible reasons, "Well we look like foreigners who are wearing a local school uniform. Even Aiko asked if we were the ones who moved into the Furigawa Ryokan, so that means others have noticed us." I thought about it a little more as we walked when I glanced at Lev then to Tia and Ani, "It could be our appearances." They all seem to be paying attention now, "I mean think about it, there are some girls who have lighter hair but there is no one with hair as pretty as both of yours. Plus, did you hear some of the conversations on the bus?"

Ani and Tia were looking a little flushed, "Are you guys okay?" I asked a little concerned.

Neither responded.

Lev laughed as he watched Ani and Tia, "Yea, we may be a similar in physical aspects to the other students, but were we ever that childish?"

"I never really had the chance. Well anyway hopefully tomorrow goes well, I am looking forward to seeing how they teach in this world."

As we arrived home we made or way to our respective rooms. While I was upstairs I heard Shivan call, "Trist, you have a guest."

A guest? Who would be stopping by my house so soon? As I came down the stairs Shivan was walking back to the dining area where he and Valdria had been talking. I came around the corner and saw Aiko and Anju standing in the entryway, "Hopefully you don't mind us stopping by."

I was a little surprised Aiko would visit so soon, I mean she said she would like to walk to school with us occasionally, but I didn't expect this, "Would you like to come in?"

"We only planned on saying hello, we don't want to intrude." Anju replied this time.

"We were going to the convenience store would you like to go with us?"

Aiko gently elbowed Anju as she glanced her way. Anju was smiling slightly.

As I was contemplating asking Lev if he wanted to go I looked up I saw Aiko and Anju's faces go blank. As I followed their eyes behind me I saw Tia and Ani with their towels and bath robes heading to the bathing room.

When they had seen me talking they stopped and were looking our direction. Ani gave me a fierce look then turned and headed toward the bathing room followed by Tia.

"I probably should pass this time, I still have some things to take care of. How about going to school tomorrow? What time do you usually leave?"

Aiko looked a bit disappointed when I declined but she perked back up when I offered going to school together, "That sounds good, Anju and I usually leave around 07:00, is that okay?"

"I will meet you then."

Aiko and Anju both left leaving me to deal with Ani's sour expression the rest of the evening.

School Life

The next few days were interesting, not our school life but the actions of Ani and Tia. The day after Aiko visited Ani and Tia began acting like my self-appointed bodyguards. Everywhere we went I had the two of them on either my right or left.

During class breaks they left no room for classmates to approach us. Only when I was tasked with fulfilling class representative activities did they leave my side.

One day when Aiko and I were asked to represent our class at a planning meeting for an upcoming event I noticed Ani biting her lip in frustration as Aiko and I departed. Aiko was ecstatic, and immediately began talking about the event and speculating what the meeting would entail.

As Aiko and I entered the meeting room we saw representatives from 1st to 3rd years. When we took a pair of open seats I suddenly heard a somewhat familiar voice.

"Trist, I'm so glad you're here." Haruka followed this up with an enthusiastic smile.

She was the girl who had shown us around campus during our first visit.

As she walked around and caught us before we had a chance to seat ourselves, Haruka clasped my hands and I heard a little squeak from Aiko as her eyes widened in surprise.

I glanced back to Haruka as she continued asking how my first week had gone. She then invited me to go with her to the nearby fast food restaurant to talk about activities outside our academic life.

She definitely knows how to drive a conversation, I thought. When Haruka noticed Aiko standing next to me she paused and gave her a satisfied smile, "Aiko, I'm so glad you're here as well. Do you know Trist?"

Aiko was hesitant, "We're in the same class."

"That's wonderful, then we can see each other during our planning events as well." Haruka looked back to me, "I hope you will join me." She said expectantly.

I smiled, "I would love too, do you mind if my friends join us?"

Haruka's expression looked a little forced, "That would be fun."

Aiko was smiling a bit as if she expected my clueless response.

As Haruka left we settled into our seats. It appeared she was leading the planning meeting for the upcoming school event.

The meeting lasted about an hour and it consisted of people throwing around a bunch of childish and unrealistic ideas. When it concluded I felt like there were no sound ideas provided by the group.

Having never sat through an event like this I took my time to listen and assess the purpose and tried to determine the benefit to the school.

Toward the end I proposed, "Why don't we accept the teachers original plan, so we could begin moving forward with planning instead of being lost in each person's individual fantasy."

While many of the male members gave me unfriendly glances there were plenty of votes supporting my proposal.

The outcomes from the meeting would be submitted to the teacher responsible for the event and we would conduct this open house in much the same way as the school had for years.

The difference was we would focus on the instructional value instead of the club activities promoting increased school applications in the years to come.

Once we were dismissed Haruka stopped me and asked when I would be free, I told her I could check with my friends today since I was heading to our temporary club.

"Oh, what club did you join?" She asked excitedly.

"None of the clubs we visited resonated with our group, so we decided to form a club of our own, but we don't have an advisor yet. We are keeping it open, so others can come and go as necessary and it was tentatively approved pending us finding a willing advisor to sign off for us."

Haruka listened intently, "Maybe I could even help, a club like that would be very useful for term exams."

As Aiko and I departed the meeting she asked, "Do you mind if I join too?" Evidently, she was not too athletic but many of her childhood friends were, so she was at a loss for a club and the two-week timeline was almost upon us.

I didn't really mind, in fact the greater the attendance the easier it would be for me to achieve my goal. When we returned to class Lev, Ani and Tia had already gone to the library where we studied until we could officially form a club.

Aiko and I gathered our belongings and we made our way to the library, she asked what we typically studied.

I glanced her way and told her we were halfway through the second-year content but if she needed help with this years I could help her catch up.

Aiko just looked at me with an uncomprehending look as she turned and remained silent for a few moments.

She finally asked, "How far ahead do you plan on studying?"

Without looking to Aiko, I responded, "I plan on making sure my friends are ready to test out at any time. That way they can help our class, so Aiko…" I stopped as I turned toward her. "…I would like your help spreading the word about our study sessions. While everyone will be attending club activities I want students to know we will make time for whoever needs it."

"This school is already the best in the prefecture. What are you trying to do?" She asked tentatively.

"I want this and every school I attend to turn out the best students in Japan. You might not believe me, but I have a goal I am working toward and I need your help and everyone else in our class. If others want to attend I wouldn't object. The more serious they can be the better." I looked her in the eyes as she slowly began to blush and quickly looked away.

"What can I do to help?" She asked bashfully.

I took her hand and began leading her toward the library. As she began walking in pace with me I gently squeezed her hand and let go.

She looked down at my hand and then hers as we stopped before the library entrance, "I want you to convince your friends first." I slid the door open and we entered our first study session with a new member.

As Aiko and I walked to the corner of the library with several tables lined up I waved to Lev who had just noticed our appearance. He said something to the group and Ani and Tia both looked up, I saw Ani's mood darken as she stood up and walked over to us, "Trist I have a question I am having difficulty with."

She began to pull me toward the chair between her and Tia. As I sat down and began, I told Lev, Ani and Tia that Aiko asked to join the study group. This gave us the necessary members. Now only if we could find an advisor.

As I looked over Ani's question I couldn't see where she was having problems, to me it appeared correct, "What were you having difficulty with?"

Suddenly she kicked me as she smiled. Ouch, I thought. Why does she always resort to violence?

As Aiko settled in she glanced at the topics Lev was working on, "Isn't that world history? We aren't supposed to start that until second term." She said a little shocked. When she looked up at me, "You were serious, weren't you?"

I nodded and smiled, "Now let's gauge your understanding so we can begin studying from there." I leaned over the table and pointed out important points that would be key on the upcoming assessment tests, "If you study these areas you will do very well on this subject." I circled key points that I knew were foundational for this level of mathematics.

"How are you at science and geography?" I asked next.

I glanced up to Aiko who looked a little overwhelmed. I think I went too far for the first subject, "Okay, for today try and memorize these formulas, they will make most of the problems much easier to solve." I pointed out several formulas, "We can even utilize some of them in our current content."

After about two hours the school chime echoed signaling the mandatory end of club activities. As we packed up I had a strange feeling we were being watched. I looked around and I only saw a few other students at the counter dropping off books they had been using but nothing out of the ordinary.

I began to focus on extending my senses, but the result was an immediate headache, not wanting a repeat of the last time I focused on blocking my subconscious thoughts.

The next few days saw a marked improvement in people attending our club. I guess asking Aiko to spread the word was helpful. We even saw students from different classes as well as second-years.

One day before classes let out for lunch there was a sudden announcement requesting my presence in the student counseling office. Murakami excused me from the remaining class.

As I approached the administrative offices I saw a man in a dark suit standing outside. He reminded me of some of the people who had visited Shivan and Valdria during our initial assessment.

When I approached the man turned to me and knocked on the door. When the door opened I stood face to face with Moriyama Kenchi, "Good to see you again Tristali, please come inside." He offered a sincere smile as he stepped to the side of the entry.

When I entered the room, there were a couple people sitting around the table already. I didn't recognize any of their faces, but they appeared to all know my name.

As I entered they all stood, Kenchi showed me to a chair across from the other guests.

While I pulled out a chair the man in the center introduced himself, "It's a pleasure to meet you Tristali, I am Mikami Sachio, from the University of Tokyo, to my left if Hiroji and to my right is Seibei both are graduate students working with me, and you already know Kenchi. I would like to talk to you about an equation Kenchi brought to our attention."

We all seated ourselves after introductions, "First, I would like to know how you came up with the solution to the problem Kenchi gave you."

I looked at the laminated paper he provided, sure enough it was the problem Kenchi had given me when he asked me to consider attending the University of Tokyo. I wasn't sure what he was asking for since the problem only had a single solution, "I'm sorry, but there was only one solution."

Mikami looked a little uncertain, "But how did you determine this was the answer?"

I frowned, "I still don't quite understand what you mean." I said with a puzzled look, the answer was obvious.

"Could you show us how you came to this conclusion? We are just struggling with where we miscalculated. This problem takes a computer several days to solve but you seem to have solved it in a matter of moments." Mikami said with a little more passion.

I was at a loss for words then I thought of an example to help Mikami understand, "If I told you to answer the problem 2x2 what would you say?"

Mikami was speechless for a moment, "That's easy, it's four." He responded with a questioning look.

"It's the same for me, when I look at a problem the calculations are made in my head. I never even really think about how to get from point A to point B, I just see the answer."

Mikami looked to his students sitting to his right and left. They both began thumbing through notebooks and wrote down several calculations and handed them to Mikami.

Mikami took the calculations and browsed through them before he looked up to me, "If I give you calculations with the work shown, would you be able to tell if the answer was correct or be able to find the error in the calculations if it is incorrect?"

I thought about it for a second, "I could try. I have never thought about looking at the processes before."

Mikami handed me three calculations on a page, they consisted of in-depth calculations to solve each problem, "The first and third are correct. The second deviated here which altered the answer." As I pointed to an equation where they mistakenly used the incorrect coefficient.

Mikami's eyes widened a bit as he glanced at the student to his left who was shaking his head, "How about this one." As he passed me a different sheet.

"These are all incorrect." I took the pencil Mikami had provided and wrote the final answer. As I looked at the error in calculations I adjusted the figures and quickly jotted down the process to the end. The student to the right was leaning over the table to closely watch my calculations.

As I slid the paper back Mikami smiled and glanced to his left, "What do you think?"

The student to the right responded, "It took us a couple days to solve that equation and the program we created kept replicating the same error. But he spotted it in an instant and even solved it." The student kept looking at me in silent wonder after he responded to Mikami.

"Tristali, do you mind me being a little unfair? I have some calculations I would like you to look at." Mikami looked up at me as if waiting for a response until he noticed me nod, "These pertain to frequency and wave length calculations." As Mikami began transposing calculations from his notebook he reviewed and then handed me the note pad.

I glanced at the equation and realized it was much the same as the early calculations for transmitting signals at sub light speed over long distances. Like the type of technology, we used on the Velisus for intergalactic communications and data transfer. I took the pencil and wrote out the answer and passed back the paper.

Mikami looked at the answer and compared it to his equation, "This looks incorrect."

He turned his notepad toward me and showed me the calculation. As I reviewed based on his assumptions his calculation was indeed correct, however… "No, both are correct. You calculated your equation based on megahertz, the one I provided would be used for transmitting data at the lowest terahertz level."

I showed him the difference in our calculations and detailed out the conversion. "When you replaced the calculation in my equation with the value for megahertz they were the same. The difference was in our expectations of usage."

Mikami took the equation I had provided and looked at it again closely, "We never even considered being able to send signals at that frequency."

Kenchi finally cleared his throat as he was trying to suppress a laugh, "Tristali, thank you for your time. I hope we will have an opportunity to work together again."

I stood up and bowed as I made my way back to the class.

When I neared the class, the bell signaling lunch rang and several students began filing out of the class.

As I saw Murakami exit he noticed me in the hall, "Well, everything okay?"

"Yea, just an acquaintance who had a few questions regarding mathematics."

Murakami laughed, "Well keep up the good work." He said as he departed.

I continued into the class and was immediately surrounded by Ani, Tia and Lev, "What was that all about?"

I smiled and was about to answer when Lev asked, "Did you get in trouble for flirting with too many girls?"

I wasn't sure what Lev meant but Ani immediately hit him while Tia gave me a disappointed look.

When the day finally ended we made our way to the library like we did every day so far. Once we found our seats, I saw several new faces, including Mikami from this afternoon.

He was sitting at the table our group normally occupied and waved as we walked up, "How are you doing Trist?"

I just looked at him with a questioning look, "What can I help you with this time?"

Both Tia and Ani were eyeing Mikami suspiciously.

"I think I am the one who can help you. I understand you need an advisor for your club. I talked to the principal and I will be your mathematics instructor starting next week." He said with a grin.

I frowned a bit, "Why would the principal so readily bring you on as our math instructor?"

Mikami smiled, "Well, having a University of Tokyo professor teaching here is beneficial to the school. Plus, it gives me the opportunity to closely observe you."

Aiko who had just entered and overheard the last part of our conversation gasped as she held her hands up to her mouth. She looked at Mikami and back to me, "Are you two close?"

"We just met." I responded but Mikami was smiling at Aiko with an understanding expression.

"It's not what you're thinking, I assure you." Mikami said as he smiled at Aiko.

Now that we had an unexpected advisor our club would be recognized. This was a major hurdle completed for advancing 1-B to the first spot.

When the end of April finally arrived, we found ourselves with several days off through the 5th of May.

So, we could still accommodate our study club we decided to hold sessions at our house, Shivan was skeptical at first but then he finally agreed when I told him the club was our idea and it would help meet a commitment I made to the school, so I could attend classes with the others.

He finally agreed, then on a Monday and Tuesday we meet and focused on the homework assignments we were given for our days off.

When I invited the club members the Friday before many sounded very enthusiastic. I extended the invitation to all in the class as well. However, I didn't expect many to accept since it was so soon in the school year.

When Monday arrived, I found myself faced with almost an entire class of students. Not only those from our class but those from 1-C, 1-D and a few girls from second-year as well.

When Valdria noticed the number of students her eyes widened a little, "Looks like I may need to have Shivan pick up a few more groceries."

I apologized and told her I could take care of that.

Even given the size of our house compared to the numbers we had I was hard pressed to find adequate space for everyone. Ultimately, we decided to study in the garden. The area outside the dining room was gravel and had several benches and tables. Luckily, I had already completed my assignment, so I only had to sit with those who were having difficulty.

I wouldn't give them the answers, since that wouldn't help the class, but I would ask questions and point out passages that contained the information they needed to answer each question. Lev, Ani and Tia also helped with the questions once they completed what hadn't been finished over the weekend.

After about an hour, Valdria brought out a pitcher and several paper cups. As the others noticed she apologized, "I am sorry about the cups, we don't have nearly enough for so many people."

Everyone was surprised since they never expected her to provide for so many. In fact, several students had brought their own snacks and beverages which they ended up sharing among each table.

As the daylight started to fade students began to pack up and thanked us for the help. Gradually the number of remaining students dwindled to a more manageable total. When there we only twelve students left we moved into the house where the lighting would be better.

The main entry had enough chairs once Lev and I moved a few from upstairs to accommodate the remaining students. Of the twelve, six were regular members of our club and the others were a mix of different first-year classes.

I was looking over the students and trying to make sure no one needed help when I noticed Valdria beckon me from the dining area.

As I walked over to her I noticed Jes also walking down the hallway, "Do you want to invite your friends for dinner?".

I looked back at the number, "That might be a bit much."

She smiled and nodded, "I am happy to see you four with so many new friends, I don't mind one bit, but would you mind running an errand for a few items for dinner?"

Jes who was close walked over and spoke, "I'm going into town for a few items already want me to pick them up?"

Valdria looked to Jes and smiled, "Yes, if you wouldn't mind." Valdria handed him a list as he looked through it he didn't seem to have any questions.

Jes had been traveling to the University of Tokyo for almost a month now. At first, he would return late and leave shortly before we departed for school.

He looked extremely tired for the first couple weeks, but he seems to have found a rhythm and was even invited to functions by some of his professors. He looked like he really enjoyed the opportunity.

As Jes took the list, he and I walked back into the entry while I stopped and waved him off, he quickly changed his shoes and departed. When I turned to the group several the students were looking at me with questioning looks.

Finally, a girl from 1-C asked, "Who was that?" If I remember correctly her name was Misaki.

"That was Jes, he is Tia's older brother and our cousin. He is currently attending the University of Tokyo." I explained choosing the best opportunity to reduce questions regarding our familial unit.

A couple of the girls looked at Tia and some of the guys viewed Tia as even farther from their reach.

Ani and Tia had a few admirers, over the last several weeks many of the boys would ask what Tia was like at home or if she had anyone she liked. Tia was extremely kind when I was around, she was cute and always willing to help in our club.

Ani on the other hand tended to scare most of the boys off. I had overheard comments regarding her fierce gaze when she was looking at anyone other than me. I guess that was due to our time together.

I am unsure what the girls thought of Lev and me though.

While the girls looked at Lev most of the time they would avoid my gaze altogether, so I assumed they were more interested in him.

We usually had a larger number of girls than boys in our study group but recently the numbers had been equalizing. I looked over the students and saw five boys and seven girls not counting my companions.

As I quietly contemplated Ani walked up and brought me out of my thoughts, "What's wrong?"

I looked up at her, "Nothing, just thinking about how our group has slowly been growing."

Ani turned and glanced over some of the newer faces and sighed, "You know most of them are here because of you right?"

"Well I did propose the study club, so I guess you're right." I responded. Ani just sighed as she looked at me before she turned to head back to the others.

I slowly cleared my throat, "Would any of you like to stay for dinner?"

Everyone including Lev, Ani and Tia looked up with surprised looks. Most of the students immediately agreed, only a couple looked hesitant. Once they all responded I asked, "Let's take a short break, that way you can verify with your families, so we have a better count."

Everyone stood, either from the floor where they had been sitting or from their chairs. A couple students asked if they could use our phone which I guided them to and told them to take their time. The others called from the cellular phones as they stretched their legs outside the entry.

After everyone had contacted their parents only four had to leave since their families had plans for the evening. Those who left, I made sure to spend my remaining time with, I wanted them to feel comfortable with the homework problems they had.

When an hour had passed the four excused themselves and headed home. The remaining students were finishing up or happily chatting amongst themselves. Somewhere along the way Kiho proposed setting up a group chat on the Line app, "It will be fun, that way we can ask questions even if we are studying at home."

I thought it would be a great way to remain in contact.

Jes arrived shortly after the group began to break up, so I helped carry the bags into the kitchen as he changed his shoes.

When I returned a couple of the girls in our class asked me if they could help.

I smiled and asked them to follow me. As I entered the kitchen Valdria was placing the items for the evening meal on the counter, "Valdria, these three were wondering if you could use any help."

Valdria looked over at me then the three standing behind me as she smiled, "That would be nice."

I had completely forgotten my manners, "Oh, I am sorry. This is Kaoru, Kiho, and Remi. They are in our class and have recently been coming to our club activities."

Valdria's eyes widened a bit as she looked at each girl, "Thank you for being so kind to Trist and the others."

The three seemed to all stammer at the same time, "It's our pleasure."

Kaoru added, "They are really helpful, the class has been much easier since we started studying together." The other two nodded.

I turned to them, "I'll leave you in Valdria's care then. Let me know if I can help with anything." I offered a slight smile as all their eyes widened as they stared at me a moment before returning my smile and turning toward Valdria.

I exited the kitchen for the others waiting in the entry. When I looked around, it appeared everyone was done, "Did anyone have any last questions or are you all finished?"

The first to raise their hand was Misaki, "Could you show me to the toilet?"

I felt immediately foolish for not considering this earlier, "I am so sorry, I didn't even think about that. Please follow me."

I took Misaki to the toilet and showed her where the washroom was once she was ready. I returned to the room, "If anyone else needs to use the toilet there are three more downstairs and one upstairs."

A few others voiced their need as well, so Ani showed them to the right toilet, and I showed the others to the left.

There was some interest about our rooms but with me upstairs and the others down stairs we declined this time with the number of people present. The girls looked disappointed. I am sure they were interested in seeing how Ani and Tia had decorated.

Once dinner was over the remaining students made their ways home. Shivan retreated to the monitoring room for a short time then returned with a portable filament monitor he took to his room.

Ani and Tia helped Valdria clean the table and kitchen. Lev followed me to my room and was sitting on my bed chatting about conversations he overheard in my absence.

After a few moments of silence Lev spoke, "Hey Trist, I think you should be careful. I hear a lot of talk about your popularity from the male students, especially among the second-years. After we were assigned to our class team I even heard that the student council president is after you from one of the girls. Did you do something when we weren't around?"

As I organized my homework I thought, "I can't remember doing anything that would cause resentment and Haruka always talks to me whenever I see her in meetings or around school. I could ask since it's better to clear up any misunderstandings."

Lev just laid back looking at photos on my personal filament monitor of Paltius, "You know, I almost forgot what it was like to be home. We've only been here a couple months and I haven't thought about missing home once."

"I don't really miss Paltius either, but I miss my family." I said with a somber expression.

Lev was quiet for a while, "I hope you consider us family, you're the closest I ever had to a brother and I know Ani cherishes you too. She just doesn't show it very well." Lev rolled to his side facing the desk, "So how is the class representative job going?"

I leaned back in my chair as I looked at Line beeping on my phone then over to Lev, "It's not bad, it's just sometimes I think I am being stalled by Aiko. She is kind of slow when we walk to and from the meetings and she always wants me to wait for the seat closest to the exit." I shook my head slightly, "That alone would make you think she wanted to leave quickly, right? But when we leave she has several things that she needs to do before club. And since were going to the same place I would feel bad if I left without her, so I am stuck following her around."

"What is the student council planning for next?" Lev casually asked.

"Well, we have plans in place for our education expo, we just have to wait for the open house. They have also started planning for the athletic festival. This is where our class team will start to come into play I guess. We will be paired with a second- and third-year class of the same color and compete during different events. At first I thought it was like survival training but after Aiko explained it sounds more like an excuse to take off from studying." I just shook my head as Lev grinned.

"Well you like to study." As he rolled onto his back holding the monitor above his head, "The study group was a lot bigger than I expected this time too. I'm glad you went over so many things with us, it seems so easy to answer the other students questions now."

"We have more to do, I was hoping to have a larger percentage of our class here than actually showed up. I'm hoping the more who attend the faster our group will grow." I said as I walked over and looked out the darkened window but could only see the faint outline of the town and a faint reflection of my room.

The next day found me up early getting ready for school. As I was about to don my uniform I remembered we still had two days off. I hung my clothes back on the rack and sat back down on my bed thinking of all the different things I wanted to do, when at some point I fell back asleep.

I faintly heard my name being called and the hurried footsteps up the stairs then suddenly the loud noise of my door being slid hastily open. What do they want, don't they know it's a holiday? I thought.

Ani and Tia bust into my room, "Trist wake up!" They both exclaimed.

Ugh, I thought. Maybe I should scare them I smiled inwardly as I devised my sinister plan.

Both Ani and Tia walked up to me, "Hey, wake up." I remained motionless. Then when they bother grabbed an arm I quickly pulled back and they tumbled across the bed on top of me totally caught off guard. I let go of their hands as they landed and reached around them like I was hugging both of them in each arm and lightly tickled their sides.

The reaction they gave was unexpected. They suddenly screamed but not in pain, as they both swatted down at my hands and continued to squirm against my embrace. This is amusing I thought, so I did it again. My action was followed by renewed kicking and squirming until Tia slipped sideways off the foot of my bed and Ani slid to her knees off the bed.

They both sat on the ground looking at me with frowns saying that wasn't nice. Ani was the first to stand, "Hurry up and get ready for school, I won't come up here again after that." She looked like she was pouting now that I found a weakness.

"We don't have school today, remember?" I said. I continued laying across my bed as I patted the mattress, "Sit down and let's figure out what we are going to do today since our homework is already done." I didn't expect them to stay after that since I was a little unfair.

Tia stood and sat at the edge of the bed next to me. I looked up at her and smiled. Ani who was looking at the wall but hadn't left after her statement finally looked at Tia and me, then slowly sat on the bed a few inches from me on the opposite side of Tia.

I reached up and gently rubbed and scratched their backs and asked, "What should we do today?" I asked as I yawned.

Ani and Tia provided several ideas as I listened, I continued to yawn occasionally. When they both agreed on going to the mall they looked down at me asleep again. Ani looked up at Tia who returned her glance and they both smiled and laid down next to me, for just a moment. Or so they told themselves.

When I finally woke up I had two arms draped over my body, Tia's face was to my left and Ani's was to my right. When I looked at them this close they really had changed over the last two years.

Tia no longer had the puffy cheeks she had the first time we met, and the expressions she made now were much less childlike, she was getting taller too, soon she might even reach the same height as me. As I looked to Ani who was slowly exhaling with her lips somewhat parted I could feel her warm soft breath.

Ani was also changing. Her hair was beginning to deepen in color and her movements were more refined when I watched her at school. Her face was never chubby but now she was beginning to look more mature and her actions were less tomboyish.

Ani and Tia were using my arms as pillows, this sort of reminded me of when they fell asleep in my room when I put them in my bed. However, this time my arms were numb. I could roll a bit but not enough to pull my arms out. I didn't really want to be mean when they were sleeping, so I turned toward Ani and whispered, "Hey Ani, time to wake up." I blew gently in her face hoping this would be enough of a disturbance to awaken her. I wiggled my shoulder trying to jostle her gently, "Wake up Ani." No luck, maybe if I try Tia then.

I turn to my left and repeat the same thing, though Tia looked like she was close to waking up. I stretched toward Tia, "Hey Tia wake up." I remember my mother waking me with a kiss on the forehead, I wonder if that would work with them. As I gently touched my lips to her forehead. Her breathing remained irregular, but she had a slight smile on her lips.

I tried the same thing to Ani, but as I gently pressed my lips to her forehead and pulled back to whisper for her to wake up I noticed Ani's eyes were wide open.

She had her lips pressed together and her face was a little scrunched up and was getting redder by the moment.

"Oh, good your awake, my arm is asleep can you help me wake Tia?" I asked her.

Ani turned and sat up suddenly, as she slowly brought her right hand to her forehead. She didn't look like she was going to be much help.

I wiggled my fingers and an unpleasant sensation assaulted my arm, first a heat then gradually pins and needles. My arm didn't quite feel like my own.

I turned toward Tia and brought my arm around attempting to rouse her, but I had very little control of where it landed. My arm draped over Tia's waist as I turned, and my face was directly in front of hers. She began to snuggle closer, so I brought my hand up to her cheek and softly stroked it, "Tia I really need to get up."

Tia's arm twitched as she smiled and brought her hand to her cheek placing it over mine. When she first opened her eyes, they began to widen as she realized the person in front of her was me, "Can I get my arm back, please?"

Tia bolted upright and stood nearly falling over backwards from the sudden movement. She looked around a bit and realized she wasn't in her room then she looked at Ani who was still sitting on the edge of the bed with a blank look on her face.

Tia pulled Ani up and turned to me, "Were so sorry we didn't plan on falling asleep." She quickly turned pulling Ani along behind her.

Having finally recovered my arms I waited for the odd prickly sensation to die down and finished getting dressed. It was about eight judging from the light coming through my window, so I made my way downstairs.

Valdria wasn't up yet, but I heard Talinde in the pantry, he must be looking information up on the Velisus. Not really feeling like making breakfast I went to see if Lev was awake.

As I knocked on his door I heard a groan, and when I slid the door open he was still lying face down on his pillow, "Hey, get up, let's go grab something to eat in town. Ani and Tia wanted to do something as well."

Lev turned his head and glanced at me with somewhat red eyes, "Sure, give me a few hours." I laughed at his response.

"Anyway, get up, I'm going with the girls soon whether you're ready or not." I said. This caused him to stretch his leg out of bed. He then stretched the other out till both his legs were sticking out of his covers and he slid to his knees.

He slowly pulled the covers off and sat there with his face and body still laying against the mattress. I just laughed as I shook my head, "Meet you in the entryway." As I closed his door.

* * *

Tia sat at her desk looking into her mirror, what was I going to do. I can't believe we fell asleep. What was with Trist, he never acted like that. When he caressed my cheek, it was so tender I thought it was my mother.

I am so embarrassed, to wake up face to face. I never could have imagined something like that before. But my body acted on its own, I felt if I didn't run Trist would be able to read my thoughts like an open book.

I know he tries to keep from doing it but if my feelings are too strong will they spill out for Trist to feel? Tia clasped her hands over her face as she quietly screamed in her hands in embarrassment.

As she slowly calmed down she thought about Ani's expression, she never said anything, usually she is so antsy sitting next to Trist she ends up acting uninterested in anything he does. But, she fell asleep too right? Why didn't she say anything when we left Trist's room?

*   *   *

Ani continued laying back clasping a pillow to her chest. She then slowly raised her free hand to her forehead where she could still feel the sensation of Trist's touch. That was a kiss right, she thought to myself. When my eye's opened and I saw Trist next to me I planned on just lying there a few minutes.

When he hadn't noticed my eyes open I quickly closed them again, then I felt the softest sensation on my forehead. I couldn't help but open my eyes to verify, I saw Trist's face pass right by mine.

I didn't have time to even get embarrassed, I just couldn't believe what had happened. Did he do it on purpose or was he teasing us again. I really wish I knew how he felt.

*   *   *

Tia gently knocked on Ani's door, "Ani, are you changed?" Tia asked quietly. Tia could hear Ani affirm so she slowly slid the door open and stepped in closing it behind her, "Are you okay Ani?"

Ani glanced up from the pillow she had been using to hide her face she knew was bright red, "I'm okay, just thinking."

"About Trist?" Tia asked bluntly.

Ani stared at Tia for a long moment before she responded, "Of course not about Trist, why would I be thinking of him?" Ani could feel her face growing hotter as she again held the pillow over her face.

Tia smiled at her closest friend's embarrassment, "I was thinking of him too." Tia said as she looked down, "Do you think he knows how we feel?" Tia anxiously asked.

Ani dropped the pillow off the side of her bed as she stared at the ceiling, "If he does I can't tell. Sometimes he is so kind it makes me want to scream how I feel. Then he shares his kindness with others, and I begin to doubt that we are even a tiny bit special to him."

"Trist is special I think. He can't afford to let his feelings slip in front of others. Sure, he is kind to everyone else because he has to. But we know him for who he really is. So, I think the kindness he shows us is special." Tia smiled as she thought of Trist.

"Plus, he isn't like the other boys at school, some of them are extremely childish and others can be very perverted. It's like they don't even try to hide it. I can see why so many of the girls in school want to talk to him." Tia said a little sadly.

Both girls sat in silence remembering individual moments of kindness granted them by Trist, "Anyway, I will do everything I can to make sure Trist is not deceived by other girls." Tia said passionately.

Ani giggled at Tia's pose, "I will do the same, I want us to be the target of his affection." Ani stated as Tia looked a little happy she was included in her statement.

*　　*　　*

Once I had gathered my wallet and clothes I went downstairs to wait for the others. I could hear Ani and Tia talking in one of their rooms.

As I sat for a few minutes and browsed the different shops at the mall downtown on my phone I heard Lev exit the toilet and head back into his room. Ani and Tia both entered the hallway and walked to where I was sitting, after this morning I expected them to be a little standoffish like they usually were, but they appeared fine.

I was so glad to have them with me daily, I could be myself and didn't have to fear them thinking less of me. As I was thinking and staring at Ani and Tia they both started fidgeting, "Are we going to go or not?" Ani asked.

This brought me back from my daydream.

"Yup, let's go." I said. In an elevated voice, "See ya Lev, we're heading out now." I pulled the girls with me out the door and had them hide against the wall and made a, Shhh sound with my finger to my lips.

I could hear crashing in his room and a muted, "Wait for me." Before Lev rushed through the door and ran right past us down the driveway.

I looked at both girls, "Should we go back inside?" I asked as they both laughed and shook their heads no.

I grabbed both their hands again and began pulling them along. I had no way to see the smile they shared between each other.

Mid-Terms

The time for the education expo was the following week, there was only one obstacle to pass before our first student council event. Mid-terms! Typically, the low point in every club's attendance and people's social lives. However, our club saw a tremendous influx of new attendees.

We never set requirements for attendance, officially we had eight members, the most recent coming from the volleyball team. They were close to being removed due to poor grades, so they asked for our help and ended up eventually becoming regular club members.

After the turn out during Golden Week many students had heard about our club, the effect was enhanced by the marks on the homework and the improved ability for those who joined in answering questions during class.

Currently, the library was no longer suitable to accommodate so many people even if we were quiet this many people is bound to stand out. Luckily Mikami was able to relocate us for the week before exams to a larger classroom.

We set the desks in groups of four and Lev, Ani, Tia and I walked around answering questions or pointing to content to be knowledgeable of during the exams.

When it came to the foreign languages I could answer most grammatical inquiries but speaking them was a little awkward since I didn't have much of a basis for comparison. From our class we had all but three of the guys and one of the girls attending. When I reminded everyone about upcoming mid-terms the last four just scoffed and chose not to participate, I only hoped they would see the benefit after the exam results were posted.

We were able to get an additional three hours of study time a day for four days prior to the exams. On Monday and Friday, we went over the items to review prior to the tests. This allowed the students to review at home, so they would be studying the appropriate content for the test.

Everyone who attended had an open invite to ask last minute questions via Line chat or even stop by if they found something challenging during their weekend studies. Surprisingly no one came. I half expected Aiko or Anju at least since they lived a short distance up the road.

I continued to review through the weekend and occasionally helped Ani and Tia with English grammar. Lev seemed to be doing fine by himself, so much so that he was asleep early the Sunday before our tests.

The next day the tests seemed to proceed without much difficulty, during breaks an occasional student would ask questions pertaining to the upcoming topic. Once the last test was over I sat my sheet down as I looked around the room a second.

Lev seemed to be near the end and Ani had an unusually calm look to her, it was hard to see Tia since she was the opposite side of the room.

I thought it would be okay to try just once, I focused on Tia's and asked as if she was in front of me, *"You okay Tia."*

I heard a startled intake of breath as several students near her turned her direction to see what was wrong.

I could almost sense Tia's embarrassment. I focused again, *"Sorry."* No headache this time is a good sign. I glanced her direction and just barely caught her eyes as she smiled in my direction. Looks like it's going well for her too I thought.

Once the day was over and Aiko and I had returned the log, we both headed to the library.

I asked Aiko how the test went, and she was almost giddy, "Everything we studied was on it, I was so surprised."

I smiled at her enthusiasm as she continued to talk about how she felt.

When we arrived at the library I planned to just let everyone have the day off from club, since we spent so much time the last week preparing. What I saw when I walked in was unexpected. The library tables were filled with students waiting for me to arrive. When I walked in the librarian on staff glanced up and just shook her head silently with a half-smile. That day we received another 12 applications for our club.

I was a little shocked as the students seemed to be all smiles, "Are you all okay with joining? I don't mind if you just come when you have free time. I would hate to take you away from a club you are passionate about."

Eichi, who was one of our brand-new members spoke up, "Trist, you made this fun. Since you didn't really give us any answer but left it to us I felt satisfied with my results today. This is the first time I actually felt good after a test."

His comments were echoed by the other new applicants. I looked at each of their faces, "Well, I don't mind you joining, but…" I paused as I considered my next words, "…you will be expected to tutor other nonmembers just like we did for you. I will of course help you prepare ahead of time but the stronger academically you are the easier it will be for the others."

Everyone nodded their agreement, this gave us a total of twenty official members. I was going to need to check with Mikami if there was a different place we could meet.

The library was beginning to shrink as our numbers increased, plus I didn't want to make trouble for the librarian who had been exceedingly understanding from the beginning.

The day was short, once I had noted and submitted the new club applications, we headed home.

The last few weeks Aiko and her friend Anju had been joining us, though Ani and Tia continued to keep me under tight control.

By mid-week the examination results were posted. Our class did remarkably well and out of a total of 500 points the class mean was 479. As I looked over the names in the top 100, I saw a majority of the students who attended our club activities near the top.

While I looked over the list I noticed the few who hadn't accepted my invitation were well below the class average. I would need to invite them again, so they didn't feel awkward joining us before the next exam.

As Lev, Ani and Tia return from taking their bags to the class I turned to them, "Great job guys. You are all in the top."

Tia clapped her hands quietly as she started searching for her name.

Lev and Ani were not showing much interest, instead they seemed to be watching the other students around us.

As we all started for the classroom I could hear the occasional, "…that's him." Spoken in quiet voices.

Lev and Ani seemed on edge as we made our way to the second floor.

When we entered the classroom, there were numerous conversations taking place. We separated for our individual seats and four classmates approached my desk.

I looked up and recognized them as the four who chose to study on their own. The shorter of the three named Tashiro was the first to speak, "Would it be possible if we attended your next study session?" He politely asked.

"I would be happy to have you all attend." As I included the whole group I could see relieved faces on each of them. They quickly bowed and offered a quick thank you. I smiled inwardly now that I had convinced most of the students to participate, this should really help boost our class average.

As the first bell rang each student settled down into their chairs. When Murakami walked in he had a slight frown on his face. He sat his books on the podium then looked out at the class, as his eyes scanned the room they seemed to rest on me a moment before they continued. With a deep breath Murakami spoke, "There have been a few objections to the test scores. Some have even been accused of inappropriate behavior." Murakami sighed a little, "So today we will be re-testing. I will be joined by the homeroom teacher from class 1-A."

Several of the students began talking at once, "This isn't fair…are 1-A students retaking the tests?" The consensus around the room was disbelief.

I just looked at Murakami then glanced around the room. I could see Lev and Ani with dark looks on their faces.

Murakami raised his hands to silence the chatter, "Now, calm down. Look at it as an opportunity to do better than the first test. That is the best way to show them your hard work." He said as he looked out over us.

A few moments later the teacher from 1-A entered. She was the coach from the track team who had advised us to join the track team, Miyoshi-sensei.

She walked up to Murakami and handed him several different printouts. Miyoshi turned to the class, "Clear your desks, if you have any questions we will answer them at the end."

Murakami and Miyoshi began passing the tests out by row, as the stack made it to me I took one and passed the remaining back. I placed it on my desk face down waiting for the start command.

As Miyoshi ensured everyone had a test she looked at the clock then told us to begin.

The test seemed easier than the previous one, the questions were different as well. The testing continued after lunch was over, this time it started off with mathematics. As we began I browsed the sheet and noticed these were some of the problems we used in our study group, the class should do well on this one.

As the day came to an end the tests were collected and Miyoshi took them and departed the room. Murakami looked at his class, "Good job today. They will have the tests graded today and new scores will be posted tomorrow." Murakami gathered his belongings and departed just as the bell chimed.

After Murakami left, the class began discussing the test and speculating on why they had to retake the entire set of exams.

Lev walked up to me and sat on the now vacant chair next to me, "What do you think?"

"We exceeded what they considered a normal deviation from our expected outcome. Probably due to the large number of 1-A students who slipped below their entrance rankings. We should be okay, maybe even better this time around."

Lev just watched me and then glanced out the window behind as he contemplated my words. A couple of the regular club members came up to Lev and me, they each asked a few questions and seemed satisfied with my answer, they must have gotten it right, I smiled to myself.

I stood and walked to the podium and picked up the class journal. We had club today but would probably just answer questions if anyone had them regarding todays tests.

I walked back to Lev and Ani who were collecting their belongings, "I'm going to drop off the journal, meet you at the library." Tia had come running up as I finished talking. I rubbed her head, "How was it this time Tia?"

Tia's smile was radiant, "It was even easier than last time."

I smiled back at her as I headed toward Aiko's desk.

"I'm going to drop off the journal, then head to the library, see you soon."

Aiko nodded as she smiled.

As I entered the administration room I made my way to the boxes containing the attendance journals and placed our classes in the appropriate box.

In the staff lounge I could overhear what sounded like Miyoshi and Murakami talking heatedly with the Principal who occasionally offered a restraining command. It sounded like we were in for a fight next test, I thought to myself.

The club activities only had a few additions today, some had questions while some wanted to talk about our next chapters.

In all, the re-test was pretty much accepted by all the 1-B students as expected.

The next morning after I picked up the journal I made my way past the poster boards where the exam results were posted. I didn't spend much time just enough to view my companions ranking and the general class. Then quickly headed up to my class.

When I entered I saw several students glance my way once they heard Lev say, "About time."

I smiled at him and several students gathered near my desk and bombarded me with questions.

The majority wondered if I had seen the scores, or if I thought our class average improved. I smiled and said, "We will probably know shortly."

Gradually the students wandered back to their desks still excitedly talking amongst their friends.

As the chime rang Murakami entered the class. He walked to his podium and placed his books on the top and then turned to the class. He appraised us for a few moments then his face broke out into a big smile he immediately tried to hide. He then turned to the chalkboard and began writing out a number, 4...8...2, then he divided it by then number of subjects tested /5=96.4.

He turned back to the class, "You guys should be proud, the class average was the highest ever for first semester mid-term exams." He placed his hands on the edges of the podium as he looked out, "With two proctors verifying no student can object, and you even did better than the first round of tests. Thank you." Murakami bowed slightly causing a few students to express surprise since this was uncommon for a teacher to show respect to their students in this way.

"Trist! You may find that Mikami has a new plan regarding the primary showcase during the education expo next week." Murakami looked at me as he finished.

I could only show a puzzled expression.

*   *   *

That day once school had ended Aiko and I made our way to the library after we carried the remaining books left by our final instructor to the administration room.

When we entered I immediately noticed Mikami waiting for us, as he saw me he turned to the other students, "Alright, let's go. I will show you your new club location." Mikami called out to me, "Follow me Trist, I have a few changes to discuss about next week."

I nodded as I looked to Aiko who was a little wide eyed.

Mikami lead us to a room in the third-year class area. The room was a little more spacious since the desks were designed for two and when pushed together made a large area where six could sit and study.

The number of tables allowed us to create nine groups of six giving us much more space than the library. "This class has been set aside for the study clubs exclusive use."

There were a few murmurs of surprise since it was unusual that a club made primarily of first years would be placed in a third-year classroom.

Mikami looked to me as the murmurs died down, "Trist, your club will be the primary attraction for the upcoming education expo. I would like to have your club field questions of your choice. Don't make them too easy." Mikami looked at me as his eye brows arched a bit, "Understood?"

"How soon do you need them?"

The other students seemed to be getting a little excited hearing our club was going to be the center of attraction.

"I would like to have them by tomorrow if at all possible, that way we can review and add to them if necessary. Just pretend you are preparing a test for each subject. Keep it below twenty questions for each topic though."

I thought about possible questions then glanced around at my fellow members, "We can do that."

Mikami nodded, "Well I will be expecting them tomorrow before you leave for the weekend then." Mikami left after he handed me a paper that basically outlined everything he just told us.

Well, I thought we should get going. I turned to the others, "Okay, break out into four groups and lets each come up with five questions for each topic." I wrote seven topics on the board, math, language, literature, civics, science, history, and geography.

This was more than the five tested topics, but geography and history usually covered a test and languages covered Japanese literature and foreign languages. After an hour had passed I asked each group to pass their selections to the next table, so we could eliminate any duplicate questions. Once we had made the rounds we had a good assortment of questions.

I helped each table with wording on any questions they had difficulty with. I should have split up Lev, Ani and Tia since their questions were a tad more difficult due to the studying ahead we had already done.

When we had close to twenty questions for each topic we ended club activities. I took the questions and sorted them by category and re-wrote them, so I could turn them in to Mikami before we left for the day.

I had Ani cover history and geography, Lev took care of civics, while Tia covered language and literature.

Tia was very fluid in the way she wrote some of the foreign languages, she had studied writing very diligently once we began school to overcome what she thought was a weakness.

I quickly wrote down the science and math questions, I corrected a few errors, but this looked to me like it would be a challenging test. When they were completed, I took the questions to the office and asked if I could copy them before handing them in to Mikami-sensei.

He agreed and was surprised to see them so soon.

As he looked through each sheet I could see his eyebrows raise when he started going through the science and math questions, "You did these didn't you?"

I just nodded, "I am confident that everyone in our club can answer them."

Mikami glanced up from the papers he held, "You know these are well into second-year level, right?" He paused as he appraised my expression, "Well, I will have these typed up and the parents who visit can test your club's ability next week."

As I departed Mikami called out, "You will be responsible for the success or failure of the open house. Make sure you are prepared." Mikami said as I gently closed the door.

When we were making our way home Lev, Ani and Tia were surprised when I pressed the next stop button.

They all stood up as Ani asked, "Why are you getting off here?"

"I need to make copies, I have a feeling this may be an interesting event. So, I want to make sure everyone has a copy." Once I stopped by the office supply store near the post office I safely stored the copies away and we made our way home. It was a little later than normal so Jes was returning about the same time as us.

During dinner Shivan asked how school was going so I explained the events of the last week.

Shivan listened and smiled when he heard the test results were even better than the first round.

When we told him about the educational expo he looked a little interested, so I shared a copy of the questions our group had put together.

He read through them and would occasionally nod, "These should be more than adequate to show the merit of your club for potential new students. In fact, these might be a little above your grade level, be careful not to give too much away too fast." Shivan cautioned.

When classes ended the following day, I handed the sample questions to Lev to distribute to our members, "I have a class representative meeting about the open house next week, can you pass these out? Tell them to be ready for Monday."

Today's meeting consisted of manual labor, we had to prepare signs and set up tables for the open house on Monday.

Sometime during early evening Tia poked her head into the room. When she saw me, she tried to catch my attention, but Aiko was the first to notice her, "Hey Trist." Aiko said as she pointed to the door.

I saw Tia standing just outside the slightly opened door, so I stood and approached, "What is it Tia?" I asked as I also noticed Ani and Lev behind her.

"Can we help at all?"

I was about to say we were good and to send them home when Haruka stuck her face right next to mine.

"Come on in." Haruka said with a big smile.

Both Ani and Tia gave a somewhat annoyed expression with Haruka so close.

With the extra pairs of hands Aiko and I were able to finish up our signs and head home much earlier than expected.

Haruka reminded us to be back by 07:30 Monday to finish setting up and hanging signs.

Monday would normally be a light day with only clubs conducting activities, however this time the focus was on clubs supporting academic related fields.

The weekend was uneventful, Shivan finished his next thesis for the government to review and distribute. I guess his papers were being submitted anonymously to the academic community. There was much speculation regarding the author, but this let Shivan be a little more open regarding ideas since the papers weren't linked to him directly.

His papers were geared toward advancing current thought regarding mathematics and physics, while basic when compared to Paltius's more advanced theories.

Shivan had cautioned me to restrict the sharing of mathematical or physics applications I was knowledgeable on until the topics had been released publicly.

The weekend went by rather quickly, while my homework was completed early Friday evening I ended up helping Talinde and Tia work in the garden. It was tedious work and required constant attention to maintain a park like state, but it also allowed me time to meditate on the past week.

Tia would giggle every time she watched me deal with stubborn weeds, most came out easily since we had sort of a routine maintaining the grounds.

Tia was moving some of the furniture on the gravel pad outside the kitchen, so she could clean up the small leaves that had blown against the side of the house. As she walked with the bulky bench moving it away from the edge of the house she lost her balance and let the bench slide against her hands.

The outdoor furniture wasn't new, so the weathered exterior had some rough spots where the wood grains had split. I heard Tia cry out and the bench fell to the ground as the wood splinter entered her hand.

I quickly stopped what I was working on and went to see if she was okay. She was holding her wrist and looking at the splinter sticking into her hand between her thumb and forefinger.

Tia wasn't weak willed by any means, but I immediately felt her pain. I took her gently by the arm and led her inside to the kitchen. I helped her wash the dust and dirt from her hands and dried around the splinter.

You could see discoloration under her skin, and I knew it had to hurt but she only winced when I gently pulled the splinter out.

As blood began to slowly ooze from the puncture I took a clean towel and covered her wound. "Tia, hold this and I will get Valdria." I told her as she stood near the sink.

I quickly found Valdria who was working with laundry, "Valdria, can I use the molecular stabilizer?"

Valdria looked over to me knowing something must have happened for me to ask, "What happened?" As she sat the basket she was sorting aside.

"Tia had a small splinter from the bench outside, but it looks like I was able to remove it completely." I said as Valdria followed me to the kitchen.

When we entered Tia was still standing keeping pressure on the wound, she glanced back when we entered, "Let me see Tia." Valdria kindly asked.

As Tia pulled the towel away blood started oozing again but the wound looked clean, "Good, you washed it before you pulled it out."

Valdria left for the pantry and I heard the faint sound of the door opening, when she returned she had a small bottle and the stabilizer. She took Tia's hand and poured the disinfectant over the wound, washing the diluted blood into the sink. Once she dabbed it clean with a fresh gauze she placed the molecular stabilizer over the wound for a few moments twisting it in a circular fashion.

When Valdria was done she closely scanned the freshly healed tissue and there was no sign of the wound, "There you go Tia, but be careful. We don't have the same access to medical technology as we used to for the time being." Tia nodded then looked at me as she gave us both a smile and thank you.

Tia began heading back outside but I stopped her and grasped her by the shoulders as I turned her and gently pushed her toward her room, "We are almost done, I can finish the last bit of raking."

Tia twisted around and stood facing me, she had a defiant look on her face, "I will be more careful, I'm not going to break. It was only a little splinter anyway."

I just smiled, but what I couldn't tell her is I could feel her pain whether she intended me too or not. When we were so close strong thoughts just passed to me freely without even trying to read them.

I gave Tia a slight hug, "Okay, but ask me to help when you move the benches, I know your strong enough, but they are long and awkward to carry." As I let Tia go I thought, was she getting shorter.

As the weekend came to an end I headed to bed early, so I would be well rested for the following day. As I fell asleep I could almost hear Lev, Ani and Tia's feelings twirling around my head. Not as coherent thoughts but as feelings of insecurity, concern, and even longing. As I drifted deeper into sleep I dreamed of my own longing to see my parents and my sister.

When I awoke early the next day I checked my phone for the time, it was almost twenty minutes until my alarm was supposed to go off. As I laid in bed I knew I would be better off using this time to mentally prepare for the day and contemplated the subtle warning issued by Mikami last Friday.

After I made a piece of toast I gathered my belongings and headed out the door, since the regular students wouldn't arrive until 09:00, I left the others sleeping. As I exited the house I noticed Aiko walking up our drive.

As she noticed me she waved, "Perfect timing." She said as she smiled.

I returned her smile and we started down the road together. We discussed the events today and what we had to prepare for, she asked if I was ready for the club event.

I nodded and asked, "What did you think of the questions, will you be okay?"

Aiko cocked her head to the side as she contemplated, "A few are difficult, but I think once asked I should be fine."

As we exited the bus I noticed a few class representatives already hanging the directional signs on the exterior poster board. We made our way up and gathered the signs we previously prepared and began placing them in their intended locations.

As we finished the signs Haruka gathered all of us in the gym to set up seats for the visiting guests.

We finished setting up the seating by the time the regular club members started arriving. The sports clubs were in their areas outside near the club house and the academic and craft clubs were doing the same around their assigned locations.

Aiko and I broke away when Haruka dismissed everyone to head to our newly assigned club location.

I saw Mikami walking from the opposite direction with an A-frame sign. As he sat it down next to the entrance of our room I noticed it detailed the average test scores for every member officially belonging to our club.

I looked at Mikami, "Why do we need the sign?"

"Not many clubs in any school hold grades like the average for your club. Think of it as a statement. Oh Trist, by the way. I invited a few friends of mine to visit today." Mikami gave me a serious look.

I furrowed my brow, "Understood Mikami-sensei." I inwardly wondered what he was planning.

As Aiko and I entered the class we organized the front desks leaving room for observers in the back.

With Three rows of tables we had just enough for our regular members. We planned on doing a short study demonstration, basically me asking a question and volunteers would answer it.

I decided to start with asking the question to the room in general and even allowing observers to respond. This would create more engagement and allowed us to spot light our level.

Shortly after 09:00 the remaining members arrived, Lev, Ani and Tia weren't the last but close to it, while Lev silently apologized for being later than they planned.

I went over the plans for the day with our group and asked if anyone had any questions.

Remi was the first to ask, "What if the audience asks a question we don't know?"

I looked at her as I smiled, "Do the best you can, if you don't know I will try to pick up unanswered questions. Just don't leave them all for me." I smiled as the club members laughed. We took our free time to study and I asked random questions from the list, sometimes changing the format or information provided. For the mathematical or science problems we could utilize the chalkboard.

It was shortly after 10:00 when the first parents made their way to the hall where we were located. The students were taking this time to self-review and chat amongst themselves. I walked into the hallway and noticed Mikami approaching with several adults following.

I quickly stepped back into the classroom.

As Mikami paused before the door he waited for everyone to come to a stop, "This is the study club. As you can see based on the school's average marks posted below they are close to 20% higher. The club consists of 20 regular members but will host study sessions and allow non-club members to participate as well." Mikami paused for questions.

I hear an unfamiliar voice, "How many students typically attend these club events prior to testing?" A man asked.

"Now, we are still early into the year but for the last mid-term exam there were close to sixty students. We had to relocate the group to a larger classroom. I expect there will be even more for term exams." Mikami paused, "Any other questions? No, then follow me and the students will give a show of their activities and an example of their knowledge."

As the adults filed into the rear of the classroom I counted close to thirty just in the class with a few outside the doorway. I stood and faced the class from the front and bowed briefly, "I thank you for granting us a moment of your time. The students sitting before you are official members of our study club. We normally have close to twice this number prior to a quiz or test. Each student here is capable of tutoring the other non-member students which allows us to assist in the growth of academic knowledge of each participant." I paused and picked up a copy of the questions.

"If you would like there is a list of questions that sit at or above our current class content. Feel free to ask any questions, we will attempt to answer all questions as long as they don't extend much past the second-year level."

I heard a few hushed whispers when I finished.

The man standing near Mikami was the first to speak up, "So any question from this list, huh?"

I extended my hand, "Please go ahead."

As the gentleman glanced through the questions he asked one I could tell was not from our list, though it was within the content we studied prior to the test. Aiko raised her hand and stood as she thought a second then responded with the correct answer.

This time another adult stood forward, a lady who appeared to be well spoken, she looked the teacher type, "If I may?"

I nodded. The question she asked was so far above the content we currently were covering I would be surprised if anyone knew the answer.

I spoke up as I looked at our members, "Anyone know the answer?"

Everyone looked puzzled, why were they pulling questions not on our list, "The question you asked will not be covered in our curriculum. However, the answer is…" I detailed the response to her question and even associated it to names and dates of related events.

"If we could stick closer to the questions on your handout it would allow you to assess more of the club members ability." There were several questions and many students were given an opportunity to answer until an older gentleman who didn't quite look like he belonged with the other parents stepped forward.

He was somewhat stooped and appeared to be in his early-sixties though I could be mistaken, "I was wondering if you could help me with a theory that was recently proposed to my institution. Would you mind me writing it on the board?"

I looked to Mikami who was showing a slight smile, "Um, please."

The elderly gentleman made his way to the front of the class and began writing an equation on the board, this was not just a random equation but the key to achieving faster than light travel.

While the equation was based on principals more advanced than Japan could replicate at this time, it will ultimately lead them in the right direction. Once it was proven and they began to apply it they could begin developing systems capable of utilizing this principal.

I watched until he completed the equation, "It looks like you are trying to determine mass at light speed. Am I correct?" I glanced at the elderly man.

His eyes opened a little wider under his bushy salt and pepper eyebrows.

I walked up to the board and wrote the answer. Since I already knew the theory was correct it was a simple response. As I glanced at the older man I could see he was utterly lost with me just writing the answer. I sighed inwardly and turned back to the board. I detailed the equation through each step and circled M=0 at the finish of the equation.

The old man reached into his pocket and took out a phone as he took photos of the blackboard. He turned to me and stared for several seconds before he, "Humphed." And walked to the back.

I could see Mikami with a somewhat awed expression on his face.

Many of the parents were lost in the content, likely never seeing it before themselves. We answered a few more questions until the bell chimed signaling time for group change. As the parents left I overheard one parent talking about better than a cram school. We might have a busy club next year, hopefully we could manage.

The event went on until 14:00 that afternoon when the final bell chimed signaling the end of the presentations.

As our group began arranging the desks back to the proper position I made my way down to the welcome table where Haruka had been passing out event maps.

When Aiko and I caught her attention, she turned, and her smile evaporated to a frown, "What did you guys give a presentation on!?" She demanded.

Aiko and I were caught off guard by her demanding inquiry, "We just covered our study content and fielded open questions as long as they were within the curriculum. Why, did we do something wrong?"

Haruka's expression gradually softened, "No, but I think your event will be the primary reason for a large percentage of our new students next year. I didn't think it would be as successful as it was. We will probably end up doing an education expo every year from now on." She said somewhat deflated.

I raised my eyebrows at Haruka's response. Once we departed the welcome desk we began cleaning up the posters and stacking chairs in the gym. I guess not many of the sport clubs had much attendance, so it was almost like a normal practice for many of them.

The next event would be our sports day. I contemplated how our class would do but my musings were interrupted by Lev jumping over my back like a hurdle.

"Let's go!" He said as he landed.

I slowly followed behind my friends toward home.

Preparing for Exams

School continued much like before the education expo, our study sessions numbers remained consistent with the occasional influx as classes hit new content. Mikami occasionally came but didn't interfere, he left his harassment for math class.

Mikami had pulled me aside shortly after the expo, "I didn't know you knew physics."

"It uses many of the same principles as math, and my mentor as I was growing up loved physics."

"Maybe I should pay you a home visit sometime." He said as he departed.

I just hoped I hadn't gone too far during the expo.

Valdria was beginning to really show the extra passenger she was carrying. She no longer had bad mornings, but she still had close to eleven months before our new addition was born.

Life in our home was gradually shifting toward summer activities. The weather had begun warming and the time came to switch to our summer uniforms. No more long jackets and long sleeve shirts. The girls also had lighter blouses and scarves. With the weather turning warmer, we tried to take the study group outdoors on good days. The light breeze and occasional cloud was just enough to keep the temperature comfortable.

Mikami had grown used to his position and only came by to check on the club a couple times a week. The members were officially caught up on first-year content. Occasionally we would review languages, but primarily we worked on content from books I borrowed from Murakami.

When I asked him for second-year texts he just shook his head.

Eventually he brought a set of older books left over from last year, "The content might change but if you are trying to get ahead these should be more than enough."

I was starting to feel a change coming on, I sometimes would catch myself daydreaming and wanting to just get away. I had a few dreams recently that seemed to be back on Paltius. I was with my father and mother and little Emeri, I remember hearing her voice sometimes at night like she was calling from a long way away as she cried. I was searching through the palace rooms for her, but her cries seemed to grow more distant the more I searched.

Suddenly I felt a cool hand on my forehead, "Trist are you alright?" I heard Aiko ask worriedly.

I looked around and realized I had been daydreaming again.

"You're not catching a cold, are you?"

"We don't catch colds." Lev responded from his seat on the grass.

Aiko looked at Lev, "What do you mean you don't catch colds? Everyone gets sick occasionally."

Lev just smiled as he realized he might have said too much.

"He just means we haven't been sick before, at least that he can remember." Ani said as she socked Lev in the ribs.

Today was sort of a self-paced study day, we all agreed it would be nice to sit outside with the early summer weather and enjoy it while we could. End term exams were coming up and we had one holiday left before exams. The third Monday in July was Sea Day, which was intended as a day to give thanks to the bounty of the sea.

"Why don't we go to the beach the week before exams?" I asked the group randomly.

Eichi looked up from the book he was reading, "That sounds fun, but it would be a crazy day to actually go. Why don't we do it as a group after we finish our summer homework?"

That sounded like a good recommendation since I hadn't previously known what the beach would actually be like on Sea Day, "That sounds like a good goal to work toward. What do the rest of you guys think?"

There were several voices of agreement and some who said it would be unfair since their families had trips planned, "What if we do two trips? One after summer starts and a little later when everyone is home?" This time all agreed, it would be easier and some of us could even go twice. I was looking forward to a change of scenery as well.

When the first week of July ended we began spreading word again about the study group, first just our class since that was our primary focus. After that word spread on its own.

During the first study group we ended up going back through old content to help the students who were coming to study for the test. At first, we only had five or six who attended, but as we grew closer the number increased as clubs began winding down for the exam season.

One afternoon after we had been studying for thirty minutes or so, a new student opened the door and looked into our club, "Is Trist here?"

I stood up from helping one of our new additions, "I'm Trist, how can I help you?"

He just looked at me and I saw a few students standing with him, "Nothing important, bye." Then he shut the door and I heard him talking with his friends as they walked off.

I wondered what that was about, "He was the first-year representative." Aiko offered, "I think the teachers expected him to be first in 1-A, but in the midterms, he was mid-twenties."

I looked to Aiko as she explained then I heard Ani, "I thought I recognized him. He was talking about you when the exam grades were posted. He said there was no way so many people passed him on the exams unless they were cheating."

That would make sense, so it wasn't Miyoshi-sensei who had issues with our scores but him.

Tashiro was the next to provide insight, "He is also trying to do a study group. He tried to get some of our class one day, but they all turned him down."

I smiled, so he wanted to improve his class too, I thought, "Well, I wouldn't mind him joining if he asked."

"WHAAAT!!!" About half of the students said including Ani, Tia and Aiko.

"I mean the better the school does the more talent it will attract right? Regardless, my goal is to help everyone pass with the highest marks possible. I want to have talented friends next year, so our club isn't as difficult to start up."

Chisa looked excitedly in my direction, "So, you're going to do this next year too? I'm telling my mom if we have to move I want to commute."

I smiled at Chisa, "Let's hope you don't have to commute then."

Chisa blushed at my comment and shyly smiled.

Two weeks before exams I asked Shivan and Valdria if they minded having a large group over to study.

They both looked at each other then gave their consent, "Why not have them spend the night?" Valdria smiled at Shivans recommendation.

This time though I think Shivan asked Kazu for a favor. The Thursday before our three-day weekend Kazu had dropped off a large quantity of chairs and an awning was built in our back yard covering the gravel area.

It looked like it had been there all along except the wood was new, but they replicated the same blue grey tiles on the roof and matched the decorative woodwork to the house.

That Friday I proposed an open study group on the coming Sunday. Several in class were talking about the last one and it generated a fair amount of excitement. When we ended the day and finally made it to our club I made the same proposal but offered an overnight study group since it was likely going to be a busy Sunday. This way even our club members would have time to ask questions instead of just answering them.

We used the Line chat for all the official members of the club, so I told them to let me know once they checked with their families about Sunday night.

As we made our way home, Aiko intercepted us and asked us to wait by the bus stop for her. When she finally met back up with us I asked, "Did you forget something?"

"No, I promised to tell Haruka when we studied at your house again. She was extremely jealous last time and begged me to let her know."

"Humm, you think she will come?"

Aiko smiled and nodded, "I think she will, and I know if she has questions I might even be able to answer them this time."

I smiled back as Aiko as Ani and Tia seemed to close in on me.

When we got home I changed and grabbed Lev from his room, "Help me pick up the garden. We need to move the chairs around too."

"Ugh, can't the students who will be using them do that?" He said, but he still headed out with me.

Early Saturday afternoon Shivan knocked on my door, "Trist? Let's go shopping. I don't want to leave Valdria with her hands full tomorrow."

I was dressed and was just laying down reading a manga which I had just borrowed, "I will be downstairs shortly." I set the book aside and grabbed my wallet and tried to remember some of the snack foods the students brought along last time.

As I bounded down the stairs Lev and Ani were waiting with Shivan. When Shivan saw me come around the corner he narrowed his eyes a bit and reached out his hand and placed it on my head.

I stopped, wondering what he was going to ask me to do.

Shivan glanced at Lev and Ani before turning back to me, "You're getting taller I think."

I didn't feel any taller, but I guess my sore muscles and joints could be attributed to that.

We all walked down the road and over to the closest grocery store. The one Ani had gotten lost at, I found myself reminiscing and quietly laughed to myself, "What's so funny?"

"Oh, I just remembered this is where Ani got lost the first time."

Lev just grinned but Ani elbowed me this time instead of Lev.

"I wasn't lost. And what do you mean the first time?" She asked with a hurt expression.

Shivan looked to be contemplating his sons and daughter's interactions with me, he mentioned that it appeared we had gotten much closer. We had grown as well, "You will probably start to catch up to the rest of the class by the end of the year if not grow taller." Shivan commented as he was trying to remember what age children on Paltius began their growth stages. It might be time to discuss finding new clothes since they could have grown several centimeters within a few months, Shivan thought.

Once we had gathered enough items to feed a small army we headed back, I also talked Shivan into buying some snack foods for later in the evening, "How many people do you expect?"

I looked down for a current count, "So far seventeen have confirmed staying the night but I am not sure how many will show up at noon tomorrow for the actual study session."

Shivan didn't respond immediately, "Well we should have enough futons for that many. Kazu dropped several off yesterday when you were at school. He was laughing about a sleep over."

"Well, it's not for fun, the evening will be the only time our regular members will have to ask questions, otherwise they will be busy helping our other classmates." I said in defense.

Shivan laughed a little, one of the few he ever offered.

It was about 11:30 on Sunday when the first group showed up. Shivan was the one to greet them and they were directed to wait while he called me, "Trist?" I heard Shivan call as he walked up the stairs.

I was out of the door before he reached the top.

"Thanks, Shivan."

He just smiled.

"You know where the spare rooms are, there are futons in each closet." He told me as he headed back toward the kitchen.

I provided a set of house shoes for everyone, good thing they were inexpensive I thought. Once they slipped off their shoes they used the remaining room in the shoe box then began arranging them on the floor.

As we made our way upstairs I heard Kaoru ask, "How many people live here?" As she was looking at the size of the house, "I mean it is so big."

I thought it was small at first, until I grew accustomed to houses in Japan, "There are eight living here. You haven't met Talinde yet, but he is Tia's and Jes's father."

Remi was looking around curiously, "Are you related to Lev and Ani then?"

I glanced back and smiled, "No, but Shivan and Valdria are my guardians now."

Remi frowned, "I'm sorry for asking something as insensitive as that."

"Don't worry about it, I'm happy. Lev, Ani and Tia take most of my time anyway now."

I led them down the second-floor wing to the four empty guest rooms, "Feel free to leave your belongings here, tonight we can pull out the futons in the side closets. There are two rooms for the boys and two for the girls. If there isn't enough room, we can put a few people in my room or Ani and Tia's."

"Where's your room Trist?" Anju asked as Aiko jabbed her in the ribs.

"My room is at the end of the hall, next to the washroom."

Ani was standing in the doorway, "Don't worry we will have plenty of room for the girls."

I looked out at Ani who had a sour expression on her face, "Do you want to show them around before the others start to show up?"

Ani's shoulders slumped a little, "Sure, follow me I will show you the personal facilities and bathing room."

I left the girls in Ani's care as I went back down to see if Shivan needed help with anything.

As I entered the first floor I remembered the bathing tub, we never had filled it since most of us just took a shower, "Shivan mind if I fill the bathtub?"

He looked up from the paper he was reading, "Sure, just don't turn the heater on until everyone is ready to use it."

The tub was intended to stay filled with water that could be reheated after each use. It would stay clean and only need to be changed every few days since you bathed before you entered the tub.

I guess it was intended as a place to relax more than bathe. The water took a fair amount of time to actually fill, and as I was about to turn it off, Ani entered with the girls who had arrived a little earlier. I heard several indrawn breaths when they first entered the bathing room.

Aiko just gaped, "It's just like a ryokan."

After I heard her statement I smiled, "Well, it used to be."

As the tub finished filling I heard the door chime, "I got it!" I said loud enough for Shivan to hear.

Outside was the remaining club members, including the ones who didn't respond on Line, "Hey, you guys never responded."

The three looked around, "We forgot." The guys said in near unison. I just shook my head as I invited them inside. I handed them a set of indoor shoes as well.

As the remaining students filed in I said, "Make your selves at home, once you're ready I will show you the guest rooms where you can drop off your belongings."

They followed me upstairs and I pointed out the washroom and toilet, the rooms are down here." We headed down the hall, "The girls are on the left and the boys are on the right. When we head to bed there are futons in the closet."

They all dropped their things and followed me back downstairs, "The bathing room is here, but we will have to take turns, it only holds five or six at a time."

"Five or six!! Wow Trist, what is this place?" Eichi said after I told them.

"Sorry, it used to be an old ryokan I was told so it had a large bathing room." I apologized.

"That's not what I meant, it's like a school trip. I'm impressed." Eichi said as the others agreed.

We all ended up in the kitchen where Shivan was reading, he placed his paper down as I re-introduced the official members of our club.

Valdria came in as well and she greeted everyone, "It's a pleasure to see you all again." She looked at Kaoru, Kiho and Remi, would you like to help prepare dinner again when the time comes?"

They all beamed smiles, "It would be our pleasure." Then they looked back toward me as Ani slightly sighed.

Tia who had just joined us was looking at the girls and seemed a bit agitated.

"We have more tables and chairs this time, so it should be easier to study, when everyone heads out tonight we can have dinner and wrap up any questions of our own."

As I started to take everyone outside I heard the door chime, "Lev can you take care of the set up?"

"Sure thing." Lev said in an, I got this pose. Where does he come up with these silly responses, I thought.

When I opened the door I was surprised, it was Haruka and what looked to be the rest of our class plus many students who hadn't attended a study session before, "Welcome, I don't know if I have enough house shoes." I said a little surprised, as I began to mentally calculate the numbers outside.

"I hope you don't mind, a few of my friends would like to take part in your group as well."

I approached Haruka and came close to her ear, "Why are there so many third years? You know I'm probably the only one who can help them right?"

She just smiled brightly, "That's perfect, it's what we wanted."

I just nodded, "As long as you're okay with me, I have no problems helping."

Haruka looked back at her friends and smiled, who I remember cornering me in the hall a few times asking about our study club.

"Well, welcome everyone. For those who have been here before the personal facilities are in the same location. For those who are here for the first time follow me and I will show you the washrooms and toilets.

They were like a mob behind me and I felt somewhat uneasy with so many older girls glaring at me. I showed them the two washrooms and four downstairs toilets, "Feel free to use them as necessary." I then led them through the dining room where we said quick hellos to Shivan and Valdria before we exited to the back covered porch.

Haruka and the four third years found a table by themselves but she left a single opening next to her. The remaining students had already found seats. From my count we had close to seventy students sitting at the tables, benches and chairs. That didn't even account for the twenty club members who were up answering the occasional questions.

After about fifteen minutes had gone by Haruka called, "Trist can you help us with a couple problems?"

I looked over to the second and third-year girls and walked to their table.

"What subject are you having difficulty with?" I got four different responses, "Okay, one at a time." I pulled a book over to glanced at the topic, "So, what questions do you have?"

The girl who offered me her book asked, "What was the event that led to the beginning of this war?"

I looked down at her book, "If you study this portion here you will be able to easily answer that. It will also tell you the date and parties involved as well as a pre and post history. If you study this, you should be able to answer any questions on this topic."

I passed the book back to her, she just looked at me as if I had done the impossible, "How did you find that so quickly?"

"I've already taken the third-year exam, so I know most of the topics you will be covering. The end term exam shouldn't deviate too much from the final content."

This time it wasn't just the third years staring at me but Haruka as well. Their looks had changed to more awe filled than predatory.

"Who else?"

The next girl slid her book over and read a question out of a notebook as she pushed the hair hanging down near her eyes behind her ear.

I quickly browsed through a few pages then identified the formula she would need, "This is the formula you will want to memorize for this type of problem, you can just plug the numbers given and solve for the missing variable." I showed her a quick example.

She looked up in disbelief, "We just started this and you make it seem so easy."

"Math is just a puzzle you manipulate with numbers." I paused and chuckled, "Shivan told me that once but I guess I only just understood it's meaning." I laughed.

As I helped each in turn they began to start taking their studies more seriously. I had the distinct impression they initially came to play and not study.

When the questions had all been answered I excused myself and walked around to help the others. Students would occasionally take a break as needed. Then at one-point Valdria brought out some cups and a pitcher of barley tea for those who were thirsty.

After we had been studying a while some students began slowly departing as it approached 17:00. Around 18:00 there were only about eight non-members left, Haruka and her friends departed a short time after.

Haruka group was extremely gracious and provided Shivan and Valdria a small gift to show their appreciation for letting them come.

I thought it was a kind gesture and noticed a bright smile on Valdria's face when she bid them farewell.

As the sky started to darken the remaining students said their goodbyes and thanked each member for their help. We all finally had a chance to sit and let our minds relax, I could have probably fallen asleep after this.

When Valdria stepped outside and asked if we were almost done I nodded, "The last students just left."

"Is curry okay?" Which made sense as it is the easiest to make in large quantities.

Everyone excitedly approved, while Kaoru, Kiho and Remi asked, "Can we still help?" Valdria smiled and opened the door so they could enter.

"Of course, I enjoyed making it with you last time." Valdria said. I think Ani was glad she wasn't in the kitchen making dinner for so many people since her face relaxed when the three volunteered to help.

I began setting chairs in the racks Kazu provided. Lev, Ani and Tia did the same. Soon all the members had the place like new, "Let's take a couple chairs and go inside." I offered.

We all moved inside and were at last able to sit and relax as we appreciated the smell of curry wafting from the kitchen.

Once dinner was done Ani and Tia cleaned the kitchen as Valdria and Shivan enjoyed a break before heading to bed.

About halfway through dinner Talinde and Jes came home and settled into a couple chairs at the table as they began chatting with Shivan.

Jes discussed a few ideas regarding technology he wished Japan had. I overheard their conversation from the lounge area, so I hoped the others didn't pay much attention.

As we all sat around the reception area the groups were split between the guys and girls. I thought it would be a good opportunity to hear what they guys in our class usually did on their days off. It turned out to be not much more than school, club and games when they got home, "What about reading?" I asked.

A couple of the guys who had been friends since grade school smiled, "We read as well, but you can't bring those books to school."

I was curious about what they meant, "What kind of books can't you bring to school?"

The guys all exchanged knowing glances and the two smiled, "Want us to show you?" I looked over at Lev and he shrugged.

"Sure, did you bring them with you?"

The two grinned, "Let's go." They said as they jumped up.

Lev and I followed Tashiro and Josuke along with the remaining boys to the guest room they would use tonight. Tashiro and Josuke were settled in the far-right room so I waited as they grabbed their books.

When they came back out they had what looked like two magazines, "Let's go in your room so the girls don't come up and see." Tashiro suggested.

"Sure." I replied.

Lev and the other six followed me into my room. Once I closed the door Tashiro and Josuke both held up a magazine with well-developed girls on the covers wearing very little clothing. I pulled my desk chair out to face the others sitting on the edge of my bed as they began flipping through the magazines.

Lev was located on the far side of them toward the head of my bed, when Josuke showed him I could see his face brighten to a light crimson.

This was building my interest since I had not seen a magazine in the library like this.

As Tashiro was about to pass the magazine to me to look through, my door burst open.

Ani stood looming in the doorway, her face was bright red. She stomped into the room and grabbed the magazine out of Tashiro's hands before he could pass it.

Ani took the magazine and opened it right to the center page. I have no idea what she saw but she looked like steam was about to come out of her ears, I couldn't tell if she was mad or embarrassed.

She approached Josuke and held out her hand as he tried to look elsewhere. She grunted as she wiggled her fingers of her outstretched hand until he removed the magazine from behind his back. She yanked it out of his hand as she quickly turned and exited the room. Before she closed the door, I could see Tia's face along with the other girls all wide eyed at Ani's actions.

I looked over to Lev who rolled his eyes, "What was it?"

Lev just smiled and shrugged, "I think it's best not to ask."

"Sorry guys, I wish we could have shared more. Don't hold it against her she's just a bit touchy sometimes."

Tashiro worriedly looked at me, "Will she give them back?"

"Want me to check?"

"Ahh, no that's okay." He said reluctantly, "Would you really have asked her if I had said yes?"

"Why not, they aren't her magazines, right?"

"Trist, you aren't afraid of her?" One of the other boys asked.

"Why would I be?" I asked wondering why they sounded so surprised.

Junichi shivered a bit, "I guess since you live with her you don't know. Every one of the first years are scared to death of Ani and Tia."

I looked at Lev then the other guys, "Seriously? Why?"

Josuke sighed, "You're the only one she's nice too, around you she's all smiles."

"Well sometimes she can be overly serious but even Tia?"

Eichi spoke this time, "Tia looks sweet and innocent until you talk to her. When she talks to the other boys she does so with almost no emotion on her face as if she only responds out of obligation."

Lev was almost laughing at the perplexed expression on my face, "Give it up guys, Trist only gets to see the sweet side of those two."

"I have a hard time imagining them any other way, I mean even when I tease them or when I wake them up they usually look so innocent and kind."

"Wait a minute, you wake them up?" Josuke asked almost fearful of the response.

"Well not always, but when they slept with me they seemed so gentle, even if it took me a while to wake them up." I thought of the ways Ani could have overpowered me but didn't, "I know Ani is strong, but she never shows me that side, unless we are training."

Everyone except Lev was staring at me like I had turned into a demon. I couldn't understand their reactions, I mean Ani and Tia always showed me nothing but their tenderest sides.

Josuke began to laugh with hesitation, "Ha-ha, come on Trist, you are a great club leader, but you make a horrible liar."

"Want me to show you?" I figured if I showed them their kind side they wouldn't be so defensive around Ani or Tia, "I will see if I can get your magazines back too. Then you'll know they aren't as scary as you make them out to be."

Lev had a big grin on his face, "This will be fun."

I stood up and headed back toward the guest rooms, since I didn't hear any noise I went downstairs. The girls were no longer in the lounge area, so I went down the hall toward Tia and Ani's room. I could hear chatter in the rooms, so I figured they were still awake. As I knocked on the door I heard Ani respond,

"Yes, what is it?" She slid her door opened and just sort of froze a second as the girls were hiding whatever they were looking at behind them.

I looked into the room for Tia as well, "Tia come here a second please." I asked. When Tia was standing next to Ani I gave them both a big hug and pulled them against me, so our cheeks almost touched. When I did this they both sort of went ridged. I could hear the girls almost squeal behind them.

As I slowly released them and they both stepped back a bit as I placed my hands on the sides of each of their cheeks, "Promise me you will smile more when I'm not around. The guys said people are afraid to approach you, okay?" I said in a kind voice, "Oh, don't forget to give Josuke and Tashiro the books you are looking at back."

Both nodded and stood in the doorway with strained expressions on their faces as if they were trying to hide something.

Before I closed their door, I asked, "Should the guys use the bathing room first or would you girls like to use it."

I saw the girls look at each other and heard someone say, "We'll go first!"

"Okay, I will turn on the heater for you." I gently closed their door.

As I walked past Tia's room I heard a burst of giggles, "...I'm so jealous..." and they talked about Ani's and Tia's bright red faces.

I turned the heater for the bath tub on and set the timer for one hour, that should keep the water warm enough for everyone to bathe.

As I climbed the stairs I heard the guys chatting, but their voices died down until they realized it was me.

Eichi glanced at me as I entered the room, "Well?"

I looked at all their faces wondering why they looked so anxious, "They will give you back your magazines tomorrow."

Josuke was incredulous, "No way! What did you say to them?"

"I just told them to smile more when I wasn't around and that the boys in the class were afraid of them." The blood drained from Junichi's face.

"When I told them…What's wrong now?" I asked.

The six echoed, "Were dead…"

Lev just sniggered, "Come on, it's not that bad. At least you don't have to live with them."

I looked at Lev, I never thought about it much. They were always there to support me, in fact I don't know how well I would have gotten along without them.

*   *   *

Ani couldn't believe they would show a book like that to Trist, how dare they. And Lev let them. I will have to talk to him tomorrow, I thought.

We all marched back down to the lounge area on the first floor, "Well, want to go to my room?" I finally asked, and the girls were all in agreement.

As we made our way to my room Tia quietly asked, "What are those books?"

I glanced down at the magazines I held in my hand, "They had pictures of girls in them, but I didn't see much."

As we all entered my room it was a little tight, so we pushed my bed against the wall, and all sat on cushions on the floor.

Chisa looked overly curious, "Well, are you going to check what they had?"

I dropped the two magazines on the floor in the middle of the group.

Tia looked down at the cover and made a pouty face, "Why would Trist look at something like this?"

"I don't think he did. I took them before he had a chance too."

Tia looked relieved, "He already has plenty of girls to look at, why does he need a magazine?"

Aiko was the first to open one of them, "Why not check what they thought was so interesting?" Anju smacked Aiko playfully.

Anju giggled, "You just want to know the type of girl he likes."

I noticed Tia look up at Anju's comment. I wanted to say something too, but I didn't want to flaunt our relationship with Trist among so many others who had openly expressed interest in him.

As we all thumbed through the pages it was a little shocking to see the models wearing so little for so many to see. That's when I heard the knock, "Yes, what is it?" I responded. I stood up and walked to the door as the girls looked through the magazine.

When I slid the door open it was Trist. Why! Why was he at my room now of all times!

Trist was looking into the room past me and I could hear rustling pages, "Tia come here a second please." Trist asked.

I could tell Tia was also surprised by his appearance.

Suddenly Trist put his arms around us and pulled us close.

I didn't know what to do, I fought the desire to hold him as well, I knew everyone was watching and I could hear them squeal behind me. I could feel the warmth of his body and the closeness of his face as he held us. Why was he always so gentle?

As he slowly released us he placed his hand to the side of my face and directed his brilliant green eyes my way and said, "Promise me you will smile more when I'm not around. The guys said people are afraid to approach you, okay?" His voice sounded full of concern for us.

Trist's eye brows lifted a bit, "Oh, don't forget to give Josuke and Tashiro the books you are looking at back."

I couldn't help but nod knowing I couldn't lie to him. I didn't know what else to do, I felt like I was still in shock.

Trist began to turn then paused as he faced us again, "Should the guys use the bathing room first or would you girls like to use it."

I could hear the girls behind me discussing it.

Aiko was the one to finally respond, "We'll go first!"

Trist nodded as he said, "Okay, I will turn the heater on for you." Then he gently closed the door.

I turned to Tia and she was still staring at the door where Trist had been standing, with a bright red face.

I could also feel the heat radiating from my body, I could only imagine what my face looked like.

As I poked Tia's cheek she turned and looked right at me as we both smiled.

"I'm so jealous you have him all to yourselves every night. Is he always like that?" The group asked.

When Tia and I turned around the girls burst out laughing, "You are both so red!" They all laughed. I wanted to bury my head under a pillow and scream. Why is he like this at the moments when I expect it the least?

Chisa took the magazines from under the pillows Tia and I had been sitting on and placed them on my desk, "So, tell us, what is Trist really like at home. Is he always as cool and calm as he is at school?"

Aiko, Anju and the others seemed to be staring intently at Tia and me.

I thought about the times he had shown excessive kindness when I was hurt or upset, and I know Tia felt the same since we sometimes talked about our encounters and even tried to plan opportunities to get closer.

Tia looked at me as if she didn't know what to say. As she glanced back at the girls Tia said, "He isn't cool or calm at home. He is diligent and always looking for ways to help his classmates. We don't have many chances to be with him but when he holds us I don't feel like anything else matters."

"Just lying next to him is like a dream, I know he doesn't see us as anything more than sisters, but we aren't." I said as I was lost in thought, not thinking about what I just vocalized.

The other girl's mouths had nearly dropped open as they watched me daydream exposing my experiences with Trist. I realized I said too much, but it was too late.

"Have you slept with him?" Kiho asked tentatively. All the girls were enthralled waiting for my response.

"We both have a couple times." Tia stated bluntly with a big smile.

The girls looked between Tia and me, "At the same time?" Several asked at once.

I thought their question was a little odd, "What do you mean? We were asleep in the same bed, but nothing happened if that's what you're wondering." The girls sighed in what sounded like relief.

Tia shot me a pouting look, "You could have let them think he was taken at least."

"Well, Trist said he was heating the bath tub, it might be tight for all of us but want to go?"

Cheers arose as they got up to gather their belongings from upstairs.

* * *

It was a few minutes before I heard the girls come up the stairs.

The guys continued to talk about manga, games and the next big movie coming out they wanted to see, "What will you and Lev be doing for summer break Trist?"

I looked over at Lev who was reading a manga that one of the guys had in his bag as I answered their question, "Well, we wanted to go to the beach a couple of times with the club but other than that we don't really have any plans."

"Yea, my parents are going to Australia for work and I have to go, so I will be gone most of the summer." Eichi said.

"Want me to help you with your English before you go?"

Eichi just laughed, "No, that's okay. My dad speaks English fairly well because of his job."

"If you change your mind let me know."

After about an hour I heard a soft knock on the door and Tia announced the bath was open, "Well, shall we head down?"

They all agreed, as they gathered their belongings I went downstairs and pulled out enough towels for everyone and placed them inside the changing room.

When the guys entered they immediately began changing out of their clothes and headed into the bathing room. After we all washed and settled into the tub I could feel the heat begin to seep into my body, "This is the first time I've actually used this tub, it feels pretty nice."

Lev looked like he was going to fall asleep and the others were astonished we hadn't used the tub yet, but for now we all just enjoyed the warmth.

Term Exams

Monday afternoon everyone left, Ani handed back the magazines to Josuke and Tashiro with a look that expressed her displeasure. The guys chatted with Lev and I more than they had previously. It looked like Ani and Tia had somewhat bonded with the other female members of the club too.

When I headed up to my room after sorting out he rooms and making sure futons were up I stretched out on my bed still a little tired. We were up extremely late chatting about everything the guys wanted to do while in middle school. When they finally asked me what I would really like to do I couldn't help but say, "I'd like to see my family."

The other guys were positive that I could make it happen by the end of our third year. I could feel Lev, give me an apologetic look, "I doubt that will happen, they're very far away."

I heard a faint knock on the door, "Yes." I said quietly as I continued to look at the ceiling.

I heard the door open, but no one said anything until I caught sight of Ani and Tia out of the corner of my vision, "Did you guys finish up."

Tia could tell I was in a reminiscent mood, they probably could feel it since I didn't really have full control over my emotions just then. Tia slowly walked around to the far side of my bed and sat on the edge while Ani sat on the other side.

They both remained silent, but I didn't press the issue. Ani turned and laid beside me on my arm and hugged me, Tia shortly followed her example.

They asked, "What's wrong Trist?" In faint voices that tickled my ears when they were so close.

I gave them both a sidelong glance and could tell they were sincerely concerned, "We just stayed up late and talked, it made me think about unpleasant memories."

I heard a faint I'm sorry from both of them. They snuggled in close with their legs slightly bent resting on mine. Ani whispered, "You can't do what you did last night. People will start to talk."

I thought about what I could have done wrong, "Oh, the hug. I won't apologize. If I can't show concern for those I hold dear, then there is no need for me to even be here."

I heard Tia say with a rough but quiet voice, "Don't say that, we just want what's best for you." I could feel a warm sensation on my arm.

I looked over to Tia who had tears quietly slipping down her cheeks, "We are supposed to support you, not the other way around." She faintly mumbled in a rough voice. I could tell Ani was fighting back her own emotions because her face was scrunched like it got before she cried.

I pulled their faces close with my arms and gently kissed each on the cheek, "I am so glad to have you both supporting me." Then I gave them both a little smile as they quietly laid there until they fell asleep.

After what seemed like a couple hours had passed based on the filtered light coming through my window I figured it was time we got up to see if we could accomplish anything today. I turned toward Tia who was quietly breathing in irregular faint breaths. Ani however was still next to me, but her eyes were wide open watching me as I turned to face her.

I turned my neck to the side as she tightened her grasp around me and slightly lifted her head as she briefly placed her lips mine. She then released her arm as she turned and sat up swinging her legs over the side of the bed as she stood up.

As she was leaving the room, "You probably should wake Tia." She turned before she exited the room, she had an extremely childish grin on her face.

I was not sure why she did what she did, but I didn't feel embarrassed about it. That was the first time someone had ever kissed me even though it was somewhat awkward. I lightly wiped my forefinger across my lips testing to see if the sensation was real. Ani was such a tease sometimes.

As Tia continued to silently sleep I turned to my side and placed my free arm around her. She was still sleeping, so I jostled her a little when I turned. I had my arm draped over her side and placed my palm on her back as I gently hugged her close.

This caused Tia to stir and she lightly hugged me back. Her face had a slight smile as she slowly opened her eyes and saw my face directly before hers, "Tia we should probably get up soon, it is getting late."

Tia nodded as she sleepily looked into my eyes and offered an even bigger smile. Tia gently reached her face closer to mine and gently kissed me at the edge of my mouth. When she pulled back Tia said, "You know we both love you Trist. Even though I am younger than Ani I care for you just as much."

I hadn't really expected her to say that. I also cared deeply for them, but I wasn't sure if our feeling were the same, regardless I always tried to express my feelings openly like my parents would openly show theirs to Emeri and I. I smiled and gently leaned toward Tia. Her face tilted slightly up as I gently kissed her cheek, "I care deeply for you both as well. But for now, we should get up, I can hear Ani behind us."

Tia lifter her head and saw Ani standing in the door with her pillow grasped in her arms staring at both of us with a jealous expression on her face.

"Tia, you need to get up, that wasn't the plan." Ani paused with a somewhat shocked expression on her face. As she began to blush and quickly headed back down the stairs.

Tia just smiled as she turned to sit up as she leaned forward, I guess I needed to get them back since Ani's comments told me they were plotting something.

As Tia stood I reached out and placed both hands on her sides and began to tickle her. She screamed slightly as she squirmed and almost fell to the floor, but I was quick enough to pull her fall toward the bed, "Alright Tia, what did Ani mean?" As I wiggled my fingers along her side.

Tia was openly giggling, and the atmosphere instantly changed to a playful engagement. She continued to squirm trying to get away, as she gasped for breath between giggles she got out brokenly, "Trist, stop…I…need to go." I intensified the tickling for a few seconds as she renewed her squirming around on the bed and me. I stopped and slid my arms around her back and pulled her close as I looked into her face that was wet with tears of laughter.

"Tia, you don't need to do things to cheer me up, I was only reminiscing, but thank you." I said as I placed my right hand on the back of her head and pulled her to my shoulder. I could feel her arms slip around my sides as she hugged me back, "You see you can hug back." I said as I released her and gave her a smile.

Tia pulled back as she realized she had given away more than she wanted, "Trist, you can be a real meanie sometimes." She said though I could tell she didn't mean it.

That evening it cooled off and I was able to get to sleep early, I had asked Lev, Ani and Tia if they wanted to go over anything, but they seemed confident the test was covered.

We all left the house Tuesday morning around 07:00 so we would have time to review any last-minute questions by the class.

Once homeroom started Murakami covered the exam schedule and began the first test. This continued after lunch up until the final bell. During each test I felt less tension in the class than I had during the midterms. I also noticed how the questions aligned with my expectations of high points of interest. I should ask Haruka how her exam went next time I saw her.

As Murakami collected the remaining exams he told us to head home safely and quickly departed the room. The exams should be posted by Thursday giving us an easy day and then Friday we would be assigned our summer homework. With the end of term assembly, it should be smooth sailing into summer.

As the students began to pack up many stopped by and thanked us for the study group, all agreed that it was much easier than they expected.

Aiko volunteered to drop the class journal off since she wanted to head home early.

I guess she had family friends visiting for the summer from Okinawa. So being freed up from regular duties I accompanied Lev, Ani and Tia with the rest of our members to our club room. The topic today wasn't studying but what we would do for the homework. Since this was our first summer break in this school none of us were sure what would be assigned.

We all agreed to set a date on Friday once the assignment was passed out and we could propose meeting times through Line.

Everyone wanted to make sure our work was done before our first trip to the beach, "Well we want to have a chance to see each other over the summer." Chisa said as she looked at me.

Ani and Tia both seemed to have goofy grins when we started talking about going to the beach, "What are you guys thinking about?" I asked.

"Oh, nothing much…" Ani immediately called to Kaoru brushing my question aside. Ani and Tia walked to Kaoru who was about ready to head out with Kiho and Remi. They were talking excitedly, and I could tell that our overnight adventure had helped them warm up to other members of the class.

"Trist were going to head out with Kaoru now, I already sent a message to father." Tia and Ani looked back smiling as they left the club with Kaoru and her friends.

"Okay..." I said but they were already out the door. I looked over at Lev, "What was that all about?"

Lev shrugged, "No clue but they seemed excited, it probably will cause you problems later." He said with a straight face, as I sighed.

"Well let's go. Anything you want to do before we head home? We have extra time now."

With Ani and Tia gone Lev and I garnered more looks than usual. I tried not to pay much attention to it, but Lev finally brought up the topic, "Aren't there a lot more girls following us than normal?"

"What do you mean?" I asked as I turned around and saw several students from other classes following behind.

As we were waiting for the bus, Misaki the girl from 1-C asked us a question, "Aren't you going home with Ani and Tia today?"

"No, we finally ditched that old bag." Lev said playfully.

Misaki's eyes widened, "Are you two going out?" Misaki asked me.

"Who? Me?" I asked not sure what she meant.

"Um yea. You and Ani?" She looked down a bit almost as if she was embarrassed about her question.

"Ahh, no. But she is one of my best friends."

Misaki looked up a little, "Tia as well?" She tentatively asked.

"The same, I would do anything for them, but we aren't dating or anything."

Lev cleared his throat since several other girls were listening in on our conversation.

I looked at Lev who had a unique expression on his face, "Let's go Trist." As he tried to pull me away from the conversation.

"The bus isn't here yet."

"I changed my mind there's a place I want to check out." As Lev tugged on my arm.

There was a flurry of chatting amongst the girls, "Do you mind if we go with you?" A few of them asked.

Lev just heaved a sigh as he stopped pulling. I looked at him and his face seemed to say he was resigned to his fate. I glanced at Misaki, "Sure why not."

She beamed a smile and introduced her friends, "This is Maiya and Akko they are from 1-A, these two are Erisa and Tomoki from my class." They all bowed when Misaki finished their introductions.

I returned their bow, "It's a pleasure to meet you all."

Lev just grunted, "Nice to meet you."

I looked at Lev, "So, where did you want to go?" I asked with five pairs of new eyes trained on him.

Lev sighed, "Well let's go to the mall, it's not too far. We can look at swimming trunks for the summer."

The girls seemed to get excited, "Are you guys going to the beach this summer?"

"We promised our club that we would do a couple summer events for missing Sea Day last week. So probably the beginning and toward the end of break."

Lev noticed Misaki watching me intently, as she walked right next to me, "It's their own fault." Lev said quietly.

I looked over to Lev as he spoke, "Whose fault?"

"No one's don't worry about it." Lev said as he forced a grin.

We made our way through several blocks pausing occasionally to look closer at some of the shops we hadn't walked by yet. As we approached the mall I thought I saw Remi walking in the far door.

Misaki was fidgeting with her bag sling, "Um Trist, would you mind if we looked at swimsuits as well? It would be helpful to have the opinion of someone trustworthy. The other boys are only interested in chest size so it's embarrassing to pick a suit and not know what others will think."

I looked at Lev, "Will we have time?"

Lev looked away as he rolled his eyes and said in a strained voice, "Probably."

Lev was acting strange, but I wasn't sure why he was so disinterested since he was the one who suggested this, "Okay." I said as I looked at Lev, then turned to the other girls who looked eager for a response, "It should be fine, I won't mind helping."

As we all headed into the mall I saw Lev whispering something to himself, but I couldn't tell what or even feel a strong sense of his feelings just an overpowering sense of dread.

* * *

When we entered the mall, I could tell there were many students from different schools here. We all paused at the map noting the different shops on this floor, the third floor looked to be seasonal accessories, Misaki pointed the location out, "This is usually where they are."

As we made our way to the escalator Tomoki asked, "Are you going to do the study group again next term?" She asked expectantly.

I nodded, "Yup, you're all welcome, though I will focus on my class the most."

Maiya had a curious question, "Misaki told us about the last two study groups you had, did you really take all the participants to your house?"

"Yea, but the regular members actually spent the night afterwards. Sort of a team building event."

Erisa sighed, "I wish I had known ahead of time."

When we arrived on the second floor we walked around the other side to catch the final escalator up. When we cleared the landing, there was a few mannequins in swimsuits and summer beach accessories off to the right.

The girls headed toward the girl's section while Lev and I headed to look at the selection of boys swimming trunks.

This is an item Kazu hadn't included in our initial wardrobe. Most of which we will probably have to replace soon, my pants and shirts seemed to be shrinking and even my uniform was starting to feel tight.

Lev quickly found a pair of trunks with a wave pattern to them and looked for different sizes of the same pattern.

I settled for a pair of longer trunks with a sea green color. Since I hadn't paid much attention to sizes before I tried holding them up to my waist to gauge if they would fit.

After a few minutes a store attendant in a neat dark blue uniform arrived and directed us to the changing rooms if we wanted to verify the fit. Both Lev and I accepted her offer.

As I entered the first changing stall and pulled the curtain I noticed a small bench and a place to hang a coat. I quickly slipped off my slacks and tried several different sizes until I found one that was comfortable. I set my choice aside and dressed and made my way out with the trunks that didn't fit. I noticed a place designated for return clothing, so I folded them and placed them with the other items sitting already.

Lev came out shortly after me, the trunks he chose were shorter, while the ones I chose almost reached my knees.

As we held our belongings Misaki came over, "Are you guys ready? I think we all have something picked out now."

"I'm ready. Lev?" I asked as he just nodded and followed me toward the girl's swimsuit section.

When he arrived with Misaki in the lead she excused herself for a changing booth. After about five minutes she quietly slipped out in a light blue two-piece swimsuit. She was holding a hand to her side and the other near her chest as she looked up at us and asked, "Well, what do you think?"

I looked at her swimsuit noticing it was very revealing, "I think it shows a lot of skin, will that be okay?"

Lev held his hand up to his forehead, "It looks fine to me."

Misaki looked a little disappointed at my comment, "What kind of swimsuit do you prefer Trist?"

"I have never been to the beach, just to go to the beach, so I can't say I really have a preference."

"Oh, well, so this will be your first time?" Misaki seemed a little more excited.

"Going for fun, yes."

"I have one more, give me a minute." Misaki disappeared back into the changing room.

As she was changing another one of the girls pulled me to the other side to look at their swimsuits. This side of the wall had several more changing rooms extending down the wall. When Erisa saw me, "Akko, Tomoki, Trist is here."

I heard someone say, "Trist!!" Which seemed to be echoed down a several changing stalls. I glanced down then back at the girls waiting. As they slowly slipped out of the changing room somewhat embarrassedly I looked at them in their swimsuits. I heard Lev quietly gasp behind me.

As I turned to see what was up I noticed Kaoru behind me, "Trist, what are you doing here!?"

"Oh, hello Kaoru, I thought you were with Ani and Tia."

The two girls who were waiting for my opinion were watching the conversation between Kaoru and me, "Trist, who is this?"

"These are friends from school, they participated in our club a few times."

After a few minutes Kiho and Remi also arrived, very surprised by my appearance.

As I watched them approach I asked, "Are you guys looking at swimsuits as well?"

"Ahh, no, we were helping…" Remi backhanded Kaoru on the shoulder as she was talking. They began whispering together so I looked back to Akko and Tomoki.

As I turned back to Akko and Tomoki I noticed their swimsuits were blue and white stripes and a darker navy blue two piece but for some reason they just didn't seem like a perfect fit, "Those are nice, did you have other choices?"

"Trist, sorry but we need to go." Kaoru said as the three moved down to the far changing stalls. I saw Remi poke her head in the curtains of a distant stall.

"WHAT!!" A somewhat familiar voice screeched.

About that time, I saw a girl in a dark red two-piece swimsuit exit her changing room and grab Remi's shoulders. The new girl wore her swimsuit exceedingly well. She looked much more mature and shapelier than the two girls who just re-entered their changing rooms. She had long deep dark auburn hair and a slightly muscular build. After a few more seconds another figure emerged from the stall next to the girl wearing a light blue one-piece swimsuit as she stood next to the girl with the auburn hair, she looked to be more petite and had a slightly girlish figure, but you could tell she was attractive and had long straight light brown hair.

I heard Lev sigh as he walked around to the other side when he noticed me looking their direction.

As I watched and waited I saw Remi point my direction as the girl slightly shook her shoulders. About the time the girl with the auburn hair started to turn I was heading back to Misaki who was calling my name. I began to walk back around the other side as Lev just sat on a bench with a gloomy look on his face.

"What's wrong? You have seemed out of sorts since you suggested walking home."

Lev looked up at me and was about to say something when his eye's widened as he looked past me. I followed his look. What I saw were the two girls with the red and pale blue swimsuits.

I looked at them from the ground up and had to admit they were very cute…wait a second, "Ani, Tia?" I asked as I finally realized who the girls were. I was so used to seeing them in school clothes that I didn't even recognize them in their current attire. Their figures looked entirely different in the swimsuits they had chosen. No longer did their school cloths hide their slightly muscular builds and well-toned bodies, they were still growing but they were both well on their way to being exceedingly beautiful.

Right as I realized who the girls I had been admiring were was when Misaki stepped out of the changing room in a light green one-piece swimsuit, "Trist, what do you think of this one?" She asked, then she noticed I was staring in a different direction. As she turned to follow my gaze she noticed Ani and Tia standing glaring at me. She slowly slipped back into the changing room.

I glanced between Ani and Tia, both were standing with fists at their side. It was hard to tell what Ani was thinking, so intent was her stare, while Tia moved her clenched fists near her chest.

The other girls finished changing and they all came around the corner followed by Kaoru, Remi and Kiho.

In slowly spaced words Ani asked, "What are you doing here?"

Why did Ani seem so mad I thought, "Lev wanted to look at swimsuits for our beach trip."

Lev just looked at the ceiling saying nothing.

I saw Ani's gaze shift from me to Lev and back, "Why were you here with these other girls?"

"They asked if they could go with us since they were also wanting to purchase swimsuits. They said they would like a guy's opinion."

Ani seemed to sigh, and her hands unclenched slightly. Tia was still clenching her hands near her chest as she glanced up at Ani and back to me. Her face looked like she could start crying.

"If you told me you were coming to look at swimsuits I would have loved to come since Lev and I both needed a suit as well. Why are you so angry?"

That was all Ani and Tia could take. I began to see Ani's lip quiver as she suddenly called me an idiot and turned and ran back around the corner followed closely by Tia who seemed to be wiping her face with her forearm.

The girls around me all seemed to sigh at my ignorance of the situation.

Lev stood up and grasped me by the shoulder, "We should go."

I looked to Misaki, "Are you five okay getting home by yourselves?"

"Um, yea. We will be fine. How about you Trist?"

"We should be fine." I looked to Kaoru, "Will you three be okay?"

She smiled a bit and sighed, "Trist sometimes you are just so…" Kaoru sighed again, "Yes, we'll be fine."

"Make sure they get home safely." I said to Kaoru as she nodded in response.

"We will." Kaoru turned to head back to the other changing rooms.

Lev and I made our purchases and walked toward home. Lev was quiet most of the way, so I wasn't sure what to say, "What did I do wrong?"

He just looked over at me as we walked then back forward. After a few minutes he said, "Why do you think Ani was mad?"

"Because we came with other girls?"

Lev sighed again, "Yea that is probably a big part of it."

"What is the rest of the problem then!?" I was starting to get frustrated.

"She probably didn't want you helping other girls choose swimsuits. Maybe it was the fact you were with other girl's period."

"How is that a problem? I am with other girls several times a day, it's not like this is the first time."

"It would be easier if she was just honest."

"About what?" I asked.

Lev just shook his head.

As he looked at me he said, "You need to ask Ani and Tia that, not me."

*　　*　　*

The next day Ani and Tia were gone for school before I knocked on their doors. I knocked on Lev's and he was almost ready. When he exited his room, he had dark circles under his eyes, "What happened, too much reading?"

Lev shook his head as he smiled slightly, "No, it was more like an inquisition." He said laughing.

"Ani?" I asked.

Lev just nodded, "Tia too. They both wanted to know how we ended up at the mall. Initially they were mad at me for not stopping you but after I explained they were madder at themselves for excluding you."

"I just want to know why it was such a big deal. Did I do anything reckless or place us in danger?"

"Nope, you were a perfect gentleman as always, one that your father would be proud of."

When we arrived at school and made our way to class I saw Kaoru who stopped me in the hall, "Well, did Ani and Tia talk to you at all last night?"

Lev raised his hand slightly, "No, they asked me!"

Kaoru shook her head, "Trist, you know every girl for the most part envies Ani and Tia, why do you think?".

"I can think of a number of possibilities."

"If they are because of their physical looks you would be mostly wrong. Of course, some envy their athletic talent and physiques but beyond that, it's you Trist."

"What's envious about me?"

Kaoru sighed, "Probably your cluelessness, you are a natural leader, look what you did for the class. I expect we will hold the top thirty spots when grades are posted tomorrow. You don't even recognize it yourself. I was even jealous for a while as well, until I saw how you looked at them differently than you looked at the rest of us."

Lev finally spoke, "But that's not entirely his fault. Sure, he is nice to everyone but that's just Trist. He spoils Ani and Tia, and they've come to expect it. So, when he is nice to others they feel like that threatens their position in your heart. I guess." Lev offered his insight into the situation.

Kaoru looked at Lev, "You are much more observant than I expected." As Kaoru offered Lev a sincere smile.

Kaoru turned back to me, "I would probably give them time to think about it. They need to come to accept it, better now than when you start a new year with even more new students or even high school with a whole different group."

I accepted her advice, while it hurt to have them distance themselves from me, if it helped, I could wait.

Class was uneventful for the most part, Ani and Tia stayed in their seats or talked with the students around them though they didn't look too excited. When school ended Lev walked up to my desk, "You ready?"

"Sure, let's go." Lev went with me to drop off the journal since Aiko was out for the day. As we made our way to the club room I noticed a few of the girls smiled at me when I glanced around the room. As they noticed me looking they just shook their heads. I understood their meaning.

We called club early since it was the end of the term, a few people were exchanging messages on Line listing the days they would be out of town with their families.

When Lev and I reached home Valdria was in the kitchen making dinner. I offered to help but she declined. Instead she asked me to have a seat, "Trist did something happen with Ani and Tia?"

I wasn't sure how to answer having heard so many different thoughts on the matter, "I guess they are upset with me." I told Valdria the entire story as she quietly listened and occasionally nodded and smiled.

"So, they have been avoiding me."

Valdria, poured a cup of tea for both of us, as Shivan walked into the dining room as well. Valdria called Shivan to sit next to her.

"Trist, Ani is older than you by a little more than a year, normally she is at an age where she is beginning to feel insecurities and experience chemical changes in her body. This process will take a few years before she fully matures mentally. The same has probably already started with Tia since her family attunement has been weakened over the years" Valdria paused as she glanced at Shivan wondering how much to say, "While you were naturally born to be a charismatic person like your father and grandfather you will also experience changes as time goes by if you aren't already."

"What should I do then, I feel a strong family bond with everyone here but even more so with Lev, Ani and Tia. I don't want any of them to suffer with insecurities, I want to be there for all of them."

Valdria showed a kind expression, "You are so much like your father. Just be yourself. That should be enough."

As I left contemplating Valdria's advice I headed for my room. I didn't really know how Valdria wanted me to be myself, but I knew I didn't like them being mad, so I should apologize to start for not meeting their expectations.

When I reached my room, I laid back on my bed and began slowing my breathing and tried to enter a calmed state as I pictured Ani and Tia. I willed all my feeling of remorse and regret over the last two days and sent with it the warmest feeling I could from my heart, and at the end I sent a few words, "I'm sorry I disappointed you."

Afterwards my head didn't ache as much as it usually did, but when I stood up to prepare for the next day I immediately got dizzy and nearly fell. I found my way to the bed and laid back down and fell asleep for the night.

The next day I prepared for school and wasn't sure if Ani and Tia had already left until I saw Valdria in the kitchen, "You're up early."

"It was a long night." Valdria looked at me, "You feel any better?"

"I feel a little better, but I am still worried about the girls."

"Well, they are staying home today."

"Why, what happened!?" I asked.

Valdria looked at me and smiled, "You tell me. You don't do things by small measures I can tell you that much."

I was a little concerned, neither of them had ever missed a day and now after everything that happened, to miss school?

Valdria could see my panicked face, "They are fine but whatever you did made a big impression."

I wanted to check in on them before I left but Valdria told me they had only been asleep an hour or so. Instead I quietly made my way to Lev's to find him snoring as well. I stepped into his room and gently shook him, "Hey, you going to school?"

Lev just opened his eyes a bit, "After all that noise last night? I'll pass." Was Lev's response.

I exited Lev's room and saw Valdria coming down the hall, "I guess he's staying too."

Valdria smiled, "That's fine, you can stay home if you like as well."

I thought about it a moment, "No, someone needs to represent the club and to check the grades and pick up homework. Best if I go." I said as Valdria agreed and thanked me as I left for school.

Summer Neighbor

As I arrived at school I noticed several students staring at me. I swung by the teacher's room to pick up the class journal and headed toward the main hall where the grades would be posted. As I approached I saw several students back away from the board as they saw me approach. One student who I remembered visiting our class once was standing in front of the ranking and glanced back as he noticed others moving away. He looked at me with a condescending look and walked off. I didn't think much of it as I looked at the rankings. I counted the number of perfect scores and checked their classes, it looked like we did well.

While I was looking at the scores Aiko walked up and checked her ranking, "Looks like it was successful."

I looked at her and smiled, "Yea but a few students were beat by this Yamato guy." As I pointed to the name.

"Ahh, that was the guy who stopped by class, remember? He is the top student in 1-A."

"He was just here but I didn't know his name."

Yamato was only four points from a perfect score, but a large percentage of our class was above that.

As Aiko and I walked to class she asked, "Where are Ani and Tia?"

"They didn't get much sleep last night, so they stayed home today."

"Are they okay?" Aiko asked with true concern in her voice.

"Yea, they just had to deal with me the last few days and it was too much."

Aiko smiled at my comment.

"Well as long as you understand that, things should be fine." Aiko said.

As class started Murakami took roll and noted Lev, Ani and Tia missing. Valdria had called so he just told the class they were out sick. When he began passing back tests he handed me the three for my missing companions. He congratulated the five perfect score earners and then congratulated the class for an average of 97%. He looked over the class and gave a short speech about his pride in our achievements and asked us to continue the great work next term. As he finished his eyes rested on me.

We continued lessons though we had several self-study classes which I decided to use for my homework that was assigned earlier in the day. When school released I was close to finished, I only had an essay on, "My ideal summer activities." Which I would hold onto for after our beach trip.

Making my way home I was forced to decline several invitations to hang out by different classmates, "No, I probably should head home and drop off the tests, it might make them feel better."

Everyone seemed to understand.

When I got home I slipped off my shoes and went to the kitchen, no one appeared to be out, so I sat the tests for Lev, Ani and Tia on the dining room table and made my way to my room.

I sat my bag on the chair and pulled my personal filament monitor out of my desk. I began researching history about my family and looked at some of the stories written about my grandfather. Why was so much of his personality mirrored in me. While I knew the reason sometimes it just seemed unfair.

I went down stairs later that evening and told Valdria I wasn't hungry, she looked at me a moment and said that's fine. I decided to go back upstairs and head to bed.

The next day, Ani and Tia were excused from class again. Valdria apologized so I drug Lev out the door with me. I was in a very depressed mood, I was happy Lev came but I hadn't gone this long without seeing or hearing Ani's and Tia's voices.

School let out shortly after we had our assembly, it was basically to remind us to be safe and adhere to the school dress code when in town but not much more. The club met for a brief time once we were released and discussed the next event, I told them to Line me their availability and we would figure a time that would work with the largest number of members.

While we walked home I decided to visit the convenience store near our house to get something cold to drink. As Lev and I approached home I noticed the grass seemed to need trimming and a couple of the shrubs were reaching toward the walkway. I thought I should ask Talinde if he wanted help this weekend cleaning things back up.

Lev and I parted once we entered the house and I clambered up to my room and sat in a half daze wondering how long things would remain this way. As I stood and glanced out the window I noticed two people walking up our driveway. One looked like Aiko but the other was older and obviously not Anju from her looks.

Aiko noticed me looking out my window and waved as the other girl glanced up.

I decided to head down and meet them at the door. When I opened it, Aiko was getting ready to press the door chime.

As I smiled she quickly introduced me to an attractive girl who looked to be a couple years older, "Trist this is Hazuki, she is the daughter of my father's brother. She is visiting this summer from Okinawa, she might be going to school with us next year."

Huh, I thought, "She's in the same grade as us?"

The girl before me had glistening long straight hair a little lighter in color than Aiko, bordering a dark brown, she had greenish hazel eyes, and was a little taller than me. She looked to be more mature than most of the girls in our current class.

I quickly bowed, "It's a pleasure to meet a relative of Aiko's she has done much to help me in school."

Hazuki smiled shyly, "The pleasure is mine. Aiko couldn't stop talking about you, so I asked her to introduce me, but I never would have guessed you were so close."

"She is actually in an advanced school near a navy base, so she was wondering if you spoke English. She gets teased sometimes for her height, so she has spent a lot of time studying instead of socializing. In a way she reminds me of you Trist."

I quickly though about the appropriate response in English and tried to mimic the pronunciation I had studied before we entered Japan, "I would be happy to study English with you. Feel free to call any time." I said in English.

Hazuki's was surprised, "Your pronunciation sounds as good as the Eikaiwa I studied at last summer." Her eyes were almost glowing.

Aiko also looked at me since this was the first time she had heard me speak a language other than Japanese, "I didn't know your fluency was that good Trist. I mean I knew you were good with grammar, but I never heard you speak."

Against my better judgement I offered short sentences in French, German, Italian, Hindi, Portuguese, Chinese, Korean and Russian. I can speak several languages but never had many opportunities to try.

Hazuki began speaking in French, "Have you ever had an opportunity to travel internationally?"

I wanted to limit her inquiry, so I offered a simple response without much detail in French, "Yes a little, but not since I was very young."

Hazuki looked enthralled with me.

"We're going into town, so I could show her a few places, would you like to go?"

I thought about how my mood had been and figured it wouldn't hurt to be outside for a bit since Ani and Tia were still avoiding me, "Sure, let me get my shoes."

We headed toward the convenience store for something to drink before going toward the train station. Apparently Hazuki was into long distance running in middle school in France where her parents lived for work. When her parents moved back to Okinawa she was held back a year since she couldn't pass the entrance exam for second-year.

"So, you're actually a year older?"

Hazuki looked a little self-conscious as she nodded.

I could tell she was uncomfortable with my question, "I'm sorry. I didn't mean to offend you. I hope you can come to our school next year." I offered her a smile.

Hazuki looked at me in awe, "Aiko, you never said he was like this." Hazuki said as she stared at me.

Aiko glanced at Hazuki and realized she had fallen for Trist and sighed. Trist wasn't helping the situation either, Aiko thought.

This was the first time I had found someone who I could practice my languages with, and she seemed smart when compared to many others at school. I hoped she had an opportunity to visit again throughout the summer.

While we walked around the mall Hazuki asked about the different locations and festivals. Aiko explained the major events which I found just as informative. After a couple hours we slowly made our way back to the house. As we said our goodbyes I saw Hazuki glance back a few times and waved as they walked down the driveway.

I entered the house and made my way up to my room. I felt a little better after being able to talk to Aiko and meeting her cousin. I hope she could transfer schools next year I really think she could be good friends with Ani and Tia.

I settled into my chair and pulled out a manga that Josuke left earlier that week. When I had gotten about halfway through the second story I heard a knock on the door, "Yes?" I said.

"You up Trist?" I heard Lev ask.

"Yea come on in."

"Where did you go?" Lev asked as he walked in and sat on the edge of my bed.

"Ahh, Aiko stopped by and she introduced me to her cousin from Okinawa. She seemed nice and about the same age as Ani. She might be going to our school next year."

Lev opened his eyes a little wider, "Sounds like she caught your attention. What kind of person is she?"

"Well, she is a little taller than me, has dark brown hair and greenish hazel eyes and a mature air about her. She is a year older I guess and likes to study, at least that is what it sounded like. She had issues fitting in at her last school when she returned from France where she used to live."

Lev seemed a little concerned, "Is she going to be visiting for a while?"

"I think so, since she is staying with Aiko we will probably see her again, she might even go with us to the beach."

Lev stood up, "Well then I probably should grab them."

"Huh? Grab who?"

Lev just smiled as he left my room.

I just continued to read until I heard Lev knock on my door again, "Yea, come in Lev."

Lev slid the door open as he stepped back and pushed Ani and Tia into the room. I set the manga I was reading down on the desk and glanced over at them as they both stepped into my room. Lev slid the door closed behind them and I could hear him depart down the stairs.

Ani looked very uncomfortable as she stood with her hands clasped behind her back, looking everywhere but at me. Tia on the other hand was holding onto the fabric of her pants, her eyes appeared slightly red. Not knowing what to say but also feeling relief in finally seeing them I asked, "I have wanted to talk with you."

It was an awkward meeting, from the look on both their faces it didn't seem like this would be an easy conversation to start. I figured the best way to ease the tension was to apologize, so I stood and faced them both. I noticed Ani glanced my way with red rims under her eyes. I bowed, "I'm so sorry I disappointed you both. I will try to treat you with more respect."

Ani's face began to loosen as tears started streaming down her face, Tia reached over to grasp onto Ani's sleeve as she began to openly sob as well.

I hadn't seen them like this since we returned from our first trip into Japan. It was extremely painful to watch as my heart felt like it was breaking knowing I was the source of these tears.

As I looked up to them Ani slipped to the floor as she openly cried and mumbled incoherently. As my heart ached I forced myself to be as strong as I could and walked to them both and knelt in front of them at the entry of my room. I gently placed my arms around them and squeezed them unable to hold back my own tears as I said, "I'm sorry." Not knowing what else to say.

This sent them into even strong fits of weeping as they both threw their arms around me and fell against me.

Between broken gasps for air I heard, "No!..." They leaned into me even more and I felt myself being pushed back, "…it's…our fault…"

I couldn't really make out their remaining words so broken were their sentences.

As I continued to hold them I felt my self-beginning to reach a point where I could no longer keep my emotions in check.

Tia mumbled, "We were just afraid you were going to leave us…" As Tia gasped for breath and buried her face into my shirt. "…we were so ashamed we acted the way we did, we love you Trist. Please don't leave us alone again."

Ani finally looked up to my face and saw tears streaking my own face, her face suddenly scrunched up as she seemed to cry even harder, "I'm so sorry."

As she buried her face I could feel her grasping my shirt and forcing her face into my chest to muffle her sobs. I did everything I could to just try to comfort them knowing they had been blaming themselves while I thought it was my actions that caused them this grief.

"I stroked their heads and backs as they continued to cry, "I will make things clearer next time." I said hoping it would calm them a little.

Tia began crying even harder, "No, we want you to stay the same don't change…" Tia rubbed her face against me before she looked up with puffy cheeks and swollen eyes, "We love you the way you are, don't ever change."

As she gasped several times trying to fight off the tears that seemed to never end.

Ani and Tia continued to hold onto me tightly for the next couple hours while their sobbing subsided I could feel them gasp occasionally as they quietly cried. I just laid against the floor holding them both and trying to reassure them that I wasn't going anywhere.

While I held them, I thought about the situation. I asked myself what would I do if someday they fell in love, and sought another to share their fear, affection, happiness and worries with.

How would I feel at that time? I began mulling over unpleasant thoughts the longer I lay there and promised myself I would support them with whatever decision they chose, I silently hoped that day would never come though. I could feel the emotion generated by these thoughts squeezing my heart as I in turn squeezed both Ani and Tia tight.

As they slowly calmed so did the fears lying in my heart, Tia pulled herself closer to my shoulder and nestled into the space between my arm and chest as she lightly lay her hand on my chest and rested her head on my shoulder.

Ani was still laying with her head buried in my side but finally turned her head a little to the side. I carefully stroked Ani's head as I ran my fingers through her hair.

While I softly held Tia by the waist as she nestled against me.

It was approaching midnight when they finally began to wipe the residue left from their tears. I knew they should get a good night's rest, so they could recover from the emotions and stress that had been building over the last several days.

"Should I carry you both down stairs." I asked, not sure if either one was still awake. My inquiry was met with their shaking heads, "Well, we probably should go to bed sometime soon." I said quietly.

Ani slowly began to sit up into a kneeling position before she stood, Tia also began to stand.

This allowed me to sit up as well, as I was preparing to stand they both extended their hands to help me up.

Their faces had red swollen eye's and marks along their cheeks from leaning against me so long. As they pulled me up they both hugged me and asked, "Can we stay with you tonight?"

I looked at each of them and leaned toward them and kissed their foreheads, "It won't be as comfortable as your own room." I said.

The look in their eyes still seemed like they feared being left behind.

"We don't care." They both quietly responded slightly out of sync.

I released them from the hug to prepare my bed, then I pulled my top comforter back. Once this was complete I slipped off my slippers and sat on the edge of the bed, "Okay, but just tonight."

They both walked over to opposite sides of the bed as they removed their slippers and sat on the edge of the bed and waited for me to lay down.

As I laid back, Ani and Tia both gently crawled under the covers and nestled against my sides. Luckily, they placed pillows over my arms as they almost instantly fell asleep.

As I looked down at their faces. I could see the tension beginning to ease as their breathing became slightly off rhythm, "I love you two as well, I hope you know that." I said to no one in particular. I also began to relax from the tension I hadn't known I carried.

*   *   *

The next morning came very quickly. Not being able to move much I slept somewhat fitfully but I still felt rested. As I looked over at Ani and Tia they appeared not to have moved much. I felt Ani's leg resting over my thigh and Tia's hand was stretched across my waist. I sighed a bit as I had to go to the toilet but didn't know how best to escape their embraces.

I didn't want to awaken them if possible, but I wasn't seeing an easy way around it. I wonder if I could slip my arms out. Luckily, they slid gently out from under the back of the pillows. I was able to lean forward enough and gently rested Ani and Tia's heads back on the pillows, I repositioned their arms and legs, so I could stand up. I kept thinking if I was just light enough I could hop off the bed and they wouldn't even hear or feel me land.

I tried to jump over Ani without pushing off too roughly with my feet and I seemed to almost float over her and land on the ground.

Okay, that was a little strange, I thought. I looked back at the two of them sleeping and thought that should have made the bed bounce a decent amount. I need to figure out what I just did. But first the bathroom!

After I had used the toilet and washed my hands and face I returned to my room and thought I should try an experiment. I focused on Ani and imagined her as light as a feather then tried to scoot her over. Surprisingly she slid with almost no effort. Now I wasn't so sure I had imagined it last time.

As Ani slid toward Tia they were now facing each other laying extremely close so I tried to position Tia and Ani more comfortably on the bed before I climbed back in. This time I was on the edge with Ani in the middle.

I gently climbed back in and lay on my side with the space I had available and eventually fell back asleep.

* * *

Ani saw filtered light coming through the window. Normally my room stayed darker until later in the day, she thought. Oh, that's right, we're in Trist's room.

As I laid in bed reminiscing about last night and how foolish we had been in not apologizing first. Trist who wasn't the one at fault, had just been his normal kind and caring self.

As I was lying with closed eyes listening to Trist's gentle breathing next to me. I could feel him turn toward my direction as he placed his arm gently around my waist. Slowly he snuggled up against me, so I continued to stay still and just enjoyed the contact.

His body felt softer and his hand seemed to gently conform to the curves of my body.

He slowly began moving his hand up the side of my ribs until his arm was resting below my chest. This situation was a little awkward but not totally uncomfortable. However, when he began pulling his hand across my chest I began to get a little nervous.

His touch was extremely delicate though like the times he would gently caresses me on the cheek. As he placed his left leg over mine and pulled himself closer and began slightly rubbing my chest over my clothing. I couldn't contain my embarrassment any longer and I pushed back as I opened my eyes.

There was something blocking my retreat, so I pushed harder and heard something land on the floor, "What was that for." I heard Trist say.

Trist! Then who was holding me? As I pulled the covers down from my groper I noticed Tia, "Tia, you pervert!"

Tia's eyes opened slightly as she glanced up sleepily at me.

"What?" Tia lazily said. As she glanced at me I began feeling a little embarrassed that my heart had been racing when I thought it was Trist.

* * *

Tia felt someone gently re-position her then Trist moved closer but turned on his back. I didn't want to get up yet and wanted to continue feeling the warmth he emitted. I turned back to my right side and placed my arm back across Trist's waist.

I wish I could sleep this comfortably, but time was unfair and passed so quickly when we had the opportunity to cuddle. I slowly moved my hand up Trist's side feeling the transition from his waist to his ribs. I thought he seemed a little thinner than he felt last night.

I decided to move closer and placed my leg over Trist's as I scooted in to enjoy his feel. Something wasn't right though. Trist was awful smooth, and he didn't feel as muscular.

I began to notice his chest was also a lot bigger and softer than I remember it being. As I slid my hand gently over Trist's chest I noticed something was wrong I tried to figure it out while I was still half asleep.

Trist suddenly began to pull away and then I heard a thump, "What was that for." I heard Trist say.

Shortly after that the covers were pulled off my head and a slight chill crept in. As I began to open my eyes I heard Ani shout, "Tia you pervert!"

As I opened my eyes a little more as I asked, "What?"

As I looked over at Ani I realized why Trist had felt so different and my face began to feel a little warm from embarrassment.

* * *

I stood up and realized Ani had accidentally pushed me off the bed, "Are you guys up now?"

Ani twisted around quickly to see me standing behind her as Tia looked up from where she was lying, "Why are your faces red?" I asked inquisitively.

* * *

Later that morning when I entered the dining area I saw Shivan drinking tea as he worked on a white paper, "Shivan can I ask a question?" I asked quietly.

Shivan looked up from his work and sat his notes and pen aside, "Sure Trist. What can I help with?"

I wasn't sure how to ask I figured I would use an example, "Has there been any Emperors who have had the ability to reduce weight of objects?"

Shivan looked at me a little puzzled, "As in their aspects?"

I nodded, "I always attributed it to our training but now I'm not too sure. Yesterday when I was jumping I thought I needed to be as light as I could to avoid a loud landing and when I jumped it was like I was weightless."

Shivan now pushed himself away from the table, "Can you show me what you did?"

I looked around the room and thought about what would make a good example, so I placed my thumb and forefinger on the edge of the table as I focused then pinched and tried lifting up.

The table resisted a moment then lifted clear of the floor a few inches. I then sat it gently back down.

Shivan looked intently at the table and tested its weight himself as he thought, "I will have to ask Valdria, her knowledge of past Emperors and their aspects is much more extensive than mine. For now, try not to use that outside of this house unless it is a dire emergency."

I nodded and promised I wouldn't use it unless I had too.

"Trist, considering your heritage there are likely many aspects that could manifest within you. I'm glad you let me know as soon as you realized it. I will think of exercises we can do to help you strengthen and refine your control once we look into the history of similar abilities."

After I talked to Shivan I checked on Lev, I wanted to thank him for helping with Ani and Tia. I made my way down the hall toward Lev's room but before I knocked I noticed him lightly snoring.

I gently slid his door opened and peered into his room which was now fully lit from the early morning sun, "Hey Lev, how long are you going to sleep?"

I heard his snoring stop and he slowly opened his eyes. He waved his arm slightly at me as it hung off the side of his bed to beckon me inside. I entered and shut the door, as he slowly turned from laying on his stomach to his back.

"Well, how did it go last night. Did you guys make up?" Lev asked sleepily.

I smiled, "Yes but it was a little emotional for all of us. They stayed in my room for the night, but Ani just pushed me out of bed a little while ago."

Lev stretched his arms straight out as he arched his back, "Good, I feel better when you guys are close. I didn't like the disjointed feeling after we went to the mall." Lev glanced over at me once he stretched as if he just remembered something, "Oh, did you mention the girl with Aiko yesterday?"

"There was never a chance to have a long conversation last night." I thought about it a moment, "I can tell them today, we all need to figure out the beach trip, so we can set a date."

Lev grinned, "Yea that's right. Wake me up when lunch is ready." Lev said as he turned to his left side he laid back down facing his window.

Lev was impossible, couldn't he tell it was getting close to noon already. I exited his room. I would tell him about the homework when everyone was awake for the day. I walked back to the dining area and Shivan was now talking to Talinde who was eating a pastry and drinking black coffee.

I had tried the coffee once, but the bitterness was a little more than I liked, green tea was okay even if it was steeped a little long, but coffee had an extremely bitter aftertaste.

"Talinde, are you working outside today or do you have other plans?" I asked.

He looked at me as he slowly chewed a bite of the cheese roll he had. As he chewed he mentally searched his daily schedule, "Jes and I are heading to an electronics store. We need to see if we could patch together some of their existing circuitry to conduct some of the same processes our scanner uses for higher frequency waves." He didn't look enthusiastic, "I am skeptical though, it might be a monstrosity to replicate a single filament circuit with what we have to work with."

I sighed, "Okay, while your gone what can I work on outside? I noticed some of the shrubs have really grown since the last time."

Talinde's eyes opened wider as he smiled a bit, "That actually sounds more fun than what I have planned. Well, you can rake and trim the small shrubs like I did last time. Do you think you can do that?"

I nodded.

"Good, you can put the trimmings in the pile on the far side of the incinerator out back."

"Okay, thanks." I smiled at Talinde as I made my way past Shivan to the back doors and into the garden area.

As I collected the rake and other tools I thought I might need, I made my way around the front of the house. This is where the overgrowth was most noticeable, so I decided to start here.

I started at the end of the driveway. I trimmed the bushes with longer shoots protruding from their meticulously tended shape. As I worked my way to the perimeter shrubs I would pull the weeds accumulating near their base as I went, I was thankful for the gloves..

I had several small piles of weeds and trimmings along the walkway. I started working my way around the left side of the house when I heard a voice calling out to me. I turned and saw Aiko and Hazuki peering around the side of the house.

"We thought that was you. Can we come over?"

"Sure, just be careful, some of the plants have thorns." I cautioned.

They made their way down the walkway toward my current working area. They were wearing sandals, and cute looking light shorts with matching blouses. It looked like Hazuki preferred blue to Aiko's beige.

"Can we help?" Hazuki finally asked, after she had told me about their plans for the day.

I looked up at them, "No, I should be okay. Plus, you already said you had plans. I wouldn't want to get your wonderful outfits dirty." That brought a smile to both their faces.

They stayed a few more minutes and Hazuki watched as I meticulously trimmed each bush with care making sure no loose branches distracted from the artistic design they had been molded into, "Do you enjoy gardening Trist?" Hazuki asked.

I looked up after I finished trimming my current project, "I don't love it, then again I don't dislike it either."

I looked back over what I had accomplished so far, "I guess I do enjoy having a garden. Looking out over it from my window or being able to walk down a path with meticulously trimmed plants is enjoyable." I looked to Aiko and Hazuki as I smiled and shrugged, "Something like that."

Aiko nodded, knowing how I felt, having had the chance to visit and study here previously she always felt the garden was well maintained, "I can see a lot of your patience in this garden Trist."

Hazuki just watched me as she nodded at Aiko's statement.

Aiko stood, "Well, we will be leaving now. Do you mind us stopping by later?"

"Sure, I will probably be helping Lev, Ani and Tia work on their homework, but you are welcome, the essay I can't really finish until later."

Aiko smiled as she glanced at Hazuki, "That's right, did you have summer homework Hazuki?"

Hazuki thought a bit, "Nothing that will be difficult, but I did bring it with me."

"Hey Trist, can you help us too? Hazuki might have some different topics but it should be generally the same."

Aiko clapped her hands before her in a praying motion.

I sighed a little, "Aiko, you only have to ask, you know I would help."

Aiko showed a radiant smile, "I know." As she giggled slightly, "Okay Trist see you later today."

As Aiko and Hazuki turned and left I faintly heard, "...who are Ani and Tia..." This sounded like it came from Hazuki.

I was able to finish the left side of the garden before I decided to gather all the clippings and weeds from today's work. I used the small garden wagon to dump the clippings and weeds in the compost pile Talinde mentioned. Then I gathered the remaining tools and placed them in the storage shed near the incinerator.

As I pulled off my gloves I could see a distinct difference from my lightly colored hands to my wrists which had been covered in dust and sweat. I thought a quick shower would be nice.

I slipped off my shoes before I entered the dining area, I noticed no one currently in the kitchen. I carried my shoes to the entry and placed them in the shoe box and ran upstairs to collect a pair of cleaner summer clothes.

Since it was early it was well before normal bathing times for the men and women, so I didn't think anything of taking a quick shower. As I entered the bathing room I made a quick glance at the baskets and could tell I was the only one present.

As I disrobed I took a towel and made my way into the bathing room. The stone floor was cool against my feet. We drained the tub a couple days ago since we just didn't use it enough to merit keeping it filled.

I sat on the small stool before the faucet and showerhead. I turned the water on and adjusted the temperature, so it was just lukewarm and quickly rinsed most of the dirt and dust off. As I turned the water off I began soaping up my body. I shampooed my hair which had grown considerably beyond what was comfortable, I reminded myself to ask Valdria to trim it sometime soon.

As I was getting ready to rinse the soap off my body I heard faint giggles in the changing room. I figured it was probably Ani and Tia, I'm sure they would notice my clothes before they came in. As I fumbled for the shower head I reached down and turned the water back on when I heard the door slide open, "Yes." I said so to make them aware there was someone in here, so it didn't become too awkward.

But they were so engrossed in their chatter that they must not have heard me. I tried to glance back, but the soap slightly stung and blurred my eyes. I could only make out blurry images of the two figures standing in the entry holding towels as they peered in my direction, "Ani, Tia, can you wait a few moments?"

I heard the door shut closed and I went back to rinsing the soap from my head down to my toes. As I finished I hung the showerhead back on the wall and quickly dried my hair and wiped the majority of moisture from my body. Once I had the towel wrapped around my waist I walked to the door and slid it open.

Ani and Tia were standing with their backs to the bathing room wall. I could tell they were a little embarrassed for walking in on me.

"Were so sorry." They immediately said when I entered.

"It's okay, not like we don't know each other, right?" I smiled a bit as I thought back to all the time we shared, "You can go in now if you want."

They seemed to hesitate, "If you don't go in I can't change." I said while giving them a silly smile.

As their faces blushed brighter I walked over to the basket with my fresh clothes and slipped my undergarments on under my towel. Figuring I was safe from this point, I unwrapped the towel from my waist and hung it on a hook next to my basket.

I immediately heard Ani and Tia scuttle through the door, "Excuse us!"

I dressed and exited the room. I took my laundry and placed my items in a basket. I needed to remind Valdria to show me how to do laundry next time. I didn't think it should be one person's job, and I disliked leaving my mess for someone else to clean up.

As the sun began stretching toward the western horizon I heard a knock on the door as I was sitting in the kitchen going over the homework assignment with Lev, "Yes!" I said as I stood and walked over to the door.

When I slid the door open it was Aiko and Hazuki, "Good evening." I offered in greeting.

Aiko held up a peace sign, "Evening Trist, I hope were not interrupting anything." As she offered a big smile.

"No, not at all. Lev and I are looking at homework so if you would like to join us your right on time."

Aiko and Hazuki were still wearing the shorts and light blouses they had on earlier today.

As I had them follow me in I saw Lev watching as we approached, "Evening Aiko. Who's your friend?"

Aiko looked ashamed, "Oh, I'm sorry. Lev this is Hazuki, she is my cousin from Okinawa. She is visiting for the summer. Her family might be moving this way next year, so she wanted to see what the area was like."

"That's nice, it's a pleasure to meet you Hazuki."

Hazuki smiled at Lev's greeting and then glanced from me to Lev, "Are you two related?"

Lev and I answered almost simultaneously.

"Yes." Lev offered.

"No, not by blood." I responded.

Our mixed responses looked to confuse Hazuki as she glanced to Aiko and then between Lev and me.

"Lev's parents are my guardians, we might not be closely related but our family lines have mixed in the past. So, in that aspect you could say we are related." I explained.

I pulled out two chairs across from Lev and me, "Please have a seat, did you bring your homework Aiko?"

She reached into her bag and pulled out a notebook with what she had already started working on.

Hazuki also quietly placed an envelope on the table as she pulled out several papers, "Trist are you able to answer questions regarding any of the content here?" As Hazuki leaned over to point out areas she was having difficulty with.

I picked them up and glanced at the papers she handed me, nothing looked too difficult. But there was different emphasis placed on geography in her handouts. I slid them to the center of the table as Hazuki continued to lean over as she placed her hand on the papers to retrieve them.

As she was leaning over I noticed her blouse hung down slightly exposing her smooth skin down to her chest. I heard Lev clear his throat. I glanced over at him and he was looking at me with a reproving look.

I didn't feel that I had done anything wrong, but I guess it was his way of reminding me of Ani and Tia's insecurities. How would they feel if they saw me looking at a different girl, even innocently?

Summer Planning

We were studying at the table for several minutes when Valdria entered the kitchen, "Oh is this a new friend?"

I quickly introduced Hazuki to Valdria, "She is visiting Aiko for the summer from Okinawa. She might stop by occasionally."

Valdria smiled at Hazuki, "Your welcome to visit anytime."

Valdria finished going through a few things before she left for her room.

It wasn't more than a few minutes before I heard the pitter patter of feet running down the hall to slow to a quieter pace as they approached the corner of the dining room.

I looked over my shoulder to see Ani and Tia poke their heads around the corner, I smiled, Valdria must have told them we had company, "Evening Ani, Tia. Are you guys finally ready to look over the homework?"

Ani had a strange expression on her face, almost that of defeat, while Tia's eyes widened a bit when she looked at our guests, "Hazuki, this is Ani and Tia, they are also in the same club as Aiko."

Hazuki stood up and approached Ani and Tia, "I am pleased to meet you both. Aiko told me much about you."

I noticed as Hazuki stood next to Ani that she was several centimeters taller than Ani and almost twice again as many centimeters as Tia. As they stood together it was almost as if they were sizing each other up, Ani had a smile, but I could see the tension in the corner of her mouth.

The two were built very similarly, though differences in their upper proportions were difficult to distinguish.

Tia was holding her homework against her chest I could see her smile, but it was only out of obligation. There was no warmth in her eyes.

It reminded me of when the guys told me about their expressions when I wasn't around. This must be what they meant.

I stood up and walked behind Ani and Tia as Hazuki's eyes followed me. I placed my arms around both of them and said, "These are my closest friends. We might not be real siblings, but I care for them like they were real sisters."

Hazuki smiled brighter, "I am so glad I finally got to meet you." Ani glanced at me with a dissatisfied look, while Tia seemed to deflate somewhat.

"Ani, Tia come sit over here." I pulled out two chairs on my side of the table. Which perked them up a bit.

We began to review and complete the homework, Lev got to the point where he needed only to complete the summer essay and slowly placed it back in his bag. He sat and just observed the others then got up for a glass of water, "Anyone like some water or tea?"

I declined and so did Aiko and Hazuki, Ani and Tia seemed to be deep in thought and didn't respond.

As Aiko was finishing the last set of questions she asked, "So Trist, when are we going to the beach?"

I saw Hazuki look at Aiko with a slightly excited expression.

I rested my chin on my hand, "I have about half of the availability dates for people in club. I guess we could start looking based on that."

I glanced at Lev, "What do you think?"

He just shrugged as he sat back down. He pulled his phone out and sent one last Line message, "I just asked, I told them we're setting a date so if they hadn't responded by now they would have to wait until the second trip." I heard two phones beep, mine and Aiko's.

Aiko looked at her phone, "That was quick, let's see if anyone responded."

Tashiro was the only new response, he was going to be unavailable until the last two weeks of summer, "Okay, I will plan with what we have. Aiko, since we're still new to the area can you tell me a good place our group could go to enjoy the beach?" I began jotting down availability dates on my notebook as she thought.

I placed the available dates in calendar format, so I could visually identify where we overlapped the most. I identified two days that would allow each member to attend at least one beach visit, "Let's go with these dates." I handed the page to Lev who already had his phone out.

Lev looked at the dates as he quickly typed out the two days. He asked everyone to confirm their availability by Sunday. We received a number of responses within a few minutes confirming attendance.

A couple members asked if they could bring friends or family. I didn't mind since it was for fun anyway.

"Well it looks like our first day will be next Wednesday, how about you Hazuki, do you plan on attending with Aiko?"

"I didn't plan on going to the beach, so I left my swimsuit at home." Hazuki said with a disappointed look.

"We don't have swimsuits yet either." Ani said, "So if you want we can go together, Trist can tell us what he thinks." Ani offered as she looked at me with a serious expression.

"What happened to the swimsuits you guys tried on the other day? Ani, the red swimsuit looked really good on you, and Tia the blue one you had really made a good impression."

Ani and Tia hung their heads as if regretting a decision, "We didn't buy them. We were a little pre-occupied." I saw Tia fidgeting with her hands in her lap.

"Oh, that's too bad. I thought they were the best ones I saw." I said a little disappointed. I had hoped Ani and Tia would wear them, so I could see them better when we went to the beach.

"Well the mall is opened for most of the day tomorrow, would you like to go together?" I asked Ani and Tia.

Both of their eyes sparkled as they smiled, "We would really like that."

Hazuki asked, "Is it still okay if I come?"

Aiko sighed, "If Hazuki goes I might as well go too. I have a swimsuit, but it is a couple years old."

As Valdria began preparing dinner I set aside my books and helped.

Hazuki, Ani and Tia were still finishing up their assignments.

While Valdria directed what she wanted me to do I deftly handled each chore. Before long the vegetables were ready for the broth that she was preparing, and the chicken was cooling in the pan, "Anything else?"

"No Trist, you were a big help, thank you." I rinsed off the knife I had just used and wiped it clean replacing it in the rack. When I dried my hands, I walked back to the table as the girls finished up.

Aiko asked as I sat down, "Do you help a lot with meals Trist?"

I pulled out the chair and sat, "Not every time but once in a while, Ani and Tia don't like doing it, so I try to help too."

I felt Ani give me a glance, as Hazuki spoke, "I think it is very admirable to find a guy who can cook. I love to cook so it has always been a dream to marry someone I could share my likes and dislikes with. Hopefully you don't dislike older girls Trist." Hazuki said while resting her elbows on the table looking at me.

"Not at all, Ani is older than me as well."

Aiko almost laughed at my response as Hazuki looked at me with a slightly forced smile, "Oh, really. But does she enjoy sports or exercise to maintain her appearance?"

It seemed like Hazuki was in full attack mode attempting to assert her physical superiority over Ani. I wasn't sure how this turned to what Ani was capable of, but I couldn't just let her misjudge Ani's attributes.

"Well, last time I saw her in a swimsuit she looked extremely tone to me, and she definitely takes care of herself."

I turned to Ani who looked nearly frozen in place and reached a hand for her head. As my hand touched her head she almost jumped a bit then I stroked my hand down her hair, "Her hair takes a lot of time to care for too." Then I caressed her cheek, "She is just smooth all over." I stood and left Ani sitting frozen in place with an off look on her face.

I moved behind Tia who had been watching me speak with a longing expression, "Tia on the other hand, is just as smooth but not nearly so strong." I stroked Tia's hair as well, "She has it just as rough as Ani, but her hair is always beautifully kept. And she's cute." I added as I looked down at Tia who slowly looked up to me with her lips pressed together as she tried to restrain her embarrassment.

Aiko was watching me, she already knew we were close and that Hazuki was still figuring out where Ani and Tia stood with me. Though my display even left Aiko a little embarrassed for Ani and Tia.

Hazuki watched me touch the other girl's hair and caress their cheeks, she was subconsciously stroking her own hair as she watched me with longing eyes.

"So, I think they are both extremely capable regardless, even if they weren't it is my job to protect them." I placed my hands on their shoulders as I stood between them.

I walked over to the side of the table with Aiko and Hazuki. They turned to follow my movements, "I will also protect my friends." I cupped both Aiko and Hazuki's cheeks with my hands, "So, let's be good friends." I stepped back and bowed slightly, "We will be in your care."

Both Hazuki and Aiko stayed motionless a few moments once I stepped back. Aiko looked down then back up at me, "Trist you are just mean." I wasn't quite sure why she considered me mean so I just smiled since she didn't sound upset.

Hazuki was still staring up at my face with a dreamy expression before she came to her senses, "Oh, I'm sorry. Of course. I may be older, but we are in the same grade after all, and if I was ever in the same class I would welcome it."

I could begin to smell dinner approaching completion when Valdria asked, "Would you two like to stay for dinner?"

Aiko politely declined, "We probably have dinner waiting. We didn't plan on staying quite this late, so we should go." Aiko thanked me for the help as she gathered her belongings.

Hazuki asked Aiko about Sunday. Aiko turned to me, "Is it still okay if we go with you guys tomorrow?"

"I don't see why not, it looks like Ani and Tia need swimsuits still. I want to make it up to them for the trouble I caused last week."

Aiko smiled while Hazuki looked a little perplexed, "Well Trist I look forward to tomorrow, send me a message an hour or so ahead of time."

"I can do that, it may come from Ani or Tia but one of us will notify you. Walk home safe you two."

Aiko waved as Hazuki still had a somewhat vacant look on her face when she finally smiled and waved.

I returned to the table and set my belongings on the stairs, Valdria was setting out dishes so I helped finish. Shivan was now in the dining room as well. We all sat for dinner minus Jes and Talinde who would likely be home shortly.

As we finished dinner I began to help Valdria clean, but Ani pushed me aside, "Tia and I can do this." She said with a slight frown on her face.

Lev and I headed to my room after he dropped his homework on his desk. When we closed the door he said, "What do you think of Hazuki?"

I was a little caught off guard, "Why do you ask?"

Lev shrugged, "I was just curious. You seemed to get along with her. Not to mention looking down her shirt."

I protested a little then paused as I asked, "Did it really look like that was what I was doing?"

Lev was grinning while he nodded yes.

I sighed, "That wasn't my intention. I just noticed how the curves of her neck seemed to accentuate her shoulders. She has an alluring presence, so I do admit I was somewhat drawn to her."

I thought as Lev was leaning back on my bed, "I'm not sure, but she seems different than the girls at school. Probably because she has matured more or if it's just her open nature."

Lev sat up, "So, what are you going to do?"

"Do? Well nothing. I mean she is only here through the summer so hopefully we can all be friends."

Lev shook his head, "You know Aiko might be right. Your cluelessness can be downright mean sometimes."

"Lev, you might think I'm being mean, but what would you suggest I do. You know very well we can't easily fall in love with someone from earth. What do you think would happen in thirty years? If that doesn't make you think, what would happen if I choose to be serious with Ani or Tia. One of them would be left out." I continued as I stared down at my desk.

"Do you honestly think I don't feel physical attachment to either of them? We're still young and I can't see disturbing the status quo we have right now. I want them to find someone special, so until then I will keep our relationship as innocent as I can. But even I have desires." I looked at Lev who had been watching me for the past several minutes.

Lev let out a deep breath like he had been holding it in, "I guess you're not as clueless as you act."

I smiled sadly, "Well, it works for now though it does have its drawbacks. It's not like you aren't in the same boat as me. How do you feel? Anyone you thought you liked?"

Lev smiled, "No, when I compare the girls to Ani, or Tia I don't see anyone who compares." Lev looked at me, "Don't you dare tell Ani I said that."

"How long do you think we will live? Even Tia will eventually grow old and die before us." I glanced back at Lev, "For now, Ani is the only one who shares a similar fate. Every time I befriend someone I am making a decision that will come back and slowly eat away at my soul. That's why I act like I do sometimes." As I looked at Lev I began to feel my eyes glaze over with tears.

Lev stood up and walked toward my chair and paused. As he placed his hand on my shoulder, "Well, let me know if you ever need to talk. I will support you. But you know Trist, love even if it is with someone from Earth isn't all that bad, I don't think. It might seem like a short span of time but the memories you share will go on once the heartache fades."

As Lev departed I contemplated his advice, it would be difficult, but I too would like a family someday.

* * *

Upon waking I felt somewhat drained, the dream I had that night had me fleeing an unseen pursuer who seemed to be right behind at every turn. As I fled down the palace halls they began to crumble to ruin and the palace staff aged and crumbled to dust before me.

I felt like I was in a cold sweat as I woke, I guess the dream echoed the fears I voiced for the first-time last night. I slowly got out of bed, from the look of the light seeping into my window it was still early. When I checked my phone, I noticed it was just after 07:00.

I sat up and used the time to relieve myself and wash and brush my teeth. Once I had changed I headed down stairs to see if the others were awake. I knocked on Lev's door and slid his door open a bit, but he was on his stomach drooling on his pillow. I couldn't help but laugh.

As I approached Ani's door I did the same, but after I knocked I heard a faint response. I could hear Ani getting out of bed and walking to the door. As she slid the door open slightly I noticed her eyes were moist with tears, "What's wrong, were you crying?" I asked with concern on my face.

"I don't know, it felt like a bad dream, but I don't even remember having one." Ani said as she rubbed her eyes.

"Okay, well let me know when you want to go, and I will message Aiko."

Ani nodded and closed her door, as I whispered quietly, "Sorry Ani, that was my dream."

I checked on Tia next, but she was still asleep, so I decided to let her be.

At noon I sent a message to Aiko, I told her to stop by when she was ready. After about thirty minutes I heard the door chime.

I answered it and greeted Aiko and Hazuki, "Please come in, I will check on the others."

Aiko and Hazuki found seats in the lounge as I went to check on Lev, Ani and Tia.

Lev was sitting at his desk and glanced back when I knocked, "They here?"

I nodded, "I'm getting Ani and Tia now."

Ani and Tia were mostly ready, today Ani wore a skirt that was mid-thigh in length with a darker plaid green and black pattern, her top was a relatively tight-fitting shirt that accentuated her curves more than a school uniform.

She had her hair in a pony tail like she would when we trained. It was amazing how much it changed her looks just by gathering her hair back the way it was now. I thought back to the times we trained and while it was only a little over two Paltian years I could see a difference in her maturity. She was becoming a beautiful woman.

Tia was in a one-piece dress with a fine floral pattern in the fabric, while she left her hair down flowing over her shoulders almost to the middle of her back. She still had a petite figure, but I understood her mother did as well. Her face when she looked over at you and smiled made my heart feel lighter.

As the four of us entered the lounge Aiko and Hazuki stood, Lev and I were wearing jeans and button up shits, of differing designs. The looks from Aiko and Hazuki were solely focused on Ani and Tia this time, I smiled a little as we departed.

We decided to take the bus most of the way, so we had more time after shopping.

While we rode Hazuki asked, "What colors do you like Trist?" I saw Ani, Aiko and Tia glance sideways at me when she asked.

"Humm, I like the color of the sunset on an overcast day as the sky deepens to crimson."

Ani blushed a bit, I recalled telling her once that I thought her hair looked like the sunset.

She had been upset when a member of the AAM had commented on her hair looking like a bloody wound. After my comments as a young child she never asked to change her hair color again.

"I guess, I like purple as well, like the deep purple of the Velisus nebula…" I felt Ani and Tia both elbow my sides. "…from pictures I've seen." I quickly added as I glanced sideways at them, "How about you Aiko, Hazuki?"

Aiko placed her finger on her lips as she thought, Hazuki was the first to respond, "I like green, I wish my eyes were the same color as yours Trist." She said as she looked at me.

I felt my face heat up a bit as she looked at me. I looked to the side only to be met by Ani's glare.

Lev just said, "I like blue."

I nodded, "I do as well, there are many different shades that I find soothing."

Aiko held her finger to her chin, "Humm, I don't know if I have a favorite color. I have several I like so it's hard to say one is my favorite."

I interrupted the conversation when I reached over and pressed the next stop button, "Looks like we're almost there."

We all stood and moved toward the front of the bus, as it began to slow we balanced ourselves while we held the overhead rail.

As we exited I heard Tia's stomach growl. I looked over at her and grinned. She just lowered her head, "I forgot to eat this morning."

"There is a food court in the basement, maybe we can go there first. Is everyone okay with that?"

I was feeling a little hungry as well since I ate too early.

We all crossed the intersection and entered the mall, there were fewer shoppers than normal since it was the first weekend school was out many families were away from town.

As we entered the basement there was a grocery store and several food stalls. Since we didn't eat out much I decided to try something I hadn't seen before, I settled on a place with several varieties of hamburgers and hot dogs. I purchased a hamburger with lettuce and a slightly sweet sauce, with a small drink.

When I sat at an open table I waited to eat until the others had arrived.

Ani bought a set meal with rice, cabbage and tonkatsu with a sweet brown sauce.

Tia surprised me when she sat down a tray with three slices of pizza. I think she noticed my eyes bulge. Tia said indignantly, "It's flat so it won't take much space."

I laughed as I smiled at Tia as she pouted a bit before she started smiling and began eating a slice of pizza.

Lev had a burger like mine, but he had a thick reddish sauce on it with a slice of cheese.

Aiko and Hazuki both had a slice of pizza.

I guess I should try one of those next time.

As we all finished I saw Tia struggling to down her third piece of pizza. I smiled, "I thought it was flat and wouldn't take up much space."

As I teased her Tia looked at me like she was asking for help, "Tia you don't have to force yourself." She looked down at the remaining slice.

Pleadingly Tia asked, "Do you want some Trist?"

I was good, but I knew if someone didn't eat it she would try to finish it herself, "Sure, if you can't finish I can help."

Tia quietly passed her tray to me as she smiled.

It was the first taste of pizza I have had, I wasn't sure what I expected but the sauce and cheese might have been too much for my stomach.

Once everyone was left we headed upstairs to the seasonal accessories. Since Lev and I already purchased our swimming trunks we only had to wait for the girls to decide on their swimsuits. Lev and I sat near the benches while we waited for the girls.

Hazuki was the first to find a swimsuit, as she changed she called out and opened the curtains without stepping out to show me. It was a dark purple, two-piece. The color and design fit Hazuki's skin tone but I thought she preferred green, "Why didn't you go with green?"

"Well, you liked red and purple, didn't you?"

"Yes, I do, but wouldn't it be better to have a color you enjoy?"

Hazuki sighed, "I have a pale green one as well, let me change and tell me what you think."

As Hazuki closed the curtains I stepped back and noticed Ani entering a changing room, I didn't see a red swimsuit in her arms though.

I heard Tia next, she stepped out and showed me a similar swimsuit to what she had last time, though it was a shade darker blue, "I like it, it makes you look even cuter."

Tia smiled as she nodded to herself and went back to change.

Hazuki called once again as she poked her head around the corner, she was wearing a pale green swimsuit with a similar cut to the last one. I thought the purple one looked better, but I wanted her to buy something she liked, "That one looks good too. Which color of the two do you like best when you look in the mirror?"

Hazuki, looked into the mirror as she twisted to glance at the side, front and back of her swimsuit. She placed her hand on her chest, "I think I like this color, but it makes my chest look smaller."

"I think your chest looks just fine, but it still shows a lot of skin, will that be okay?"

"Isn't that a good thing?" She said as she looked over her swimsuit in the mirror. Then she gave me a satisfied smile as she closed the curtain.

Ani still hadn't come out and Aiko was still browsing through several different designs. I walked toward where Ani was changing, "Ani everything okay?"

"It's fine, I just can't decide." Ani responded. She slid the curtain open a bit and showed me a light green swimsuit that had a nice cut but didn't really match my image of her.

"What about the red you had the other day? I thought it looked really good on you."

She frowned and looked down, "I don't want a swimsuit that reminds me of that day."

As she closed the curtain to try her next suit on I walked back and found a swimsuit with a similar cut she just tried but that was the same red as the color she had the other day. I wasn't sure of the sizes, so I took a couple in the range I thought would work.

I walked over to her changing stall and stuck them past the side of the curtain.

"Hey, what..." She began to ask then she noticed I was holding something. She stuck her head out of the curtains as she held them closed, "I told you I didn't want that color." She said as she looked into my eyes.

"I really think this color is best, I want to see you wearing it again. Would you at least try it?"

Ani reluctantly closed the curtains, "Fine, I'll try it, but can you get me a different size? These are too small." I smiled and my failure at guessing her size.

"What size do you need?" I asked. As she showed me the tag on the first one she tried I returned the other two and looked for a swimsuit in the right size. I finally found a suit with the right color, but the cut seemed a little different. It appeared to be the only one in the color I wanted her to try. I returned, "I'm passing it through, okay?"

"Okay." Ani responded, and she took it from me as I stuck to past the curtain.

Aiko finally called, "Trist are you outside?" I saw her also poke her head out of the changing room.

I waved, "Coming." I said. When I stood in the front of her changing room she was wearing a black one-piece bathing suit, it had a slightly different cut than what Tia settled on. While it was a one piece it was cut to expose more of the back and sides the cut was a medium rise.

"I like it, are you happy with the color?"

Aiko smiled as she nodded.

I headed back toward Ani's changing room and heard her say, "Impossible!" To herself in a soft voice.

"Is everything okay Ani?"

I could hear her almost loose her balance.

Ani's response was full of embarrassment, "I'm fine, but I can't do this Trist."

"What's wrong? The wrong size?"

"Um, no the size is okay it's just…" She paused for a minute, "You can look in but don't open the curtains wide."

I poked my head past the closed curtains and saw Ani bashfully holding her hand near her chest and other hand down by her crotch. As I saw the difference in cuts I agreed, this wasn't a swimsuit she should wear around others.

"Thank you for showing me, I think you look wonderful in that color, but I wouldn't want to share it with others either. Would you try another color I picked?" I asked with a slight blush on my face from seeing such an exposing suit.

"Yea." She sounded with a slight nod.

I knew the size I needed, I just needed to find a color to match her style. I looked around several racks till I identified a few suits with a dark purple color. I looked through the size listing and pulled the one that matched, this time I looked at the cut of the crotch, it looked to be a lower cut and looked like what she had the other day.

I carried it back to her changing room, "Ani, can you try this one?"

I slipped it past the curtains once she answered.

A few minutes later Ani slid the curtain back, "Well, what do you think?" She asked me quietly. She looked good, the suit accentuated her natural beauty and made her toned muscles stand out as she turned.

When she twisted to look at the back I could see the muscles in her legs and abdomen tighten. Even her chest was a perfect fit for the top. Here before me was a girl with my two favorite colors.

Ani was looking at me as I glanced at her swimsuit and I could tell she felt a little uncomfortable, but she didn't shy away. My face must have said I liked it because she smiled as I looked up.

"I think I will get this one." She hurriedly said as she closed the curtains.

After everyone had finally made their purchases we decided to head home. This time we walked, and Lev and I chatted about next Wednesday and what we should bring, "Aiko, what should we bring when we go to the beach?"

Hazuki looked at Aiko as she thought, "I always went with my parents and they drove, so we always had a bunch of things, like a barbeque and ice chests, but you don't plan on taking those kinds of things do you Trist?"

"I don't plan on taking more than we can comfortably carry, will there be places to change?"

Aiko suddenly said, "Oh yes, there are bathrooms nearby as well as several beach house restaurants that stay open throughout the summer."

Hazuki looked at Aiko as she made a recommendation, "You definitely want a large cloth or towel to lay out, plus you probably should bring sunscreen. I got burnt once when I was much younger, and it was very painful."

As we continued to make our way home I made a mental list of items to begin setting aside, I already knew we had a couple bags capable of holding our towels and a sheet, I wasn't sure about the umbrella but apparently you could rent those.

As I was mentally planning Hazuki asked me a question, "Are you a good swimmer Trist?"

I thought a second and answered, "No, I only ever used a suit that allowed me to float but haven't tried to swim on my own power." I looked at Tia, Lev and Ani, "Can you guys swim?"

They all shook their heads, "So sounds like this might be interesting."

Aiko looked at us with a worried expression, "Do you plan on going into the water?

"I've never been to the beach for fun, I'm not sure if I will or not. Maybe we should look into learning before next trip."

I guess, we should spend some time focusing on more than just studying this next year.

Beach Party

Wednesday arrived much quicker than I expected, when I woke I began gathering the items I planned to take and placed them in my backpack. Once I had packed the towel and a large sheet Valdria provided, I slid in a few drinks we purchased the day prior in along with the sunblock.

I carried my bag down to the entry and went to make a simple snack before I left. The group was going to meet at the beach at 10:00, a couple people were already on their way to save a spot. Once we left I figured the train and buses would take about an hour, so we needed to leave the house by 08:45 to meet at 10:00. It was still early, so I decided to make breakfast for everyone. It was simple, but at least everyone would have food in their stomachs before we left.

As I finished up I went to Lev's, Ani's and Tia's to call them to eat. Tia was the only one awake but Ani and Lev both rolled out of bed when I mentioned food. This also gave them a chance to wake up and get ready early enough to make our intended departure.

When we left, Lev and I had the larger of the bags while Ani and Tia carried their own clothes and any extra items they thought they would need. We met Aiko, Anju and Hazuki near the train station.

The trip by train was about thirty minutes with several stops but it was much quicker than taking a bus. When we reached the other side of the peninsula we switched to busses with one transfer before we arrived down the street from the beach.

We made good time, we were about twenty minutes early, so we decided to find Josuke and Junichi who had volunteered to come early and save us a spot. The beach already had hundreds of people that stretched down the coast in an arc over about three kilometers. We began watching for familiar faces, but it was difficult with so many people wearing clothing you weren't used to seeing.

After about fifteen minutes we finally found Josuke sitting on a sheet with a couple smaller sheets spread out around him.

Josuke looked over when we called out to him, "Yoh, how was the trip here?"

I smiled at him, "It was pretty quick, most people were off the trains already. Where's Junichi?"

"Oh, he's changing. We have only been here about thirty minutes. Go ahead and take any of the spots around us, I hope this is enough space for twenty…" Josuke paused as he saw a girl he didn't recognize, "Hey Trist." Josuke called me over, "Who's the girl with you guys?"

I looked over at Hazuki who was happily chatting about being at the beach, "That's Aiko's cousin from Okinawa. She is here for the summer, so we invited her. Do you mind?"

"Not at all, I can't wait to see her swimsuit." Josuke smiled.

"It's not bad, it's a pale green two-piece."

Josuke looked up at me, "How do you know that?" He asked wide eyed.

"Oh, I went with them to pick them out last Sunday."

Josuke was shaking me by the shoulders, "How do you always end up in those situations?"

I began spreading the sheet we brought on top of the one already down, it wasn't too hot yet, so we might not need an umbrella. Josuke pointed Aiko and the other girls toward the changing room while Lev and I held down the fort.

After the girls had been gone a few minutes Tashiro arrived in his swimming trunks holding his bag. He waved and asked how we were doing so far. After he sat down he said, "I saw a bunch of girls our age heading into the changing room, I can't wait to see them come out."

"That was probably Aiko and the others. Being out of a uniform makes a big difference in what they look like, so it doesn't surprise me much that you didn't recognize them."

"You mean the tall girl with auburn hair was Ani? What about the girl with dark brown hair, about the same height as her?" Tashiro was holding his hands up indicating height difference.

"Oh, that was probably Hazuki, she's Aiko's cousin from Okinawa." For some reason I felt like I was repeating myself.

As we sat waiting the remaining club members who could attend arrived, we now had about fifteen people at our first club event. The girls all sat their belongings on the sheet we had laid out, I told them we could watch them as they made their way to the changing rooms.

A few moments later I heard Ani and Tia's voices close by, "You guys can go change now if you want, we can wait by our belongings."

I noticed Josuke and Junichi glaring wide eyed at Ani as she walked up.

"Careful guys." I said as I smiled. They caught themselves before anyone else noticed them and only stole glances when they thought no one was looking.

Lev and I quickly changed and put a pair of sandals on, so the sand wouldn't burn our feet as it grew warmer in the day.

We approached the sheet and saw Ani and Tia sitting on their towels with a few older students harassing them. Ani and Tia seemed to be avoiding looking at them and just stared off to the sea. Josuke and Junichi were gone.

I looked at Lev, and we kept walking. I overheard several rude comments being made about them ignoring the three standing around them. I walked up and placed myself in front of the taller of the three who was close to looming over Ani and Tia.

"What can we do for you guys?" I calmly asked.

Ani and Tia jumped up behind me, "Trist we can handle this."

"Ohhh, you hear that guys she can handle us, maybe we should find a nice quiet place." The tallest sneered.

"I'd appreciate if you left without trouble, we are on a club event." I calmly said.

"Leave, who's going to make us? We're not leaving until the little ladies join us for some fun." The guy next to Lev said.

The guy in front of me was tall but he didn't look particularly tough. I had been trained to take down opponents larger than him.

As the tallest guy sneered down at me I asked a final time, "Would you mind leaving now? It might be embarrassing if you got hurt." I glared at the guy standing in front of me. I could feel the adrenaline in my body begin to increase.

"Get out of here kid!" As he tried to throw me to the side.

I immediately grabbed his wrist and twisted it around using his own momentum to bring his arm and wrist into a lock, bent at such an angle that the slightest additional pressure would tear or break muscle and bone.

I heard the guy to my right cry out in pain as he lay on the ground with his wrist bent in a funny angle. The third guy just backed up not believing what happened.

As the tallest was on his knees before me I stared down into his eyes which were filled with pain and fear.

"Like I said, it might be embarrassing if you got hurt." I squeezed the angle I had his wrist in until I could feel cartilage crack, "Now get out of here!" I released my grasp as I smiled and used as much strength as possible to push him several feet back, the force left him near unconscious due to lack of breath.

He stumbled up gasping for air and ran off without his friends.

"Trist, I'm sorry. I didn't mean for you to take care of that. I thought if we ignored them they would go away."

I turned to Ani and Tia who had been standing since I arrived and hugged them close. I could feel the slightly slick feeling of perspiration until I pulled back, "I'm sorry you had to hear that."

I never expected something like this to happen so soon.

As I released Ani and Tia a bunch of our club members came running up.

"What was that about?" Several girls and guys asked.

Junichi and Josuke walked up behind me. They looked at me when I turned toward them, "Trist remind me never to make you mad. I don't think that guy will ever do that again. I mean you scared me, and you weren't even talking to me."

Everyone just waited listening while I asked them to include Lev and me if they needed to wander too far. The guys and girls were glancing between Lev and I after our self-defense demonstration.

Hazuki looked at Aiko, "I thought you said he was the study club leader?"

Aiko just nodded her head as Anju spoke, "Yea, but I saw him running once when they were first looking for a club. Trist might be strong, but…" Anju glanced down at Ani, "…it is probably better Ani didn't do anything."

Hazuki looked curious, "Why is that?" Hazuki asked, as she looked more closely at Ani and Tia. She now noticed the contours of muscles along their legs, arms and back. "Ahh, Ani, do you work out?"

Ani looked at Hazuki then the rest of the club members who were all smiling, "Not recently."

Kaoru giggled a bit, "Everyone has accepted it, when we go out for physical education you just don't compete against Ani's times." She looked at Tia as she smiled, "Our first goal is Tia, but that might even be too much."

Tia made a little whining noise, "I'm not going to let you beat me either." Tia said as she showed conviction on her face.

A couple of the girl's giggled and walked over to settle down on the sheets.

Hazuki sat down next to Aiko and leaned forward to see Trist as she asked, "Trist, do you run?"

I leaned forward, "Run? Well we ran when we first looked at clubs for the track team. But we used to have hand to hand training every day."

Hazuki looked shocked, not expecting someone she associated as an honor student with superior physical abilities, "What was your time?" Hazuki had a curious look on her face.

"Humm, if I remember Miyoshi-sensei correctly she said Ani's time was 46.2 seconds, I think mine was just 57 seconds, so just under a minute. Lev and Tia were a little ahead of me when we finished."

I tried remembering Lev's and Tia's times but didn't remember hearing Miyoshi-sensei list them. Hazuki was looking at me with a blank look, as she shifted her glance back to Ani.

"I'm glad I didn't ask her to race me, I probably would have cried."

Aiko was smiling at our conversation, "Well don't think of any of them as ordinary, or they will constantly surprise you." She giggled, "It's better to just follow their lead and you will naturally get better, regardless of what they do."

Aiko then turned to Trist and excitedly asked, "So, what are we going to do for second term? You know if you keep letting other classes take advantage of our club and the exam study sessions sooner or later everyone will be in the top where even someone with a 100% isn't number one. You know."

I leaned forward and rested my arms on my knees, "I could talk to Murakami about having extra credit questions added I guess."

"But would they just do that?" Aiko asked with a curious face.

Lev leaned back glancing to his left as he spoke to Aiko, "If Trist asked, they would probably do it."

Aiko looked contemplative, "Well okay."

"Aren't you going to play with the others?" I asked.

"Well." Aiko held a small bottle, "Would you mind putting some sunblock on my back where I can't reach Trist?"

Lev quietly cleared his throat, before I responded, "Wouldn't it be better if Hazuki did that while you are both sitting there? You could do each other's difficult to reach spots."

Aiko sighed, as she turned to Hazuki. Aiko rubbed some on Hazuki's back and shoulders then down to the line of her suit.

I decided to pull the small bottle we had and tossed it to Lev who did his legs shoulders and chest then handed it back. I did the same.

Hazuki glanced our way, "Make sure you put some on your face, nose and ears or you will really regret it."

Once we were done Lev rubbed some on my back really quick and the cold sensation made me cringe a bit as it had already mixed with the small particles of sand on my back feeling like fine sandpaper. I put some in my hand and slapped it in the middle of Lev's back, "Ouch." I just laughed and finished up.

As I watched the club members playing with an inflated ball and tossing it back and forth, the girls who used to be from the volleyball team looked to be having a blast.

Ani came running up, and grabbed me by the hand, "Trist you have to feel this. It's like your moving backwards but you aren't." As Ani tugged me to a standing position, she had a huge smile on her face, no longer worried about how she looked in her swimsuit.

I offered her a smile, "Okay I'm coming." We moved out to the edge of the waves as they lightly broke against the sand. As the water rushed past your feet and you looked down facing the ocean it was like you were sliding backwards. I could feel the sand also pulling out from under my feet with the retreating water.

After a while I made my way into the water, it was much cooler than I expected but as you slowly worked out deeper your body acclimated to it and really helped cool you off. A couple students were floating out deeper with inflatable rings or splashing each other as they played tag while running through the waist high water.

I looked back and Lev who was still sitting on our sheet, though he was putting sunscreen on Tia's back. She had the bottle and was rubbing it on her face and legs. I hadn't seen Ani put any on and we had been playing for close to four hours.

I waded to shallower water where Ani was sitting in the sand enjoying the waves as they washed up against her and slightly pull her back toward to ocean.

"Hey Ani!" She looked up as I called. I could see her complexion was slightly flushed, so I reached out for her hand, as she stood with my help I asked, "Did you put any sunscreen on?"

"No, not yet, it isn't that hot, plus the water keeps you cool." She said. I pulled her closer and turned her slightly as I looked at her back and shoulders.

She didn't look too red yet, but when I touched her, the skin on her back was burning up. I tried to drag her out of the water, but she resisted.

"No, let's have some more fun." Ani pleaded.

If she got hurt after I realized she was doing something wrong I would have a hard time forgiving myself if I didn't act. I scooped her up in my arms as she floundered and kicked a bit, "Stop it! We can go back in a few minutes." I said as I reprimanded her.

Ani slowly stopped resisting when she heard my tone, I never used a voice like that with her, so she must have sensed my concern.

I knelt as I gently sat her on a towel and dabbed the water from her back, I could see a slight discoloration from the strap of her top that had shifted when I picked her up.

"You idiot, what did we talk about when we first came." I was as mad with myself as I was with her. I began rubbing sunblock on her back as she squirmed under the cold sensation. I covered her back and told her to lay on the towel. When she did I covered her sides and the back of her arms then the back sides of her legs.

Ani was tensing up as I rubbed the sunblock on her legs, she wasn't used to me touching her like this, so she was a little uncomfortable as I rubbed down the interior and exterior side of her thighs and down to her heels, "Now sit up."

Ani sat up as she showed me a chastised and embarrassed look.

I put some more sunblock on my hands and rubbed my hands together as I asked, "Ani, hold your hair back." Ani's hair was slightly damp from splashing in the water. I cupped my hands as I reached around her neck and then applied sunblock to her face, nose and ears.

Once that was complete I placed the bottle in her hand, "Now don't go anywhere until you finish doing the same to the rest of your arms, chest, stomach and front of your legs." Ani gave an embarrassed nod.

I reached for our bag and placed a bottle of water between her knees, "Drink this when you're done." Lev was watching with a smile and pitiful look directed toward Ani.

I glanced at him as he shook his head. I slumped my shoulders knowing what he was thinking.

I stood, "You better hurry if you want to play some more, we will probably head to get something to eat pretty soon."

I headed back out to the others, we decided to play a game involving passing a ball using volley ball like tosses to see how long we could keep the ball going between us. The person who missed would drop out making it more difficult for the rest. As it bounced the member closest would knock it back up until it finally was out of reach and fell to the ground.

I glanced over at Ani who had her head hung down, I could tell Lev was talking to her. Ani looked like a scolded puppy, and seemed to be contemplating something serious with Lev.

We continued to play until someone suggested a drink and something cold to eat. So, we headed back to our spot and began gathering our belongings, I asked Lev if he wanted to go first.

"No, that's okay. I can watch the stuff and go with the second group."

"Ani? Want to go?" I asked.

She kept her head down as she shook it silently no. I was a little upset with myself thinking I had been the one to ruin her fun. As she sat on her towel with her knees pulled up to her chest I stepped in front of her and knelt straddling her feet with my knees.

Now that we were at eye level I reached out to cup her chin and raised it slightly to meet my eyes, "Ani, I'm sorry if I put a damper on your fun. But I don't want you to get burnt. So, stop being so depressed and let's enjoy our time here. It makes me feel bad when I see you like this."

Ani nodded but was looking like she was about to cry.

I stood up and reached down as I took the hand she had been resting on her knees and pulled her up. I was about to release her hand as she stood but she suddenly tightened her grip and stood next to me with her head somewhat downcast. We made our way to the stalls for something to bring down the temperature of our bodies.

* * *

Ani was thinking, this was so much more fun than sitting in the bath with friends, and there was nothing like this on Paltius. I really wanted to be able to swim out with the others. When we took the transfer relay from the Velisus to the Ryuuga I saw so much sea life all I wanted to do was explore it openly.

The sensation of the waves tugging at your legs or the funny feeling it gave when you stood and felt like the water was making you move backwards was amazing. I had to show Trist.

As I made my way back, "Trist you have to feel this. It's like your moving backwards but you aren't."

Trist looked up at me with an amused smile.

"Okay, I'm coming" He had replied.

We both moved to the edge of the water and stood in the waves as the shallow water rushed past your feet and retreated. Trist made a somewhat curious face. We began to splash around as I moved out of his range but had to defend from water being thrown at me by Kaoru.

I decided to try sitting in the waves to see if it gave a similar sensation. The water crashed up around my waist but still felt like it was tugging at my body as it pulled back. I smiled and noticed Trist walking toward me with a serious expression.

"Did you put any sunblock on?"

I hadn't really thought about it, but we have only been here a few hours and the water kept you from feeling overheated, "No, not yet, it isn't that hot, plus the water keeps you cool."

Trist reached down and roughly pulled me to my feet and turned me to face away from him. I was surprised, he was usually so delicate in everything he did. I could feel him touch my back with his cool hand. Then he began pulling me with him, "No, let's have some more fun." I told him.

Trist had a conflicted expression then his face turned resolute. He scooped me up in his arms forcing me to lean against his slightly slick chest. I resisted by trying to push away and wiggle, so he would put me down.

"Stop it! We can go back in a few minutes." Trist said in a commanding tone.

This was the first time he had spoken to me like this, so I was somewhat taken back. I stopped squirming as I leaned against him placing my arm around his shoulders and my free hand against his chest.

Trist carried me back to the sheet where Lev was watching. As my eyes caught my brothers I saw him shake his head disapprovingly.

Trist gently knelt and sat me down on his towel. He began drying my back, but he was extremely gentle. As he was behind me I heard Trist mumble, "You idiot, what did we talk about when we first came." I felt a little ashamed.

I could hear him shake a bottle of sunblock and pop the cap as he squeezed it into his hand. When he placed his hand on my back it was COLD! I couldn't help but arch myself as he slowly rubbed the sunblock around the center of my back. As it felt like his hands had covered most of my exposed skin Trist told me to lay on my stomach on the towel.

As I laid down he repeated the same with my sides which caused me to tense up since I was ticklish when he touched me like that. He covered my shoulders, underarms and the backs of my arms. As he moved to the back of my legs the cool sensation began to feel good, it wasn't until he started sliding his hand up the middle of my thigh that I tensed for a different reason.

"Now sit up." Trist stated. He looked me in the eye, but I could feel my face heat for reasons other than the sun.

Trist was in front of me putting more sunblock on his hands, "Ani, hold your hair up away from you neck." He told me.

As I did he reached around my neck as he cupped his hands gently, slightly pulling me toward him as he worked the sunblock around my neck. His hands were extremely gentle as he held my chin to steady it and applied sunblock to my forehead, nose, ears and face.

When Trist finished he sat the bottle in my hand, "Now don't go anywhere until you finish doing the same to the rest of your arms, chest, stomach and front of your legs." Trist gave me a hard look. I could only nod. He pulled something from the bag he brought and placed a bottle of water between my knees, "Drink this when you're done."

I couldn't help but thinking Trist was unhappy with me.

Trist stood and said in a somewhat softer voice, "You better hurry if you want to play some more, we will probably head to get something to eat pretty soon."

As Trist left I heard my brother clear his throat, "Ani, why do you think Trist is angry?"

I glanced at my brother, "Because I didn't put on sunblock?"

He just shook his head, "Probably because you did something that put yourself in danger. Even if it was something simple you did something that was careless and could cause yourself pain. How do you think Trist feels about that?"

I wasn't sure what to say.

My brother was looking directly at me, "Ani, you are the older one, you need to make sure you don't do anything careless that would risk pulling you apart." Lev paused as he considered something.

"I'm going to tell you something Trist told me the other day." As my brother's eyes narrowed and turned serious, one of the few times I have seen him this way with me, "You have to promise me you won't say anything."

I quietly nodded as I looked down at the sand and listened.

"Trist is the way he is because he is afraid. I can tell he loves both you and Tia, but he doesn't want to hurt either of your feelings by choosing one." Lev paused, "Trist will likely out live Tia and definitely outlive every friend he makes since we arrived. He is afraid to form bonds, so he plays his clueless act." Lev emphasized, "He is not clueless." As he stared at me, "What do you think would happen if you someday did something foolish enough to get yourself killed?"

"How do you think Trist would deal with that. He told me every time he makes a friend he knows they will someday eat away at his soul! So please Ani, try not to be the one that destroys his soul. Don't burden him with worry by making poor decision regardless of how insignificant you may think they are, Trist takes them very seriously."

I nodded and tried to say something, but it felt like my tongue was stuck in my throat, so it came out a grunt. I didn't know how to respond, I always though Trist was just oblivious to our affection, but my brother just told me he does it on purpose for our continued happiness.

I never thought about it but if Trist did fall in love with another girl from earth how would he feel as they grew old and died before him. I felt like I wanted to start crying because my compassion for him was overwhelming.

A few minutes after my brother finished Trist walked up, "Lev want to head over to grab a drink?"

My brother just said he would watch the bags.

"Ani? Want to go?"

I didn't think I could look into his eyes the way I felt right now so I shook my head.

I saw his feet in front of me as he knelt placing my legs between his knees. He reached out with his right hand and gently took me by the chin and gently raised my face to be even with his.

"Ani, I'm sorry if I put a damper on your fun. But I don't want you to get burnt. So, stop being so depressed and let's enjoy our time here. It makes me feel bad when I see you like this."

I felt like I could cry when I thought, what an idiot I could be sometimes.

He stood up and slowly bent down to take me by my right hand, he pulled me up and I stepped off the sheet to stand next to him. As I felt his hand begin to loosen its grip I squeezed tighter refusing to let him slip away. Trist looked at me and smiled as we began walking toward the others.

As we walked up to the food stalls I saw Tia looking into a small freezer of ice cream, the others were in line for shaved ice. When Tia turned and saw us she waved, then noticed Trist and I were holding hands.

Tia walked over with a pouty face, "That's not really fair you know." As she looked up at me.

I offered Tia a smile, "Well he does have two hands." Tia's eyes widened a second as she smiled and stepped next to Trist and took his other hand. We walked into the shop and didn't care what anyone else thought.

Second Term Surprise

The second term started the last week of August, we never got to go to the beach the second time due to rain. While the students were disappointed I think I was more so.

The homework essay was easy to complete, it was on, "My ideal summer activities." After our day at the beach I bet many of the students turned in an essay about the same thing.

I was also glad the second beach trip was canceled for other less obvious reasons. Ani had come home with a very bad sunburn on her back, shoulders and face.

Valdria had refused to use the molecular stabilizer on her at first. I think this was more to help her learn a lesson than anything. She couldn't sleep and had a difficult time moving for several days.

Tia had a slight burn, but it didn't hurt her nearly as much, she ended up looking a little darker, and it made her freckles stand out when you normally wouldn't notice them.

I spent several evenings applying aloe lotion to Ani's back and other sensitive spots affected by her sunburn. She would apologize every time, I was upset I hadn't noticed sooner since she wouldn't have had to suffer if I had.

By the time school started up Ani was pretty much over her sunburn, she just had a dappled look to her face and shoulders though most wouldn't see that until physical education.

I heard from Aiko that Hazuki was supposed to leave last Friday but they never stopped by, so we didn't have a chance to wish her farewell.

So many changes in such a short time, my classmates all looked a little taller and more mature, though we still had the occasional goof ball who stood out in class.

The club members who couldn't make the first beach party were gathered around their friend's desks asking about it and sharing photos of the event. I guess there were several Line photos going around from the day we were at the beach, but I hadn't turned my phone off silent, so I didn't see them for a few days.

There were pictures of Ani, Tia and me when we entered the shaved ice stall as we were holding hands. The messages below that were amusing, things like, "Finally," and "Not fair," the funniest was, "That's going to hurt." I think they were referring to Ani's sunburn since you could see the slight pink cast to her skin in the photo.

The first bell rang, and the final students filed into the classroom, I saw Aiko file in later than normal as she looked my way with a big smile.

When the bell rang Murakami was nowhere to be seen. We sat relatively quietly but as the time passed students began chatting and the noise gradually grew. That was when the door slid open and Murakami entered the classroom.

I thought it unusual when he left the door ajar but didn't think much more of it. We conducted our normal homeroom start with a stand, bow and, "We will be in your care." Before we seated ourselves again.

Murakami then asked how our summer had been then told us to gather our homework and asked Aiko and me to collect it. As we placed the homework on his desk we made our way back to our seats.

"I have an announcement, we will have a new student joining us today." Murakami looked to the door, "Edamitsu please enter."

When the door opened Hazuki walked in. I looked over to Aiko who was already looking at me as she shrugged and smiled.

Murakami introduced Hazuki and told us briefly she was starting here ahead of her parent's arrival from Okinawa, so she would have an easier transition next year. "Edamitsu, you can take the back seat in row three for now."

"Thank you, Murakami-sensei." Hazuki began walking to the back but turned to look at me before she passed offering a bright smile.

Murakami addressed the class, "Okay, now the new term is upon us, I want you guys to continue your effort leading up to this. Trist, I hope you plan on continuing your club, if you need any help let me know."

"Thank you, Murakami-sensei."

"First order of business, do we have new nominations for class representatives?"

I had hoped that I might get a break from the extra planning but those fell through rather quickly.

"Anyone like to propose new representatives?" Murakami asked again. "Very well, Aiko, Trist keep up the great work."

Both Aiko and I responded, "Yes, sensei." So much for simple freedoms I thought.

"Next then. Seating assignments will be changing, we will use a lottery system and you can change if both parties agree." Murakami wrote an outline with all the seats from one to thirty-two. "Trist will come by with a box, please choose a slip from the box, that will be your new assignment."

I stepped forward to collect the box Murakami had produced from under his podium. I started on the isle closest to Tia and allowed each person a chance to draw until I had passed through the entire class. Everyone was fairly quiet about the new seats, I guess they were waiting to see who was around them.

"Okay, please arrange your desks and settle in, I will be back in thirty minutes for the assembly." Murakami picked up his folder and departed.

I turned and asked Lev, "What seat?"

Lev looked at his paper then waded it up and tossed it at me, I uncrumpled it, 21 huh. Lev looked at me, "Yours?"

"No change, ha-ha."

Ani chose 5, Tia had 19, Lev had 21, and I was in the same seat number 27. Even Aiko and Hazuki were separated. To my back I had Chisa, and diagonally was Kaoru. I felt pretty good having club members surrounding me, maybe they could help think of ideas over the remaining year.

Ani and Tia looked disappointed and tried everything they could to convince Lev to trade, but he held firm. He may regret it later I thought knowing Ani and Tia. I gently smiled at each, "We still have club together, right?"

The morning assembly was to welcome us back and addressed any issues that had come up during break involving students. Luckily our class was good. When it released we made our way back for the true start of the new term.

Murakami had Aiko and me bring a cart of new books up from the teacher's room. I hadn't seen these before, but they are clearly not middle school texts. As we rolled the books into the class and found our seats Murakami began explaining the agenda for the second term.

"I know you all are probably ready and excited to carry on in your old books, but after the last exam the principal and the board of education approved new books. These will be exclusive to your class." Murakami explained. He held them up and began setting them on the first desk to be passed back.

As Murakami set six volumes on my desk I began passing them back one at a time, as I looked at each cover I noticed they were clearly high school text books. My eyes widened a little as I began to thumb through the table of contents. While I should be fine, only Lev, Ani and Tia would probably be ready for some of these questions.

I heard Murakami speak and I looked up, "Yes, Aiko?"

Aiko raised her hand and asked, "Murakami-sensei doesn't this content extend past the planned curriculum for the three years?"

"It does, the school is trying to see the extent of your abilities. You will still be held to the same scoring standard among first years. However, the school will take this into account if your overall class average slips too low."

Everyone was muttering their concern. I glanced back at the class and noticed several of our club members with worried expressions. I raised my hand.

"Trist? What is your question?"

"What's in it for the class? I mean if they rise to meet this challenge what about next year?"

"If you achieve a 70% class average on the content provided the remainder of the year you will begin working on second-year high school content next term." Murakami appraised the class who looked in shock, "Those that remain attending this school in order to keep your progression uninterrupted will remain in the same group through graduation."

I nodded, so that helped protect the class dynamic, so each class didn't need to come up to speed, I thought, "If we clear the high school content, what about when we actually reach high school?"

Everyone began mumbling asking, "Yea what then."

"If you achieve a class average of 90% or higher upon finishing your third year, you will be offered a position at the Prefectural High School at no cost to your families. From there you will have special instructors who will closely monitor your progress and if you achieve similar results from the specialized curriculum you will immediately enter a graduate program at the University of Tokyo upon graduation."

The room was silent, what he just detailed cut out a tremendous cost to each student's family. Not to mention it cut four years of college.

I knew this was in large part due to my mistakes during the academic expo, so I didn't want the students to suffer from my excessive academic display.

"Murakami-sensei would the school give those unwilling to attempt this an opportunity to change classes?"

The entire class started objecting, several of the students looked at me with worried faces, "We can do it. We don't mind the challenge if you are going to face it too."

I was a little bit embarrassed, "Murakami-sensei I rescind my previous request."

Murakami looked at me with a father like expression and then to the remaining students, "If you are willing to proceed you will be locked into this class the remaining three years, those who would like to reduce the risk of potential failure can do so now. By a show of hands, who would like to remain in this new course?"

Hands shot up everywhere, mine was probably one of the last since I was concerned for my classmates, "Those that would like to change classes?" No hands appeared. The enthusiasm in the class was beyond expectation, "So, your parents are aware of the challenges and potential risks over the course of the next six years the board of education has already mailed packets detailing the change and benefits upon graduation of middle school, high school and college entry."

That afternoon when school released we had twelve more applications to our study club.

Aiko looked a little worried, "You know Trist, without your assistance and help this wouldn't be possible, are you sure you don't mind?"

I glanced at Aiko across from the table in our now full club, "I wouldn't have it any other way. I told you I wanted our class to do well, so I had talented friends, remember? This is more than I could have wished for. I should ask all of you, are you really okay being stuck in the same group for six years?"

A number of the students laughed, while several bluntly said they would prefer it no other way. I did feel proud of these new friends and hoped I wouldn't let them down. I looked at my three closest friends and thought I would really be leaning on them from here on.

I had hoped Aiko and I would be excused from volunteer work with the student council, but Murakami just laughed, "You can't get by without representing your class at school. You will need time to enjoy your school life and that's what these events are for."

As planning for sports festival continued during after school meetings so did our daily study club. At times I wished I could be in two places at once. I knew I needed to find some way to make myself accessible during club so not one minute was wasted.

*   *   *

The second week of the new term I was sitting at my desk in my room shortly after dusk. I had decided to really try to utilize and develop the ability Valdria had so vehemently warned me about. I focused my thoughts, and pictured Lev, Ani and Tia as I called them to my room. My head felt a little light, but I wasn't dizzy when I stood up.

It was just a few moments before I heard a mad rush of footsteps coming up the stairs. Lev threw open my door, "What's wrong!?" He asked with a worried expression.

I saw Ani and Tia directly behind him peering into my room, "That was fast."

"Don't…that was fast… me. You know what Valdria said about that don't you." Ani slapped her hand on my desk with a seriously concerned look on her face.

"Trist please don't do that again, I was so scared last time." Tia said as she tightly held her hands near her chest.

Lev just walked over to my bed and dropped onto the edge, "Well? What did you want to talk about?"

"Sit down guys."

Tia sat next to Lev while Ani reached for a pillow. Lev pulled out a cushion and smacked Ani in the face with it. Ani glared at her brother but sat quietly on the floor. Their relationship had been changing lately, I wonder if their talk had anything to do with it.

I looked at them, "I need a way to be able to answer questions when I'm not in the room. You are the only ones I can trust with this knowledge right now and you are farther along than the other students academically."

I looked at Ani who was staring up at me, while Lev was just listening. Tia looked a bit worried about where the topic was leading.

"I am going to need your help, or this new plan proposed by Murakami will fail. We are already two weeks into the new term and there are only six weeks until mid-terms. The class is struggling since they haven't seen most of the content before. You guys need to be the backbone while I'm helping the student council, sometimes it takes most of our club time and with the sports festival, it effectively pulls me out of club till the end of September." I looked at the three.

"So, I need to start working on strengthening my ability to pass and receive information to you, so you can ask advice and questions while I am elsewhere." I glanced at everyone, Tia looked a little mad while Ani had a concerned look.

Lev looked a little concerned still, "Trist, I know you want us to succeed but do you think it will really be that easy?"

I looked at the three and thought, *"Yes."* They all immediately threw their hands up to their temples.

"Dang Trist! You didn't have to shout." Lev said as Ani and Tia continued massaging their temples.

"It's simple, the ability is developing whether I want it to or not. If I don't learn to master it while I'm young it will end up doing the same thing to me as the 2nd Emperor. I want your help." I said as I bowed slightly.

"Stop that, you know we will help. You only need to ask and let us know how." Ani said indignantly.

Lev smiled at Ani's rebuke.

Tia had a somewhat unsatisfied expression, "Fine, what can we do to help?"

"Just like a moment ago, I have no idea how my thoughts come across, so tell me if it is too difficult to hear or if I am coming across too strong. I can't see into your heads."

Trist paused as he rested his elbow and propped his chin up on the back of the chair, "I still need to work on reading your thoughts too. I know I can do it but that was the difficulty I had last time."

Tia stood, "I'm not helping with that."

She tried to walk past but I gently caught her wrist and pulled her onto my lap as I rested my chin on her shoulder with my arms around her waist. I cocked my head to the side, so I could see her expression. She was a little red, I knew I could convince her, "Please Tia."

Tia turned her face away from me, so I couldn't see her. Ani looked a little jealous but remained quiet. I thought about Tia's personality and how she could be obstinate for the oddest things.

I closed my eyes and in the softest tenderest voice I could imagine, *"Please Tia."* Tia slapped her legs and stood up as she pulled away from my embrace and stepped back to the bed as she sat down wiping tears from her eyes.

"Trist you are so mean, it's like you're asking us to help you hurt yourself, but when you talk like that I can't help but melt. Don't use that tone again or I won't forgive you." While Tia rubbed her eyes, I could see she was also blushing slightly.

Ani was antsy, "Tia, what voice! What did he say?"

Tia just smiled at Ani.

"He just asked the same thing but the way he sent it was just a little…" Tia said without finishing.

"A little...what?" Ani asked expectantly.

Tia just smiled and had a look that said it's a secret.

"Tia, you're not being fair, Trist can you show me too?" Ani pleaded.

Lev laughed, "Ani give it up."

Ani began pouting.

It couldn't hurt but they needed to tell me how it came across, so I didn't send messages with a different meaning than I intended.

"Okay Ani, but you need to be honest when you hear, I don't want to accidentally send a message that someone misinterprets. Okay?"

Ani nodded enthusiastically.

I again pictured speaking in the softest tenderest tone and said, *"Ani, tell me how this sounds."*

Ani's face blushed bright red.

"Trist don't use that on anyone but Tia and me." She said as she began fidgeting.

"Okay but I need to know why?"

"Well…it was like you were whispering into my ear suggestively, it was more than just a message but also…" Ani struggled for a way to express the feeling.

"It was very sensual, it almost made my whole-body shiver. So, don't use that on anyone else!" Tia stated looking even more embarrassed.

"Okay, so I will refrain from that, can one of you close your eyes and picture me as you try to tell me something. Just one please." I asked not wanting to be overwhelmed.

Lev volunteered. He closed his eyes as I tried to extend my senses focusing on just him. I heard or sensed a faint voice, *"Trist this is crazy."*

I opened my eyes as Lev opened his, I wanted to make sure I didn't pull back my senses which I would have normally done but to make this work I would have to extend them even further.

"Lev, this isn't crazy." I said after I felt no after effects.

Lev's eyes widened, "Okay that is still too weird."

"Ani, you want to try?" Ani looked at me a moment then slowly closed her eyes.

I tried not closing my eyes this time and just left my consciousness open. I began to be bombarded by all kinds of thoughts, I could somehow tell they were Ani's but there were a multitude of emotions and desires mixed in, even some I know she didn't want me to see.

I slipped to my knees from the chair and grasped her by the shoulders since I didn't think my voice would work. As Ani's eyes popped open the thoughts began to subside, only the feeling on the surface of her mind were still mingling in my consciousness.

"Trist, what's wrong!?" Ani said as she saw me in front of her.

Lev and Tia stood showing concerned looks.

"You guys are killing me here, Lev, Tia I'm okay. I'm not the one who needs to develop control you three are." As I got that last part out the assault seemed to lessen. Now it felt like a dull white noise.

"Ani, I'm sorry but I probably saw more than you wanted me too. What were you trying to send?"

Ani looked flustered not knowing what I had seen or heard, "I was just trying to tell you to be careful, but then I started thinking of all the times we were together and feelings and stuff…" Ani stopped her embarrassed bluster.

"You need to focus just like I need too, if your thoughts are all over that's what I hear, and when you all start in I am overwhelmed."

I took a few deep breaths as I tried standing back up. I didn't feel nauseous, so I stepped back to my chair and sat.

"Ani try again please." We needed to get this down, it would be pointless if the messages only went one way.

She closed her eyes and within a few moments I heard, *"I'm sorry Trist, does this work?"*

"Okay Ani, yes. That was perfect" I offered her a smile.

She looked wide eyed, "I did it!"

I looked at Tia, "Can we try?"

Tia was still a little concerned especially after Ani. She turned and looked right at me, *"I don't like this Trist!"* Her thoughts were as clear as day.

My eyes widened followed by hers, "Did you hear that?" She tentatively asked as she covered her mouth in surprise.

"I was surprised, let's try a conversation Tia." So, I sent my next thoughts to Tia only. Though I tried to keep them caring and sensitive to her fears, *"Tia, we need to make this work both ways. If we can figure this out, think of the things we can accomplish."*

Tia turned back toward me, *"I still don't like it. What if something happens to you while you're trying to communicate, and we can't tell you're in trouble. I don't think we should do this."*

It was sort of weird hearing Tia speak in my mind even though her mouth wasn't moving, the expressions she showed mirrored her words though.

I smiled, "Tia that was wonderful, you are my official representative while I'm away from club."

Tia's eyes widened, "No, I don't like it!"

I figured I could tease her since she said not to do it with anyone but them, *"Please Tia."* I said in a similar tone to the first time.

Tia stood up and slapped me, I was a little shocked, "Trist if you do that again, I won't forgive you."

"Whoa, Tia what's wrong?" Lev asked. Ani stood up knowing something must be wrong for Tia to lash out at Trist.

"You ask that way knowing full well what it feels like in our minds, don't you think that's a little mean. I already told you how I felt about this and then you do that." Tia was almost in tears.

Ani stepped over not knowing the extent of her anger hugging Tia around the head for a few moments.

I felt pretty bad, I could obviously tell I pushed Tia too far, "Tia I am sorry. I promise I won't do that again to you."

I could hear Tia mumble in Ani's arms, "You can always call me that way but not when you want me to do something that could hurt you." She said, "I don't care what you want me to do, but if I think it will hurt you in any way I won't do it. I never want to have those feelings again."

I stood and rubbed Tia's head, "Okay, I'm sorry. Continue to be honest with me." I glanced caringly at Tia.

"However, you three are the only ones who can help without fear of exposure. If Tia refuses, then Lev and Ani are my only options." I looked at the two as they offered serious expressions, "The only other way is to identify someone I think I can trust in class."

Lev stood up, "That's not necessary. Even if Tia and Ani won't help I will. We just need to make sure it's safe for you."

"Then let's keep trying so it will work."

Lev, Ani and I practiced for a couple more hours before we decided to head off to bed. Tia sat a little dejected knowing it was her choice to exclude herself from the practice.

We were able to determine how some of the emotion was transmitted as well as intensity, I knew now if I just called they would receive a message that was loud and clear with no feeling which they both said made it difficult to tell if there was trouble.

My head started aching a few times during our attempts, so I tried to note the clues that indicated I was pushing too hard.

When we were done, Tia didn't say much and just left when Lev and Ani got up to go. As she was getting ready to close the door I tried to express my kindest thoughts, *"Tia, thank you for caring and being you."*

Tia looked back, "Good night Trist."

We practiced the next several nights for an hour before bed, I always called all three even if Lev and Ani were the only ones that responded.

The next weekend Valdria caught me as I was making an early breakfast, "Trist can we talk?"

"Sure, what is it?" I asked as I pulled up a chair at the dining room table.

"I understand you are working on a different form of communication?" Valdria asked as she arched her eyebrows.

"Did Tia tell you?"

"She did, she seemed very worried, I told her about Verndactilia 2nd and she was even more concerned. I think I calmed her worries but pointing out that if you can master this ability young you won't have the same problems. So, give her some time to process and keep asking her to help."

I smiled, "I always call her too, honestly she is the easiest to talk both ways with."

Valdria's brows furrowed a bit, "What do you mean both ways?"

"Well we can literally hold a conversation without opening either of our mouths, and we can do it from a long distance off I bet."

"Can you show me an example of how you communicate like that?"

I kept eating my toast and sent Valdria a calm message, *"Like this."*

Valdria's eyes widened a bit more, "Oh I see." She looked contemplative as she glanced at the table, "Trist, this isn't the same ability as Verndactilia 2nd, he could only hear people's voices, he could never talk to people. You never told me you were sending the messages, you told me when you tried to hear their thoughts you had problems."

"That's true, the sending messages is simple, but if I extend my senses then I begin to have trouble sorting all the stimuli." My head was normally in receive mode unless I was in school, so I asked Valdria subconsciously, *"Ask me a question."*

She thought a second then I could hear a faint, *"How do you determine who things come from?"*

I smiled and responded mentally, *"When I hear your response my brain is converting it to what I recognize as your voice, not sure how it works for people I just don't know yet."*

"Trist try not to use that ability too much outside of the house. I am already looking into the issue you discussed with Shivan and I will check on this as well, but this is beyond what I think I have seen in any of the records." Valdria seemed a little perplexed.

Sports Festival

Classes continued to be challenging, not just for the students but also for the instructors who were now teaching an entirely different curriculum for our class alone. The club was made entirely of our class and we maintained near a 100% attendance rate most of the week.

The student council activities were beginning to take much more time as we approached the school's sports festival. We even had to meet with merchants who donated goods for the event. I had heard the class was struggling but Lev, Ani and Tia did what they could. After we got home I went over the class content for that day in hopes it would make it easier for them.

The class was stuck on a particularly complex mathematical problem and Lev and Ani didn't know how to ask about it.

As I was sitting in a student council meeting I suddenly received a message from Tia, but she wasn't talking. It was as if she took a picture of the problem and sent it telepathically. I smiled as I jotted down the problem and quickly solved it including a detailed breakdown of each step.

I'm not sure if this will work but here goes, I looked at the problem and followed it all the way to completion in my head and tried to send it to Tia.

"Thanks Trist." Tia responded a few moments later.

I began to smile as Aiko elbowed me gently, "What's wrong?"

I smiled as I looked over at her, "Just had a break through idea for club."

Aiko raised her eyebrows.

The sports festival was next Friday so we had to have most of the details completed the weekend prior. Luckily Shivan didn't have a car so we wouldn't have to help pick up donations but that didn't mean we were free either.

During the weekend we were elected to help with banners and coloring decorations for our team color. It was a lot of work but even the second and third years pitched in for their team.

As Friday approached I was feeling emotionally exhausted, not only was I helping with all the representative activities I also was answering club problems when they were sent my way by Lev, Ani or Tia.

The team our class had been assigned to earlier in the year was the blue team, the way I understood it was throughout the year teams earned points based on academic merit and activities like the sports festival and other school events.

When I finally got home Thursday night I was exhausted. I hadn't been to club once all week. My classmates seemed to understand since it was visible on Aiko's face as well that we were losing sleep.

As I entered the kitchen I let Valdria know I wouldn't be down for dinner and immediately knocked on Lev's door, "Yea?" He responded.

"Do you guys need any help from today's club?"

Lev just looked at me, "No, get some sleep, the week is almost over."

I then checked with Ani and asked the same, she just told me to sleep that everything was okay for today.

As I knocked on Tia's door she opened it and was already wearing her pajamas, "Aren't you going to diner Tia?"

Tia was a little hesitant to respond, "I am but I wanted to ask you a favor first."

I tried to give her my best smile regardless of my exhaustion, "Sure, what is it?"

"I know I got mad once about it, but could you please wish me sweet dreams tonight before you go to sleep like you did the night we worked on your ability to talk without speaking?" She tentatively asked as she fidgeted, "I'm worried I won't be able to sleep, since I'm not as good at sports as Lev and Ani."

I smiled at Tia, "Are you sure?"

She looked up at me and offered a tiny smile.

"Please." She looked like she was more than worried, but I didn't want to push her too much.

"Tia is the class work going okay in the club?"

She nodded slightly.

"Though sometimes I have a hard time with some of the math." Tia admitted.

"Can you show me?"

I sat on the edge of Tia's bed as I could start to feel my body entering rest mode, every day for the last two weeks had been nonstop.

Tia sat at the foot of her bed next to me and opened her book, "I am having a hard time with applying this one." Tia pointed to a formula.

I glanced down as my eyes got blurry. My head felt heavy and I remember saying, "I'm sorry Tia, good night."

I woke up the next morning feeling very fuzzy, my alarm was set for 05:30 and hadn't gone off yet so I figured I still had time since my room was fairly dark. As I looked at the ceiling I realized I never changed out of my clothes, but I wasn't currently wearing my uniform.

I looked sideways at the door and noticed that my belongings weren't where I normally placed them, in fact the door looked much closer than normal. I turned my head to the left and felt a tugging sensation as I saw Tia next to me in her pajamas.

I tried to remember coming home and I slightly remembered Tia asking me about a problem, I must have fallen asleep. Tia was nestled against me but not draped over me like usual.

I turned to face her and gently stroked the top of her head and cheek. Tia began to stir, and she put her arm around me as she pulled herself a little closer.

Now she was nestled up against my chest as she had a hand near her face and one slightly on my waist. I laid my head back down on her pillow as I quietly looked at her sleeping face.

I admired her smooth complexion and dainty features, I reach over to stroke the top of her left ear as she stirred and brought her left arm up under mine. I rested my head on her pillow and reached out to give her a hug with my free arm.

As I raise my arm again I heard Tia faintly call my name. Is she awake? I guess I could ask like she requested last night. I think of her wanting to protect me and my pride at having her as my friend. I mentally told her, *"Thank you Tia I hope you have a good morning."*

Tia's face contorted a bit as she wiggled in closer pulling in with her arm, as she squirmed against me, she tilted her head back ever so slightly like she is ready to whisper something.

As my arm rested on her side softly stroking her hair and caressing her cheek she began to stir in earnest. With her head tilted up I was in easy range of her forehead, so I leaned in and kiss it gently.

Tia's eyes began to flutter open slowly, as they seemed to be searching my face as her brow twitched intermittently. Tia looked down at her arm across my sides and she began to process her situation. Tia's eyes opened wide for the first time as she sat up and looked at her room.

In a squeaky voice she asked, "This is my room, right?"

"It is, good morning Tia."

"Didn't you just say that already or was it a dream." Tia asked in earnest.

"I did say good morning instead of good night like you requested, or shouldn't I have?"

In another squeaky voice I heard her say, "No, that was good." She said with an extremely red face.

She jumped up and grabbed my clothes from her chair and sat them next to me. "I didn't want you to ruin them while you were sleeping." She said apologetically as her eyes dart around her room.

I slipped my pants back on. Even though it must have been embarrassing for her to do this it was appreciated. I took my phone out of my pocket and saw we still had almost an hour before my alarm went off.

I hung my shirt on the back of Tia's chair. As she stood fumbling with her hands. I patted Tia's bed and she slowly sat down. I told her to lay down again since we still had an hour, I felt less awkward with my pants on as well.

Tia gently scooted back into bed as she laid on her back, this time though I snuggled up to Tia who's face began to border crimson, I can even see her ears have changed to a dull red. I laid down next to her and gently placed my arm over her like she did to me. I rested my face slightly touching her shoulder.

"Good night Tia." I heard her inhale as she began holding her breath. Sometime after that I fell back asleep.

Tia must have turned to her left side and nestled her back against me, she held my hand like she did when she was nervous or scared, up near her chest.

I heard my alarm start to vibrate which was usually enough to wake me. As I turned, Tia began to squirm again. I felt extremely relaxed, almost like I had slept the whole day. I rested my head back down and whispered, "Tia, are you ready to get up?"

I could feel her nod, she twisted to her right and laid her head against my chest as I put my arms around her in a gentle hug, "I really like this." She quietly said. I stroked the back of her head and hair as it cascaded onto the bed next to her.

"Me too, but I really need to get ready, you can sleep a little more if you want." I could feel her shake her head no. I let her go as I sat up and grabbed my phone and headed up to prepare for the day.

I left the house by 06:00 and found myself at school with Aiko close to 06:45. We began moving the items for the sports activities into the grass area as well as setting up the tents. I felt so much better than the last few days it was like my energy had been completely renewed.

The class activities through the day were primarily team events showcasing team strength in tug-o-war, the 100-meter, 400-meter relay and the solo events like jump rope and also the three-legged race.

The class representatives were busy keeping scores or moving props from one location to the next. The number of activities weren't numerous but to get each group through sometimes took a considerable amount of time.

Around 15:00 the sport day concluded. Once we had things organized we were free for the weekend. I think we should do more exhibition matches next time, I thought. Maybe that wasn't what was expected in a sports festival though.

As a majority of the students began to depart, individuals identified in each class began to help wrap up the remaining cleaning. The student council took responsibility for the tents while individual team colors were responsible for the cleanup of one assigned event.

Our class was very quick since we were the 400-meter relay, Lev, Ani and Tia were participants. Tia ran remarkably well for someone who had been so nervous the night before, Ani ran anchor and was able to fly past the regular track team members.

The tug of war was a win for our team as well, overall the blue team came in second of six teams. The green team who had most of the athletic oriented students came in first. Several of their students were on the track, soccer and volleyball teams.

As the day concluded for the students and staff we were thanked for all the help and Haruka reminded us we would be doing the cultural fair early next year during the founding date of the school. I inwardly dreaded it but knew it was too far off to worry about.

I chased Lev, Ani and Tia off early, so it was only Aiko and me heading home, "How has the new content been going? I know you are in the same position as me with being held away from club." I asked her.

Aiko was a little subdued in her response, "Hazuki tries to help but I'm not sure if she even grasps it 100%."

"I need to start going over things with Lev, Ani and Tia this weekend, do you want to join? I know it has been a rough two weeks for studying. The extra day might help."

Aiko looked up at me, "I might take you up on that offer once I wake up tomorrow but for now all I can think about is sleep."

I laughed, "Yea that's how I felt last night but I slept extremely well yesterday."

"Lucky." Aiko said with a pouty expression.

"Anyway, think about it, regardless I will be reviewing even if the others choose not to."

That night after dinner I excused myself for bed, I knew I needed to quickly catch up, so I could settle back into a rhythm for school. Around 06:00 I woke up. About an hour before my alarm but I felt well rested, so I turned it off.

I gathered up all the material we had covered in class the last month and began to prioritize content by difficulty. If we can get the easy stuff cleared that will boost the overall average, we can catch up on the hard stuff as well now that I was back in club.

When 10:00 arrived, I heard the door chime, I looked out the window but didn't see a car, it must be Aiko I thought. As I made my way downstairs I met Shivan who smiled up at me since I saved him the effort of climbing all the way.

Not that I thought it bothered him, "Morning guys." I offered Aiko…Hazuki…Anju. "Oh, a few more than I expected. Come on in."

Valdria was cleaning up after breakfast it looked like only Shivan, Valdria and Talinde were up already. I heard Talinde outside around 09:00 finishing where I left off two weekends ago.

"Valdria, mind if we use the table?"

She just smiled, "Go ahead."

Anju and Hazuki were looking at Valdria, "Is she going to have a baby?" Anju finally looked at me and asked quietly.

"Humm, yea in eight months I think." Trying to remember the due date Shivan had, "I think she is due around Golden Week."

"Oh, it's a girl?" The three said excitedly, "I bet she will be cute."

"Hopefully she doesn't look like Lev." Anju said as Hazuki and Aiko giggled.

"I think she will be cute regardless, she will be the first member of our family born here."

As we began studying I told the girls what I would like to work on with them and they agreed with my reasoning. After an hour I began to hear doors open and close in the right wing of the house.

Ani and Tia came walking into the room in their pajamas and headed to the kitchen.

Anju, Aiko and Hazuki watched them pass without comment. As they turned to head back they both seemed to stop as they just noticed a group of people sitting at the far dining room table.

"Are you guys going to join us or sleep all morning?"

They both had blank expressions until they realized what we were doing and then they both hurriedly headed back to their rooms and returned a short time later.

Their hair was still a little frizzy from sleeping, but Ani combed Tia's and they switched places.

After they sat with us Tia paused, "Just a minute." Tia ran off to her room then returned with my shirt, "Trist you left this in my room the other night."

Tia handed me my shirt as I placed it over the back of my chair, "Thank you, Tia."

I noticed intent stares coming not only from Ani but the other three as well. Tia just sat there with a curious grin on her face.

*　　*　　*

The Monday following the sports festival was my first opportunity to really see where everyone was at during club. Classes went well, the teachers provided an adequate number of examples and seemed to leave the class with plenty of guidance I thought.

When school released for the day and I was able to make my way to the club with Aiko I could feel a sense of frustration when I entered the room.

Each table was focusing on a different subject, I guess this was Lev's idea, and students moved as they began to understand a topic. I first approached the table with the most students.

As I sat and listened I understood the areas they were being challenged. I began to explain, "For this problem, I think the best areas to pay attention to in the book are these three sections."

I found the areas that pertained to each problem, "When you see a problem, they might be giving you the actual answer, so make sure you recognize the steps, and you can work forward or back depending on the question."

The table seemed to understand, and my example pointed out a step they hadn't thought of yet. As we worked through several of the book problems I wrote down a few problems of varying difficulty and in different stages of completion and asked for the origin and the result.

As each member worked through the problems they began to seem a little more satisfied with the process.

Hazuki sighed as she told me, "That was so much easier, I kept getting stuck when the problem didn't look like the formula. Thanks Trist."

I smiled, "Glad I was able to help." I stood up and wandered to the next table, some of the students at the last table were now moving on themselves.

The table covering history and geography were working on dates and events. I showed them how the text book highlighted significant events, "If your familiar with this summary, your good. Otherwise go back and make sure you can answer who, what, where and when for the topics they summarize here. If you do that for each chapter you will do okay."

Naoki scratched his head, "What about geography? Is there an easy way to memorize that?"

"Humm, knowing what country the historical event occurred will help but as far as geography in general, it would be easiest to focus on the countries actually discussed. Knowing every countries capital and region might not be worth focusing on yet. So just memorize the areas relevant to our current studies." I recommended, Naoki sighed but nodded.

I continued this for each table, after about two hours the final chime rang out signaling the end of the day.

"Well, I'm glad I am back with you. Hopefully we will be able to catch up this month, we can discuss a study group before the exam too. Should we limit it to just our class this time or would you like to keep it open?"

Sae, one of the members who joined before the last exam spoke up, "I had a lot of fun helping the other students, I think it really reinforced what I already knew too."

Aiko also raised her hand, "The content we are working on is significantly different, so if we help it will give us a chance to keep a decent grasp on the basics."

I nodded, "Okay, I won't announce it until the week prior in case we have a change of heart. Until then give it your all, you can also ask questions on Line, someone other than me might even be able to assist."

The group all nodded.

Classes began to ease up, and as the club met and progressed so did the general understanding of the class content. More people began answering questions in class, so this improved engagement with the teachers as well as advice on certain questions.

As October ended many students took a day off from club to enjoy seasonal festivities in town. I recommended that everyone who could go and enjoy the local festival, but I still had a number of students who wanted help after school. This worked out nicely since I could more easily focus on a smaller group.

Lev was getting to a point where he no longer had to verify questions with me and was really turning into a valuable resource. Ani was good with the humanities subjects, but she had to really focus on the math and science and sometimes made mistakes. Tia was pretty good with each topic, the only problem was she couldn't work well with the guys, she was just to standoffish. I really couldn't see why when she spoke so easily to Lev and me.

When we were a week out from mid-terms, I set a study date of Saturday and Sunday the two days prior, "Okay, so do we want to meet any place specific for our study group before the test?"

The answer was a resounding, "Your place!" I just sighed.

"Let me verify with my family, but it will probably be okay." I said.

That Monday evening once we all arrived home I found Valdria and Shivan working in the kitchen on dinner.

As I entered the kitchen, I must have looked like I had something inconvenient to request, Shivan glanced at me then went back to preparing his portion of dinner, "It's not a problem just let us know how many." He said without me even asking.

Valdria was hiding a laugh, "It will be next Saturday and Sunday. If you don't mind we might do the same thing as last time. I am fairly sure Sunday will be at least 32 students but Saturday…" I shrugged. "…could be as many as 70 or more."

Shivan's eyebrows raised, "Are you tutoring the entire school?" He said in an amused tone, "I will ask Kazu if he can bring some chairs and tables again."

"Thank you Shivan, Valdria. I know this is an imposition, but it really helps the students in our class." I headed out and walked to Lev's room. He was just lying on his bed reading a manga he borrowed from Josuke, "How do you have time for that after today?"

"It's easy to read and it kind of helps my mind slow down." I pulled out the chair at his desk and began writing a confirmation on Line for those in class.

I immediately received confirmation from about two-thirds of the class. After the first sleep over the grades the students earned were high enough that convincing most parents to allow their kids to stay over was an easy task.

After a couple minutes almost everyone had confirmed, those that hadn't I could verify with tomorrow. I left Lev's room and headed on upstairs.

When I entered my room, I sat my book bag next to my desk and began reviewing study content for this weekend. I looked ahead in the chapter and identified key subjects to add to the list, so I wasn't adding at the last minute.

The week seemed to take longer than expected, we had one student council meeting on Wednesday, but it was only the preliminary meeting for the Cultural Festival in February.

By Thursday evening the club was doing pretty good, only occasionally did they really have difficulty answering problems with their books.

During our Wednesday class I told the others that if anyone asked about a study group we would be holding it on Saturday starting at 10:00, "If no one shows up we can focus on our own material."

Tashiro looked doubtful, "Trist, we have probably all been approached for the last week asking about a study session, I doubt it will be empty."

Thursday night I checked with Valdria asking if there was anything I could pick up on my way home Friday. She gave me a list of items that she thought we could purchase on our way home.

The ingredients looked a little different from curry, so I wonder if we were going to have something new.

After class released and club concluded we walked to the bus stop with most of the club members in tow. Along the way a few students called out, "See you tomorrow."

We just waved and continued to chat about what we needed to set up for tomorrow. Tashiro, Josuke and Junichi all volunteered to help set up.

At first, I declined but their persistence paid off, so we compromised. We all agreed on a 09:00 meeting, they said they would stop earlier if I wanted but I declined.

That night after we all separated for bed I had a number of things running through my mind. This made it difficult to settle down but finally I found myself drifting to sleep.

I was up relatively early and took care of my personal hygiene before I made my way down stairs. As I walked toward the kitchen I saw through the curtains Ani and Tia were already moving things around outside. I grabbed my shoes and opened the door, "Why didn't you wake me?" I asked.

They both just smiled but didn't offer a reason. I slipped my shoes on as I stepped outside. There were a few more tables this time and an extra rack of chairs. Hopefully Kazu doesn't expect us to fill all of them, I thought.

Ani was wearing a light outfit which looked out of place given the temperatures had begun to decline. The sky had a slight overcast look to it but there was no rain in the forecast for today or tomorrow.

Luckily the patio cover was spacious and would still accommodate a large number even if it did rain.

Ani was moving a number of chairs at the same time, to me it looked a little cumbersome, "Ani be careful, we don't need to rush."

Ani just glanced my way as she carried an armful of chairs around the walkway to the patio, "It's fine, there not that heavy."

I helped Tia move the tables and organize the benches so that we could fit the largest number of students under cover. As I was walking to grab another table I heard someone walking up the gravel road.

I leaned the table against the house and looked out front. Josuke, Tashiro and Junichi were standing at the front door, "Hey guys." I said as I walked around the corner of the house.

"You already started? I knew we should have come earlier." Tashiro said.

I laughed with them and we set their bags down along the inside wall and went back outside.

As we swept the large leaves from the patio, Tashiro wiped down the tables and Junichi and Josuke helped carry the remaining chairs. We placed a few stacks along the wall since we didn't know if we would need them.

Based on what we had we could accommodate close to 60 people with relative ease.

Ani was carrying several chairs inside to place in the lounge area where we gathered after the study session. As I looked around I was wondering if we had any lights that would allow us to work later.

I suddenly heard a crashing noise and Ani was on the floor of the dining room with her arm twisted and cut from the chairs. I rushed to her side without thought, "Ani are you oaky!?"

She was gritting her teeth and had pulled her hand to her chest. She had scrapes on her shins and elbows and both her hands looked red, but one was swelling.

When she had tried to step up into the kitchen the legs of the chairs caught, and her forward momentum caused her to fall and slip off the step.

I gently picked her up as I turned to Lev who had come to see if she was oaky. "Can you get Valdria? I'll be in the washroom."

Ani was trying not to cry but I could tell she was in pain. She held her hand tightly and the scrapes were oozing blood on her shins and elbows, her hands looked like they were smashed or pinched when she fell.

As I looked at her cuts it made my heart ache inside seeing her like this. I gently wiped the dust away from the scrapes but realized it was going to take more, "Ani can you stand by yourself a minute?"

Ani gave a little nod. So, I grabbed one of the chairs she had been carrying and brought it into the washroom, "Here sit for a moment." I told her. I knelt down and slowly cleaned the dirt and blood from her scrapes.

I took the gauze we had and placed it over the scraped area to keep the bleeding down. I had her extend her arm the best she could, so I could do the same with her elbows. When I had her first elbow wiped clean Valdria came into the washroom followed by Lev.

Valdria was more concerned with her finger, "I can't tell if it's fractured, the cuts can wait. Ani, since others saw you fall we can't really heal these today, it will have to wait until tomorrow. Okay?"

Ani just nodded as she tried to wipe a stray tear from her eye.

"For now, though, you should rest in your room. Trist can you wash the scratches and wrap them good?"

"I can, I will carry her to her room when I'm done." I said.

Lev looked relieved and walked out to give an update to the concerned students.

I continued to touch up the scratches after Valdria left. I tried to keep a fair amount of pressure on the cuts since I knew they would ooze for a long time. As I cleaned her other elbow Ani noticed me frowning and shaking my head.

"Aren't you going to say anything?" Ani quietly said in a scratchy voice.

"What should I say?" I asked as I continued to work.

"You told me not to carry so many chairs, I thought you would yell at me." She said as she winced from the burning sensation of the antiseptic.

I looked up to her, "I only said that because I didn't want you hurt. But since it happened it does no good to say it again does it? Let me see your hand."

Ani held out her hand which was trembling slightly, "I'll be right back." I went to the kitchen and grabbed a towel and plastic bag and made a small icepack to put against her hand and returned.

As I carried it back Ani had a somewhat relieved expression, "Here, hold this here." I had her hold the towel with the ice inside, "I'm going to wrap this around, so it won't fall off easily, it should make the pain subside a bit." Ani nodded a little.

"Okay, here we go." I picked her up and carried her out of the washroom to her room. As I slid her door open I carried her over to her bed and gently sat her down, "If you need anything call. Okay?" I said as I smiled sympathetically.

Ani looked unhappy she wasn't going to be with the group, "If you feel better I will help you come out later. But please Ani for now rest a bit." I gently kissed her forehead then pushed her back gently. I began to head out then heard Ani.

"Thank you, Trist."

Over the next hour our remaining classmates arrived followed shortly after by the first batch of outside students. Initially it was a reasonable number, the outside students totaled about twenty.

The work load was distributed and even allowed some club members to focus on their own studies.

Around noon the door chime rang again. Outside was another eighteen students, some whom actually had been dropped off by their parents when they realized today was the study session.

It didn't take long for our classmates to ask about Ani, it was unusual to not see her and more so considering this was her house.

I explained what happened and several of the girls asked if they could visit her, "I think she would like that, follow me." The girls were Kaoru, Kiho, Remi and Chisa.

They followed me back to her room. I gently knocked and heard Ani's faint response. I slid the door open a bit, "Do you mind visitors?"

Ani shook her head, so I walked in followed by the four girls, "Let me look at the bandages."

I gently picked up Ani's leg and looked at the gauze then her other, when I finished looking at her arms I asked, "Need more ice?"

"No, it is pretty cold still."

The four were sitting around her room as I looked her over and once I finished I turned to them, "Let me know if she needs anything, okay?"

The girls all nodded with admiration in their eyes.

As I slid the door closed I could hear the girls as they began to chatter and giggle.

Ani looked in good spirits when they came in, I was glad she had made friends.

When I made my way back outside I noticed a number of overfilled tables, Lev was explaining some of the content for our current class, the funny thing is the students around his table weren't in our class.

I walked up and asked if I could help. Misaki was the first to ask, "Why are you guys the only one studying this book? Isn't that a little unfair?"

I assumed she meant they thought they should be as well, "You could probably talk to them about moving you to our class if you wanted too."

Misaki shook her head vehemently, "No thank you. I have a hard-enough time doing what we have now. Why are they making you do stuff so advanced?"

"I guess to prove we can do it? We all had a choice but everyone in the class accepted the challenge."

"It doesn't seem fair. I mean your club, and now your class do so much for everyone, and you are struggling with the biggest challenge of all. It just doesn't seem right." Misaki said as she looked up at me.

I shrugged, "I think we will be fine, once we catch up it'll be easier."

A little while later Kaoru came back out, "Hey Trist, Ani wants you."

I looked at her and asked, "Is she okay?"

"Yea, I think she wants you to bring her out, she still seems depressed she's in her room."

I sighed as Kaoru smiled, "You know you like it when she depends on you." Kaoru teased.

I tried to conceal my smile at her comment, "Yea I guess I do."

Kaoru's eyes widened a bit as she smiled at my honesty, "I will make some room for Ani."

I walked back to Ani's room, the door was still slightly ajar and three of the girls were still present, "Mind if I come in?"

"Yes, do you mind taking me outside Trist? It's hard to walk without bending my knees a lot and I hate not being able to help."

I walked over to Ani and leaned over as she put her arm around my neck and I picked her up, "Kaoru is fixing a spot for you, but you need to be careful you don't bump your injuries. Okay?"

Ani had a bright smile as she nodded, "I'll be careful this time."

I carried her out as she rested her head against my shoulder and stepped sideways out the door, so I wouldn't jar her legs. Kaoru had a table set up and had cleared the chairs near where Ani would sit so no one would bump into her.

I sat her down as gently as I could and looked at her knees and arm, "Ice?"

She smiled, "It's still good."

So, I nodded and pulled a chair up and sat next to her.

A couple of the students who had worked with Ani before brought their work and sat at her table, so she could help. Ani enjoyed the gesture and did all she could.

As it approached 18:00 I noticed students beginning to thin out. Tia and Lev were still helping a large group of students, but the majority of our classmates were now reviewing their own material.

The three girls working with Ani were now talking about school and the most recent fashion. Something Ani never had a chance to talk about.

I thought I would tease her a bit. I looked at Ani as I thought, *"Instead of a dress ask them if they have a padded one so you won't hurt yourself if you fall."* Ani looked over at me as I sent my message, instead of the smile I thought I would get she looked a little unhappy.

Ani looked down at herself then at the girls talking to her, *"Do you think I really need padding?"* She asked with a dissatisfied look on her face. I was starting to think we were talking about different things.

"What does padding mean to you?" I asked, wanting to make sure I didn't dig too deep of a hole for myself.

Ani didn't answer instead she held her hand up against her chest as she looked at me. I could have hit my head on the table, *"No! I meant padding as in wrapped all around you so if you fell you wouldn't get hurt, I think your chest is perfectly fine!"*

I shook my head as Ani slowly released the hand she had gripping her shirt and smiled a little as she turned back to the three girls before her.

I heard someone call out so as I turned I noticed Aiko asking me a question, *"What can I help with."* I sent…I just thought that! Didn't I?

Aiko stopped and cocked her head to the side like she wasn't sure what had just happened, "Trist?"

"Yes?" I answered in a slightly elevated voice as I faced her. She looked a bit perplexed like she wasn't sure what just happened. Then she continued walking toward me and pulled out a chair next to me.

"I'm having a hard time answering this question. I looked through the last two chapters but can't seem to find it."

I could hear fragments of her thoughts, *"Did he really answer, or did I just think he answered?"*

"Umm, let's see." As I tried to change the subject. I reflected on Valdria's words I guess I need to be more careful in my home too, "I thought I saw this mentioned on the second page of the most recent chapter."

I thumbed back and quickly scanned the text, "I am not sure you need to worry about this one Aiko, it is only mentioned once, and the author doesn't place much emphasis on it."

"That's good, I have been overthinking some of these topics, it might be time to take a break."

"Want me to get you something to drink?"

Aiko looked at me, "How can you always do that?"

I was a little confused, "Do what?" I asked thinking I said something awkward again.

"You are always looking out for others or making people comfortable and even standing up against people who are much bigger. If I didn't know better, I could see you as a prince." Aiko said as she innocently looked into my eyes.

"A prince huh? Well I'm not that special."

"Liar!" I heard Lev tell me. I glanced over my shoulder and saw him grinning at me.

Mid Term Fall

The Saturday of the study group was a mixed success, the students from outside our class were happy but our class was beginning to feel the strain of the upcoming exam. We moved inside after dinner had finished since it had been a pleasant evening. Valdria fixed meat and potato stew, Kaoru, Kiho and Remi were a little disappointed that all the prep work had been done. I was glad they used the time to study though.

The evening ended fairly early, it was apparent many of the students were emotionally exhausted from the stress of studying. A couple girls stayed in Ani's room in case she needed help with anything, this prevented Valdria from healing her wounds before she had to sleep.

When I woke up the next morning I checked in on the students who were beginning to mill about. Tia was up, sort of, as she made her way past me to the toilet then stumbled back into her room. I made sure to take a quick picture of her sleeping face, so I could show her later.

Some of the students began making their way downstairs, I asked if they wanted anything to eat but the response was no. We ended up doing one on one question answer drills.

I gave everyone a list of items to be knowledgeable on as well as page and paragraph numbers to review that evening. I focused on the easiest categories, so the class would pass the largest number of tests.

Aiko, Anju and Hazuki were the final students to depart. I made my way to Ani's room and noticed Tia was there as well looking at her bandages. She had long since discarded the ice since it was difficult to keep up when you were asleep, "I'm going to get Valdria." I told Tia and Ani. Tia nodded, and Ani just smiled.

Valdria had already exited the pantry and met me halfway, "Everyone's gone now, can we heal Ani?"

Valdria held up the molecular stabilizer, "Let's go."

As we entered Ani's room Tia moved aside as I helped peel the bandage wrappings off.

The blood on the bandage had turned to a blackish ooze and Ani's shins looked black and blue, her hand and elbows also were very discolored.

Valdria took her time healing the scrapes and bruises first before she moved to her hand, "Ani, this might hurt, but since I don't have a way to view the bones in your hand I will need to feel, and it will require me to trace the bone to make sure where it's broken. Okay?"

Ani's face seemed to contort, in anticipated pain, "How much will it hurt?"

"Honestly it might hurt more than last night, I am not sure."

Ani nodded but I could see her eyes moisten. I sat down on her bed next to her and held her other hand, "If it hurts just squeeze my hand, okay? I'll give you a reward if you can do it without crying. I whispered to her."

Ani turned and looked at me, "What kind of reward?"

Valdria started tracing the bones in Ani's hand as we were talking. When she found an area that she thought was damaged she pulled her finger slightly to make sure the bones were still lined up.

Ani's face contorted as we looked at each other, "I will let you decide." As Ani squeezed my hand with all her strength I watched her do her best not to cry.

"It looks like it was broken, but the bones matched up nicely so there was no splintering. Ani try wiggling your fingers now."

Ani looked down at her hand as she slowly closed and extended her long slender fingers. She turned her hand around looking at the top and her palm but the blemishes from the swelling and bruising had begun to subside once the muscle and bone was healed.

I squeezed Ani's hand, "Good job." I rubbed the top of her head as she sighed a bit, "So, what do you want as a reward?"

Tia was looking at Ani expectantly as Valdria smiled and exited the room. Ani glanced at Tia then back at me, "Can I save it?"

I honestly didn't expect that, "Sure, but don't make it too unrealistic. Okay?" I cautioned.

Tia relaxed somewhat, as Ani smiled.

Monday was exam day, our class was in a different mode, none of the usual chatter and everyone was sitting in their seats or scanning over problems with the person next to them.

Before the bell rang I stood and cleared my throat, "Everyone, don't over think the problems remember they will all be what you have already studied but don't get stuck on the format, if you don't recognize it as a question we covered, ask yourself if it was one of our answers and work back from there. We only need a 70% but I think everyone here is capable of much more."

The bell rang shortly after I finished, and several students continued to watch me even after I sat, their expressions slowly hardened with determination. Murakami entered, and we paid our respects, then role was taken, after that he detailed the exam schedule for our class.

I had confidence in each student, it was a matter of them identifying it themselves. As the first test was passed out we waited to be given the instructions to start, each test would be an hour in length and would include one extra credit problem per test.

I thought they must have added that since there were so many high scores last term exam.

The command was given and there was a massive rustling of papers being turned over. I quickly skimmed over the first page, short answer, and the following was multiple choice and a matching date to events.

I laughed but hoped the class didn't get stuck, there were more dates than events, so they must have included them to throw the tester off. The third page included a couple short answers and a single essay.

I turned back to the first page and began answering the questions. The test wasn't extremely difficult since we covered so much the first two months but there were really only two or three questions per chapter. The hard part was the test had a lot of possible content so there is no way to tell which two or three questions would be chosen.

I finished with twenty minutes to spare, I also went back and reviewed each portion and adjusted the essay twice to include additional facts.

As time ended for the first test there were a few sighs of relief. We had a couple minute break before the next exam, so I looked around the class to try to determine how people were feeling.

The looks were still focused, a couple people were verifying their responses or reviewing what they felt weak on for the next exam.

As the bell chimed Murakami began passing out the next exam. The same process repeated itself through third period ending with lunch. I turned to Lev and asked how it was going.

He just shrugged, "Okay I think."

"Let's get something to eat, I need to get Ani and Tia up and about, so they don't break." I said, but Lev just laughed.

I walked over to Ani who was looking through her book, I put my hand on her shoulder, "Let's get something to eat Ani."

"I can't"

"Ani! Let's get something to eat."

She looked up at me as I thought, *"Don't make me tease you."*

Ani huffed, "Fine." As she sat her book down.

We walked over to Tia's desk and she was in a similar state, "Let's go Tia." I reached down and took her hand as she looked up. I gently tugged her up to a standing position.

"Huh, where are we going?" Tia asked a little flustered.

I held Tia's hand and began pulling her with me toward the door. Ani was looking a little disappointed I didn't do the same for her, but she was still following. I reached back and quickly grasped her hand as well. She looked embarrassed, but she didn't let go.

When we made it to the stairs I let go of both their hands, so we didn't draw too much attention as we neared the school store. Which was not much more than an empty room filled once a day by a local shop owner who sold quick snack items and a small variety of sandwiches.

We usually didn't come down here since it was always busy, but during exam time a lot of the students ate in the classrooms or cafeteria while they studied.

After we all purchased something to eat we decided to sit in the covered courtyard outside the main wing. It had been an overcast day, so it was a little cool and slightly humid. Luckily the cooler temperatures made the humidity more bearable.

We ate and enjoyed the cool, having a break from the class was also helping Ani and Tia clear their heads, "Only two more to go, I know you guys will do great." I rubbed both Ani and Tia on the head.

I reached over toward Lev's head teasingly and he slapped my hand away and made a ferocious pose, "I will not be tamed." Lev said as he made a meowing noise.

All three of us laughed.

There was about fifteen minutes left in lunch, so we started to head back to class. I sat at my desk and Lev rested his head on the top of his, "What are we going to do after this is done?"

I remained silent a moment, "I want to go home honestly. I doubt many will want to do any club studying after this last week."

Lev turned his head, so his forehead was against the desk, then I noticed Hazuki walking our direction.

"Do you guys want to go for a parfait after school is over? A couple of our classmates wanted to get something to forget about the tests today."

I sensed Lev laughing more than I heard him, "Shouldn't we wait until the results are posted?"

Hazuki held her finger up to her lips, "I wouldn't mind doing both with you…guys." She said as she glanced down at Lev who still had his face on his desk.

I smiled, "Let me check with everyone. I wouldn't mind as long as the other club members don't mind canceling."

Hazuki beamed a smile, "I doubt that will be a problem, most will probably go with us."

I rested my elbow on my desk as I propped my chin on my hand, "So much for going home."

Lev was smirking as he looked at me, "Trist, you're a glutton for punishment. If you never say no, people will continue to ask."

The bell chimed it's five-minute warning and the class slowly filled back up. As the final chime called out Murakami re-entered the class with a huge stack of papers.

"Okay, lastly math and science." Murakami said as he began passing out the thicker set of papers. As we were given the start command I reviewed the material. I realized the test wasn't too long and that a couple papers were scrap paper for calculations.

I saw several people writing down the formulas, so they wouldn't forget once we started. We probably should work on a way to help them memorize them since the appropriate formula made the test so much smoother.

The math was easy for me, I had gotten used to detailing the process since that always seemed to come up. The written problems had way too much information given for what the question asked. This will probably cause problems for a few people.

The last test was science which contained a mix of biology, physics and chemistry, the questions weren't too complex, but they were definitely more advanced than what we had last term.

I finished solving the problems and even drew a neat cellular diagram detailing the components discussed in a couple of the questions. I sat my pencil down and leaned back, I saw Lev glance at me as he slightly shook his head.

When Murakami called time, there was a significant sigh released across the classroom, "Great job guys, we will have these ready on Wednesday and posted with the regular test scores."

Murakami gathered up the tests as the final bell chimed and made his way out of the class.

I stood up and announced, "No club today. Everyone needs to get some rest."

There were mixed cheers of satisfaction and disappointment, "I will answer questions as we walk out if you want."

"I'll meet you, Ani and Tia downstairs." As I grabbed the class journal. I bounded down the stairs and made my way to the teacher's office to drop off the class journal.

As I quietly knocked and entered I saw Murakami glancing through the test papers. I bowed slightly as I placed the journal in the box and turned to leave.

"Hey Trist, come here a second."

I froze midstride and turned to approach his desk located between the second row of teacher's desks, "Yes Sir?"

"How do you think you did?"

"Me or the class as a whole?"

"Well, both. How about your thought then thoughts on the class?"

"The test was pretty easy, but the class might have been challenged with it. Due to student council activities I wasn't able to help them as much as normal so that may have impacted it."

"Humm, maybe we can discuss that later. You guys are in an unprecedented situation and you my boy are the reason." Murakami looked hard at me, "You know, that right?"

I nodded, "I am fairly certain that's the truth." I admitted, "But I also have faith they can meet the challenge." I said as I smiled.

"Be safe going home." Murakami nodded as he shooed me off.

I made my way to the entry lockers and changed my shoes, I saw Ani and Tia near the front doors. I headed there way as I was intercepted by Hazuki.

"Perfect timing, everyone is waiting." Hazuki said.

"Sorry, Murakami had a few questions."

"Shall we go?" Hazuki hooked her arm around mine as she started to drag me past Ani and Tia with their mouths agape. They quickly followed as they moved in close to my free side. Hazuki seemed to be leaning in close as she gripped my arm.

I could feel the outside of my arm lightly rub on her coat. As I glanced over I could see the school emblem on her left breast pocket brushing against my arm.

I glance over at Ani who is walking with a very unhappy expression. She looked my way as I was glancing at her chest wondering if she was bigger than Hazuki. I looked up to see her giving me a nasty scowl.

* * *

When we finally made it to the shops flanking the mall, the group filed up a narrow set of stairs to a second story shop. I wouldn't have even guessed this place was here.

There was a large number of students, but they had already set aside several tables for our group. I was a little curious how they knew we were coming so I looked at Hazuki, "I called." She said with a big smile.

"What if I had refused?"

She winked, "I would have turned to Ani and Tia. You would still have come if they were, wouldn't you?" Hazuki said mischievously.

With Hazuki clinging to me the entire trip, Ani and Tia didn't have an opportunity to guard my sides. As we approached our chairs Hazuki ensured she and I sat in the corner.

I could tell Lev was getting a kick out of this, but Ani and Tia looked visibly upset. As our group filled the three tables I noticed we had a little more than half the class here.

The menu was fairly extensive, you could pick snack foods or deserts, the main specialty of this shop was their parfaits. I looked at the menu and the first thing that caught my attention was the price, close to seven thousand yen. I looked a little more closely then realized this portion of the menu was party sized parfaits.

The group pooled their money together and purchased two giant parfaits.

When they delivered them to the table the waitress had to have a kitchen staff help bring them out. They stood a little over one meter high with different cookies and decorations poking out of the top.

The waitress provided us all bowls, spoons and a very long narrow serving spoon to scoop out of the elaborate glass. I could see cookies, fruit, ice cream, pudding and a number of other ingredients layered decoratively in the container.

I glanced at the students as the parfaits were delivered, many didn't seem to look surprised but a few students who were here for their first time had wide open eyes. I looked at Ani and Tia and they had totally forgotten about Hazuki.

Hazuki stood and began serving the students at our table while Chifumi was helping those at the second and third tables. Everyone passed their bowls down and took a filled bowl as they came back around.

When Hazuki handed me, mine she had placed a large chunk of brownie on the top. I looked around and mine seemed to be a little over filled in comparison to the others.

I picked up the spoon they provided and was about to take a bite when I saw a spoon slip in front of my mouth and angle toward my lips. Having a spoon suddenly thrust in my mouth was a little surprising but as I felt the contents begin to slide into my mouth I had no choice but to close my mouth around the spoon to keep it from falling out.

As I sat my spoon down I turned to Hazuki who was smiling happily as she took a bite of her parfait with the spoon she just used. As she was sliding the spoon past her lips to ensure it was clean she offered me a huge smile. She leaned a little closer and said, "Thank you for the indirect kiss."

She said this in a tone just loud enough for the others to overhear, they all cast surprised glances our way. I'm not sure if my face expressed what I felt but if it did, people would have seen my mouth drop open.

Ani was holding her spoon in a fist as she was staring down at her parfait while Tia looked extremely flushed with her hands resting on the table next to her bowl.

Even Aiko was shocked at her cousin, she never imagined she would do something as blatant as that, "Hazuki, would you stop. Your embarrassing Trist!"

I looked at Aiko with what was probably a pleading expression as she just had an I'm sorry look on her face.

As we finished up the parfaits, several people began talking about the exam and parts they wish they had focused more on. It sounded like most of them did better than they initially thought they would, which was encouraging.

When everyone began sliding out of the booth and getting up from their chairs Ani took this chance to quickly grab me by my right arm as Tia moved close to my left.

Hazuki pouted a little but smiled at both Ani and Tia as her expression changed to a calculated grin.

After we wrapped up our afterschool fun we began walking home, we were close enough now that taking the bus would have been a waste of money.

As we walked home Ani had taken my arm like Hazuki had and Tia just held my left hand. As we were walking I felt a similar sensation against my arm but when I glanced over I could definitely tell Ani had the advantage over Hazuki.

* * *

Wednesday arrived with little fanfare. When the four of us arrived at school we went to check the scores after I quickly grabbed the class journal from the teacher's office. After I met with Lev, Ani and Tia we looked at our ranking. I noticed the majority of class 1-A were now in the top.

As I was identifying our top and bottom performers I heard someone clear their throat to my left, "I guess your study group met its match." Yamato from 1-A said.

I smiled, "It looks that way doesn't it." I smiled slightly as I walked past him and joined Lev, Ani and Tia.

Lev glanced back at Yamato as we began walking, "Who does he think he is, he hasn't hit 500 once on the tests and this time you hit 525 while taking a high school exam." Lev was shaking his head.

I turned to Lev as we climbed the stairs, "Let him be, competition is a good thing. Even if he competes on a different field."

As we entered class several students asked if I saw the results. I nodded and praised each one. Even the lowest score was still in the low 70% range. Lev had come in at an 82%, Ani was almost 80%, Tia did surprisingly well regardless of her fear of tests with an 83%.

The class average would probably sit in the mid 70% range I thought. That alone made me pleased since it was past the required benchmark we had to meet by the end of the school year.

As the first chime rang everyone found their seats. A little before the second chime rang Murakami walked in and started pulling out papers. When class officially started he looked at the clock and then grabbed the stack of papers and began calling names.

As students went up one by one he gave them a smile and a good job. When he called me he told me, "Great job Trist, the principal was amazed when he reviewed the class scores."

Once the tests were finally out Murakami wrote an average on the board, this time it was 77.2%. He turned and addressed the class, "Guys…" As his hand reached back to touch the board, "…you should be extremely proud of this. While some of you are at the edge of the acceptable limit on individual subjects, overall you scored amazingly well."

The class seemed to be upbeat all day after that, when we were released everyone seemed to meander around the class like they were waiting for something to happen. As I reached over and bumped Lev's shoulder, "Ready to go?"

Lev grabbed his bag as I stood.

When we turned toward the door everyone was facing me. They all bowed and thanked me in unison. I was surprised, "Stop it guys, you did it not me."

They agreed but also said it wouldn't have been possible without our help.

I was a little embarrassed being called out like that, but I knew they meant well, and their appreciation made the extra work worth it.

During our club we began reviewing the missed questions and we stayed until everyone felt confident in the correct answers. We even asked questions around the tables to quiz ourselves.

As club began winding down I dismissed everyone feeling pretty good about their standing and the mid-term results.

As Lev, Ani and Tia walked with me to the bus stop a couple of 1-A students standing with Yamato were laughing and making comments about how we couldn't keep up with real students.

Ani turned and started walking their way, but I quietly called her, *"Ani, it's not worth it."*

She stopped and turned back but as soon as she did the younger boys all laughed, "She even knows it's the truth." As they laughed they turned as they continued walking with Yamato.

Ani was in a horrible mood the rest of the day, she kept clenching her fist as we made our way from the bus stop to our house. As we entered Ani kicked off her shoes and stormed to her room. I looked at Lev and Tia.

Tia sighed, "Trist, sometimes you are just too nice. I would have liked to see Ani hit him honestly."

Tia's comment surprised me a bit. Lev almost snorted with laughter so uncharacteristic was her statement, "Tia, what good would that have done, we aren't going to school for them and they don't even know our classes situation. I can't justify being mad because he thinks his class did better."

Tia frowned, "But still. Doesn't it make you mad? He isn't directing it at the class but at you."

I placed my hand on Tia's shoulder, "All that matters is that the class honestly did their best and that you guys support me." I hugged Tia with one arm before we headed our separate ways.

Lev continued to follow me upstairs, so he must have had something to say.

As I slid my door open I walked in and Lev closed it once he passed. He dropped his bag near the wall and sat down on my bed as he sprawled backwards, "You know you need to talk to Ani, right?"

I inhaled and exhaled slowly as I considered what I would even say, "Yea, but what should I say that I already haven't?"

Lev sat up and looked my direction, "You have to figure it out. Just do it soon so she doesn't do something she will regret when you aren't there to stop her." I looked at Lev inquiringly.

"She wouldn't hurt them, would she?"

Lev shrugged, "No clue. But she has been growing awful fond of you. You can see it in her face when she looks at you from across the class. It wouldn't surprise me if she started a fight."

"She could hurt someone pretty bad if she did. I can't see her going that far."

Lev laughed, "It's you were talking about. Did you see her yesterday? She was ready to rip Hazuki apart. Even though Hazuki was being nice, imagine what she would do to someone she thought threatened you." Lev smiled as he finished explaining.

"I'll talk to her today then, though I'm not sure what I should say." I mused over possible options.

Lev was grinning as he thought, "Just tell her you consider her yours and you don't want her to do something rash." Lev bust out laughing, "Okay maybe not, that might cause other problems."

"Be serious, you're the only one I can really ask."

"You could just tell her not to, but you will need to think of the reason." Lev finally offered.

I sighed, "Humm, okay."

"Well, I'm heading downstairs."

"Wait up, I'm going too." I followed him after I hung up my school coat.

We walked down in silence, and as we passed Lev's room he departed with a quick good luck. I knocked lightly on Ani's door.

"What!" Was the blunt response Ani made.

"Can I come in?"

"No! I prefer not talking right now."

I sighed as I slowly slid her door open making sure she was not changing. Her room had the blinds closed and no lights on as she lay back on her bed with her arm resting across her forehead.

"Leave me alone, I don't want to talk!"

I just nodded as I closed her door once I entered and sat on the edge of her bed at her side. She turned to her other side facing the wall away from me.

"I'm sorry Ani."

"You have nothing to be sorry about! I have been so frustrated since this morning, and then those guys after school." I could hear fluctuations in Ani's voice and could tell she was beginning to cry.

She reached up to her face with her free right hand, "I don't like when people constantly put pressure on you. You never complain, and it makes me so mad I can't hold it in."

"I have my parents and Lev to support me, but you don't have any of that now." Ani was beginning to sob as her speech hastened to finish her sentence.

Ani was quietly weeping as her voice occasionally caught, "Sometimes I still wish we could have stayed on the Velisus, at least I only had to share you with Tia, but even the girls in class are clamoring for your attention now. I don't think I can take it. My heart feels like it's being squeezed every time someone gets close to you and I know I can't be selfish."

I can tell she is breathing roughly between sentences. I contemplate everything she has said, "Ani?"

"What?" She asked quietly.

"Your wrong you know. I can only do what I'm doing because I have you and everyone else supporting me." I stretch out and lay on my side facing her back.

I gently reach around her and grasp her hand which is slightly moist from her tears, "But I need your support most of all, so please don't do anything that could put you in harm's way. Even if you think it won't, remember to stay by my side. Okay?"

I rested my head against her back as I felt her nod and she began to cry more. After several minutes her breathing began to settle down, "Trist, can I ask for my reward now?"

I thought for a second, reward? I remembered when she hurt her hand last weekend, "Sure, what is it?"

Ani turned on her back and placed her hands on the side of my face as she raised up and gently kissed me on the lips. It was a lingering kiss, and I could feel her tear moistened face touch mine.

When she pulled back she smiled and wiped the few tears still in her eyes, "I wanted to do that yesterday when Hazuki fed you a spoonful of parfait, but I held back."

I was not expecting that to be her request, but it was a simple request. It made me more acutely aware of Ani's growing femininity. I brushed her hair from her forehead, as I looked into her face. I felt a time would come when these simple pleasures would be my only salvation.

As I fondly looked at Ani I asked in a tender voice, "Did you plan to use your reward like that all along?".

Ani nodded slightly then laid back down next to me.

As I rested my head next to hers I placed my arm around her waist and gently hugged her to me. She nestled up against me with a smile. We continued to rest in her bed for several more minutes before I heard a knock-on Ani's door.

"Yes?" Was the muffled reply Ani offered.

I could hear Tia's voice, "When are you coming out!? You can't keep him in there all to yourself!"

Tia slid the door open and walked in as she looked around the room. As she closed the door she walked over to Ani's bed, "If were both here it's okay though."

Tia began pushing my side trying to get us to scoot over. Finally, Ani sat up and scooted over so all three of us could lay on the bed.

"You guys know this isn't really comfortable right?" I said.

Tia looked like she didn't care, and Ani just smiled as I lay on my back with Ani to the right and Tia on the left.

Tia finally said, "Deal with it." As she rested her head on my shoulder and wrapped her arm around me with a satisfied smile.

It was still early so I gave in to their selfishness and let then nap while I gently stoked their heads until I heard Lev knock, "Dinners ready."

He must have known this would happen.

I gently tried to wake them up, but they refused. Actually, I could tell they weren't asleep since they were breathing in a normal rhythm. I quietly mumbled to myself, "I guess I have no choice but to tickle them."

Tia pulled her arms into her sides and Ani opened her eyes as she looked at me, "How could you tell?"

"How many times do you think I've listened to your breathing when you are asleep. Tia even talks in her sleep sometimes." I said.

Tia sat upright, "I do!?" She said with a worried expression, "When!?"

I thought a moment, "The night before the sports festival for sure and occasionally when you stayed in my room after the bathing suit issue."

Tia's face went white as she nervously asked, "What did I say?"

I thought back, "You called my name, but you were groaning a bit and were squirming around in your sleep."

Tia covered her face and I could see the white gradually replaced with crimson. As she sat up and quickly left the room.

Ani glared at me, "When around the time before the sports festival was this?"

"The night before if I remember correctly."

"Tiaaa!" Ani said as she rolled out of bed, "Come here please." Ani left her room before I even had a chance to sit up.

Holiday Mayhem

December was right around the corner signaling time for second term final exams. Aiko and I were excused from a majority of the student council meetings thanks to Murakami's intervention.

When I brought the subject up during club everyone groaned.

"I feel a little better now though, so as long as we keep at it I think I can score even higher." Kina said in an excited voice. She looked like she was ready for a big sports event the way she posed.

Josuke spoke up, "Think of the bright side, Christmas is the following week."

Naoki laughed, "Not like you have anyone to go anywhere with."

Josuke's expression faded, "Maybe we could do something as a class? I hear there is a big light show by the harbor where we went to the beach."

Several of the members were hesitant to commit at first.

Hazuki was the first to ask directly, "How about it Trist, do you think you could go?"

A large portion of the class looked expectantly at me.

"Humm, I need to check with my family, if they say it's okay I wouldn't mind going."

A couple of the guys cheered, and the girls looked around and talked with their friends excitedly.

I looked at Lev, Ani and Tia, "Would you guys like that?"

Lev was sitting on his chair watching the planning progressing, "I wouldn't mind as long as it's not too cold."

Ani and Tia both agreed but looked at Lev and smiled, "Even if it is cold Trist can keep us warm."

Ani made a face at Lev who just shook his head while Tia smiled at Ani's comment.

As the group headed home for the day Ani asked, "What do you think about the light show Trist?"

"Humm, sounds like it might be fun, and it would be good to see more outside our town."

"I hope we can go, I think it would be a lot of fun." Tia offered.

"If we can't go no one else will." Lev said flatly.

"What do you mean?" I asked.

Lev looked at me as he rolled his eyes, "Do you think the other girls would go if you weren't Trist?"

"They might, I'm sure not all of the girls feel that way."

"I wouldn't go with any of the other guys." Tia said with an emotionless expression.

I reached out and placed my hand on Tia's head as I pulled her next to me and gave her a hug, "You could try to make friends in class you know Tia. What if something happened to me?"

Tia put her arm around my waist, "That won't happen. I wouldn't let it." Tia assured me.

Ani was watching our discussion, "Trist, I know you were teasing but I don't think you should even joke about that."

I looked sideways at Ani, "Ani, have you ever looked at the accident statistics in Japan? There are a multitude of random events that could just as easily end my life as they could yours."

Ani looked a little upset with my comments, "I'd do whatever was needed to keep you safe." Ani said as she glanced away.

I stopped and reached over for Ani's arm as she jerked back a bit not expecting my grasp. I gently grasped her by the chin as I looked into her eyes, "Ani, don't you ever do anything that would put you in harm's way for me, understand? I'm serious." I said gently.

Ani gave me a downcast nod though I could tell she wasn't being entirely honest.

I sighed as I gently released her chin and stroked her cheek before we continued to walk. I knew someday I would be forced to make sacrifices for my friends. Even if the price I paid was high.

During club after the first week of December I told the class, "We would have our study session the weekend before the 20th.

Everyone in the club seemed extremely nervous.

"You guys will do great, think of the work we have accomplished since the mid-term." I offered in support.

Inaho glanced around at her fellow students before she asked, "Trist, do you think we really will be okay this time?"

I looked at Inaho with a sincere smile as I patted her on the head, "I know you will."

She stood with her eyes closed and head bent slightly forward as she provided me with a huge smile as a reward for my encouragement.

"I already have my family's approval, so we don't need to worry. The following week we can celebrate with our trip to the light show." I told the class.

Everyone one cheered, you could feel the positive energy and excitement in the room.

The following day as I looked out the window at the bare trees as I saw a large vehicle pull up to the school's front gate. As I continued to watch I saw Kazu exit the passenger side as he let out a passenger, Shivan! Why were they here? I thought to myself.

The class we were in was mathematics, while Mikami was knowledgeable he still was only teaching high school math. I had a hard time focusing during his classes, but I was still able to do much more than simply explain his examples during our study club.

As I contemplated Shivan's and Kazu's presences I felt a little apprehensive, Shivan had not visited our school once that I knew of.

A few minutes later there was an announcement calling me to the office.

Mikami paused until the final chime of the announcement ended and excused me from class.

Lev glanced at me as I stood up leaving my books on my desk as he gave a curious glance. I saw Ani and Tia both watch me as I quietly departed.

I made my way to the administration room and met with Shivan and Kazu.

Shivan looked to be filling out paperwork as Kazu glanced at me and placed a hand on my shoulder.

When Shivan turned he just said, "Trist come with us."

I obediently followed since I had no idea what this regarded.

When we began to exit through the main entrance I asked, "Are we leaving school?"

Kazu responded, "Yes, we have a very important meeting we wanted you to attend."

I looked to Shivan then back to Kazu, "Can I grab my books and let the others know?"

Shivan looked at me, "No we don't have the time for that, we only have a few hours to get to where we need to go so we must leave now."

As we walked out into the front courtyard the chill wind bit at my cheek as I looked forward to being back inside. I only hoped this wasn't a long meeting.

As Kazu opened the door I looked back to our class and saw a few students as well as Mikami glancing out the window.

* * *

Ani was deep in thought regarding the new mathematical processes Mikami-sensei was going over. As I began to hear rustling and surprised voices I glanced up and noticed Mikami glancing out the classroom window. I looked up and saw my brother standing next to Trist's desk and was curious what had even caught his attention.

As the class bell chimed Mikami gathered his materials and made his way out.

Tia had stood and was walking toward my desk, so I joined her and we both walked over to my brother.

"What was so interesting earlier?" I asked curiously.

My brother looked up at Tia and me, "Trist, father and Kazu left a little while ago."

Tia began to get agitated, "Why would he leave without saying anything!?"

I looked at Tia since I could feel her emotions echoed in me, "Well we can ask him when we get home." He said.

As the last class ended Murakami called Aiko up front and was discussing something with her.

I noticed her eyes widen as she responded, then Murakami shook his head and Aiko suddenly had a very dejected look.

Aiko departed with the class journal, but I would be sure to ask her if she was okay during club.

My brother, Tia and I headed toward our club room, even if Trist wasn't there for the day the other students would need help.

As much as I wanted to run home I knew Trist would be disappointed if we failed to help achieve the class goals.

As we began going through questions with the other members I heard Aiko enter the room. She immediately headed in our direction.

"Is it true Trist won't be back until the end of the year?" Aiko asked in a rushed voice.

When I heard her question, it felt like my heart was at the base of my throat, "What do you mean by that?" I asked in a slow measured voice trying not to let my anxiety show.

"So, you didn't know either. I thought it was odd." Aiko said as she sat down biting the end of her thumb.

I glanced at my brother who just shrugged then to Tia who looked like she was trying to hide her fear.

"Father was with him, so I don't think we need to worry too much. We can just ask when we get home." He calmly explained.

I wanted to run, I wanted to see him. The anxiety I felt thinking he was going to be gone for that long tore at my mind. What would I do, it would be the longest time we had been apart since we left Paltius.

I tried contacting him on his phone, but it went right to voicemail, that's when I thought I could send my message telepathically but the more I tried the messier my thoughts became, Trist warned us once about overwhelming him with multiple messages and feelings. I needed to calm down but found I couldn't.

I did my best to maintain my normal composure as I helped the class, but every time the members asked if Trist was truly gone through the end of the year I became more frazzled.

Tia seemed to maintain her composure and my brother wasn't affected at all from what I could see.

As club finished for the day we traveled home with Aiko and Hazuki. Hazuki seemed to be a little concerned Trist was gone and asked if we would still do the study group or go to the light festival.

"I don't see why not, if he really is going to be gone that long I think he would be disappointed if we didn't." My brother explained.

I knew he was right, I had to get myself together.

When we got home all three of us looked for father, but mother explained, "Your father and Trist are at a physics conference in Austria and aren't expected home until the 26th of December."

Tia looked unaffected as she headed to her room.

My brother just sighed and carried Trist's books up to his room.

Me on the other hand, I felt like I was ready to break. I took my books back to my room and sat at my desk. As I rested my head on the desk I began to think about Trist's voice and our everyday interactions that I couldn't enjoy for a few weeks. I stared to feel extremely miserable.

As I stood up and walked to my bed to lay down I felt a faint thought, *"Ani, Tia, Lev, sorry I couldn't call but it looks like I will be away for a few days. We're on a plane now heading to Austria for a conference with Shivan and Kazu."*

All I could do is send my feeling because if I tried to send words I knew my feelings would rush out and overwhelm him. I sat on my bed and covered my face with my arms regretting my weakness.

I heard a quiet knock on my door, "Yes." I said in a raspy voice feeling like my throat was being restricted.

Tia gently slid the door open and entered as she closed it behind her. Tia walked over to my bed and looked down at me with my face semi covered. I could see her holding her hands in front of her as she turned and sat next to me.

"It's only three weeks, right? Do you think he will be okay? He'll be alright, won't he?" Tia said sounding closer and closer to tears with each question.

Tia began to cry quietly and as I looked up at her with tears running off the side of my cheeks I couldn't contain my anxiety any further.

Tia laid next to me as we both shed silent tears as we both held hands.

The following few weeks went by extremely slowly, we attended classes, worked with our club and went home.

Trist occasionally sent us messages late at night after they finished conference activities, but it was always brief. He would ask us to continue helping the class, so they did well on the test.

As he told us he had faith in us and missed us I could tell it was sent with tenderness and it would momentarily make my heart race. We couldn't let him down.

The weekend of the study session included our class only, the group had agreed earlier that week to keep it just our class since Trist wasn't present.

It was amazing to see how the atmosphere differed without Trist's presence. Even my brother was very low key, and I could almost sense him dazing off more frequently than normal.

The day of the test arrived, and I felt we were nowhere near as ready as we could have been. Our classmates had spent countless hours since they knew Trist wasn't going to be present to focus on studying.

It seemed like their intensive drive to study increased once everyone knew he wouldn't be there. I had my own struggles as well. Some material took me longer than normal to understand, how does Trist make this look so easy, I thought. He applied himself a hundred times more than my brother, Tia and me while he also holds down a class representative job.

As the final test concluded there were many sighs of relief. The class knew we wouldn't have study club today, so we all departed together.

As we walked toward the bus stop Junichi asked, "Has Trist called since he left?"

Tia was the one to answer, "Not really."

Chisa laughed, "What does that mean Tia?" As she teased Tia.

Tia blushed, "Well I can tell he is doing good, but he hasn't called on the phone." Knowing she couldn't mention the link they shared.

"I think I know what you mean." Hazuki said with a far-off gaze, "He is the kind of person who can make you feel close even if you are laying alone in bed." Hazuki blushed as she quickly looked around at the other girls smiling at her.

"I know, sometimes I almost feel like I can hear him in my head." Aiko said as she remembered the mid-term study session.

"Well, I think we should call when we get the results, I am nervous but also excited to see how the class did." My brother commented.

I looked forward to hearing his voice.

The Wednesday before winter break the exam results were posted. My brother, Tia and I eagerly approached the board, we noticed a number of students already gathering around it.

Several people noticed Trist's name wasn't on it and I saw Yamato with a smirk on his face as he turned and looked at us.

"I guess he wasn't up to the challenge this time." Yamato said sarcastically to my brother.

I really wanted to hurt him sometimes. While my brother just smiled.

The class in general scored in the low 80% range on the five exams. My brother was almost an 86%, Tia did very well with an 89% and I scored a 77%. I was a little disappointed in myself and felt frustrated I was lower than the others.

When we arrived in class Aiko approached us, "Did you see the results?" She said in an excited voice.

Tia and I just nodded, while my brother said, "Yea it looks like we did even better than mid-terms."

When class started Murakami congratulated everyone for their hard work, "Not one of you were below the 70% mark, I am exceedingly proud. The class average was 77% this time."

I was glad I wasn't a burden on the average but also disappointed in not being able to provide more support.

As the last class of the year ended my brother, Tia and I headed home. The class still planned on going to the light show on the 25th but I was not sure if there would be as much participation since Trist wasn't here.

The week before our outing seemed to drag on, Tia and I would occasionally chat, but the topic always turned to Trist. I guess she missed him as much as I did.

The day of the light show the class agreed to meet outside the neighboring towns train station. My brother, Tia and I arrived a little early and found several classmates already waiting.

Ultimately only three classmates were unable to come and surprisingly they were male students. When it reached 13:00 the class began to make our way to the area where the light show would be taking place. As we walked we slowly separated into small groups, so we wouldn't take so much room as we made our way to the park. There were a number of shops open serving hot foods which looked to be bustling since even the weather was somewhat chilly.

Tia was talking to Chiyo, Naho and Kyouka, I thought it sounded like they were discussing Trist. Tia seemed to be doing most of the talking as the other girls listened in rapt attention.

I was with my brother, Josuke, Tashiro, Aiko and Hazuki. They were talking about the difference in festivals in Okinawa and Furigawa. Hazuki pointed out the weather was the major difference while Josuke disagreed. I guess he lived there when his father worked in Okinawa when he was a kid.

After a while I decided to walk to the harbor edge where the crowd was thinner. There must have been thousands of people walking about already. I noticed several couples walking around hand in hand and longed to hold Trist's as well. Only a few more days I thought.

I was going to make him pay attention to me for a week as a reward for helping in class. Though I knew he wouldn't just focus on me since he cherished Tia as well, but maybe just a day, I compromised.

As I was leaning against a concrete pillar near the docks edge I heard voices coming from all around, the crowds passed as someone called out to me.

I didn't pay much attention at first until someone tapped me on the shoulder. I turned to notice several students maybe a couple years older asking if I would like to join them.

I had little interest in others at this moment and less for other guys, "No thanks, I'm here with friends."

The guys glanced at me then around the area I was standing, "You can bring them along if you want. I'm here visiting friends and my girlfriend couldn't join me, but I wouldn't mind if you did."

Does this guy not get it I thought, "No thanks I'm fine."

When he grabbed my wrist, I was a little surprised as he began pulling me with his group. The other guys were laughing.

I pulled my wrist out of his grasp.

"What part of no thank you don't you understand!?" I was past mad, all I wanted was to watch the light show, so I could tell Trist about it and now these guys had made me regret even coming.

I stood there facing off with the guy who had grabbed my hand. He had a slightly annoyed look on his face since he thought I was making him look bad in front of his friends.

I was a moment away from beating him.

I suddenly felt someone grab me by the shoulder, "That's it!" I spun around fully intending to knock the person to the ground.

As I swung my fist around I felt someone deftly grab my swinging arm by the wrist.

As I began to calm from the adrenaline I had built up I realized who it was. Trist!!

Trist pulled my wrist and led me behind him.

"Sorry guys she's with me." He said casually.

I don't know what he did, but their interest died in an instant. I suddenly felt like my legs were going to give away, my heart was beating so fast with a mix of adrenaline and desire. I could feel my hands shaking not fully believing Trist was in front of me.

"Ani how do you always get into situations like this. Do you realize how much that makes me worry?" Trist said as he turned and looked into my eyes.

"Hey, what's wrong?"

I dropped to my knees and couldn't hold back my tears. All I could do is reach out with my arms for him as tears streamed down my cheeks.

Trist looked at me with a sympathetic expression, "I'm sorry I thought I would surprise you, but I didn't expect this."

Trist reached down and placed his arms around me as he helped me up, I engulfed him with my own embrace and swore I wouldn't release him until I was done shedding all my lonely tears. As I did I could feel him turn slightly toward my ear.

"I missed you too, Ani." He whispered.

As he held me with my head resting on his shoulder he would occasionally stroke the back of my head and run his fingers through my hair.

After an hour of just standing my eyes had begun to dry but I loved this sensation. It was my safest place.

I felt him turn again to my ear, "Ani, we should find the others soon. I think I heard an announcement about the light show starting."

I didn't care about the light show in this instant and I definitely didn't want to be with anyone else right now, but I nodded slightly as I raised my head and gently released my arms from around him. As I backed away a bit I looked up into Trist's face and felt so much passion for him. I wanted to be his alone and sometimes wished he wasn't so kind to others.

Trist reached up with his forefinger and gently wiped the residue from the corner of my eyes, "I think you have gotten even more beautiful over the last few weeks." Trist said in a faint voice.

I could see his face redden a bit probably not intending to say that as loud as he did.

As he turned to go he held out his hand, "Let's go Ani. We're going to be late."

I walked next to him and moved closer instead of taking his hand I placed my arm around him, so I could slightly lean against him, at least until we found the others. I could feel him hesitate a moment until he finally settled his arm around me and we headed towards our friends.

We walked for what was probably a half an hour, the announcement listed the countdown as less than five minutes to start. I was oblivious to everyone around me. I even walked with my eyes closed knowing Trist would watch over me.

As we approached a large grassy area at the seaside park I felt Trist stop.

As I opened my eyes and raised my head from his shoulder I saw several angry faces staring straight at me.

Tia was almost red with anger, "Why didn't you say something!?"

Tia had moist eyes and was holding her hands in fists at her side. Beside her stood Aiko, Hazuki and my brother.

Lev was the only one who had a somewhat relaxed expression almost as if seeing Trist gave him the reassurance that everything was alright.

Tia on the other hand was mad. She looked at me and not Trist as her lip seemed to quiver a bit.

"How long has he been with you?" Tia asked me sternly.

I wasn't sure what to say since my concept of time was a little distorted since I first saw him.

"I've been with her about two hours. What's wrong Tia?"

Tia's angry face began to melt into a pout as she grabbed my arm and pulled me.

"I think you can let me welcome him home too." Tia said as I stepped toward her.

Tia immediately ran to Trist and hugged him. She was a little shorter than Trist so seeing them together like this made me think their heights seemed to be a perfect combination.

What Tia did next thought caused those from our class to gasp in disbelief.

Tia released Trist and reached up to his face as she stood on her toes to give him a kiss on the cheek.

Trist's eyes widened in surprise since actions like this were usually for private moments.

When Tia stepped back and turned she looked at me and stuck her tongue slightly out of her mouth then broke into a big smile.

The others also gave him a brief hug then Tia and I moved to his sides as we walked with him to the rest of the group.

* * *

The final day of the conference was incredibly stressful. Not to mention it felt like it took the first two weeks for anyone to really take me seriously. I guess that's not surprising since I appeared so young. But for the senior scientists to ignore my recognition of flaws in their work was just arrogance.

When Shivan, Kazu and I headed out as the conference concluded on the 24th I told them I really wanted to be home by the 25th.

Shivan was the first to inquire, "Do you have plans tomorrow?"

I explained the club was going to the light show as a reward for doing well on exams. When I told them both how the class had fared on the high school content Kazu reluctantly agreed.

We were able to change our tickets to a late non-stop flight for our way to Tokyo. We arrived early on the 25th and had been hard pressed to get home and back in time, so Kazu was kind enough to drop me off near the event since he was familiar with the festival.

As I made my way through the crowd toward the festival I took out my phone and tried to use the location function. I saw three pins, Lev and Tia were closest and appeared to be together, while Ani was off by herself.

Why is she always wandering off I thought?

As I made my way in her direction I occasionally glanced at my phone to verify her position, then I finally saw Ani standing talking to a group of guys close to our age.

I would be lying if I said I was happy, but this didn't look like anything I should ignore. As one guy grabbed Ani by the wrist I felt somewhat agitated and was glad when I saw her pull away. The situation she was in looked like it was going to escalate so I probably should step in before Ani did anything rash.

As I walked up behind her I placed my hand on her right shoulder. I heard Ani mumble something as she spun around with her fist directed toward my head. I was easily able to block her swing by grabbing her by the wrist since she was responding out of anger and not thinking.

As I gripped her wrist I could feel the tension in her arm, then just as suddenly it was gone. I looked at Ani's wide eyes for a moment and then I gently pulled her behind me and stepped to face the guys who had been talking to her.

"Sorry guys she's with me." I stated flatly as I narrowed my eyes and mentally told the guy who had grabbed her to get lost with all the animosity I could muster.

As the guys left I turned to Ani, "Ani how do you always get into situations like this. Do you realize how much that makes me worry?"

I began to notice Ani was just standing there shaking slightly as she slowly dropped to her knees.

"Hey, what's wrong!?" I asked as I looked down at her face I thought, what was I going to do with her.

"I'm sorry I thought I would surprise you, but I didn't expect this." I reached down toward Ani's outstretched arms.

She didn't look like she would stand easily so I leaned down against her as I placed my arms around her chest, she almost immediately encircled my neck in a tight hug.

I could feel Ani's chest press against me and could hear her slightly rough breathing as she fought against her tears. I wasn't sure what I could do to make her feel better, but I did know I missed her.

As Ani clung to me and quietly cried I whispered in her ear, "I missed you too Ani."

I quietly comforted her as she continued to embrace me. I gently stroked her hair and occasionally the back of her head, she had such beautiful hair, I hoped she never tired of caring for it.

After about an hour went by I heard a distant announcement stating the light show would start in one hour.

I turned toward her ear again as I gently said, "Ani, we should find the others soon. I think I heard an announcement about the light show starting."

After a few minutes more, Ani gently released her grip around my neck and pulled her arms down past my shoulders. As I looked at her face I could see a few stray tears in the corner of her eyes. As I gently wiped them away I could see her face was slightly angled up as she leaned toward me ever so slightly.

"I think you have gotten even more beautiful over the last few weeks." I said not even thinking I voiced this thought out loud.

I suddenly saw Ani's eyes widen a bit as I realized what I said. I turned to hide my embarrassment and held out my hand for Ani, "Let's go Ani. We're going to be late."

Ani walked past my hand and moved against me as her arm slipped around me and she lightly rested her head against my shoulder. I never had her do something like this before, so I felt a little awkward. What do I do with my hand I thought. Finally, I accepted the fact she wasn't going to move anytime soon so I settled my hand around her waist and lightly squeezed as we began walking.

I knew the general area I had seen Lev and Tia on my phones locator, so we slowly walked in that direction. There were a number of people visiting the numerous stalls, so I had to be cautious where Ani and I walked.

As we approached the park I saw several faces I recognized. Lev was the first to notice me and I could see him speaking and point in my direction. Tia twisted around frantically and looked our way. The smile on her face was spectacular but it suddenly faded to a scowl and a pout as she stood with several others and began walking our direction.

Tia who I expected to stop in front of me, instead was standing in front of Ani.

"Why didn't you say something!?" Tia said in a rough voice.

I felt Ani raise her head as Tia asked, "How long has he been with you?"

Ani looked at a loss for words when I glanced over at her, so I answered, "I've been with her about two hours. What's wrong Tia?"

Tia began pulling on Ani's arm while she was pouting. As Ani released her grasp on my waist she stepped toward Tia.

"I think you can let me welcome him home too." Tia then took two quick steps toward me as she threw her arms around me and placed her head against my shoulder. As I hugged her back with just as much force.

As Tia began to release me she stepped back slightly. Tia looked up into my eyes and she suddenly placed a kiss on my cheek.

We have done that many times before but always in the privacy of our home so when she did it in public I was extremely embarrassed. Tia then turned toward Ani before she walked back to the others.

The others moved forward to give me a slight hug one after the other.

Once everyone had finished I asked, "Shall we sit?"

We walked to the blanket spread out on the grass. I could feel a slight chill in the air as the sun had begun to set.

When we all settled in, "Well so what was the conference all about?" Lev was leaning back on the blanket with his legs stretched out in front of him.

I laughed, "At first I was annoyed. The first day they kept trying to usher me with the students visiting the conference. Even with my participant badge."

Lev looked at me and laughed, "Did that really happen?"

"Yea, I was a little irritated since the girls in the visiting classes kept trying to pull me with them. After that was sorted out I had to deal with close to two weeks of being ignored or looked at as being a nuisance. It wasn't until the old professor we had during the education expo. Do you remember the old guy who asked me to solve that problem?"

Lev thought back a bit, "The guy with the camera?"

"Yea, well anyway after the first week he was with us a part of each day. The next time someone ignored me he told them they should listen and check what I had to say."

I paused as I glanced at the others chatting around us.

"After that I had a couple participants ask my forgiveness for not listening. The last week was fairly eventful though. I was even able to help prove a couple of their equations. Nothing they discussed was beyond Paltian theories so there was a lot of repetition."

"Humm, so did they get around to any of the papers you recognized?"

"There were several papers Shivan had prepared and they were being discussed but a lot of physicists dismissed them as fantasy. I proved a couple of the equations and I think we have some interest from some of the physicists in Europe and the United States."

As Lev and I talked a number of other students had been gathering to listen.

"Wait a second Trist. You were participating in the conference?" Hazuki asked as she glanced sideways at Aiko.

I nodded, "But they didn't have many new ideas there."

"Anyway, congratulations on your tests. You guys did fantastic." I told the students sitting around me.

"Oh, I have your homework." Lev said as he glanced over at me.

As the light show began Ani and Tia moved and sat next to me. The show was nothing like I had seen before, but it reminded me Earth had technology they hadn't fully developed yet. This might be an area where we could enhance communications.

The show lasted close to an hour as it began to wind down we all headed home. The trains were packed, and it took us two tries to get everyone in a train before Lev, Ani, Tia and I boarded.

The ride home was long, since we had to stand the entire way, I had Tia and Ani in front of me with Lev to their sides. The remaining students were gathered around us. I had heard a number of times that young women needed to be cautious when traveling alone so I wasn't about to risk anyone laying a hand on our friends.

As we walked the last few kilometers and neared our house we said our farewells to Aiko and Hazuki.

During the train trip we discussed what chances we had to complete our winter break homework before the third term started on the fourth of January. We had until the third off of school for New Year's celebrations, so we decided to meet the next Sunday.

As I retrieved my belongings that Shivan had left by the door I made my way upstairs. I sat the homework on my desk but was just too tired to do anything after the long day.

Tomorrow would be Thursday, so we could do more planning when we were up and about.

New Year

As the Sunday before New Year's arrived we had a number of students who decided to use this opportunity for help. While there was less than half the class when we first proposed a homework group many of the students replied that it was completed. This made me feel better regarding the classes current level.

The questions weren't difficult, but they were numerous, the funny thing was that besides Lev, Ani and Tia most of the students that arrived had already completed most of it.

The session wrapped up before 14:00. Several asked if we had plans for the New Year.

I thought about it and the only item I remembered was the garden, "Not that I know of. We just need to finish picking up the fall leaves in the yard before the weather gets worse."

As a few of us worked in the yard the others finished what remained of their homework. When we all completed our individual chores, it was Hazuki who proposed a hatsumode or a midnight trip to the local shrine.

I hadn't seen anything about such a ritual when I did my reading before we arrived on Earth. Aiko explain it was just one of the firsts for a New Year, as the bells chime you make your first wish for a happy and safe New Year.

It sounded like an interesting event, so I proposed we contact the others and leave an open Line invite for an hour ahead of time.

Aiko completely objected, “If we decide to go we will need to leave much earlier. It will be very busy.”

As I looked to the others Lev was the only one who seemed to object since it meant he wouldn’t be in bed early enough. After a little convincing by the other students he agreed to go. He would have gone anyway but I’m sure he appreciated the attention.

Everyone including Jes spent the next two days cleaning house, preparing for a fresh start on New Year. Valdria prepared traditional dishes from a cook book Kazu had brought during one of his weekly visits. They would be eaten over the first three days of the year.

I also noticed a number gift basket being sold at the grocery store.

As I began researching the traditions associated with yearend it became apparent this was probably one of the biggest celebratory events of the year.

The morning of the 31st I tried to sleep in but still ended up getting out of bed by 06:30. I was really looking forward to seeing more of the traditions in Japan and everything I had researched about New Years. I even stayed up late reading on different activities in the area around our town.

After I found a warm set of clothes I changed and headed down stairs. The house had a refreshed look about it. I was glad cleaning it had only taken a little effort when everyone pitched in. Even Shivan did a large part of the cleaning in the kitchen and dining room so Valdria didn't have to kneel down as much given her current condition.

I looked forward to having a new addition to the family this year but wasn't really sure what to expect since I barely remembered what it was like when Emeri was born.

It was still early so even the adults didn't seem to be up. The refrigerator was full of New Year foods that Valdria prepared with Shivan's help. There were even a few decorations Kazu had dropped off, he said they were traditional decorations called kadomatsu that brought good luck. It sat on the table and was made from three pieces of bamboo with some type of fragrant pine needle wrapped in decorative paper and fancy string.

The decoration that was hung from the door was called a shimekazari and was made of straw and was supposed to ward off evil spirits. I was amazed at how much spiritualism was steeped into Japanese cultural festivities.

I decided to walk down to the local Family Cart for something to drink other than what we had in our house. As the doors slid opened I could even tell retailers took advantage as much as they could to market gifts themed for this holiday.

While I was shopping I decided to purchase a green tea and when I was at the counter I noticed they had some beef croquettes available, so I purchased one for my walk home. The croquette was very tasty, but I noticed there was a little oil staining the bag. Valdria would have a fit if she saw me eating this so I made sure to dispose of the bag before I entered the house. No reason to upset her regarding my eating habits.

When I walked in the house I saw Ani and Tia sitting in the lounge with their arms crossed. They wore unhappy expressions.

As I slipped off my shoes they both stood up and made their way to the entry.

"Where did you go?" They both asked in near unison.

I was a little surprised, I didn't wake them because they normally like to sleep in a little on weekends and holidays.

"I just walked down to the convenience store, why?" I asked a little surprised at their questioning looks.

Both of their shoulders slumped as they gave me disappointed looks.

"What's wrong with you two, you almost always sleep in on your days off. So, I wasn't going to wake you since we will be out late tonight. I figured letting you sleep in would be best."

They both walked back to their seats and sat down with expressions that showed their disappointment for not being up early on their own.

I sat across from them and told them, "We will be out all afternoon and evening, so you will have your chance to run around later."

"That's not the point, when we didn't see you in your room we were worried. We thought you might have been drug off again by Shivan and Kazu." Tia told me as she sat slumped down in her chair.

Ahh, that was why they were unhappy, I was already up, and they thought they would sneak in and snuggle.

"Sorry to disappoint you guys but I was up early since I couldn't sleep well."

As the time approached for us to meet near the train station I made sure I had my wallet and a scarf incase the wind started blowing later that night.

Ani came out in light looking clothes at first and I knew she would regret the decision, so I warned her, "Ani it will probably be very cold tonight, don't you think you should wear something warmer?"

She looked at me with a slight frown but returned to her room.

Tia was dressed much more sensibly, she had jeans and a nice shirt and matching sweater that she had purchased when the weather had started cooling down. This was her first opportunity to wear it, so I made sure to tell her I thought it was a cute outfit. She provided a bright smile and held the scarf she had wrapped around it against her face as she blushed slightly.

Lev was dressed similar to me, he had jeans and a shirt. Instead of a sweater and scarf though he wore a light jacket.

Ani finally exited her room with a much more sensible outfit, this time she had a longer skirt and knee socks with a turtle neck sweater foregoing a scarf. She also had a light jacket just in case.

Shivan and Talinde were up in the dining room and told us to be safe. We had already gotten their permission to be out after midnight, but they wanted us to check in occasionally throughout the night.

When we arrived at the train station it was a little after noon. So far it looked like we were the first. After about twenty minutes of waiting and chatting on Line, I saw Aiko and Hazuki waving from across the street.

As they approached they looked excited but turned toward me, "Why didn't you tell us you were leaving early. We even stopped by your house."

I didn't recall that even being mentioned, "Oh, I'm sorry I just figured we would all meet here since that was the decided location."

Hazuki sighed as she glanced to Aiko then at Tia and Ani, "You guys look cute." Hazuki commented after seeing their outfits.

Both Ani and Tia blushed a bit

"Thanks Trist said so too." Tia's responded.

Shortly before 13:00 everyone who had committed to going was present. As we made our way into the station we caught up on the past couple days events.

The shrine we were heading too was two stops toward the edge of town and a long walk. With so many people we decided to just walk since it was easier to talk outside, than on a bus.

There were already a large number of people heading the same direction as us, I was glad Aiko objected to my initial time. I almost dreaded the trip home and knew we would be exhausted come tomorrow.

The area outside the shrine leading up to and around the edge of the main path was filled with brightly colored stalls. They were selling a wide variety of snack foods and good luck charms. The decorative paper lamps were lining the perimeter of the open area in front of the shrine.

I noticed once we passed the main torii gate that there were an additional number of stalls in the main courtyard. One stall had several open burners with some large pots. The smell coming from this stall was slightly spicy like ground cloves.

There was an area roped off where a few people had already started standing, this must be the line Aiko mentioned. If there were people standing in line already I could imagine what tonight would have been like.

We decided to all meet back at the line when it reached a certain length, that way we could freely explore until we had to begin our long wait.

As our group walked from stall to stall I saw a sign hanging on one of the side buildings indicating good luck charms, so I made my way to the window. I glanced around and noticed one for healthy birth. I thought this would be a nice gift for Valdria. As I moved closer to the window I accidentally bumped into someone doing the same.

"I am so sorry." I said as I turned and slightly bowed.

I was hearing a similar response from a girl who I had bumped into. When I looked up I realized it was Kaoru, Kiho and Remi. Each one had a similar charm in their hands.

As I looked down I smiled, and they all began to giggle.

"I guess we had the same thought." Kaoru responded as she held the charm by the string in front of me.

"Are you getting that for a friend?" I asked not wanting to assume too much.

Kaoru's smile wilted a bit as she said in a somewhat stern voice, "Of course, it's for Valdria."

I continued to smile as I thought about how wonderful the friends I had made this year were.

I found Lev, Ani and Tia once I made my purchase. Lev was looking at some type of decorated arrow called a hamaya. Lev explained it was an arrow used to ward off misfortune as he made his purchase and held it up triumphantly.

About 17:00 I noticed there were well over a hundred people standing in line. I sent a message and discovered that a number of our class had already decided to wait. I grabbed the three and headed toward the end of the line.

As we stood in line Ani seemed to have a worried expression on her face. She had been in high spirits until Tia and she had gone to purchase an omikuji or fortune slip from the shrine store where I found the good luck charm. I guess Tia had drawn a good luck talisman while Ani gotten a small fortune. They didn't sound like something to be discouraged over so I wasn't quite sure what was wrong.

We stood as we chatted with the other students, occasionally the adults would randomly ask us where we were from. They always had surprised expressions when we responded in Japanese.

While we stood I had plenty of time to observe the crowds, I was amazed at the number of foreigners I saw walking around. Not that there were a lot, but we didn't typically see them to and from school or when we did our occasional shopping. So, when they glanced our way I'm sure they thought something similar about us since we tended to stand out in a crowd.

As it started to get dark the numbers waiting increased and extended past the torii gate at the front of the shrine. I was amazed how orderly everyone stayed.

Later that evening Josuke and Sakiko stepped out of line and returned with several steaming paper cups. They handed one to Lev, Tia and me. As I smelled the liquid I immediately recognized it as the scent from the pots we saw earlier in the afternoon.

I looked at Josuke, "What is it?" I asked inquisitively.

Josuke smiled, "Try it but be careful it's hot. It's called amazake."

I found the aroma very pleasing and as I tested the heat with the edge of my lip I could slightly taste a mix of spices and a slight hint of something like mirin. It was an extremely pleasurable spiced drink. I wondered why I hadn't tasted it before.

Josuke told us that it was usually only prepared during festivals or on New Year's at this shrine.

With only a couple hours to go I began to feel my legs cramping up. I really wanted to sit down but with so many people there just wasn't an opportunity to stretch out.

Ani had kept to herself since I first noticed her worried expression. She just seemed to peer off into the crowd and hadn't joined any of the conversations since. She even passed when Josuke offered her a cup of amazake.

Tia on the other hand was talking to Lev and a few of the other students as the conversation turned to a topic they found interest in.

Occasionally Tia would glance my way then at Ani who was withdrawn and then she looked at me with a questioning glance.

I shrugged, and Tia turned back to her conversation.

As the time drew closer to midnight many of the people returned to the line and there was a noticeable reduction in people visiting the stalls.

My phone told me the year was about to end. Many people began a quiet countdown. As my clock switched over to 00:00 I began to hear an intermittent hollow gong in the distance.

Aiko looked at me as I was trying to determine the sound, "That's the Buddhist Temple on the other side of the hill. They ring the bell 108 times to symbolize the 108 sins and desires." She smiled as I listened intently.

"Does that only happen at Buddhist Temples?" I asked.

"Yea, but since Japan has a mixed religious heritage with Shintoism and Buddhism it can even happen at some older Shinto shrines."

Aiko continued to explain a little more regarding the history of Buddhism and Shintoism in Japan.

I should have been more knowledgeable on the topic since I took pride in knowing my surroundings. I felt a little deflated having something I should have known have to be explained to me, so I was glad Aiko took the time.

The line slowly began to move, there were probably three hundred people ahead of us at this point so considering the line we were in a good spot.

We paid our respects with the traditional two bows, two claps and a bow before our prayer for a safe and happy New Year.

The students moved down the shrine exit out of the way of the remaining visitors waiting in line. We all made our way to the train station which was running later than normal due to the large number of travelers today.

As we arrived at our stop a number of people exited the train, but it was still close to standing room only. Even about town there seemed to be a fair number even though it was approaching 02:00 in the morning.

As we separated at the train station a number of students waved goodbye, "See you guys tomorrow."

I returned their wave but wasn't sure we would actually see them until school started on the fourth.

As we walked toward our street Ani seemed to be on auto pilot while Lev just said, "She's fine."

Tia also was a little anxious about Ani's behavior.

We came to our street and waited for the signal to turn green before we crossed. As the signal turned and the chime announced all clear Ani stepped out into the street and we followed behind. From the corner of my eye I noticed a truck approaching the intersection, but it didn't appear to be slowing.

"Ani wait, there is a truck coming make sure it stops before you cross the last lane." I said as she approached the far lane.

Neither Ani nor the truck seemed to stop. So, I took a fast step toward Ani and grabbed her around the waist and spun her around out of the way of the oncoming truck. I could tell it was close since I could slightly feel the mirror of the truck graze the back of my head.

Lev and Tia were shouting as I spun and tossed Ani toward Lev. They both tried to reach out as Lev had Ani in one arm and Tia reached both hands toward me. Luckily, I was out of the direct path. The truck didn't slow down or even act like the driver noticed us as it flew through the intersection.

Ani was finally paying attention to her surroundings as her eyes grew wide when she saw a vehicle nearly hit me. She began crying as Lev and Tia quickly moved her to the other side of the intersection out of the road.

Tia was holding my arm as she asked, "Trist are you okay, didn't that mirror hit you?"

I had only felt like it grazed my head, but I noticed there was broken glass in the street from it shattering as it bent from coming in contact with an object.

I assured her I was fine, but when I reached to rub the back of my head I could tell it was bleeding. I was pretty good with my own pain, but Tia and Ani weren't.

Lev saw my hand come away red and he grabbed me as he turned me around, "Trist, your scalp looks like it is gushing blood."

He was pulling his jacket off and then his shirt as he balled it up and placed it against my head to stop the bleeding.

Ani was crying and apologizing saying it was her fault. As much as I wanted too while I held the shirt against my head I was unable to comfort her or Tia who had also gone deathly pale when she initially saw my hand.

We started walking toward the house while Tia held my free arm Lev guided Ani who was still an emotional wreck.

When we entered the house, Tia looked for Valdria who had been sleeping in her room.

I think Tia probably over exaggerated the situation because Valdria looked a little panicked as she and Shivan approached the entry.

When she arrived, I tried to explain what happened, but I was feeling really light headed. I almost felt like I was about to faint as she led me into the dining area which was brighter.

Lev tried to take Ani to her room, but she wouldn't budge. She refused and sat quietly sniffling with Tia across from where Valdria examined my scalp.

As she pulled my shirt off I noticed the blood stain ran down my back and could feel a slightly sticky sensation as my shirt pulled away from my back.

Valdria sighed as she saw the blood, "Trist you are extremely lucky. I am surprised you're actually conscious." Valdria said as she pulled the shirt from my scalp.

Shivan had brought some clean towels and the molecular stabilizer.

"What happened?" Shivan asked as he watched Valdria examine the wound.

"Trist pulled Ani from the street as a truck ran a light. If he hadn't Ani would have been hit." Lev explained as he winced looking at my blood matted hair.

"What were you doing? Why weren't you paying attention?" Shivan directed his dissatisfaction toward Ani.

Ani began crying and apologizing all over, Tia put her arm around her shoulder as Ani leaned against her.

Shivan sighed, "Well at least everyone is alive. But you need to be more conscious about your surroundings. Understood Ani!?"

Ani was nodding against Tia's chest as Shivan talked.

Valdria made sure there was nothing in the wound then used the stabilizer to make sure there was no additional damage before she sealed the gash closed. She helped me to the bathing room, so I could rinse off my hair and back before I went upstairs. We left mine and Lev's shirts on the table since we would have to do more than just wash them in the morning.

Shivan ensured I made it to my room as he told me to call if I needed help.

I smiled, "I'll be fine. I'm just tired and somewhat lightheaded from the accident."

He narrowed his eyes then nodded slightly, "Okay, I will check in on you in a bit then."

That night I slept poorly, while the wound on my head was healed it didn't replace my lost blood. I woke several times and noticed each time Shivan was standing in the doorway watching me before he slid the door closed and headed back downstairs.

It was probably close to noon I thought when I opened my eyes to glance at my phone. Oh, good I thought it was only 10:00. I slowly got out of bed and made my way to the bathroom. I relieved myself and went to brush my teeth and wash my face. I thought about taking a shower, but I just didn't really have the energy.

As I looked at myself in the mirror I could definitely tell I looked haggard, my face was pale, and I had slightly dark lines under my eyes.

I dressed and made my way downstairs. Lev was awake and cleaning the mess left in the dining room.

I looked around for the girls and as Lev saw me he said, "They aren't up yet. Ani stayed with Tia and I don't think they got to sleep until after 04:00."

I just nodded slightly when the door chime rang. Lev sat the shirts down, "I got it go sit down before you fall down." He said jokingly.

As Lev opened the door I saw Hazuki and Aiko standing with a small package. Lev invited them in, and they approached the dining room where they saw me standing. As they both smiled and looked at me they seemed to hesitate.

"Trist are you okay?" Hazuki asked ahead of Aiko.

"Yea why?"

"Well you look a little pale." Aiko said next.

"Oh, yea we had a little trouble last night." I said.

Lev walked past me as he grabbed the shirts and held them up with a sarcastic face, "Yea a little trouble." As he tried to mimic my earlier response.

Both Aiko and Hazuki's faces drained of color when they saw the black stains covering the shirts. They snapped their attention to me.

"Seriously, what happened? Are you okay!?" They both nearly shouted.

I sighed at Lev's idea of a joke since his comments made this seem like a bigger deal than it was.

"I'm fine, I hit my head and Valdria had to patch it up. You know how head wounds bleed more than anything else right?"

They both began peering at my head, "Are you okay? I don't really see anything wrong." Hazuki asked as she tried to step around me.

"They fixed it with a few stitches." I told them, silently apologizing for the lie.

Both Aiko and Hazuki winced as I placed my hand on the back of my head.

"Well, we brought a thank you gift. My parents wanted to bring it, but I talked them into letting me drop it off." Aiko said with a smile.

"Thank you, Aiko, I know Valdria will be extremely happy to receive it." I said with a warm smile.

I guess the end of year gifts or oseibo were a way of expressing thanks for the assistance provided throughout the year.

I noticed a lot of gift giving was intended to build relationships through gift exchange and obligation. It was a very interesting cultural value.

"Well please express our thanks to Valdria and Shivan for always putting up with us during the study sessions." Aiko said with a more serious face.

I smiled, "I think they know that, and they enjoy having everyone over."

A few hours later I heard a door open and close down the right wing, so I expected to see someone come out but never did.

A little after noon there was another knock on the door. I answered it this time and noticed the postman had left a bundle of mail in our box. As I grabbed the letters I could recognize some of them as nengajo, traditional post cards wishing for a happy New Year. Some of them had depictions of the current zodiac and others had lottery numbers on the backside.

I was amazed at the number of cards, many of the names I recognized but many more I did not. I took these into the dining room table where we usually left items to be reviewed by the adults.

Ani had refused to come out and told me she didn't want to talk when I asked if she was okay

A number of students visited our house that day, including several parents who thanked Shivan profusely for allowing their children to study with us. When the day ended we had a number of gifts sitting on the table, everything from dish towels to mandarin oranges.

Valdria put the towels and tea to good use and she sat out a large bowl on the table filled with oranges. After about the fifth orange I was done for the day.

Later that evening I heard a gentle knock on my door.

"Yes, it's open."

Tia gently slid my door open as she hesitantly walked in. I could tell she wanted something since she was usually like this when she had a favor to ask.

"Umm, Trist. Can I ask for your help?" Tia said shyly.

I frowned, this wasn't usually what she asked for, "Sure, what can I help with."

Tia looked hesitant to ask but resigned herself to the deed, "Can you cheer Ani up? She is blaming herself for the accident and I can't get her to come out of her room. I know she was kind of responsible since she wasn't paying attention, but she was talking about a fortune or something. So, I don't know what to do." Tia said slightly frustrated with herself.

I was almost as lost as Tia, "I can try talking to her, but Tia she told me to keep away from her earlier. Wouldn't it be better to let her think it through?"

"No! That was what happened last time. I know how I felt so I don't want her to feel that way anymore than she has too. I know you can help Trist. You always know what to say."

I thought Tia might be setting her expectations too high, but I agreed, "Fine, I will go and talk to her in a little bit." I told Tia with a smile.

After Tia left I made my way downstairs. When I came to Ani's door I lightly knocked. No answer. I slid the door open a bit and could see a ball on the bed. I went ahead and entered and quietly closed the door behind me.

I stepped over to her bed and quietly called Ani's name. I could see her curled up in a ball and she moved slightly when my voice called out.

There was plenty of room on her bed, so I sat down on the edge and turned toward the ball of covers. I called her name again, but she didn't answer. I reached out and gently patted the ball and could tell her back was facing me. I slowly laid down as I propped my head up on my hand, my other hand gently rubbed her back.

I could feel a hand reach back to brush my hand away as Ani mumbled, "Leave me alone."

"Ani turn around please."

She ignored my request and remained silent.

I reached out and gently tried turning her to her back, but she pushed against my efforts, "Trist go away! Leave me alone!"

"Do you really want me to go away?" I asked quietly.

I could hear Ani sniffle slightly under the covers she had wrapped around her. It sounded like she was crying but I wasn't sure.

I sat there for many more minutes before I finally stood, "Okay Ani, I will leave you alone. Good night."

As I was turning to walk out I heard Ani say in a faint voice, "Don't go."

This time though it was followed by audible weeping.

I paused and turned again as I sat back on the edge of her bed, "Ani tell me what's wrong, please."

"It was my fault that you got hurt." She managed to get out after a few minutes.

"Ani, what did I tell you about accident statistics, this could have happened to anyone. I was just glad I had been able to grab you before it was too late."

Ani began to weep a little more when I reminded her of that, "My fortune said the one I loved would be hurt if I didn't pay attention. I didn't know what to do and no matter what I thought about I couldn't get the thought out of my mind."

I had no idea what she was talking about, "Your fortune?" I finally asked.

Ani told me about the omikuji she had bought during the hatsumode visit the day before.

"Was that why you were spacing out all night?" I asked in disbelief.

I could see her nod slightly under the covers.

I wanted to ask if she was an idiot, but I knew that would only make her feel worse, though what I said next was almost as bad.

"So, Ani that could be taken two ways and your actions are making it come true for both meanings." I said bluntly.

Ani began to cry harder as I sighed inwardly to myself, "Listen Ani, first, thinking a piece of paper can dictate your future is stupid. You control your actions not a slip of paper. Because you were worried about that paper you nearly got hit and I was lucky enough to be able to grab you in time, and now you're not listening to reason."

I paused as I was starting to get a little frustrated over a simple slip of paper, "Do you think the paper had anything to do with it or was it your actions after reading the paper?"

"It happened because I love you…" Ani continued to sob.

I sighed again, "Ani, stop it! I am starting to get a little mad at you."

She continued to cry.

"Okay, fine. When you are ready to accept what happened had nothing to do with a piece of paper let me know."

I left her room much more frustrated than I had ever been.

Tia poked her head out of her room as I walked by, but she didn't say anything as I passed.

The next day Lev and I made our way to several of our classmate's homes and thanked them for the nengajo. They were all surprised to see us but thanked us for stopping by, several of the parents joined in on the thank you.

As we walked home I noticed Ani standing outside the entry waiting. Lev looked over at me as he sighed. My expression must have been a little dour.

Ani watched us walk up but I walked right past her and tried not to let my eyes wander in her direction as we entered the house.

We slid the door closed behind us as Lev said, "Your being mean."

"No, this is me being mad."

Lev just shook his head, "Want to stop by the last few places tomorrow?"

"Sure. Let me know when you're up."

I headed upstairs and really felt like I wanted to go on a long trip.

After that morning Ani didn't try to wait for us again. She stayed primarily in her room and would occasionally come out for meals.

As the fourth of January arrived we all headed off to school. I avoided Ani since she was still stuck on a silly piece of paper directing her fate kick. Until she realized she was the one who controlled her destiny I was going to drive the point home. Ani didn't walk next to me, so Lev and Tia took my right and left side. Ani followed with her head hung slightly.

As we walked to the bus I heard Aiko and Hazuki call. We paused to allow them to catch up.

As we walked Hazuki stepped closer, "What's wrong with Ani?" She asked somewhat concerned.

I shook my head, "We're what you probably could call fighting."

Aiko was shocked, "Why!" She asked in a hushed tone.

"She thinks I got hurt because of a fortune slip." I said as I shook my head.

Hazuki laughed, "I had a friend who used to believe in those until a Shinto priest told me they were put together randomly. How could someone believe a piece of paper. Not to mention most of the time people overly stress about them and create a self-fulfilling prophecy." Hazuki made sure she replied loud enough for Ani to hear.

I responded in a normal voice, "I know so until someone realizes this, I can't do anything about it."

Ani turned around and started running back toward the house. Aiko called to her, but I just watched knowing she had to figure this out herself.

The first day back was busy, after turning in homework Murakami asked where Ani was during role.

"She wasn't feeling too well this morning." Lev offered.

Murakami nodded and started in on the days plans.

I was extremely irritated all day and when Murakami asked if Aiko and I could attend the student council meeting that day I wanted to say no. However, I restrained my irritation and attended.

The meeting was to discuss class plans for the cultural festival and there was information passed that we needed to discuss with the class to decide how we would participate.

As the meeting let out we walked to our club room, Aiko would look at me occasionally before she finally spoke.

"Trist, why don't you make up with her, I know you want too. Ever since this morning you seemed agitated."

I sighed, "I want too, but until she realizes that what caused the accident was her lack of awareness nothing I say will be helpful."

When we arrived at our club room we only had about thirty minutes before activities ended. We covered any questions from today and then ended for the day.

As Aiko and Hazuki headed home with us I listened to their conversations, but I proved to be a poor conversation partner.

When we got home I made my way upstairs. As I entered my room I saw Ani sitting on my bed. I said nothing as I walked to my desk and sat my bag next to it as I pulled out my chair. When I sat with my back to Ani I heard her shift on the bed.

I felt Ani's arms slip around my neck as she leaned over and rested her cheek on my head, "I'm sorry."

"For what?" I asked plainly.

"I went to the shrine and asked about the fortune slips, the man working the counter said they were primarily for entertainment but that some people took them seriously."

"So, what are you sorry for?" I asked again.

"I'm sorry you got hurt because of me."

"Do you realize why that happened?"

"Yes, after you forced me to see, that's why I went to the shrine. Because I was worried about something happening my distraction actually made it happen."

"Remember what I told you about accidents? That is real, you need to be conscious of your surroundings at all times."

"I know, father also talked to me when I came home today. He said many of the same things you did the other day."

I turned in my chair to face Ani, "You know, I care about you very much. But when you told me I was hurt because of a piece of paper I was mad."

I shook my head slightly, "I was hurt because I couldn't live without you so to me it was worth risking myself to keep you safe."

I stood as I faced Ani, "My actions are my own, so don't let yours be dictated by an object."

Ani hugged me, "Umm, I won't."

Ani held me for a time as I hugged her back, "I hated when you ignored me, I felt like my heart was unraveling. Please don't leave me like that again." Ani asked in a quiet but passionate voice.

"Then pay attention to me too, I don't just tell you things for fun, it's because I worry."

Cultural Festival

The following day things seemed to be mostly back to normal, Ani walked with us, but she was still a little quieter than normal. She seemed to be less concerned when female students talked with me in class, Tia though was at somewhat of a loss. She wasn't as outgoing as Ani so fending against unwanted affection directed toward me was difficult for her.

Ani turned in her homework and apologized to Murakami for missing the first day.

As class began I just couldn't help but feel Ani was forcing herself.

Before class came to an end Murakami announced that there was some student council business to discuss prior to our departure. After that he invited Aiko and I up to the front to address the class.

We had the topics we needed to cover regarding the expectations and restrictions on cultural festival events, so we quickly passed those along.

When we asked the class what they would like to do several hands were raised. The general consensus was a takoyaki booth. It sounded like a few students had grills they could bring from home so making them would be relatively easy.

"Okay, do we want to go with a theme or just the school anniversary theme?" Aiko asked as a few other students raised their hands.

The class decided to stay with the school theme just celebrating the anniversary would make less work.

"Okay, we need an indoor option as well, are the grills electric?" I asked this time.

The answer was yes for all three, "Is this something we could do inside or out? We want to be ready in case we have to change venues due to weather." I explained.

Kina raised her hand, "I think we can do it inside or out, we cook them inside at home and there isn't a problem. You just don't want to burn them." Kina said with a slightly embarrassed look.

"How about the booth, does anyone have access to wood or a canopy we can use?" I asked next.

Tashiro raised his hand, "I can probably bring a canopy, my dad has one he uses when we go fishing."

Josuke also raised his hand, "I have some plywood we can use as a front, but I don't think I have enough to circle the whole booth."

Aiko and I took notes and thanked the class for their input, it looked like we would try to do a takoyaki stand whether it was good or bad weather.

When class dismissed Aiko and I made our way to our student council meeting. The only meetings we had to attend covered class specific information since we were excused from general support.

There were a few classes who proposed takoyaki among a number of other festival themed foods. Luckily the indoor option changed so we would have a better chance of doing well if the weather was actually bad.

When the student council had our information, they informed us they would submit it to the school administration for approval. We should know in a couple days if our idea was accepted or we would be deciding on a different plan.

As we entered our club room I noticed several students chatting instead of studying. What I could hear was their excitement for the cultural festival.

"Did anyone have questions?" I asked as I walked in and placed my books on an open spot at the first table.

I noticed Ani glance my way and offered a slight smile as she sat with her arm propping her head up as she worked on today's problems. Tia was helping one of the tables that were actually studying, and Lev was sitting back in his chair.

For some reason I just felt like there was a disconnect between Ani and I, it was a feeling I just couldn't shake and definitely didn't like.

The week prior to the festival was mid-term exams. We conducted a normal study group prior and ended with remarkable results. The class was approaching a mid-80% average. I noticed Ani wasn't too interested in the scores even though she did much better than the previous mid-terms.

School progressed toward the cultural festival, we had found out our plan was approved. Many of the other proposals for takoyaki booths didn't have equipment readily available so their ideas were declined. This raised the spirits of the class. With only one takoyaki booth, we had a good chance to earn a significant number of points for our team color.

Ani continued to be her calm disinterested self, the only change I could see was when the girls in class were talking to me she only had a somewhat sad expression when she normally would appear jealous and intervene.

At home Tia was now the only one who ever tried to snuggle. One evening when she knocked on my door she asked if she could cuddle a bit before she went to bed. I sighed but let her lay next to me until she fell asleep.

"Do you think Ani is happy? I'm worried about her, she just doesn't seem like herself. I hope she is keeping warm." Were the last words Tia mumbled before she drifted off to sleep.

As I laid in bed I contemplated Tia's words and observations. They seemed to mesh with what I had seen. I just couldn't figure why Ani had withdrawn so much. Even though she still smiled and would accept an occasional hug it was as if her passion was stolen away.

After school exams and before the festival our class took turns working on decorations and studying. Ani helped Lev and the others with some of the heavier jobs, but she didn't really seem excited.

A few days before the festival I woke up to cooler than normal weather and found myself turning on the heater. As I looked outside I noticed a blanket of white covering the entire yard. This was the first time I had seen snow other than on the distant mountains.

I quickly prepared for the day and wore an additional shirt under my school uniform as I made my way downstairs. I knocked on Lev, Ani and Tia's door and told them to come and see.

They all were up so they followed me to see what was so exciting. When I opened the front door all their eyes widened in surprise, even Ani had a truly excited look on her face. One of the first since the beginning of January.

We all finished preparing and made our way to school, noticing that the roadways were much more slippery, Lev ended up falling on his back side when he tried running and sliding in the snow. Tia and I laughed as Ani provided a slight smile.

As class started that morning we had one day until our school festival. Murakami announced that the venue was to be shifted inside. This wouldn't be a big issue, in fact it saved some additional trips for some of the student's family members.

Instead of using a tent we decided to set up three tables and placed the banner board we had painted with our class number and advertisement at the foot of the front table.

All the preparations were made, that night several students walked in the snow to purchase the ingredients. We thought we needed to have enough ingredients for two hundred servings, but we settled on twice that since the class was bound to purchase thirty on their own.

The Friday of the festival we all arrived early, there weren't classes that day, but all the staff was present. We took the few hours we had before the festival started to set up our booth along the covered walkway between the school building and the gym.

This was our lottery location for the internal venue. While not totally free of the elements it was somewhat covered, and we even had a few small kerosene heaters along the walkway that students could warm themselves by.

The student council had prepared banners that hung at the entry gates of the school and our festival was set to start at 10:00 and run through 17:00 our normal time for club activities to end.

We decided to prepare a few batches of takoyaki to make sure the batter and octopus would cook well. It was fun making them and I even had an opportunity to try, but I always seemed to try to turn them before the batter was completely cooked so they came out a little misshapen. The girls in class refused to let me help cook.

We had everything ready, as we waited for our first customers to arrive. We were selling six small takoyaki balls for three hundred yen. The proceeds would reimburse us for the ingredients and the remaining would go toward our school celebration at the end of the year.

The number of sales would also be recorded since you were awarded points based on your success and team work that went toward your yearly team score.

Ani was pretty good at making them, so she had been voluntold to run one of the three takoyaki cookers. As we started to notice younger kids running around we could tell our opportunity to shine was beginning to start.

Lev, Josuke and I had signs and we volunteered to walk around the gym and advertise for our class. I saw a number of other foods, all in the covered areas of the school grounds. In the gym most of the stalls were craft goods that the students had made or procured at a low price and were re-selling.

The food booths closest to us were doing donuts and yakisoba on an old grill that looked very heavy. A number of families began walking through the corridor toward the gym and the smell of cooking food caused many to pause and look at each food stall. We were a little more expensive than the donut shop being ran by 2-D but cheaper than 3-B's yakisoba stand.

After a couple hours the students switched places for cooking, so everyone had a chance to walk around. Overall there wasn't much to really see, a couple of the presentations were on some of the local cultural events or even some focusing on historical sites in town. The student council had a booth dedicated to the school's history that dated back to the early Showa-era.

I noticed students from other schools walking around as well. As I walked a group of girls in uniforms for the school a few kilometers away called out to me. They were asking about our school and what class I was in. One of them finally asked if I was single.

This set the girls to giggling as I blushed at her question. As I answered they walked next to me and asked me to show them our booth. The one girl hooked her arm around mine as she smiled and said she was cold. Since I was holding a sign it didn't really bother me as long as she let me continue to advertise.

As we walked toward our booth I noticed Ani turned the corner heading into the gym when she saw me with girls she didn't recognize. As she saw that one of the girls had linked arms with me. Ani's face seemed to turn anxious as she looked up at me with a frown and turned and headed the opposite direction.

When we approached our booth, I saw Tia look up from the takoyaki grill she was working on and her eyes widened when we drew near. She had a little scarf wrapped around her head to keep her hair from hanging down as she was cooking.

She set down the skewer she had been using to turn the takoyaki and walked around the tables and over to me. She grabbed me by the other arm and looked at the girl who had been next to me.

"Um, Trist we need your help back here." As Tia continued to pull.

I handed my sign to Naoki who was waiting near the front of our stall.

The girls looked at our booth and even bought a few servings.

As they left Tia turned to me, "What were you doing!?" Tia demanded with an upset expression.

"I was bringing them to our stand, I couldn't very well be mean and shake her arm off. They did ask if I was single, so I was honest, and I told them that I had people close to me."

Tia sighed, "Trist, what if Ani saw you like that?"

"She did, but she turned around and went the other direction."

"Trist you should go find Ani and explain what happened. I know she has been a little withdrawn lately, but I know she still loves you more than anything. I know how it felt when I saw you with those girls, I can only imagine what she felt." Tia pleaded with me.

I thought about it and I remembered when I saw guys talking to Ani at the light show last Christmas, I felt more than a little agitated. Did Ani feel the same way?

I nodded to Tia, "Okay, are you okay handling things for a while?"

Tia nodded as she paused like she smelled something. Her eyes suddenly widened, and she turned and ran back to the grill she had been working on.

"NO!" I saw Tia's face take on a defeated look as she tried to turn an almost black takoyaki ball.

I decided I needed to find Ani, I knew locating her just running around would be difficult. The location app on my phone would give me a general area but if she was in the school it could be any floor.

The app showed her location near the area where our class would be, so I figured starting at our class made the most sense.

As I climbed the stairs closest to the gym I walked down the East wing toward our class. This floor was fairly quiet right now since most of the activities were downstairs or in the gym.

I slid the door open quietly and glanced in, but I didn't see her in the class. I looked at my phone again and it said she was right on top of my location. I knew she wouldn't be down stairs, so I went up to the next floor which were also first year classes. I glanced into the classroom on the third floor but still didn't see her.

I wasn't sure what was going on until I found her phone in her bag next to her desk. I knew this was going to be more difficult now.

I put my phone away and started walking through the first-floor area but didn't see any sign of her. As I made my way to the gym I stopped and asked Tia if Ani had been by. She just shook her head, so I moved into the gym.

I walked the perimeter of the gym but didn't see any sign of her. I didn't have much choice, *"Ani, where are you?"* I asked in a concerned voice.

I didn't immediately get a response, so I asked again, *"Ani please, I need to talk to you."*

This time I heard a faint response, *"I'm fine don't worry."*

"Ani! Please, I'm worried!" I felt like I almost shouted mentally.

There was a long pause, *"I'm sitting by the old dojo out front."*

I quickly made my way to the front of the school as I exited out the south wing and walked to the front of the dojo used by the judo and kendo clubs. I saw Ani sitting staring out into the garden which was slightly covered with snow.

I sighed in relief as I saw her glance my way. I walked over to her and sat next to her noticing the floor was extremely cold.

"Aren't you cold?" I asked a little concerned.

"Not really, I'm kind of used to it now."

I didn't know where to start but I knew I was the one who should, "Ani, sorry about earlier. It wasn't on purpose."

Ani just nodded slightly as she turned her head away from me.

I thought about Ani's actions for the last few weeks and finally asked, "Ani, what wrong? You haven't been yourself for a while now."

Ani didn't provide a response as she kept her head facing away.

"You know Tia is worried and I think you are better when you show your normal passionate self. Even if you are a little blunt sometimes that's the Ani I love"

I smiled as I thought about her personality and what a large presence she played in my life. It almost seemed like she was purposefully trying to shrink her presence.

Ani still remained silent. So, I gently reached my hand over to her chin and gently turned her face my direction. I could she was very close to crying as she blinked tears began to form in the corners of her eyes.

"Ani, what's wrong? You know how it hurts me to see you like this don't you?"

Ani tried to speak but she stared gasping as she brokenly got out, "I'm scared…"

I had no idea what a person as strong as her had to be afraid of, she was always the strongest of our group.

"Why?" I asked compassionately as I placed my open palm against her cold cheek.

Ani was openly crying, "When I saw you hit by that truck and then saw the blood on your hand I couldn't take it. You were hurt because of me…"

Ani began to rub the tears from her eyes, but they just returned, "You wouldn't have gotten hurt if I had been paying attention, so I thought I should try to be more responsible, but I can't…" Ani began to sob harder as she gasped for breath.

She leaned into me and grasped my jacket sleeve with her left hand as she buried her face against my arm.

I moved my right hand to gently rub her head as she continued talking between gasps.

"I wanted to be next to you, but I was afraid that I might do something to get you hurt. I can't handle that again. When I saw all the blood on your shirt as it dripped down your back. I still have dreams almost every night about that and I get so scarred."

"Ani, I'm okay alright, it was just a little accident, remember what I told you before I would do anything to keep you safe?"

Ani cried a little harder, "That's what I'm afraid of! If you got seriously hurt because you tried to protect me I couldn't live with myself."

"I would do everything I could to ensure both of us were safe, but Ani I feel the same way. If something happened to you because I failed to act, I don't think I could take it either. So please don't worry as much and be yourself. I miss the old Ani."

I stood as I straddled Ani and sat behind her, so I could put my arms around her and keep her warm. I gently whispered in her ear, "Don't ever forget I love you."

She began crying a little more though she had seemed to be calming down as she turned around and threw her arms around my neck.

"I love you too, I'm sorry I have been so depressed since school started. Then I saw those girls today and it was too much." Ani kept her face buried against my shoulder as she sat kneeling as we both hugged each other.

After she had calmed down I said, "Want to go back?"

"No, I want to stay like this."

I smiled, "Maybe tonight since we don't have school tomorrow."

Ani pulled back from her hug, "Promise?"

I didn't think snuggling would be such a bad thing, "Sure but if you're too obvious Tia will notice."

Ani smiled slightly, "Humm, okay I will be quiet about it then."

As we stood I noticed it was closing on 16:00 and there was only a little more than an hour left.

"Let's see how the booth did?" I told Ani as I helped her stand up.

When we made our way back Ani still had slightly puffy eyes, so Tia looked a little concerned as she came over to me.

"Is she okay?" Tia asked in a quiet voice.

"I think so." I smiled as I responded.

Tia offered a brighter smile mixed with relief as well as happiness.

"Tia, want me to take over?" Ani asked after a few minutes.

"Sure, but don't burn them like that." Tia pointed to a container heaped with black round half cooked balls.

Ani laughed a bit and she now wore a smile that truly represented her bright and strong personality.

As the day closed we ended up with about forty servings left. We cooked up the remaining batter and made a batch for each student, so we had less to carry home. Ani must have eaten four servings all by herself now that she was feeling better.

We didn't beat everyone in sales, but we definitely made more than enough money to have a small school party. As well as provide a decent amount of points toward our team score for the year.

I took us about an hour to clean up and we returned the tables to their racks, the parents of the students who loaned the grills helped move the equipment out of the walkway.

We dropped off the lock box in the office, so Murakami could secure it, we also provided him with the remaining takoyaki that he humbly accepted. After we had everything picked up we made our way to class and collected our belongings as students headed home for the weekend.

As we took the bus home I could feel a closer bond with Ani as she tried to recover the lost contact from the last month. Ani and Tia positioned themselves again at my right and left as we walked the short distance from the bus stop to the house followed closely by Aiko and Hazuki.

"So, Ani what happened, you look like you feel better. I thought for a while that you were going to let me have Trist." Hazuki said in a playful tone.

Ani glanced at me as I laughed then turned slightly toward Hazuki, "Not in your lifetime." She said with a big smile.

Hazuki gave an over exaggerated sigh, "Well it's nice to see you back to your old self."

Ani stepped closer as she grabbed my hand and leaned her head slightly on my shoulder for a moment.

Tia noticed this and gave Ani a stern look, as she hooked arms with me as she smiled broadly, "I wanted to try this since this afternoon."

When we arrived home Shivan welcomed us back as he and Talinde were playing some type of game at the dining room table.

We all headed toward our rooms and prepared for the evening meal.

Once dinner was completed, it was Lev and my turn to help clean up. We quickly finished the dishes and straightening the kitchen as Shivan put the remaining ingredients away. He had been doing a majority of the cooking so Valdria didn't have to stand as long as normal.

As I was in my room getting ready for bed I heard a faint knock on the door. I expected it to be Ani but when the door opened it was Tia who just looked in my room then smiled at me, "Just checking."

Around 22:00 I finally laid down for bed, it was still early but today had been a little exhausting. I was facing the window when I fell asleep.

It was probably an hour later that I felt someone slide under my covers behind me from the feel against my back I could tell it was Ani. She reached around me and placed her hand on my chest as she slowly drifted off to sleep herself.

When I woke up our positions were somewhat reversed. Not having two extra bodies in bed I was able to turn freely and as Ani lay on her back with the covers pulled up to her neck I was turned facing her with my arm around her.

As I stirred faintly Ani turned to her right side and grasped my hand as she held it to her chest. I could faintly feel her heart beat as she pressed my hand against her.

I scooted a little closer, so I could feel her warmth and curled my free arm around her head as I gently fell back to sleep.

The light was just peering over the horizon when I heard my door slide open.

I heard Tia make a clicking noise with her mouth as she entered my room and climbed into the bed behind me. I noticed she was cool, and her feet had been bare and were cold against my skin. She gradually warmed up as she snuggled against me.

Ani was the first to wake up as she felt my hand move against her skin. She grasped it and reached down as she kissed my slightly bent fingers. When she turned she looked not at my face but at Tia who was giving a defiant stare across the bed.

"You said you weren't going to his room, you're a fibber." Tia boldly told Ani in hushed tones.

Ani just smiled, "How long have you been here?"

"About two hours, why?"

"Just curious." As Ani gave Tia a mischievous smile.

Tia looked a little shocked, "You didn't do anything did you?" Tia said a little anxiously.

Ani just smiled as Tia started to pout and laid back down.

Tia reached across Trist's chest as thoughts raced through her mind. Trist wouldn't do anything would he? As she began to think of all the fantasies she had dreamed of with Trist. Tia suddenly found herself a little uncomfortable as she sat up.

"Ani?" Tia said in a loud whisper, "You really didn't do anything did you?"

"No, she didn't unless you call holding my hand doings something." I said in a croak as I was waking up.

Tia's face was turning bright red as Ani smiled broadly as she looked across Trist to Tia.

"I need to get up, mind letting me out now?" I asked in a tired voice.

As Ani slid out of bed I noticed she was wearing a beautiful pink night gown. I don't think I had seen it before.

"Hey, when did you get that?" Tia asked a little surprised.

I was thinking the same thing but didn't say anything after Tia.

Ani smiled, "I bought it before the light show. Why?" Ani asked as she looked back at Tia.

Tia's face was getting redder, "You know you can see through it right?"

Ani's expression faltered a moment as she looked down then at me as I tried to casually glance toward the ceiling. Ani's face grew a shade redder as she quickly left the room.

Tia threw her arms around me as she rested her head on my chest, "Thank you for making up with Ani."

I rubbed the back of Tia's head and stroked her back, "You don't need to thank me, I just helped Ani with her insecurities." As I gently pinched Tia's sides before I grabbed her and began tickling her in earnest.

As I stopped Tia gave me a hurt look, "Why do you always do that?" Tia said as she covered her sides with her arms.

I smiled at Tia, "Because you react that way. Plus, I like your smile and laugh."

Tia smiled faintly as she turned and headed out of my room. I then got up and began getting ready for the weekend.

As the new week started we began making our way toward the final month of the school year.

Valdria was at a stage where the baby could be born at any time so Kazu made frequent visits to our house. The plan was to take her to facility operated by the government where we could use our technology to ensure her birth was safe. Birthrates were usually low due to the slow cellular growth so there were extended periods of danger for expectant mothers. That was one of the reasons why births were so celebrated on Paltius.

Given how slow our bodies healed having a baby was a risky affair without the appropriate technology. There was even discussion of taking her back to the Velisus until after the birth. Valdria refused and said she wanted her baby born on Earth not on the Velisus which was considered an extension of Paltius.

Valdria was fairly certain the development of her daughter had progressed well since she had intimate experience with birthing as a midwife. We kept an emergency kit ready just in case and Kazu told us he was basically on standby or would have someone available if he wasn't.

As the end of the school term approached we decided to hold a one-day study group since anything more could potentially put pressure on Valdria.

I apologized to the students, but they were more excited about her baby than the study group. We decided to meet on a Saturday and would run until 20:00 in the evening if there we a lot of questions. The group worked in the house since it was still fairly cool outside as we broke into different groups and settled in the lounge downstairs and upstairs, and the dining room tables.

I was fairly confident we would do great, we had already surpassed the initial requirement of 70% set by the principal. So, it was just a matter of time before we entered spring break and started as second years.

As the Monday of exams arrived the class seemed to be in high spirits. Lev, Ani and Tia had a few questions Sunday, but they were more advanced than what I expected on the test.

As Murakami entered the room when the bell rang he was accompanied by another proctor. My eye's widened as I finally confirmed Murakami Shotaro's relationship with our teacher.

I raised my hand and Murakami called to me, "What shall we call you Murakami-sensei while you are both in the class?" I said with a slight smile.

The original proctor who issued our assessment followed his older brothers gaze to me, as his eyes widened in recognition, "Trist, good to see you again."

Our teacher glanced at his younger brother, "Have you met before?" He said with a truly puzzled look.

He smiled as he looked at his older brother, "Sorry but I couldn't say anything about it. But I wondered when you told me stories about your class."

Murakami-sensei shook his head as he addressed the class, "This is Murakami Shotaro, as Trist pointed out he is my younger brother, but he is also a proctor for the National Center Exams. Considering your unique situation, we will have a two-person validation at the end of each year so there are no questions raised regarding your progression."

The two began to separate and pass out exams as the class patiently waited.

Once we all had our exams Murakami glanced at his watch and gave the begin command.

The tests were easy, and I finished each one with enough time to review multiple times. The class seemed to be doing well also, there were very few sighs of disappointment when time expired.

As the final test came to an end there were brief cheers from a couple of the male students, and everyone began chatting amongst themselves as the tests were passed forward.

As Murakami and his brother gathered their belongings and departed I checked amongst my classmates.

"Did anyone have any major questions or obstacles?"

Hirotada asked about a problem, "I wasn't sure of the response on a problem on our second test."

"Do you remember what problem?" I asked remembering back.

"I think it was the second to last on the third page."

I quickly jotted down what I remembered, "This one?"

"Yea, how can you remember it that well?" He asked incredulously.

The other class members standing around were also shocked that I was able to recite a problem like that from earlier in the day.

"It was the third choice; these other three options were regarding different periods." I wrote the correct response down.

Hirotada sighed in relief, "Thanks Trist, it looks like I did get it right."

A couple of other students also asked about a few problems they were unsure of. Once we finished, everyone had a pretty good feeling about their exam results.

The next day was review and several self-study classes. When Wednesday arrived Lev, Ani, Tia and I made our way to school early.

Aiko headed to grab the journal as Hazuki joined us in checking the results. Our group did remarkably well, Lev scored a 91%, Tia had a 94% and Ani even came in with a 90% average for the five tests. The class had moved its way back up the board and several of them were among the top scorers.

Yamato was walking toward the boards as we were heading toward class. He offered a nasty look as he passed me. I felt Ani pause behind me as I turned. Lev was still at the board as he turned to Yamato.

"Looks like you slipped." Lev said in satisfaction to Yamato as he snorted and kept walking.

Lev walked up to me, "That felt good." Lev had a huge smile on his face.

Ani still scowled back at Yamato, "I still want to hit him." She said enthusiastically.

Hazuki sighed as we walked up to our class for the final announcement before spring break began signally the first success of my plan.

End First Year

Murakami congratulated us on our progress and said he hoped he could be part of our class next year.

I could tell he really meant it.

The final assembly ushered out the graduating class to make way for the new students.

We were informed that acceptance for new first years had to be reduced to only top performers since so many applications had flooded the school and even with them adding two classes they were unable to meet the demand.

I had been asked to give a student address by Haruka who normally would have as the student council president. She had tried nominating me for her position earlier in the semester but was denied by the principal. Ultimately a new second-year had been voted into the position and she settled with me wishing the outgoing students farewell.

It was an emotional event, and while I only knew a few of them I could see the bonds among the students before me as they wept knowing their close friends would be moving to a new school.

As I wrapped up my short speech, I reminded everyone that this was but a brief stop and that our feelings for one another would continue if we made the effort to kindle our bonds.

Several of the graduating students nodded in agreement and the assembly released with the graduating students meeting friends and family while the first and second years returned to their classes for the final day.

As we made our way back to class Murakami allowed us to have a yearend party which really just consisted of snack foods and drinks purchased with our funds from our food booth.

People were somewhat emotional, but Tia reminded everyone that we would see each other in a little more than a week.

After that the atmosphere was more upbeat since we were a class bound to be together for the next several years.

I was a little excited to see new faces at school but for the most part I didn't expect much change over the next term. I realized having study groups at our house might be difficult with an upcoming family addition but figured Valdria wouldn't mind the help.

As I sat watching our class talk and laugh I thought this wasn't so bad. I could definitely get used to this sight.

Our little group made its way home Friday midafternoon with Aiko and Hazuki. They had asked what we had planned over the next week, but I figured it was time to start cleaning up the yard for spring.

I had already started noticing pink blossoms around town as blooms began to appear on some of the more established cherry blossom trees.

Aiko suggested a group outing to the local park to sit and watch the falling petals but Hazuki joked about that being too boring.

I wouldn't mind since I enjoyed watching them from my window last year, but she was right. It might be a little boring for some of the other students.

I contemplated all the events looming on our horizon plus what would school be like this next year. It was amazing a year had already passed since we arrived.

Lev had grown but he still acted like he always did. Ani had matured both physically and mentally, Tia was still growing but when she looked me in the eyes I could see a deeper desire.

How would I change as I continued to mature, I thought to myself?

What challenges will we face over the next year How would my companions grow? I contemplated this as I began to feel at ease with our situation knowing it was but a short-term respite.

Made in the USA
San Bernardino, CA
25 February 2019